SF Books by V

LOST STARSHIP SERIES:
The Lost Starship
The Lost Command
The Lost Destroyer
The Lost Colony
The Lost Patrol
The Lost Planet
The Lost Earth
The Lost Artifact
The Lost Star Gate

THE A.I. SERIES:
A.I. Destroyer
The A.I. Gene
A.I. Assault
A.I. Battle Station
A.I. Battle Fleet

Visit VaughnHeppner.com for more information

The Lost Star Gate

(Lost Starship Series 9)

By Vaughn Heppner

Copyright © 2018 by the author.

This book is a work of fiction. Names, characters, places and incidents are either products of the author's imagination or used fictitiously. Any resemblance to actual events, locales or persons, living or dead, is entirely coincidental. All rights reserved. No part of this publication can be reproduced or transmitted in any form or by any means, without permission in writing from the author.

ISBN-13: 978-1730723490
BISAC: Fiction / Science Fiction / Military

-PROLOGUE-

Six thousand, two hundred and fourteen light-years from Earth, a Swarm science fleet entered a haunted star system in the Sagittarius Spiral Arm.

The Hive Master commanding the fleet knew nothing about weirdness, eeriness or such concepts as haunted, wretched or even evil. They were Swarm creatures, insectile, primarily driven by hunger and chemically induced obedience to higher Swarm authorities.

The Hive Master had his orders and he obeyed. Certainly, he understood the statistically improbable number of times a Swarm expedition had failed to return from this star system, and for no known reason. But he did not attach any good or evil ideal to this. He merely took necessary precautions as the massed science fleet—five thousand vessels strong—neared the only artificial object detected in the otherwise normal-seeming system.

It was true that the closer the science vessels approached to the strange object, the higher the number of instances of disobedience rose throughout the fleet. But even Swarm creatures experienced anomalies at times or had mutations that caused stupidity, imbecility or an antisocial streak that when discovered brought swift eradication to the mutant insect.

The problem for the Hive Master and the Regulators under him was that Swarm society did *not* understand group madness.

Many hundreds of ship sensors indicated unclassified emanations radiating from the…from the giant silver pyramidal object slowly rotating in the stellar darkness.

The shape and color of the object matched the specifics for what the unconventional Swarm creature known as Commander Thrax Ti Ix had once informed the Imperial Queen was a Builder nexus. As important was the knowledge that a nexus could produce a hyper-spatial tube, which would allow the Imperium to expand faster because a hyper-spatial tube permitted a swift journey many thousands of light-years in length.

The Hive Master clacked his pincers once he understood that the object out there was indeed a Builder nexus. The Imperium had precise orders regarding the sighting of such a structure. Thus, despite the statistically improbable number of reported "accidents" within the fleet since entering the star system, the Hive Master gave orders to advance with haste.

Yet, the closer the fleet approached to the silver pyramid, the more quickly the number of reported "accidents" rose. Finally, the Hive Master admitted to himself an un-Swarm-like reaction to the artificial object slowly rotating in the stellar night.

From an observatory node in the command vessel, the Hive Master studied the silver pyramid for several hours, wrestling with sensations within himself that he did not understand. Finally, he coined a term that was new among the Swarm to describe the will that radiated from within the Builder nexus: *malignant*.

With growing weariness, the Hive Master returned to the control station, ensuring that the individual ships of the fleet continued their approach.

Three hours and fifteen minutes later, communal madness engulfed the Swarm crews of the science vessels. They did not understand why or how they could have averted such a thing, but the insectile creatures began attacking each other with savage intensity.

Five hours and nine minutes later, the last Swarm creature died from inflicted wounds. A Soldier had impaled the Hive Master one hour and twenty-three minutes ago, hacking him with glee. The Soldier had died four minutes later to a massed rush of Sensor Operators—who then turned on one another.

In any case, the five thousand science vessels bearing the dead Swarm creatures cruised past the ancient haunted nexus in the Sagittarius Spiral Arm, unaware that their passage stirred the dreams of an evil thing that manipulated reality through the hidden undercurrents of the universe.

Those stirrings would have drastic consequences for a race of hominids called *Homo sapiens* given to individual choices, creatures that understood madness, evil and good and courage. Would those concepts and their individuality help the humans against the thing in the nexus?

Like most such questions in the universe, the answer was, that would depend…

-1-

ORION SPIRAL ARM
TAU CETI SYSTEM

Brigadier Mary O'Hara—the Chief of Star Watch Intelligence—wondered for the umpteenth time if it had been a mistake coming alone to the abandoned space station.

The orbital was in the Tau Ceti System where thousands of junked and alien warships drifted aimlessly. Several years ago, a Swarm invasion fleet had steamrolled through the ambush set by Star Watch and the New Men. The radioactive furnace of the planet below was a grim reminder of the genocidal nature of the Swarm.

That the ghost station still had functioning gravity plates astounded the Iron Lady. Somebody must have fixed the plates, and she didn't think the Swarm had done it.

Four days ago, O'Hara had arrived in-system aboard a *Bismarck*-class battleship, an elder vessel. No other warship had dropped out of the Laumer Point with the *Moltke*.

As per O'Hara's instructions, the battleship was presently one billion, three hundred and forty-seven million kilometers from the station. She'd traveled from the battleship in a shuttle, alone, of course.

Mary O'Hara was an older woman of nondescript size wearing a bulky vacuum suit. She had a blaster in her gloved right fist and attached to her helmet was a lamp that swept an otherwise dark, debris-littered, station corridor.

She'd carefully picked her way through the gutted station for an hour and a half already. It was neutral ground, he'd told her, yet another precondition for a face-to-face meeting with *him*.

That she had agreed to his many terms showed not only her desperation but also that of Star Watch and the greater Commonwealth of Planets.

She reached another hatch, noting that this one was already open. Hmm... All the other hatches had been tightly sealed, only unlocking after she'd punched in an override code.

That had been another odd factor to find on what had originally seemed like a junked space station.

O'Hara looked around, her solitary beam washing over ruptured deck plates and torn bulkheads. She activated a suit-sensor, but only detected her own bio readings.

Despite that, O'Hara's stomach tightened as a feeling of unease grew. Was someone watching her? It had been *decades* since she'd gone on an assignment like this. She was supposed to trust her instincts, but she wondered if this was a case of nerves, especially as backup was days away.

Re-gripping the blaster and resolving to fight through any trap rather than allowing anyone to capture her, O'Hara ducked her helmeted head, stepping into another debris-littered corridor.

She exhaled with relief and silently chided herself at the same time as she moved along the new corridor.

The man she had come to meet was a charlatan and a scoundrel on many levels. But he had good reasons to fear her. He had only agreed to a face-to-face with such stringent requirements as she was performing. Still, if she ever got her hands on him—

Lights snapped on along the ceiling, one right after another, illuminating the corridor, showing old burn and blast marks on the bulkheads.

O'Hara jerked in surprise.

A beam flashed down the corridor, a perfect strike, hitting her blaster. The metal and plastic began to melt, some of it dripping onto her glove.

Within her helmet, O'Hara screamed at the violent heat transfer. She let go and snatched her hand from the ruined weapon, but not quite fast enough. The palm of her glove smoked.

Then, her training took over. With deliberate speed, she unhooked a canister with her left hand and sprayed the smoking glove. The goop resealed any possible breach and cooled her heated palm.

O'Hara sweated heavily—her suit's air conditioner had snapped on, blowing cold air against her—and she might have fainted from the pain. Fortunately, her bio computer ordered the suit's medikit. It injected her with painkillers and a special stim.

The brigadier blinked rapidly as the nausea passed, finally becoming aware of a tall individual at the end of the corridor. He did not wear a spacesuit, but a silver garment. He had dark hair and golden-colored skin—he was New Man, and he held the weapon that had destroyed her blaster.

O'Hara turned around. Another New Man blocked the way. He must have stepped through and closed the hatch after she'd entered the corridor.

That didn't make sense, though. Her sensor should have spotted him.

For just a moment, O'Hara closed her eyes. She'd taken a wild risk and lost. Was it time to take a kill pill? Maybe she should try to play it out first and see where it went. She could always swallow the pill inside the false tooth in her mouth.

With her chin, O'Hara activated the helmet speaker.

"Where's Professor Ludendorff?" she asked the first New Man, the one who had beamed her blaster.

Maybe she should have kept her eyes on the second golden-skinned bastard. She heard a click and felt a sudden sharp pain in the back of her left thigh.

Her eyelids drooped as a terrible sluggishness swept over her. With agonizing slowness, she turned to the second New Man. He held a dart pistol. O'Hara looked down at her suit. A dart had been stuck in the back of her left thigh.

He drugged me with a fast-acting trank.

A horrible sense of loss filled the brigadier. O'Hara did not want to die. But under no condition would she let New Men capture her.

Both golden-skinned supermen raced for her. She smiled because they reminded her of Captain Maddox.

That was all she had time for.

Brigadier Mary O'Hara, the Chief of Star Watch Intelligence, bit down on the false tooth, cracking it. She pried out the kill pill with her tongue, crushed the substance with her teeth and swallowed hard.

The New Men reached O'Hara as her eyelids fluttered. It was the last thing she knew.

-2-

O'Hara opened bleary eyes. She lay on her back on a table, feeling horrible. She ached all over and was beginning to shiver.

Groaning, she twisted her head to the side and tried to vomit. There was nothing left in her stomach, though. She began trembling after the heaving passed.

How was this even possible? She had swallowed the kill pill. She should be dead. She should—

The New Men!

O'Hara closed her eyes as she gathered her resolve. The two must have revived her. The pill had taken effect, but not quite fast enough. Through their superior science, they had kept her from dying. Now, they would likely pump her for critical Star Watch information. They would learn things. They might implant an obedience chip in her brain, turning her against Star Watch as a secret spy for the enemy.

O'Hara groaned with despair.

"Tut, tut," a familiar voice said. "It can't be all that bad."

O'Hara opened her eyes again, but her vision was blurry. She could not see anything definite.

"She is going into shock."

"Well, *fix* her," the familiar voice said. "This is crucial."

After a fuzzy time, the shivering ceased. The aches in her body lessened. She no longer felt like vomiting.

Had she passed out and come to again?

Yes. O'Hara had the sense of the passage of time, but she didn't know for how long. It could have been seconds. It could have been hours. Could it have been days?

She opened her eyes. They focused. She saw the ceiling above her. It was ordinary enough for a space station. It seemed clean, unmarred, as if nothing bad had ever happened to it.

She had a blanket over her body. She pulled off the covers and noticed that she was still wearing her Star Watch uniform. She yanked the blanket all the way off. She was not wearing boots, but she still had her socks on.

O'Hara glanced around. Medical machines hummed around her. This was a moderate-sized chamber.

A hatch hissed as it went up.

Professor Ludendorff came walking in, blowing over a cup of hot coffee. She could smell it. Her mouth watered and she was thankful it didn't make her nauseous.

The professor looked like a fit, older man with tanned skin, a golden chain around his neck and thick white hair. He was a Methuselah Man, ancient, filled with cunning knowledge gained over who knew how many centuries.

"Good morning, Brigadier," Ludendorff said in a cheerful voice.

He moved to a chair, sat down and blew across the coffee again before taking a sip. He closed his eyes in contentment before opening them and looking at her.

"It's the first sip that's always the best," he explained. "One has to sleep for a full night before another sip will taste as good the next morning. Isn't that a strange phenomenon?"

O'Hara groaned as she sat up and swung her feet off the table. With a sudden jerk, one of her hands flew up to her scalp where she carefully felt for surgery scars. She found nothing.

"I'm not like Strand," Ludendorff chided.

"But you have New Men in your employ like Strand."

"What?" Ludendorff asked. "That's preposterous."

O'Hara stared at the charlatan. She never should have agreed to meet with him. Star Watch could figure out its own answer to the great dilemma. Even as she thought that, O'Hara knew it was false. The problem was too big for Star Watch.

"I know what I saw," she told him.

Ludendorff leaned forward as he set the coffee cup on a nearby stand. "Pray tell, what did you see?"

O'Hara wondered if he was trying to trick her.

"Why am I here?" she asked.

"Because you begged to see me," he said. "Don't you remember your calls over the long-range communicator?"

She shook her head. "That's not what I meant. Why did I fall ill?"

"You swallowed a suicide pill, my dear. What else did you expect from such an act?"

"Exactly," she said. "Why did I swallow the pill?"

"As far as I can tell," he said, "your action was induced by paranoia. I suspect the paranoia struck because you're not used to being on your own like this."

Once more, O'Hara shook her head. "No. New Men burned my blaster and shot me with a knockout dart. I swallowed the pill so they couldn't capture me and turn me into a mind slave. They must have saved me from the—"

"Excuse me," Ludendorff said, interrupting. "*I* saved you."

"Fine. Where are the New Men?"

"Gone," Ludendorff said.

"You're lying, although I'm glad you finally admitted I did see New Men."

Ludendorff scowled before picking up the cup and sipping.

"How long have I been out?" O'Hara asked.

"Twenty-one hours and sixteen minutes."

"Oh. You must realize that the *Moltke* is coming for me."

Ludendorff nodded, taking another sip.

"Unless you have star cruisers nearby, you're going to have to run soon if you want to remain free."

"There are no New Men in the Tau Ceti System," Ludendorff said.

"Were those two working for you?"

"On no account," Ludendorff said.

"But New Men were here. You already admitted—"

"Yes, yes, they were here. They were here, and they shot and drugged you. Now, does that satisfy you?"

"Why did you lie to me a few moments ago?"

Ludendorff shrugged.

"Did you try a new drug on me, wanting to test its effects?"

Ludendorff said nothing.

"Give me some coffee," O'Hara said suddenly.

Ludendorff cocked his head, stood after a moment, held out his cup and approached her.

"No," O'Hara said. "I want a fresh cup, a hot cup. I like boiling hot coffee."

Ludendorff stared at her before abruptly turning and leaving the medical chamber the same way he had come in.

O'Hara slid off the table. She took a step and almost lost her balance, staggering several steps before catching herself on a medical machine. She studied the machine.

Yes. This was a revival unit. She *had* swallowed the kill pill. She had done so for the reasons she stated. Why then—

The hatch slid up sooner than she'd expected and Ludendorff walked through, stopping upon seeing her up. He grinned a second later, walking near and gingerly handing her a cup of steaming coffee.

Once O'Hara had a firm grip of the handle, she flicked her wrist, hurling the steaming liquid at him. Ludendorff must have anticipated the motion, because he was already dodging as she flung the coffee. Some stained his suit, and he noticeably winced as a few hot droplets struck his cheek.

Before he could fully recover, O'Hara backhanded the cup against his head, although not hard enough to break the cup. Ludendorff staggered backward just the same. The Iron Lady rushed him as she dropped the cup. But Ludendorff slipped to one side even as he stumbled back. He also stuck out a foot, and O'Hara's left foot struck it. She went sprawling onto the floor with a thudding crash.

She lay there, panting from the exertion.

Chair legs scraped across the deck plates.

She looked up and saw that Ludendorff had turned the chair to face her new location. He was sitting, sipping his own coffee, obviously trying to pretend his head didn't throb from the strike.

"Would you like to continue this farce?" Ludendorff asked in an altered voice. "Or would you like to act like a civilized person?"

O'Hara sat up, noticed she was near a bulkhead, slid across the floor until she rested her back against the wall.

"I realize you have studied the best Star Watch personal combat techniques," Ludendorff said, his voice returning to normal. "But I am the clear expert in such matters, knowing vastly more than you. In truth, you are a child compared to my advanced skills."

"Why did the New Men ambush me?"

"Does it matter?"

"Very much," she said.

"I don't agree. Thus, I won't answer. Do you wish to continue the meeting or should we adjourn and go our separate ways?"

"Adjourn," she said.

Ludendorff set down the cup, stood, bowed his head and made to go.

O'Hara almost let him. "Wait," she said.

Ludendorff raised his left eyebrow.

"I… I…need to talk to you."

"Oh," he said, sitting down again.

"But I don't know if I can trust you."

"What's to know?" he said. "You were in my power and you still possess your free will. I haven't tampered with you. In fact, no one tampered with you."

"Did the New Men wish to do so?"

"I rule here," Ludendorff said, his voice hardening for just a moment.

"Then why?" O'Hara said. "I don't understand why the New Men drugged me."

"I am the Methuselah Man."

"Meaning that your motives are above my puny understanding?" O'Hara asked.

"You mean that as a joke, but you are precisely correct."

O'Hara thought about that and about the New Men and their actions. "I'm sorry, Professor. I must conclude that you did something to me while I was unconscious."

"You're right. I healed you."

"That you did something nefarious to my mind," O'Hara amended.

"Think what you like," he said with a wave of his left hand. "It doesn't matter to me. Now, why did you beg to see me?"

"Why did you need the New Men to help you capture me?"

Ludendorff sighed as he crossed his legs. "Brigadier, you have a decision to make. I will have to leave soon. As you pointed out earlier, I do not wish to remain in the vicinity with the *Moltke* drawing near. If you wish to speak to me about other matters, now is your opportunity."

She studied the old scoundrel. She still felt the same way about him as ever. Could he have deceived her in some fashion? He was playing an angle. The professor always did, and he often told mistruths. This was maddening. She should have never come alone. Yet, the stakes had led her to do this, to take a gamble with the arrogant old Methuselah Man.

"Very well," O'Hara said. "It's time we talked."

"I'm listening," Ludendorff said.

"I could use a cup of coffee first," she said, "and something to eat."

"Yes," he said. "Come with me. I could use a bite to eat, too."

-3-

O'Hara ate much more than she expected. It would appear that she'd been famished.

After wiping the corner of her mouth with a napkin, she took a moment to look around. The bulkheads were different here. The air was clean—pure. The food dispenser—

She turned to Ludendorff. He sat across the table from her, having eaten a wedge of lettuce with blue cheese dressing and bacon bits.

It was a small galley.

"This is part of your ship," she said.

He set down his knife and fork, pushing the empty plate from him.

"Are we still in the station?" O'Hara asked.

"Of course," he said.

"But this is part of your ship," she said.

"No."

"It has to—"

"I had this place installed inside the station," Ludendorff said, interrupting.

"Oh."

"I'm not kidnapping you, Brigadier. I gave you my word that you would be safe."

"You still haven't explained about the New Men."

Ludendorff glanced up at the ceiling as if in exasperation.

"But I'm no longer interested in them," O'Hara lied. "We have a short time. We must talk before you flee from the *Moltke*."

"Please," he said. "I'm immune to your petty insults."

"I see. You're too mighty to flee from a *Bismarck*-class battleship?"

"Mighty," he said, as if tasting the word. "Yes. That would be correct. I am too mighty to fear your lone battleship."

O'Hara wondered if that was true. With Ludendorff...maybe, but maybe it was his constant arrogance speaking.

She cleared her throat. He was going to leave soon. That was the point. Thus, she should use her remaining time wisely.

"I'm not sure how much you know," she began.

"Rest assured, more than you."

"Oh. So you know about Admiral Fletcher's latest battle?"

"Tell me how you perceive it."

She paused for a half-beat before saying sharply, "A Swarm fleet appeared."

"Another one?" he asked.

"What?"

"Nothing," he said. "Please, continue."

"What do you mean 'another one?' Has the Swarm appeared somewhere else?"

"Admiral Fletcher fought a battle," he prompted.

O'Hara glanced at her empty plate. Ludendorff had asked if another Swarm fleet had appeared. He surely could not have meant another from the original invasion fleet of 80,000 Swarm warships several years ago. Could a different Swarm fleet have attacked the New Men? Was that why two New Men had been here with the Methuselah Man?

She cleared her throat, regarding the cunning charlatan. All the while, Ludendorff watched her closely.

"I'll be brief," O'Hara said. "Less than three months ago, a hyper-spatial tube appeared a quarter of a light-year away from the Hydras System."

"Indeed," Ludendorff said, seeming intrigued.

"Our long-range Builder Scanner on Pluto spied the invasion fleet," O'Hara said, "but it was at the extreme limit of the device. According to it, five thousand Swarm warships were heading from the tube's exit-point to the Hydras System. I'm not sure if you know, but Star Watch annexed the Hydras System after the war with the New Men."

"I'm familiar with the Hydras System," Ludendorff said dryly. "Approximately fifteen million people inhabit it. Most are of Greek descent."

"That's right. We spotted the five thousand warships and decided to send the Grand Fleet against it. This time, we didn't use any Destroyers. We kept those near Earth in case the five thousand ships were a Swarm feint to outmaneuver us."

"That was a logical deduction," Ludendorff said.

"The Commonwealth doesn't own five thousand spaceships even if one includes most haulers. But five thousand ships is a measly number for a Swarm Invasion Fleet."

"Why are you stating the obvious?"

O'Hara shook her head. "I'm happy to report that Admiral Fletcher rose to the occasion. He took the bulk of the Grand Fleet and rushed to the Hydras System, reaching it before the enemy. He mined the outer system just as we did here in Tau Ceti. There wasn't as much dust and debris there as here, but the Swarm ships fell easy prey to Fletcher's massed missile assaults. That astounded the admiral to such a degree that he changed the operational plan. He openly approached the remaining enemy vessels with the Grand Fleet, and he butchered the Swarm ships with…with pathetic ease. That bordered on the fantastic."

O'Hara had a frozen half-smile. "Toward the end of the butchery, Fletcher had a stroke of genius, using space marines to board several of the final enemy vessels. He captured all but two of them. Those two blew up, taking the marines with them. Fletcher's surviving marines captured Swarm royalty. That may well have been the turning point of the war for us. He brought the Swarm captives back to Earth."

O'Hara laughed sharply. "Our scientists have studied the Swarm and finally hacked their bizarre language. Do you know what we discovered after long interrogations?"

Ludendorff shook his head. For once, he didn't seem like someone who knows everything.

Once more, O'Hara laughed sharply.

"The five thousand ships were science vessels. Oh, they had a few laser cannons per ship, but that was due to regular Swarm design, not for any real military purpose. The five thousand vessels were like one of our Patrol ships. Instead of sending a single scout ship to check something out, the Swarm Imperium sent out five *thousand* vessels. Those scout ships went to a distant silver pyramid. I mean distant from the borders of the Imperium."

"By silver pyramid, you mean a Builder nexus," Ludendorff said quietly.

"Right," O'Hara said. "According to what we learned, that particular nexus was approximately four thousand light-years from the Hydras System."

"Was?" Ludendorff asked.

"I'm getting ahead of myself. The point is that the Swarm Patrol Fleet—to use our terminology—went to the distant nexus. There, the Swarm scientists studied it in detail. What we didn't know until we interrogated their royalty was that the first time the Swarm invaded with their eighty thousand warships, Thrax Ti Ix had created the hyper-spatial tube for the Imperium by manipulating a nexus. Apparently, Thrax did not pass along this information to the War Masters, to anyone in the Imperium. Well, the Patrol scientists stumbled onto the secret of creating a hyper-spatial tube. The tube shot out to the Hydras System four thousand, one hundred and nineteen light-years. From what we've been able to discover, the hyper-spatial tube entry point sucked in the Swarm Patrol Fleet. It did not suck in the scientists aboard the nexus. Those Swarm creatures remained at the fringe of the Imperium inside the nexus."

"By Swarm creatures, you mean their scientists," Ludendorff murmured.

"Weren't you listening? That's what I just said."

"The alien scientists," Ludendorff said, ignoring the interruption, "now know how to create a hyper-spatial tube. Once they return to the Imperium, others will know as well."

"Yes," O'Hara said hoarsely.

A hyper-spatial tube was the unique creation of a Builder nexus. The Builders were ancient beings of vast intellect, mostly long gone from this part of the galaxy. With a hyper-spatial tube, a ship or a fleet could cross thousands of light-years in an instant. It had allowed the Swarm Imperium to send ships all the way to Human Space twice already. The first invasion had cost humanity several, formerly populated star systems, including the Alpha Centauri System 4.3 light-years from Earth.

The brigadier had squeezed her fingers into fists, pressing her fists against the table. "Do you understand what this all means? Fletcher thought he'd won another glorious victory. It was important that we won the battle, certainly, but—"

O'Hara rubbed her forehead before glaring at the professor. "To the Imperium, losing five thousand ships was like us losing a single Patrol vessel. They weren't even military vessels."

"I was listening. I understand the situation."

"The attack against the Hydras System was a warning," O'Hara said. "We used our Grand Fleet to demolish a tiny enemy probe. The Imperium could just as easily have sent *hundreds of thousands* of warships down the hyper-spatial tube, not a mere eighty thousand like their first invasion attempt that we barely defeated."

"That does constitute a problem," Ludendorff said.

O'Hara gave a strangled laugh. "'Problem?' Hundreds of thousands of Imperial warships means the end of the human race."

"I take it Fletcher took losses during the latest battle."

O'Hara blinked, thrown off by the statement. "Forty-seven ships," she finally said, "half of them destroyer-class or smaller. The admiral thought it was a glorious victory. In the end, it was a staggering defeat, if one thinks of it in attrition terms. If we lost one ship to their ten thousand, we would still go down to certain defeat."

"Yes," Ludendorff said. "The New Men did much better in terms of ratios, but in essence, they had similar results."

"The Swarm Imperium attacked the New Men?" O'Hara asked.

"Indeed."

"And?"

"I just told you," Ludendorff said. "The New Men annihilated the enemy vessels just as Admiral Fletcher destroyed the five thousand."

O'Hara stared hungrily at the professor, hungry for information.

"Oh, very well," he said, sounding exasperated. "Ten thousand Imperial vessels appeared in the Throne World System."

"No," O'Hara whispered.

"Oh, yes," Ludendorff said. "Fortunately, the Emperor led the attack, using all the tricks the New Men had prepared for Admiral Fletcher—if Fletcher had been foolish enough to take the Grand Fleet to the Throne World before this Imperium business all started."

"Was it an Imperial science-team probe?" O'Hara asked.

"Yes, although a considerably larger one than Fletcher faced."

"Did the New Men take losses?"

"I am not at liberty to say," Ludendorff replied.

O'Hara snapped her fingers. "That's why New Men were here. They wanted help, but they're too arrogant to ask us ordinary humans directly. Are you their intermediary?"

"By no means," Ludendorff said.

"Then, why were New Men here?" O'Hara demanded. "Why did they dart me?"

Ludendorff drummed his fingers on the table as he studied her. "I doubt you would believe the truth. Thus, I am hesitant to say."

"Try me."

Ludendorff looked away. Abruptly, he stood. "Follow me, please," he said.

O'Hara rose and then had a second thought. "I want a weapon first."

"There's no need. You are quite safe, my dear, as I'm here."

"The New Men showed up once already. They attacked me, remember?"

"Yes. I half expected their attempt. It was the reason I took such delicate precautions. You should be grateful I did so."

"What are you talking about?"

"Come," Ludendorff said, "I'll show you. I think it's the only way you'll believe me."

O'Hara was deeply suspicious, but she nodded in the end, following Ludendorff out of the galley.

-4-

In disbelief, O'Hara stared at two dead New Men. Each lay on an operating table with his head sawn open at the top. Dangling wires protruded from each exposed brain.

"That's disgusting," O'Hara whispered. "Aren't you as savvy as Strand?"

Ludendorff seemed shocked by the comment and then offended. "Do you think *I* attempted to install obedience devices in them? That I attempted and *failed*, killing them during the process?"

"Didn't you?"

"Certainly not. I exposed their shame, nothing more."

"Wait, what? I don't understand."

"They are quite dead. Don't you agree?"

O'Hara frowned at the professor before stepping closer and pressing a forefinger against each…corpse. Each was quite cold, quite dead indeed. This wasn't a sham.

The brigadier moved to a head, bending down and examining a wire. Her stomach twisted with revulsion. She hated overt mind control like this.

"Are these the same two that ambushed me?" she asked.

"Of course," Ludendorff said.

"And you killed them?"

"Not right away," he said. "I felled them just as they reached you."

"How?"

"Please, do not try to pry all my secrets from me."

"Then, you…you saw me walking the corridors?"

"Naturally."

"And you saw them?"

"Not at first. They wore stealth suits for a time. I had to wait until they revealed themselves before I moved."

"I was bait to lure them?"

"In a manner of speaking," he said.

"And this is why you agreed to meet with me here?"

Ludendorff smiled. "Brigadier, I think it's time to remind you of a painful truth. I am far superior to you. I am superior to the New Men, but not as much as I am superior to you."

"What's your point?" O'Hara snapped.

"Quite simply, that there are subtle games afoot that you fail to understand. Fortunately, I have helped humanity all along the line. These two New Men do not represent the Emperor or the interests of the majority of the New Men."

"Whose interests did they represent?"

"I thought you'd see it immediately," Ludendorff said. "My mistake. Sometimes, I expect too much from others."

"Just tell me," O'Hara hissed.

"These are or were Strand's creatures, of course."

O'Hara looked at them again. "What was their goal?"

"Why, to gain Strand's freedom, of course."

"You've lost me. What does any of this have to do with the Swarm invasions?"

"Very little, I'm afraid. Strand and his remaining mind slaves are a complication in the greater problem. However, they are a complication that we can possibly use to our advantage."

"I'm still not following you."

"I'm not surprised. There are few who can."

"Professor, a smart person can make himself understood. It is your failure that I do not understand you, not mine."

"That is patently false," he said. "Surely, you are aware that people separated by two standard deviations in IQ seldom know what each other are saying. There is an even greater gap between you and me."

O'Hara glanced at the corpses a third time. Sometimes, she wondered if humanity would have been better off without the last two Methuselah Men.

"I need to get out of here," she whispered.

"Yes, I understand. This way, if you please."

O'Hara followed him down a short corridor into a small but comfortable chamber. This one had cushioned chairs facing a stellar chart of Human Space and the surrounding Beyond. The chart did not indicate the location of the New Men's Throne World.

The brigadier plopped into one of the chairs. Ludendorff sat in the other.

"Is Dana around here somewhere?" O'Hara asked.

"Let us stick to the issue, shall we?"

"Fine," O'Hara said. She felt exhausted. Was Ludendorff right?

"Brigadier—"

"Just a minute," O'Hara said. "I've risked my life coming here. I suppose those two we saw back there intended to enslave me in a manner similar to the way that they had been enslaved."

"That would be my guess, yes."

"You don't know?"

"Not yet," Ludendorff said. "Their stealth ship is hidden nearby. I'm wondering if they're going to make a stab at the *Moltke*."

O'Hara's eyes bulged outward. "You lied earlier. You said there were no New Men in the system."

Ludendorff made an offhanded gesture.

"You're using the *Moltke* as another lure," O'Hara said in sudden understanding.

"I suppose that's true."

"I have to warn the commodore."

Ludendorff shook his head. "The Human Race might well perish if you do that."

The physical and mental exhaustion intensified. O'Hara lowered her head, placing her face in her hands. She groaned aloud, shaking her head. Was this part of his plan? Was Ludendorff trying to demoralize her? No. She was made of sterner stuff. She had to play this game to the best of her ability. Ludendorff had a goal. That's why he was doing it this way.

A feud, she realized. She was caught in the ancient feud between Strand and Ludendorff.

"Does the Emperor still hold Strand captive?" she asked through her fingers.

"Ah," Ludendorff said. "You're beginning to understand."

She looked up, squinting at the professor. "This is Strand trying to regain his freedom?"

"A freedom we now need," Ludendorff said softly.

She stared a moment longer before saying, "What in the Hell are you talking about?"

The professor crossed his legs as he leaned back against the cushions. "Don't you see it yet?"

"Why not explain it to me and save time?"

"Humanity cannot defeat the Swarm Imperium in a head-to-head war."

"We've known that for a long time," she said.

"Granted. How, then, does humanity survive the Imperium?"

"Is that a riddle?"

"Indeed."

"Do you have the answer?"

"That I do."

"I'm not going to like your answer, am I?" O'Hara asked.

"No."

She nodded. "Go ahead. Tell me. I'm ready to hear it."

He did tell her, and he was right. She hated the idea. But as he continued to explain, she began to see that Ludendorff might be right this time. Then, he added a kicker, a condition she must meet for his continued aid.

"Captain Maddox isn't going to like your condition," she said.

Ludendorff's eyes seemed to gleam, although he hooded that after a moment. He managed what seemed like an offhand shrug.

That didn't fool O'Hara. Ludendorff had a grudge against Maddox because of what had happened in the Alpha Centauri

System near the end of the original Swarm invasion, and this seemed like the professor's way of getting back at her favorite agent.

Would Ludendorff try to kill Maddox?

"Well?" the Methuselah Man asked. "Do you agree to my terms or not?"

"If more New Men are hidden in this system, we may not live long enough to implement your plan."

"We'll live, trust me."

That was the one thing O'Hara had no intention of doing. Not Ludendorff—or Strand, for that matter. They were two of the slyest, most untrustworthy beings she knew. Yet, she couldn't lie to the Methuselah Man, as he would likely detect such a thing. Therefore, she had to mean what she said.

"Yes," O'Hara told him. "I agree."

"Without equivocation?" he asked, watching her closely.

The brigadier swallowed a lump in her throat, nodding a moment later, hoping that Captain Maddox could forgive her someday.

"Excellent," Ludendorff said, as he rubbed his hands together. "I can hardly wait to begin."

-5-

FIFTEEN DAYS LATER: 103 LIGHT-YEARS AWAY

Captain Maddox strode down a dusty city street on Usan III, the only inhabitable planet of the Usan System.

Starship *Victory* was parked three planets away, having pretended some time ago to use a Laumer Point to leave the star system.

There were two giant haulers in orbit around Usan III, along with several tramp freighters, a decrepit torchship, two Patrol scouts and one defensive satellite.

Not so many years ago, Usan III had been an independent frontier world near the Beyond. The independence had been something of a sham, however. Commonwealth corporations had run Usan III, forcing the poor souls stranded here to work as slave labor in the crystalline mines or hunting the wastelands for varths. Varths were small predatory creatures the size of rats, with stings like scorpions and uncommon speed. The stinger was the thing for humans, as the substance in the hollow of the stinger was incredibly complex, immune to synthetic duplication.

Many labs had tried to duplicate the varth venom, but all had failed, no matter how much money had been sunk into the research.

Varth venom was deadly. A mere touch could kill. Diluted and mixed into a secret formula, it helped to prolong life—provided an elixir of youth for a season. During that season, the varth elixir in a human system built up to a dangerous level. When the tipping point arrived, a user keeled over and died. But it was sudden and relatively painless, even if the signature grimace on each corpse said otherwise. Until such moment, the individual had a second youth, with increased strength, speed and stamina.

As Maddox walked along the dusty street, he removed his wide-brimmed hunter's hat, taking a handkerchief from an inner pocket and wiping sweat from his forehead. The rust-colored sky, the glaringly bright star and the slightly metallic-smelling dust particles floating along the street added to Usan III's alien bleakness.

This was a dry world with ancient low hills mostly devoid of vegetation and with too much red rock, exposed iron ore and shale. Capricorn was the only real city thanks to the spaceport outside its city limits.

There were tin-roofed, stone-and-clay shacks everywhere, blisteringly hot during the day and chilly at night. There were a few taller brick buildings near the center of town. This was where Maddox presently walked. Each of the towers belonged to a different corporation. Air conditioners hummed during the day, while heaters provided comfort at night. Lastly, along the Strip, were several garish casinos. Each of those sported a tall if flimsy statute. Two of the statutes had movable arms, beckoning people to come and enjoy the cool air, the food and whores, and the many card games allowing the lucky the opportunity to win enough money to buy a berth off-planet.

The casinos attracted professional gamblers, bored corporation shills, rock workers, port loaders, bio-fabricators and varth hunters, while on paydays the miners arrived via company airbuses.

Usan III now officially belonged to the Commonwealth of Planets, but like many frontier worlds, law and order was spotty at best. Naturally, company guards protected corporation interests. And for the most part, the corporations had a system in place to keep antagonisms between them to a minimum.

Spotty law and order often meant the law of the jungle. Usan III had advanced a little beyond that. Custom here had brought back the duel to settle most grudges and feuds, and sometimes—an unintended benefit—duels helped to relieve boredom. Those duels could be by gun, sword, knife or even viper stick.

Due to his cover as a professional gambler-slash-occasional varth hunter, Maddox had a rapier belted to his right hip and a short-barreled gun on his left. He wore a dark hat, dark garments, a dark jacket and dusty black boots.

The captain was a tall, lean individual with dangerous blue eyes and an unnatural quickness due to his New Man heritage. He was a half-breed, although he despised the term. When the time came, he would kill his rapist father, a full New Man who had taken advantage of his mother in a breeding facility.

He'd landed on Usan III thirteen days ago, having come down from orbit in a now-departed tramp hauler. After a week in the casinos and a week of poking here and there, asking questions, he'd rented a sealed dune buggy and traveled into the wastelands, looking for a particular varth hunter. He'd found him a day ago, dead on the sands, shot through the face.

When Maddox had turned him over, two young varths had wriggled out of the corpse. One of the horrible creatures had leaped at him, using all six legs to do so, the stinger flashing at his face. Maddox had barely dodged the tiny monster in time, at the same instant he'd used a boot heel on the second, slower varth, crushing it without harming the stinger.

He'd drawn his rapier afterward, although he'd meant to draw his gun. The still-living varth had circled him, scuttling across the sand with unnatural speed. It had faked a leap—yes, it was a nasty creature—and then it had leapt and flashed its stinger at him again.

Maddox hadn't dodged that time. Instead, he'd speared the little creature with the rapier, his follow-through stabbing it against the ground, and then he killed it with a boot heel.

After Maddox had regained his breath, he'd carefully detached each stinger and deposited both in a glass tube where they'd rattled like pieces of iron.

Only then had he returned to the corpse, studying it for a time. He'd recognized the clone of Strand even though the face had been mutilated.

Had that been the last Strand clone, one that had seemingly escaped the original Strand's conditioning?

Maddox suspected so. Soon thereafter, he'd recorded the location, climbed into the dune buggy and headed back for Capricorn, traveling over three hundred kilometers.

As the captain trudged toward The Strip—he'd returned the buggy to the rental agency—he eyed the Nerva Corporation Tower to his right. It was the tallest building on the planet, a full six stories and with a private landing pad on top.

He knew that most of the Nerva Corporation personnel lived in the tower or in orbit aboard a hauler. The original Strand had once worked for Nerva Incorporated. What did it mean that a Strand clone had come here to be shot—many times—in the face out in the wastelands?

Maddox put his hunter's hat back on. He had reason to believe that the last androids—the same kind as he'd faced last mission—had infiltrated the Nerva Corporation. That would mean that he had not dealt with the last of the androids back on the *Shiloh*, the battleship he'd destroyed before gaining two radioactive Builder devices.

He hadn't figured out what those devices were and likely never would. Each was stored in a special compartment deep underground in the Alps on Earth.

Why had the Strand clone traveled to Usan III? Why would some of the last androids be here—if he was correct in that assumption?

The planet was far from other human-inhabited star systems. The varths, and the unique crystals deep underground—

Maddox squinted as he headed for the Star Light Casino, the largest, secretly owned through many shell companies by the Nerva Corporation.

After several months of investigation in other star systems, Maddox had come to believe that Usan III held a secret, one that hinted of Builder or possibly ancient Swarm origins.

Maddox didn't know—yet. But he planned to find out, and hopefully soon.

The key was discovering who had killed the Strand clone out in the wastelands. Once he found out, he believed that he would be that much closer to discovering the hidden androids, and they would likely lead him to the planetary secret. Why else would the androids be on Usan III?

Maddox increased his stride. It was time to start making the right people nervous so he could analyze their mistakes.

-6-

In the Star Light Casino, after winning several big hands at a poker table, Maddox reached into his jacket and took out the glass tube with the metallic-sounding varth stingers.

The other gamblers at the table eyed the tube hungrily.

It was moderately noisy in here, with several hookers leaning against various big spenders. There were a half dozen poker tables, but only this one was occupied at the moment.

There were other tables, though, with roulette, blackjack, spinner and more. Most of the noise came from there. It was cool inside the main room, with several large casino security personnel stationed at strategic locations and keeping track of things.

Maddox rattled the tube, grinning at the others. "This is my good luck charm," he declared. "As long as I have it, I can't lose."

He tucked the tube inside a hidden jacket pocket and leaned back against his chair.

"Aren't you going to cash those in?" asked a beefy miner sporting red hair and a red silk handkerchief tied around his bull neck.

"Don't need to cash 'em in when I can take your money so easily," Maddox replied.

A few annoyed players grunted.

A painted woman approached the captain. She was beautiful and voluptuous, but there seemed to be a strength in her that the other hookers lacked. Her clothing wasn't quite as revealing, either. She wore a short dress that showed off her shoulders and legs to good effect, but her breasts remained tantalizingly hidden.

Her name was Meta, and she was Maddox's wife. She'd arrived five days ago, having come down from the decrepit torchship. Meta had been born on a 2-G world, and had great natural strength. Like the captain, she was a modified human and worked for Star Watch Intelligence.

From behind his chair, Meta rubbed the captain's shoulders. "Let me see that again, love," she stage-whispered in his ear.

Maddox looked up at her, shrugged as if he didn't care, and took out the glass tube, rattling the stingers.

Meta oohed with delight and pressed herself against his nearest shoulder.

"Hey, little lady," a large gambler said, a giant of a guy with ruddy features and expensive blue clothes. "Why don't you come over here to a real man?"

Meta ignored him.

The giant—he was over seven feet tall—took a large roll of bills from a pocket. He waved them at her. "Is this what you love, darling?" he asked Meta.

She wrapped her arms around Maddox's neck, pressing one of her cheeks against his.

The giant—his name was Ajax Clanton—scowled angrily. He'd been drinking for quite some time, and he'd lost a large amount of money to Maddox several hands ago. It was possible he was still smarting from the loss and was on tilt.

"Hey, *bitch*," Ajax said in an ugly voice, "I asked you a question." And he threw the wad of cash at her head.

Maddox reached up in a seeming lazy move—it actually happened startlingly fast—and caught the wadded bundle before it could hit his wife's forehead.

Without a word, the captain pocketed the wad.

Ajax grew red-faced. "Give it back," he told Maddox.

"You threw it away," Maddox said matter-of-factly.

Ajax sat dumbfounded, his mouth open, showing his shock. Then he leaned across the table as he clicked his teeth together. "Do you want to die, friend?"

Maddox ignored the threat as he picked up his latest hand.

"Did you hear me?" Ajax growled.

Meta withdrew her arms from Maddox's neck.

"Come here, bitch," Ajax demanded. "I paid for you fair and square. Now, you're mine. I'm going teach you some lessons you'll never forget. I'm going to—"

Ajax might have continued the tirade. The man seemed to enjoy the sound of his threats. But Maddox picked up his shot glass. It had a film of whiskey at the bottom. He'd had several drinks, but his faster than ordinary metabolism had quickly burned up the alcohol. In any case, Maddox dashed the last contents of his whiskey at Ajax Clanton, the droplets hitting the giant on the face in mid-sentence.

That was too much for the man. He abruptly stopped talking and bellowed as he grasped the nearest edge of the table with both hands. Standing to his imposing height, the giant heaved, lifting the table and hurling it at Maddox.

The captain moved fast, pulling Meta and himself out of the way.

The chips, glasses and cards all flew, furniture crashing against the floor and some of the smaller things reaching other tables.

Ajax stood like an angry primate, panting, aiming at the captain with a heavy gun that he'd quick-drawn from a hidden holster. "You freak!" Ajax shouted, with spittle flying from his mouth. "No one steals from me." He jerked the trigger so the gun roared like a cannon.

Maddox was already twisting, unnaturally fast. It barely proved to be enough as the heavy caliber bullet plowed through the edge of his jacket, tearing a hole through it. The bullet kept going, smashing a chair and its roulette player in the back, causing the unlucky soul to pitch forward against the table, bumping the ball out of the spinning wheel.

Ajax Clanton's eyes bulged outward at Maddox. "What are you?" he whispered. "I've never seen anyone move like that. Are you a New Man? You look like a New Man with a skin job."

Before Ajax could say more, several more gunshots boomed. Bullets riddled the giant, making him stagger. More shots roared as casino guards fired at Ajax Clanton. Clearly, they did not want him shooting up any more guests.

All the gambling stopped as Ajax crashed to his knees. Only then did his big gun slip from his fingers to thump against the floor.

That must have been the signal, for the casino guards stopped firing.

Ajax peered around in the sudden and deafening silence. The man must have incredible vitality. He tried to speak, but to no avail. Finally, like a vast redwood tree on Earth, the giant fell forward onto his face, twitched several times and then lay still.

Smoke drifted from the guards' guns. They kept their weapons drawn as they eyed the stunned and watching crowd, many of the spectators with cards or chips in their hands.

Maybe three seconds later, a short blocky man walked briskly into the area. He wore a black suit, slicked back hair and an air of extreme competence. Despite his shorter stature, he had thick shoulders.

He walked up to the corpse, glanced at it and then listened as one of the guards whispered to him. The man turned toward Maddox.

"Who are you?" the chief, obviously, of casino security asked.

"Bishop King," Maddox said. "Who are you?"

Two of the casino guards squatted by the back-shot roulette player, lifting the groaning man onto a cloth stretcher. They had grabbed the stretcher from where it had been hidden in a nearby wall slot.

The security chief glanced at the injured player. "Take him to the infirmary," he told the guards.

They hoisted the stretcher with the still-groaning player, hurrying out of the main room.

The security chief re-regarded Maddox. "I'm the sheriff in the Star Light. It's best if you act as if my word is law."

The remaining guards had moved closer and taken up station a step or so back and flanking the security chief. They still had their guns out, all of them aiming at Maddox.

"Call me Mr. Tubb," the security chief added.

Maddox nodded.

"Now," Tubb said, "tell me what happened."

"I can do that," Meta said, stepping up.

Tubb's head moved minutely toward Meta as he leaned back toward the guard that had whispered to him earlier. The guard explained something. Tubb nodded, and the guard retreated a step.

"You started this?" Tubb said.

"No," Meta said. "He did." She pointed at the dead giant.

"And who are you?" Tubb asked.

"A traveler," Meta said.

"That's not good enough. I want a name and your reason for being on Usan III and in the Star Light."

Maddox felt it then. Something had gone wrong and he didn't know what. This all seemed like an act. Someone had set Ajax Clanton on him. Now, the hidden someone was setting Mr. Tubb on him. Why then had the guards murdered Ajax?

Could Ajax's actions have been an accident? Yes, maybe the giant was supposed to have started something, but he wasn't supposed to kill other customers. Yet, if that was true, why hadn't Ajax just kept firing at him? The giant had paused, and in pausing, he'd signed his death warrant. If the guards had acted differently, they would have given themselves away. That might have also given away the hidden someone that Maddox hunted. Yet, how could that have been the case?

This was a nebulous feeling, to be sure. But Maddox trusted his instincts. He focused on Tubb as Meta gave the man her fake name and a made-up reason for being on Usan III.

Another nebulous feeling grew within the captain. Something was off with Tubb, very off.

Maddox suddenly felt as if he should leave this place. Meta needed to leave, too.

"Thanks for nothing," Maddox said, interrupting Tubb's interrogation of Meta. "I was on a winning streak before this. But all this gunplay and useless killing has made me tired. I'm turning in." He grabbed Meta's left wrist, jerking her to him. "You're coming with me, Sugar. I need a bed companion and you're elected."

"No," Tubb said in an even voice. "I'm not finished with my investigation. You may be at fault here. You will stay until I determine the truth."

Maddox turned to the gamblers from his table. Someone had righted it and put the glasses, cards and chips back in place. He pointed at the miner with the red silk handkerchief tied around his bull neck. "You saw it. Tell the man what happened."

With a nod, the miner started talking about Ajax's foul mood.

"You," Tubb told the miner, "stop talking, now."

The miner stared at Tubb, maybe noticed the gunmen behind him, but he kept on talking anyway. The miner seemed like the stubborn sort, not easily intimidated.

Other gamblers from other tables were listening to the explanation. Two men at Maddox's table nodded in agreement as the miner continued his rundown of the event.

There was no flicker of annoyance, no flicker of *any* emotion as Mr. Tubb moved up to the strong-looking miner. The security chief put a hand on the man's left shoulder, squeezing gently, it seemed.

The miner cried out in pain, twisting under Tubb's steely grip. The red-haired man tried to wriggle free, but despite the difference in size, Tubb was clearly stronger than the bull-necked miner.

At last, the miner whimpered, nodding vigorously.

Tubb let go.

The miner collapsed forward as he gingerly touched his tortured shoulder.

Meanwhile, Tubb eyed the other gamblers at the table before focusing on Maddox, who still stood with Meta's wrist in his grip.

It was time to preempt the security chief.

"Know what I think?" Maddox shouted. "I think Mr. Tubb here wants my varth stingers." With his free hand, he took the glass tube from his inner jacket pocket and held it high. Maddox rattled the two stingers. "Man wants to murder me for these. Can you believe it, here at the Star Light?"

A murmur began throughout the casino as many of the patrons nodded in agreement with Maddox.

"Are you going to murder me, Mr. Tubb?" Maddox asked the chief directly. "Don't they pay you enough in this joint?"

"Boss?" an upset guard asked the chief.

Mr. Tubb shook his head, holding up a hand even as he stared evenly at Maddox.

The captain did not read any anger in Tubb's eyes. He did note something critical that convinced him of a hard certainty—Tubb was an android. Maddox would have bet his captaincy on that.

"You must come with me, sir," Tubb told Maddox in a mild tone.

"You want to murder me out of sight, is that it?" Maddox asked loudly. "That ain't fair."

"Have you forgotten?" Tubb asked. "My will is the law in the Star Light. Notice those guns, Mr. King. I have the ability to enforce the law."

"Being the law don't give you no right to murder me," Maddox said in a loud voice. "I haven't done nothing wrong. All I done is win money and hold two stingers everyone wants."

Tubb scanned the watching throng. It seemed that gears clicked in his computer brain—and they did, if Maddox was right about the humanoid being an android. "Bishop King," Tubb said, "you are free to go. Before you do, I would like a private word with you."

"You can talk to me outside," Maddox said, "without your bully boys and your damn law."

For a half-second, Tubb assessed the situation, nodding, dismissing his gunmen. He noticed the two stretcher-bearers returning, walking to the giant corpse and putting the empty stretcher beside it.

"A round of drinks," Tubb said loudly and emotionlessly. "It's on the house."

The miners, varth hunters, corporation shills and gamblers cheered. Afterward, the spectators left the tables as they rushed as a mob to collect their free alcohol at the bar.

Compared to a moment ago, the main room was almost empty. The stretcher-bearers grunted under their heavy load, staggering for an exit. The bloody corpse was face-down on the stretcher, with his hands dragging on the floor. Two guards had remained in the general area, while a crusty old salt sat alone at a blackjack table slyly inspecting some of the decks.

"Outside," Tubb told Maddox.

The captain eyed Tubb, deciding on his plan of action as he nodded. The security chief was likely an android; likely enough that Maddox would play that angle.

As he turned to go, the captain glanced at the two guards. By their stance, they were clearly waiting for orders. They would not move until they received new orders from Tubb. As Maddox continued to turn, he also checked out the lone blackjack cheater.

The old-timer was one-eyed, as he had a patch over the other side. He had the worn clothes of a down-on-his-luck varth hunter and the leathery skin of a man who had spent far too much time under a harsh star. Once, the old-timer must have been strong and agile.

The man was, of course, Sergeant Treggason Riker in disguise. He had a bionic eye under the false patch, and a bionic arm. Riker had lost both the eye and the arm during a desperate mission on Altair III many years ago.

For just a moment, Riker looked up. As the sergeant did so, Maddox gave him a prearranged signal—he rubbed the underside of his nose as if trying to stifle a sneeze. They had many prearranged signals to choose from.

Maddox did not look long enough to see if Riker gave him the *yes, I understand* countersign. The captain expected Riker to be on top of his game and to get it right the first time.

With the turn completed, Maddox headed for the casino exit, with Mr. Tubb following him. The captain had no doubt that Tubb had signaled the two security honchos, who would now trail behind. That was fine, as Meta and Riker should both be following the guards.

Maddox had released Meta's wrist a moment ago, pushing her from him as he'd turned to go. That, too, had been a signal, one he knew his wife had clearly understood.

Meta and Riker surely knew that they were going to try to kidnap an android in plain sight during the middle of the day. It would be a novel approach, one that should work but that had never been tested in the field before.

This could prove to be interesting, which whetted the captain's appetite to try it.

-7-

At the blackjack table, Sergeant Riker rose unsteadily to his feet. He had been checking decks, acting the part of a drunken fool. Unfortunately, he'd had far too much practice doing the real thing the last few years.

The truth was that he was too old for these sorts of junkets. He should have retired after the terrible invasion war with the Swarm Imperium. The horrors that he'd undergone then—

The sergeant shivered as he remembered, and he brushed his bionic hand with the real one. He'd burned off the old bionic hand with a blaster when a Ska ego-fragment had tried to indwell his body. The fragment or spawn of the Ska would have possessed him like a demon in those Bible stories.

Riker shivered once again, and he felt one of the security people studying him. It wasn't one of the two that followed the captain and Mr. Tubb, but a different person in the shadows.

Was Mr. Tubb really an android? According to the signal, the captain clearly thought so. How would Maddox have determined that? How could Maddox think at all after barely surviving an assassination attempt by that giant madman?

Riker did not know. He did know that the captain had uncommon reasoning abilities and was one of the coolest people under fire that he'd ever met. The youngster—well, Maddox wasn't really a youngster anymore. He was a seasoned Intelligence agent. Maddox might actually be one of the best agents in Star Watch's impressive arsenal of agents. The captain still took far too many risks, though.

The security person that had been studying him from the shadows now turned away, perhaps satisfied that he had seen a bum. Riker's private worries and fears must have translated into the role he was playing, making him a convincing non-threat.

Riker didn't celebrate the small victory. He was a technician doing his job. He seldom made fancy moves, sticking to the book or to his plain old horse sense.

He shuffled across the casino floor, wearing shabby clothes and even worse footwear. Riker knew that he had something of a gift for looking like a rundown hobo.

Oh-oh, the two guards following the captain and Tubb drew holstered weapons. Did they mean to gun Maddox down on the street?

Riker did not speed up, but his gut began to twist. If Tubb was indeed an android, his best chance at remaining free was to follow a ruthless pattern of behavior against the captain. It should be obvious to all the security personnel—and certainly, to Tubb—that he and Meta were Star Watch agents. How could the enemy *not* know?

Riker began muttering, spitting on the spotless casino floor. If a guard saw him, the man might come over and reprimand him…but no, the guards were through watching him. To them, he was a harmless bum, a rabbit in a den of wolves.

At that point, Riker increased his speed. He also increased the volume of his muttering in order to disguise that he'd slightly picked up his walking pace. He no longer shuffled as such, but scuffed his worn-out boots against the polished floor.

The captain had reached the main door. He glanced at Tubb just behind him, opened the door and strode through as if he didn't have a care in the world.

Tubb glanced back at the two security honchoes following him, giving them a slight nod. The likely android noticed Meta. It did not seem to surprise him. Instead of checking further, Mr. Tubb followed Maddox into the hot sunlight.

The two security men picked up their pace, jogging toward the closing door.

"Hey," Meta called to them, using a seductive voice.

One of them looked back at her.

She used her left hand to raise her skirt, showing the guard the color of her panties.

That guard slowed down to get a better look. The other continued for the door.

Meta smiled, licking her lips at the guard.

That must have been too much for the security man. He scowled, and he began to turn his head toward his companion, who had reached the main door as it closed.

From her glittering purse, Meta drew a tiny but powerful stunner. She drilled the head-turning security man, hitting him in the neck.

The man gurgled, staggered—Meta stunned him again—and he went down with a thud.

The other man already had his hand on the doorknob. Instead of turning it, he turned back, saw his downed friend and looked at Meta closing in on him. He began to bring his weapon around to bear against her.

Meta kept the stunner trigger down, drilling the second guard in the face. It was a brutal stunner tactic. He crashed back against the door. Meta hopped over the fallen security man and punched the second man in the kidney. He arched back in pain. Meta slammed another fist against him, and he began to fold.

Riker reached them, stepping over the first guard, and he passed Meta as she bodily tossed the second guard out of the way.

There was no place to drag them out of the way to hide them from others. Speed and the element of surprise were their only friends today.

Meta yanked the door open. Riker needed that, as he busily assembled a special android-altering weapon. Taking a deep and hopefully calming breath, Riker charged through the opened door and into the painfully bright, dusty street where Maddox faced Mr. Tubb.

If Maddox was wrong about Tubb being an android, the captain was going to bring a storm of trouble onto their heads. Even if the captain was right, things were about to get nasty in the worst possible way on an out-of-the-way desert planet like Usan III.

-8-

Maddox whirled around as Mr. Tubb stepped out of the shadow of the Star Light Casino porch and into the glaring light of the bright star.

The captain expected Tubb to continue his role as chief of security. He was surprised to see Tubb point a forefinger at him as if it was a weapon. That meant it likely *was* a weapon and that Tubb was indeed an android, a synthetic human constructed long ago by the Builders.

"Ah. You understand the situation," Tubb said in a flat voice.

"What are you talking about?"

"Please, Captain Maddox. Let us forgo the pretense. You belong to Star Watch, and I am an android, as you clearly have already surmised."

The captain switched mental gears at astonishing speed. "Are you a Yen Cho model android?" Maddox asked.

"I am going to warn you, Maddox. You are in grave danger on this planet. We all are. The—"

At that point, Sergeant Riker appeared. He aimed the anti-android weapon at Mr. Tubb. It was likely that the sergeant understood the meaning of the pointing finger. The android concealed a weapon-tube there and threatened the captain with death.

Maddox noticed the sergeant, saw the man's weapon, the intent on Riker's face, and he signaled with a raised hand. There had been a change in plans.

Tubb turned around as he stopped talking, likely seeing Riker with the weapon drawn.

Riker must not have seen the captain's waving hand, or if he did, not understood the new sign. The sergeant pulled the trigger, firing a strange yellow energy into the android's chest plate. The beam burned away the clothing, but it did not blacken the pseudo-skin underneath. The beam wasn't supposed to.

The effect of the beam on Mr. Tubb was startling. He—or it—stiffened at once.

Riker fired again, even as Maddox shouted at him to stop. From a second tube under the first, the sergeant fired a small disc that attached to the exposed android skin. The disc made humming sounds, and it injected a computer virus into Mr. Tubb.

The special virus was supposed to turn the android into a willing Star Watch helper.

"No," Tubb whispered. "That isn't going to happen. We have anticipated such a weapon and have developed a counteraction."

Maddox heard the words, and he suspected the worst. "Down!" he shouted. The captain threw himself onto the sandy street. "Down, Sergeant. Get down before you die!" Then, Maddox covered his head with his arms.

Riker blinked stupidly, finally dropped the strange weapon and threw himself down. Meta was coming through the door, must have seen Riker going down and did likewise.

At that point, the upright Mr. Tubb exploded, android body parts, many of them human looking, flying violently outward.

The blast concussion shook Maddox. But his evasive tactic proved effective in one particular. The shards of Mr. Tubb did not blow downward. They blew down the door of the Star Light Casino. Some of the shards peppered the interior of the place. Other android shards struck the casinos on the other side of the street.

The blast alerted security systems, as alarms began to blare in the Star Light and other casinos.

As Maddox, Riker and Meta lay stunned on the ground, the surviving legs of Mr. Tubb toppled over onto the dusty street.

It was a grotesque performance. There was some blood, fake blood, to be sure, but there were also mechanical gears and mechanisms that fell out of the two legs' upper openings.

Across the street, several people stumbled out of casino entrances.

Maddox's ears still rang as his mind attempted to kick-start its thinking. The blast had disoriented him. He realized vaguely that he only had a few more seconds to do something. Otherwise, Meta, Riker and he were going to be arrested by someone. Later, that someone would interrogate him and the others.

Maddox dragged his hands beside him, pressing his palms against the hot dust. He had to get out of here. He had to contact Starship *Victory*. This spectacle would blow his cover. This had blown the androids' cover. Both sides would likely move openly now. Did that mean the Nerva Corporation people would do likewise?

Maddox groaned as he shoved his hands against the dust. He levered his torso upward. He gritted his teeth and dragged his knees forward, helping to keep his higher position.

More people were coming out of the casinos. Many of them pointed at Maddox and pointed at the two legs lying near the captain.

What had just happened? Had Mr. Tubb been trying to help him? It would appear so. The android had tried to warn him, warn him of danger.

What was the threat? It was imperative that Maddox learn about the danger as quickly as possible.

Why had Riker used the android-capturing weapon? Hadn't the sergeant seen the new signal?

Well, that didn't matter now. He could criticize the sergeant later for failing to be properly alert. First, they had to survive.

Using his hardened resolve, Maddox forced his leg muscles to propel his body upward until he swayed where he stood. His eyes weren't quite working right yet, but he stumbled to his wife.

Kneeling, Maddox shook her. She groaned pitifully.

"Get up," Maddox told her in a rough voice.

Meta opened her eyes, but it was clear she couldn't see him yet.

"Get up, Meta," Maddox ordered. "We're out of time."

He shoved up to an upright stance again, stumbling to Riker. The sergeant was an old-timer. The blast might have finished his oldest companion for good.

Maddox put surprisingly gentle hands on the older man's body. He shook just as gently. "Riker," the captain said.

The sergeant did not answer.

"Sergeant Riker," Maddox said, more sternly. "This is a gross violation of duty. You will get on your feet and start helping around here. We're in trouble, and I need you to cover my back."

Riker lay on his back. Maddox had just rolled him over. Riker opened a bloodshot eye.

"Did you hear me?" Maddox demanded.

Riker just stared at him.

"Fine," Maddox said. The captain reached down, grabbed hold of the sergeant's rags and heaved with considerable strength. He hoisted Riker to his feet and then heaved again, placing the oldster over his left shoulder.

Maddox turned, seeing that Meta was on her feet. "Ready?" he asked her.

"Where are we going?" she asked in a slur of words.

"Straight for the Nerva Corporation Tower," he said.

"Won't that be a nest of androids?"

"Given Mr. Tubb's last action, I'm beginning to wonder."

"People are pointing at us."

"The reason we have to move now," Maddox said. "Someone is going to try to stop us, and the longer we wait, the more certainly they will insist."

"If—"

"*Move*," he said.

Meta did, dragging her left leg. She had little left in the way of garments, mostly dressed in a bright red bra and equally red panties. That interested many of the watchers; a few who had started to whistle and holler their appreciation.

Maddox did not like their leering or whistling. "Come here," he told Meta.

She did as ordered. He put his other arm over her—the first steadied the sergeant draped over his shoulder. Maddox now leaned some of his weight against Meta.

"Help me remain upright," Maddox said. "I'm feeling winded."

Together, Maddox and Meta moved toward the Nerva Corporation Tower in the near distance.

"Hey, you," a man shouted with a stentorian voice from across the street. "Where do you think you're going?"

Maddox halted, shuffling around with Meta's help. "You talking to me?" the captain shouted.

"Who do you think I'm taking to?" the loud-voiced man bellowed. He wore a costly suit and had many guards behind him. He was a casino owner, Mr. Harvey.

"I'm calling out Nerva Corp," Maddox shouted back. "That was their hitman that did this."

"What?" Mr. Harvey said. "That's nuts."

"Follow along if you want," Maddox said. "I aim to get justice for what just happened."

Many of the mob stared at each other. Maddox's words did not sound like a guilty man's false plea of innocence. They sounded like an angry man who'd been wronged.

"Let's follow him," Mr. Harvey told his security honchoes. "We need to get to the bottom of this."

Maddox had Meta shuffle him around again so they faced the six-story Nerva Tower.

"How does having them following us help?" Meta whispered in a pant.

"Don't talk," Maddox told her. "I'm thinking, looking for an angle that will get us off planet before the other androids, or whatever this grave danger is, tries to kill us."

-9-

Maddox still felt the effect of the blast, as it was making it harder than normal to concentrate, especially with the ringing in his ears.

He carried Riker on one shoulder and sheltered Meta under the other arm. A mob followed. Many were simply following Meta's wonderful butt.

He needed to concentrate. What had Tubb been trying to tell him? The android had attempted to warn him of a grave danger. Tubb had included himself as being threatened. What sort of menace endangered an android and Star Watch operatives?

The androids had factions. Had he stumbled onto an android civil war? Was Tubb on the weaker side?

Maddox had had his fill of androids last voyage. Actually, he'd had his fill of them before that. Why didn't the androids make a deal with Star Watch? The constant skullduggery hindered both sides. Possibly, the androids did not do so because their objectives were quite different from Star Watch's goals.

Builder androids…

Could Usan III have ancient treasures buried in the sands? Given what had happened last voyage that seemed likely here. The mines went deep into the earth. Maddox wracked his brain. What did he know about the crystalline mines?

In the extreme depths, miners chipped at unusual crystal formations. Those crystals were used in…in long-range detection and comm sets, if he remembered correctly. The unique crystals helped boost such technologies.

Was it possible the crystals helped or were used in ancient Builder devices?

As Maddox neared the Nerva Corp Tower, he wondered why he would have thought of such a thing, the Builder angle. He had no reason to have made such a leap. It almost seemed as if someone else had…had *slipped* the idea into his mind.

Maddox almost halted because *that* was an even stranger thing to think than the idea of ancient Builder use of the Usan III crystalline mines.

He shifted the sergeant on his shoulder.

"Ow," Riker complained. "Your shoulder is too bony for you to move me around like that."

Maddox did stop this time, as he suspected the sergeant had been slacking, riding his shoulder instead of asking to be set down. Only a well man complained so overtly about a lack of comfort.

The captain tilted his torso forward.

"What are you doing?" Riker complained. "I'll lose my purchase if you keep doing that."

Maddox slammed the sergeant onto his worn boots and released the older man. Riker might have fallen backward if Meta hadn't jumped out from under Maddox's arm and steadied the sergeant.

"Keep walking," Maddox said. "We need to stay ahead of the crowd."

He didn't wait to see if the other two listened, but starting walking, lengthening his stride and increasing his pace to its normal abrupt manner.

"Maddox," Meta called. "Wait for us."

The captain glanced behind him. Riker had an arm around Meta's shoulders as the two of them tried to keep up with him. Behind them by thirty feet, the well-dressed Mr. Harvey led his gunmen. Some of the gunmen did not look as enthusiastic as they had earlier.

"Hey, you," Harvey shouted in his loud voice.

Because Maddox was waiting for Meta and Riker to catch up, he looked at Mr. Harvey.

"Where *are* you headed?" the casino owner asked.

Maddox pointed at Nerva Corp Tower looming nearby.

"Why there?" Harvey asked.

"Because they're responsible for the blast," Maddox said.

Harvey stopped. So did his uneasy gunmen. The trailing mob also stopped, keeping their distance from Harvey and his men.

The heat, the passage of time, the destination—it was possible all three had dampened everyone's former enthusiasm to see Maddox get some justice. The explosion back at the casinos meant someone had seriously killed someone and might well use similar explosions to kill more people.

"You can prove Nerva Corp had something to do with what happened back there?" Harvey shouted.

"You saw the two legs, right?" Maddox asked.

Harvey nodded slowly.

"You didn't check," Maddox said, "but those weren't human legs."

"What?" Harvey shouted.

"They were an android's legs," Maddox said, "an android that just blew up."

Across the small distance between them, Harvey squinted suspiciously at Maddox.

"What have you been drinking?" Harvey asked.

"If you're scared, go back."

"No one talks to me like that," Harvey said in front of his gunmen.

"Boss, *look*," a security honcho said. The gunman pointed at the tower.

Four big battlesuited marines were walking out of the tower entrance. The combat suits had exoskeleton power, an enclosed atmosphere, cooling units and heavy firepower along each armored sleeve. Each unit weighed approximately one and a half tons. Those looked like the newest high-grade military suits. All they lacked were jetpack-assisted takeoff nozzles in back. Such suited marines could make twenty or even thirty foot leaps.

The combat suits began to lumber toward the mob, the four of them in a row. Dust swirled as each heavy suit-boot struck the ground.

The casino mob in back was the first to turn around and take off. Two or three people hurried to the sides of the street, but they looked ready to run after those sprinting down the street.

Several gunmen forcefully complained about the situation. Mr. Harvey looked back at them. Whatever the gunmen told the casino owner next must have proven convincing. He gave an order, and the group of them began walking away from the approaching combat suits. They walked away much faster than they had walked after Maddox a few minutes ago.

"Now what do we do?" Riker complained. "We've given ourselves into their hands."

"Did you expect combat suited marines to show up?" Meta asked Maddox.

The captain remained silent as he studied the approaching space marines. Back at the casino, he'd kept the three of them from a sudden lynching by boldly demanding justice. He had envisioned using the mob to storm Nerva Corp Tower. Once they were inside, he had planned to race up the flights of stairs or elevators and steal whatever air-car was on the top pad. Upon reflection, he realized that it had been a stupid plan. Surely, Nerva Corp had heavy weaponry here. A surprise blitz would have been unlikely to be successful under any circumstances, especially if the Nerva Corp people were trying to pull something strange.

Why had he marched straight to his most likely foe? That wasn't like him. Did it have anything to do with the unbidden insights he'd had earlier?

Maddox recalled that the Spacers had developed an electronic form of mind manipulation. He also remembered that the androids sometimes adopted Spacer methods. This was looking more and more like an android civil war.

"Maddox?" Meta asked. "What are we going to do?"

As if upon some command, the four space marines raised their left arms, aiming heavy caliber anti-personnel cannons at the three of them exposed in the middle of the street.

"Maddox?" his wife asked.

The captain raised his hands high into the air and walked in front of Meta and Riker. "I surrender," he told the marines.

The four suited marines halted.

Maddox watched, wondering if the cannons were about to open fire, shredding his body into bloody chunks.

Instead of that happening, two of the space marines backed up toward one side of the street and the other two backed up the other way.

Maddox understood the signal and starting walking toward the opening between them.

"What should *we* do?" Meta called.

Maddox did not answer. He hoped the marines would be satisfied with just him. He trudged past the towering suits, continuing for the Nerva Corp Tower entrance.

"Hold," an altered voice said over a helmet speaker.

Maddox stopped.

"You two," the speaker said. "You are also our prisoners. You must join Captain Maddox in the coming interrogations."

Maddox looked back, watching as Meta and Riker stumbled after him. He had made a critical error, and it looked like it might cost him two of the people he cared about most.

Who controlled Nerva Corp on Usan III, and what had Tubb been trying to warn him about?

-10-

Maddox stumbled as a suited marine shoved him into an underground holding cell. The captain strained but couldn't stop himself in time, slamming his left shoulder and hip against the far wall, bouncing off it and finally bringing himself to a halt in the center of the cell.

The hatch slammed shut, the door sounding heavy, too heavy to open with normal human muscles. Perhaps only exoskeleton strength could open and close the stone hatch.

Gingerly Maddox sat cross-legged in the center of the dimly lit cell. It was a small holding area without any toiletry but with a musky odor and a sense of great solitude and heaviness.

The feeling of heaviness would be the weight of the planet pushing psychologically against him. The space marine and he had ridden in an express elevator, going down to a great depth.

What had happened to Meta and Riker? The marines had separated them after walking through the tower's front entrance.

Maddox calmed his breathing as he forced himself to ignore the throbbing in his body where he had struck the wall.

Someone had captured him. That someone had known his name. That someone now had him prisoner deep under the sands of Usan III.

What could he decipher from the situation?

Maddox started thinking. He had to think in order to stave off the claustrophobia that threatened him. His heritage was

New Man. New Men liked to move, to act, to do. Long periods of confinement proved difficult for almost all New Men. That included the captain, although not to the same degree that it would a full-blooded Dominant.

Great depth would seem to indicate an affinity for the crystalline mines.

Maddox breathed deeply through his nostrils, holding his breath and only slowly letting it out. He did this several more times, attempting to calm his mind.

He feared for Meta and Riker. But there was nothing he could do for them now. He must release the fear. He must let go of everything—

Maddox straightened into rigidity. He stood up, raising his arms until the palms of his hands touched the rock ceiling. He pressed upward against the ceiling, straining harder and harder. He let rage grow in his chest. He continued to push, panting, drinking gulps of air as the strain began to tell against him.

Part of him wondered what he was doing.

Maddox deliberately opened his mouth and began shouting, the sound loud within the confines of his cell. He continued to shout—

You're not fooling me.

The words were clear and distinct in Maddox's mind. There was no concealing them, and the captain knew for a certainty that he had not generated those thoughts.

He let his arms drop, lay down on his back and closed his eyes. He was tired. He was starting to get hungry and he was certainly thirsty.

One thing he knew, an android had not generated that thought in him. He wasn't sure how he knew this, but the certainty of it bubbled in his chest.

"Spacers," Maddox said aloud. "It has to be Spacers. Shu 15 had two modifications in her. One powered the other. The other was the ability of transduction."

Maddox cocked his head, feeling as if he was right about the causation of the thought in his mind. He recalled the trip into the deep Beyond with Shu, and the various ways that she'd used her transduction.

"Ah, yes," he said, speaking loudly. "Transduction was the technological ability to see electromagnetic radiation and electromagnetic wavelengths and process the data as fast as a computer. That's how Shu used to say it, anyway. She also told me once that she could interfere with the neural connections of androids."

As he lay on the floor, Maddox folded his hands on top of his chest. He had to needle the hidden operative who had these Spacer-like modifications. He was sure that was what was happening. It had that feel, and he was going to trust his intuition.

"How far of a stretch is it to learn to manipulate an android's electronic brain, to manipulate a human brain? Whoever you are, you've been putting ideas and thoughts into my head. I suppose that wouldn't exactly be transduction but hyper-induction, imposing your will over mine. Yes. That's what you've been attempting with your particular technological modification. You should know, however, that I am already beginning to know what is my thought and what is your thought."

Maddox waited, but nothing happened. How could he needle the operator even more? Ah. He began by forcing a chuckle.

"I find that interesting. You're silent now. Or are you attempting a deeper level of hyper-induction within my frontal lobe?"

Maddox paused. Why would Spacers bother with Usan III? It came to him.

"This is about the crystalline mines, isn't it? I'm guessing the peculiar crystals can help power the Spacer-like modifications. Occam's razor would suggest that you are a Spacer agent. Star Watch hasn't seen hide nor hair of you Spacers since the Ska caused Alpha Centauri A to radically expand. The last I heard, the Spacers had left Human Space to start over in the Beyond. Is this, then, a retrograde movement on your part? Did some of you slip back into Human Space because your crystalline supply has run low?"

Again, there was nothing in his mind to indicate that this was doing anything.

Maddox wondered if the mind-altering agent was lying low, hoping he would tire of this line of inquiry. Instead of the unanswered words causing Maddox to doubt, he became even keener to think this through.

He would proceed as if he faced a Spacer agent. That could easily be the wrong conjecture, but he would see where the line of thinking led him.

Androids and Spacers hated each other—a well-known fact. Thus, Tubb would have seen Spacers as a grave danger to both android and human. The Spacers had good reason to hate him, Captain Maddox. Not so long ago, he had slain the Visionary's son as she had attempted to trap Starship *Victory*. He had succeeded in the null region where the Visionary had spectacularly failed against the Ska. With the dreadful expansion of the star Alpha Centauri A, the Visionary and her group of Spacers had died in an alien-run Destroyer. It was also true that Spacers hated Methuselah Men even more than they hated androids. That might explain what had happened to the Strand clone. If Maddox were right about this new modification ability—hyper-induction—the Spacer agent might have detected the clone with his newfound power.

The more Maddox considered the angles, the more certain he was that he faced a Spacer agent like Shu 15. That did not bode well for him, Meta or Riker. If the Spacers hated anyone more than anyone else, he would be that person.

"I suppose you realize that Starship *Victory* is going to tear this planet apart to find you," Maddox said.

The captain wasn't sure, but he felt, or thought he did, a momentary sensation of fear.

Maddox reconsidered the idea. Hyper-induction wasn't telepathy as such. The agent attempted to alter his thinking through electromagnetic or neural pulses.

If the unknown agent were this good at hyper-induction against him, would the agent be able to use transduction against the Adok AI Galyan?

The momentary fear he'd felt must have been a trick. If that was true, he had to keep Starship *Victory* away from here. He needed to escape and warn—

Maddox began to laugh in order to cover his thoughts.

"That was *your* thought," he said a little later, wiping a tear of laughter from his eye. "You're good. I'll grant you that. But I doubt you can take on—"

Without warning, the heavy hatch began sliding open.

Maddox sat up, surprised. As the stone hatch continued to scrape open, he climbed to his feet. Finally, the hatch stood ajar, with a space marine in exoskeleton-powered armor standing beside it.

The other person, the one standing beside the space marine, interested Maddox even more. She was a small Spacer in a tight blue uniform. The top of her head wouldn't reach his shoulder if she stood beside him. She wore dark-colored goggles over her eyes, and long dark hair framed her elfin features.

She resembled Shu 15 in that she appeared to be of Southeast Asian heritage. She had narrower features than Shu had possessed. This woman was prettier in the face but with a more slender form. She was too boyish in shape for Maddox to appreciate sexually. Perhaps that was partly a property of her tight uniform. Maybe she looked more womanly in the flesh.

In her right hand, the Spacer held a projac, a small stubby weapon.

"You're a Provost Marshal," Maddox said. "I recognize your insignia. But that's what Shu did, pretending to be provost marshal. Are you really a First Class Surveyor?"

The woman seemed startled by the guess.

Shu 15 had once told Maddox that she had been a special agent, a cross between a Patrol officer and a Star Watch Intelligence operative. It would make sense if this woman were a similar sort of agent. If the Spacers had departed Human Space, coming back here would be a Patrol-like mission for whoever did it.

"You are *di-far*," the Spacer said in a lilting voice. She also said it as if that explained Maddox's guess about her. "You will come with me, *di-far*. Know, though, that if you attempt to subdue me, I will kill you without hesitation. You are a known enemy of ours, a man who has committed terrible deeds against the Spacer Nation. Do you understand the narrow thread by which you live?"

Maddox nodded, although he said, "Your projac ejects slivers. Given the design, the spring-driven slivers are normally hardened knockout drugs. Will you drug me to death or will you inject me with killing poison?"

"This," the woman said, twisting the projac, "will not do the killing." She holstered the weapon in a small pouch at her belt.

"Will you kill me with your hands?" Maddox asked.

"With my mind," she said.

"You can do that?" Maddox asked, impressed in spite of himself.

"Not as you think," the woman said. "Observe."

The armored marine stepped forward, and the visor slid down with a whirr, revealing an empty helmet—no one stood in the suit.

"The suit is remote-controlled?" asked Maddox.

The woman tapped the side of her head. "I control it through transduction. One thought, and it will aim its guns at you and shred your body to bloody ribbons."

Maddox nodded again. He understood.

"Now come," the woman said. "It is time that you learned your part in the coming struggle."

-11-

Maddox settled comfortably in a chair at a small table. On the table were piled various delicacies and drinks. He rubbed his hands together, picked up a waiting fork and knife and made to dig into a dish…and paused.

The woman and her combat suit had taken him down several drilled rock corridors, finally entering this medium-sized chamber. It had the table and food, some ship-like chairs to the sides and several screens on the rock walls, along with several air-vents higher up near the ceiling.

The woman had sat in one of the chairs along the side. The marine combat suit stood at the entrance, blocking the closed hatch.

"What is wrong?" the woman asked.

"Can't you sense it?" Maddox replied.

"I am no longer allowed to probe your mind."

That was interesting—given that she was telling the truth. "Why not?" asked Maddox.

"I am not allowed to tell you."

"Oh. Who gave the order?"

"I am not allowed to tell you."

"Ah," Maddox said. Once more, he raised the fork and knife, and then slowly lowered the cutlery onto the table, releasing them.

"What is wrong?" she asked.

"I have a suspicious nature." Maddox indicated the food and drink. "As you stated earlier, the Spacers have no love for me. Possibly, you blame me for the Visionary's death. Maybe you blame me for the loss of Spacer vessels. Given those things, I wonder why you should offer me food and drink. One reason might be because you've laced the items with mind-altering drugs."

"If true, would that matter?"

Maddox nodded.

"Why would we bother giving you drugged food, as we could have just as easily used the marine suits and injected you with drugs? We need not even have done that. We might have laced your air with drugs."

Maddox didn't answer, although he could have pointed out that some drugs weren't as effective if the imbiber knew about them beforehand. Clearly, some drugs would not inject well through the air supply.

Abruptly, Maddox used his right forearm and swept the dishes and drinks from the table so they crashed and spilled onto the floor.

The woman jumped up, clearly startled.

That satisfied Maddox on several levels. The most important was that it proved that she no longer probed his thoughts, as she had said. He frowned a second later. Might she be an excellent actress? If so, she might have just faked being startled in order to lull him.

"That is only a temporary solution for you," she said, while resuming her seat. "In time, you will grow hungry, too hungry to resist our food."

"You're wrong," Maddox said. "I am well capable of starving myself to death."

She cocked her head. "That is poorly reasoned. We can subdue you and inject drugs into you, if that is our wish."

Maddox said nothing.

"You are thirsty and hungry. I know you are. You should eat."

Maddox still did not reply.

"You need nourishment."

"Take me outside to a casino," Maddox said. "I'll eat there."

"I cannot do that."

"Then tell me what you want from me."

"You must eat first."

Maddox crossed his arms and sat back in his chair.

"You are stubborn, *di-far*."

Maddox's nostrils widened. That was the second time she'd called him that. The Visionary of the Spacers had once named him as a *di-far*. The Visionary had called herself one, too, a greater *di-far* than he was. According to Spacer lore, a *di-far* was a living node in human history, a person through whom events from one path of destiny could change tracks and lead to a different destiny. According to the Visionary, he'd helped to save the human race. Later, the Visionary had turned against him until she'd died at the end of the Swarm invasion—if she'd ever really been his friend in the first place.

Spacers did not control territory like other political groupings. They were nomadic, living in their spaceships, traveling from place to place. Ludendorff had called them mystics, cultists and fanatics. The Methuselah Man despised them. The Spacers claimed to have originated from a Builder. Builders had created the Methuselah Men and the androids. None of the Builder-generated peoples liked each other much.

Maddox wondered what that indicated. He wasn't ready to hazard a guess about it just yet.

"This is silly," the Spacer said. "We have plans for you, Captain. For your sake, it's better if you cooperate with us."

"Maybe," Maddox said. "What's your name?"

"If I tell you, will you eat?"

He eyed the food as if he was hungry. He was to an extent, but he could control his appetite for a time. He wanted her to think that he was on the brink of eating.

"Maybe," he said, wishing he could force his stomach to growl on command.

"I am called Lulu 19," she said.

"Nineteen…" Maddox said. "Does that make you higher or lower ranked than Shu 15?"

"We know that Shu 15 is dead, slain on Earth."

"You are well briefed, I see."

Lulu dipped her head, accepting the compliment. "As to your question, I am higher ranked, as nineteen is higher than fifteen."

"You're higher by four degrees then?" Maddox asked.

"That is correct."

"Are the higher degrees more difficult to earn as the numbers increase?"

"Considerably more difficult," Lulu said.

"How high do the ranks go?"

"That is quite enough of that. Besides, I am not allowed to tell you such a thing."

"Do you have a list of things you cannot tell me?"

"Captain, please, this is becoming ridiculous. I am an agent much as you are in Star Watch Intelligence. I have answered your questions. Now, you must replenish your strength through nourishment. It is time for us to advance to the next level, and the process will considerably strain you. I do not wish for you to faint halfway through."

Maddox gave her a frank scrutiny as a man looking at a beautiful woman. "Why not take off your goggles so I can see your eyes. I assume they're pretty eyes."

Her head jerked back. "No!" she said. "I could never do such a thing."

"Why?"

"I will not say," she told him, sounding offended.

"It isn't that you *cannot* say," Maddox said, grinning wolfishly, seductively, "but that you *will* not."

She remained silent.

"Are you the highest ranked Spacer on the planet?" he asked.

She had been looking away, but now regarded him. "I am not."

"The second highest, perhaps?"

"Why does any of that matter?"

"I'm curious, and I'm the *di-far*. It is my nature to inquire."

"You are mocking me, Captain. If you continue to mock, pain will be your reward."

Maddox glanced at the spilled drinks and food on the floor.

"Should I summon more nourishment?" Lulu asked.

"That will not be necessary," Maddox said in a subdued voice as he studied the spilled food and drink more carefully. He rose slowly, moved to the sprawled dishes, knelt and began to right the plates, putting the food back on them.

"Leave that," Lulu said. "It is tainted food. I will have more brought here."

As if he had become contrite for his previous actions, Maddox continued to put the food back on the plates.

Lulu shifted on her chair—

And Maddox struck. He'd been waiting for something. He had knelt in order to be a fraction closer to the First Class Surveyor. The Spacers were clearly his enemies as they had attempted to thwart Star Watch from gaining the needed tools to face the Swarm invasion. He could only assume the Spacers were still working against Star Watch. They had messed with his mind. He assumed Lulu meant to turn him into a Spacer asset against Star Watch. He would never allow that, and this seemed like his best opportunity to strike.

The Spacer screamed as Maddox lunged at her. He moved fast, faster than any ordinary man could have, although not as fast as a prime New Man could have done it. Maddox reached the small Surveyor, grabbed one of her wrists and yanked her off the chair, slamming her against his chest. He wrapped his other arm around her.

By this time, the combat suit had moved, raising an arm as a gun port along the sleeve activated.

Maddox backed up against the far wall, using Lulu as a shield against the space marine weapon.

"If the suit fires, you die," Maddox hissed into an ear. "Do you want to die?"

Lulu struggled in his arms. It was a pitiful attempt, as her strength was nothing compared to his steely muscles. A twelve-year-old boy would have had better luck. Spacers were not known for their size or strength.

"I'll crush you if you continue to resist," Maddox said into an ear.

He'd seen her hand slide to her left thigh. He suspected she had a concealed pin or other secreted weapon there, one tipped with a deadly poison. She could easily pull it out and stab it against him as she struggled. He had been wondering if she possessed such a secret weapon, and now he knew. It was time. Thus, he hardened himself in order to take the necessary action.

He squeezed her tightly in a threatening manner. Lulu ceased moving as she panted from exertion.

The woman was warm in his arms. His original assessment about her garment's restrictive quality seemed correct. According to his sensory input, she had larger breasts than appearances warranted.

"Put me down," she said.

He noted that her left hand was near the hidden seal on her thigh. It was time to act, but he found himself hesitating, and thus, he started speaking.

"I have no incentive to do so," Maddox said. "I'm a captive. You're trying to drug me to make me more compliant. That is the last thing I intend. In fact, I would rather die than become someone's puppet. I suspect you wish me to ingest the drugs so you can complete whatever mind manipulation you started."

"You are wrong. Now, let me go."

"Until it is proven otherwise, I will believe that you're lying to me."

"Captain Maddox, I could make your head explode with pain if I so desired. I need merely think it for it to happen. I might even cause an aneurism to kill you."

"While I can snap your neck and kill you just as fast."

"If you kill me, you will die in this cell from starvation."

"Incorrect," Maddox said. "I will open the suit and use it, rescuing my friends and destroying the Spacer operation on Usan III."

"No," Lulu whispered. "It is too late for that. If you had snapped my neck immediately, that might have worked. Now, I have alerted the others. They are coming. If they see you holding me like this, they will kill you. It is unalterable ship custom."

"You're lying."

"A Spacer never lies about something as profound as ship custom."

Maddox heard the truth in her words. By grabbing her like this, had he already gone too far? It might well be so.

He hated this underground confinement and he knew what he had to do. Others were already coming. He might have already sealed his fate by grabbing her.

It was time.

Maddox squeezed her again before releasing her, letting her drop to the ground. She landed and stumbled, catching herself a moment later.

She turned to face him.

At the same time, the space marine suit lumbered forward, both guns aimed at Maddox.

"I should kill you for what you just did," Lulu said quietly. "It was sacrilege. Ship custom bids me destroy you, an outsider. You are even worse than that, a heretical enemy of the Spacer Nation. Instead of a quick, clean death, I am going to use you in a manner you find revolting. You have made a terrible mistake, Captain."

Maddox waited like a coiled spring. He seemed tense, decidedly so.

"I am about to tame the evil Captain Maddox," Lulu said. "You will do things—"

"No," he said, interrupting.

"Are you going to try to *force* me to kill you?"

"It's too late for that," Maddox said. The coiled tension in him seemed ready to explode.

Lulu cocked her head, and suddenly, she groaned and swayed. "What's wrong with me?"

Maddox said nothing.

"What have you done to me?" Lulu asked hoarsely. She looked down at herself, noticing the lose flap on her left thigh. Her hand dropped there and tried to grasp a tiny thing in the hidden pouch. Instead, she dropped to her knees as her strength seemed to ooze away.

Lulu's head moved slowly as she swayed on her knees. She seemed to stare at Maddox.

"You…" she said. "You have…"

The Spacer Surveyor wilted then, pitching sideways onto the floor, gasping for air.

"Die," she whispered.

Maddox dove forward as the combat suit's guns opened fire. He was no longer in the line-of-sight as the heavy caliber slugs dug into the rock wall, ricocheting everywhere. Maddox crawled until he was under the armor suit, using it for shelter. Some of the slugs *whanged* off the suit. One of the slugs smashed against Lulu 19, killing her instantly.

That caused the marine suit to abruptly quit firing its guns.

Maddox crawled out from under the suit and pushed off the floor. He'd survived the ricocheting slugs, but little else had. The table and chairs, and most of the wall screens were shattered. Amazingly, none of the air-vents had been scratched.

As Maddox surveyed the damage and the dead Spacer, he released the tiny needle that he'd taken from her hidden pouch. He had pricked her with it when she'd dropped to the floor.

Had the substance been a killing contact poison or merely a strong knockout drug? Maddox didn't want to know. He hadn't had any desire to kill Lulu 19. He just wanted to remain free, to save Meta and Riker and to make sure that Star Watch won whatever present contest they were in.

Pricking her had been his only option.

With a start, Maddox lurched for the upright combat suit. Lulu had said others were coming. He had to be ready before the others opened the hatch. With the First Class Surveyor dead, he was sure the others who were coming would kill him.

-12-

Maddox steeled himself as the last lock on the space marine suit snapped shut.

This was going to get ugly.

First Class Surveyor Lulu 19 was dead, a mangled corpse in the cell with him. He had no idea if she had been lying or telling the truth. One thing he did know. A secret Spacer base was hidden in the Nerva Corporation Tower. He was fairly certain the Spacers were mining the unique crystals here. Lulu 19 had partly controlled his mind through her hyper-induction. It was quite possible she'd also caused Mr. Tubb to self-detonate, through transduction. Maddox was now almost one hundred percent certain the Spacers had face-shot the Strand clone in the wastelands. They presently held Meta and the sergeant prisoner, and he was deep underground with possibly only one way up to the surface.

Even as he was processing all this, Maddox was checking the interior of his suit. It was the latest in combat armor, probably stolen from a Nerva Corp warehouse.

A thought struck. There might be another Spacer who could practice a hyper-induction and/or transduction similar to what Lulu 19 had done. Such a process might interfere with the smooth operation of the combat armor.

Maddox put the idea in storage. There were too many unknowns regarding that. Maybe the only mind manipulator on the planet lay dead in the cell.

"Let's get started," Maddox said to himself.

He powered up the suit, faced the hatch and put a powered glove on the latch. It did not budge.

Should he tear the hatch open?

That would alert the others if they were already here.

In the suit, Maddox turned around, searching the shot-up cell. He did not see any spy devices or cameras. Oh yes, he did see them. The screens had been recording events, but there were all shot up now. Hopefully, any watching Spacers had lost reception.

Score one for the good guys.

Maddox stepped back from the hatch. He would wait. As he waited, he rechecked the suit, finding the batteries at 78 percent power, the ammo supply at 89 percent capacity and rockets—no. The suit lacked rockets.

Perhaps that was just as well, given that most of the fighting would take place underground.

Maddox glanced at a chronometer. Two minutes and thirty-two seconds had passed since he'd donned the combat armor. How long was it going to take the reinforcements to get here?

Maddox did not glance at Lulu's corpse. He had a job to do, but he was beginning to feel worse about her death. He reminded himself that the Spacers were fanatics. They had also done more than simply run out on everyone else when the Swarm Imperium had invaded with eighty thousand warships. The Spacers had tried to hinder the rest of humanity from surviving the bugs.

According to some Star Watch analysts, the Spacers would side with the bugs, if it ever came down to a choice for them.

Maddox checked the chronometer: three minutes and seventeen seconds had passed since—

A lock clicked on the hatch. It began to open.

"They have your wife and best friend captive," Maddox told himself. "Either you save them, or Meta and Riker will die."

With an exoskeleton-powered glove, Maddox grasped the hatch and flung it open. It crashed into a provost guard, a small Spacer in a blue uniform with dark goggles over his eyes and a glistening projac that flew out of his left hand as he struck a corridor wall.

Maddox charged through the hatch.

Other provost guards waited in the corridor. Some shouted at each other. A provost marshal cried out at the sight of the suit. Two of the guards aimed their projacs and opened fire at the marine armor.

Maddox reacted, opening fire with the twin arms of his suit, blowing down the guards and the marshal. In seconds, it was over. Had he killed them before any of them had warned others upstairs?

Maddox had no idea. He clanked down the corridor, hoping to reach Meta and Riker before the enemy used them as bargaining chips.

It might already be too late to save them. But he was going to damn well try. There was one thing he knew. The Spacers here were going to know—if they didn't already—that they were in a fight to the death.

"To the death," Maddox whispered in the helmet.

He clanked down the corridors, recalling the route Lulu 19 had used earlier. Once he reached his former cell, he traced the route from memory back to the elevator.

So far, he had not seen anyone else. He'd slain four provost guards and a provost marshal, maybe a real one instead of a fake. He'd also slain a First Class Surveyor. Was—had—Lulu 19 been the highest ranked Spacer on Usan III? Maddox would guess not, as someone had prohibited her from certain actions.

The elevator door opened and it was empty. Maddox had been pressing buttons to get it here. He entered the elevator, studied the control unit and tapped the console. The doors closed, the elevator lurched and Maddox in the latest space marine combat suit headed up, presumably, for the Nerva Corp Tower.

-13-

Maddox had half-expected a Spacer to contact him via a helmet comm channel. He'd also expected to hear thoughts in his head that were not his own.

Neither happened.

The express elevator reached its destination and opened. No one greeted him in the tower elevator lobby.

Maddox lowered his arms, thus lowering the sleeve guns. He made a quick adjustment to his plan. Instead of charging like a rampaging robot, he marched smoothly as he'd seen the four combat suits doing when they'd first exited the tower, pretending to be a suit under transduction-control.

He passed a Spacer, a woman walking the other way. She did not appear to be in any particular hurry.

Maddox made another quick evaluation. He didn't immediately recognize her rank. She wore dark goggles, had short-cut dark hair and carried a computer slate under her arm. She struck him as a flunky.

Maddox looked around, saw no one else, and turned back toward the woman.

She must have heard something to alert her. She stopped and faced him.

In three strides, Maddox reached her, scooped her up and pivoted. She sucked down air to scream, a natural reaction.

Maddox's faceplate whirred as it came down. "Don't do that," he said.

Her eyebrows rose higher than the protective goggles as her features tightened in horror at the sight of him.

"If you scream, you die," Maddox added.

The woman whimpered, and she wilted in his armored grip.

By this time, Maddox had found and entered a side room. He closed the door quietly. There was a desk in here and boxes piled atop one another along the walls.

She jabbered at him in a foreign tongue.

"Use English," Maddox said.

She nodded rapidly. "English. Yes. I will speak English."

"Who are you?" he said.

"I am an adjutant to Mako 21."

"Mako 21 is a First Class Surveyor?"

"First Class Surveyor *Senior*," the Spacer said.

That told Maddox that Lulu 19 had not been in charge. If luck was with him, this Mako 21 had been with the provost guards he'd slain in the depths.

"What is your name?" Maddox asked.

"Risa Long," she whispered.

"You don't have a number?"

The shorthaired woman shook her head.

"It doesn't matter," Maddox said. "Do you know who I am?"

"The *di-far*," Risa whispered in a tremulous voice.

Maddox didn't know if it was good or bad that she knew him. He decided to settle on 'good,' because it was better to remain positive in the middle of a desperate mission.

"How soon until the fleet arrives?" he asked on inspiration.

"How do you know about that?"

"Never mind," he said. "Just tell me how long?"

"T-They're already late," Risa said. "The new Visionary was supposed to have already touched down on Usan III."

Maddox felt a jolt. Time was running out for him and for Starship *Victory*. He had to get upstairs—in orbit—and get back to his ship.

"Where are Meta and Riker?"

"I assume you mean the other two Star Watch agents."

"Precisely," he said.

At that point, Risa Long's face screwed up. "I am sorry," she whispered. "But I can tell you no more. I have already said too much."

"Risa," he said. "That's where you're wrong. If you don't tell me what I want to know, I'll kill everyone here."

"What? No. You must...you must surrender."

"I am the *di-far*. I am loose. I am dangerous. You do realize how dangerous I am, yes?"

"Please," she whispered. "Kill me and be done with it. I can say no more."

"I have placed Mako 21 and Lulu 19 in a prison in the depths," Maddox said. "I have also placed a timer with a bomb in the same cell."

"What?"

"Unless my friends are freed, I will let the bomb explode."

"But-but—"

"Quickly, Risa, tell me the location of my friends."

"You won't kill the surveyors if I speak?"

"They will go free because you acted wisely," Maddox said.

Risa hung her head and she trembled, but soon, she began to speak, telling him what he needed to know.

The safest course would be to kill her, but Maddox could not casually kill like that. Thus, he bid Risa turn away. He tied and gagged her and exited the room, shutting the door behind him.

If Risa Long was right, time was running out—maybe had already run out.

Thus, he resumed his robotic pace, moving along the tower corridors. He passed others, but these were Nerva Corp people. They did not rush. They did not gape at him. Instead, all of them seemed glassy eyed, drugged, hypnotized...or, most probable, modified by Spacer hyper-induction. None of them seemed to notice him.

Maddox increased his pace.

Had the new Visionary come for the crystals? Or had the woman—he assumed the Visionary was a woman—come for a different reason? Might she have come because she knew he was here? How could she know such a thing?

The old Visionary had claimed to be able to see into the future. Had that been true? Or was that Spacer mumbo-jumbo? If a Visionary could see into the future, she only seemed to be able to *see as through a glass, darkly*, as Visionaries had made many erroneous predictions.

Maddox approached two combat suits flanking a door. The suits were immobile. Did that mean both first class surveyors were dead?

Maddox worked on that assumption and went through the door, passing the armor suits. He found an empty room with security panels. There were no Spacers watching the monitors. Maddox examined the screens, and he froze, seeing Meta and Riker in one of the displays. Each sat facing the other, but neither spoke. Each had a metal band around their head, and electrodes were attached to their naked bodies. Meta and Riker both sat motionless, and although their eyes were open, it did not appear as if they could see one another.

Maddox dampened his growing rage, as this was a time for straight thinking.

Without conscious thought, Maddox clanked to the nearest door, a closed one, opposite the door he'd come through. He did not open the closed door, but smashed through using the armor, causing wooden splinters and metal to fly everywhere.

Two Spacer guards whirled around.

Maddox fired, their riddled bodies slamming against a wall.

Afterward, the captain began to clank at speed, wanting to get Meta and Riker out of whatever programming machine the Spacers had hooked them into.

-14-

After smashing the lock, Maddox slipped into the programming chamber as softly as possible. He didn't want to accidently send shards flying against Meta or Riker.

He clanked toward a wall-sized machine covered with multicolored flashing lights and emitting soft humming sounds. Meta and Riker sat beside the machine. Each wore a metal band around their head, with leads attached from the machine to their naked bodies.

There was something Maddox hadn't noticed while viewing the screens. Both people twitched and made odd grunting sounds, as if the grunts were forced out of them, and their eyelids kept trembling.

Maddox aimed the arm guns at the machine, readying to blast the hideous monstrosity apart. *Might that send overload signals into Meta and Riker?*

Maddox spun around, looking for attendants to murder. There were none, although robot eyes cataloged everything.

The guns chattered for a moment, obliterating the watching cameras.

The exoskeleton arms swung down, remaining motionless. Locks began to unsnap. Like a giant turtle shell, the armor opened down a body-length seam. Maddox wriggled free, scratching his torso as his feet thudded onto the floor, and he regarded the grim machine.

He needed Doctor Dana Rich or even the boastful Professor Ludendorff, although he supposed Andros Crank could have told him how to shut this thing down. He couldn't tell on his own, though. He couldn't just stand here doing nothing, either. The awful grunts and the eye twitching told him the machine was attempting to program their minds.

It was time to gamble.

Maddox stepped beside Riker, flexed his fingers and debated—no, no debate. He moved decisively, ripping the metal band from the sergeant's head.

In the interest of time, Maddox grabbed fistfuls of wires attached to the leads on Riker's body and yanked them off.

Maddox held his breath, wondering if the sergeant would go into a violent seizure. That was why he'd picked Riker first. He couldn't experiment the same way on Meta.

The seconds seemed to last forever as the sergeant just sat there with his eyes closed. The man no longer grunted and his eyelids stilled, so that was something positive.

Abruptly, Riker gasped, his mouth opening and closing like a landed fish. He shivered—Maddox expected him to go into convulsions about now. Instead, the sergeant's eyes opened, wide and staring as if half-mad. Riker gurgled in a choking manner.

"I'm right here, Sergeant," Maddox said.

The head turned as if upon a rusted neck. The crazy eyes seemed to latch onto the captain. Riker tried to speak, but it came out as gurgles again.

"This is real," Maddox said. "You were hooked to a machine. I detached you from it."

Riker blinked, and some of the wildness drained from his eyes.

Once more, the sergeant gurgled before he closed his mouth, cleared his throat and whispered, "It's a horror show, sir. What I saw…"

"What did you see?" Maddox asked.

The sergeant frowned and cocked his head. "I…I can't remember now. Isn't that odd? It was so clear a second ago."

Maddox didn't like the sound of that. If they survived, both Meta and Riker would have to undergo strenuous treatments to confirm that their minds hadn't been compromised.

That Meta would have to undergo such treatment for the second time in her life made it worse. Couldn't he protect his woman any better than that? Maybe he should forbid her from going on more undercover assignments.

Taking a calming breath, Maddox removed the metal band from Meta's head and peeled the adhesives from her body.

Her recovery process took longer, as she sat there as one unconscious and barely breathing. In a moment, though, her eyes flew open and she looked about in stark fear.

"It's me, Meta," Maddox said gently. "I'm right here. It's okay. You're going to be okay."

Her mouth worked but no sound came out. Her eyes finally locked with his. Then she slumped weeping into his arms, although the longer she held him, the tighter and stronger her grip became until it was nearly bone crushing.

"Where are we, sir?" Riker asked.

Maddox twisted around as Meta clung to him. The sergeant appeared to have remained in one spot, although he now stood upright and he seemed saner than before. The question was weird, as the sergeant should know.

"Where do you think we are?" Maddox asked.

Riker shook his head.

"Look around," Maddox suggested.

Riker did in a perfunctory manner, but that seemed to have no effect on his memory.

"Usan III," Maddox said.

"Where's that?" the sergeant growled.

A sense of unease shot through Maddox. Was this mere disorientation or something worse?

"We're in Nerva Corp Tower," Maddox said. "You must start thinking, Sergeant. It is imperative. Meta's life may be forfeit if you cannot."

"I think I understand," Riker said, although it still didn't seem like it as he continued to stand wearing a vacant expression.

"Sergeant!"

"Sir?"

"Think! Use that head of yours. Figure out what's going on, or are you too stupid of an old coot to do anything right?"

Riker scowled, and he began looking around, noticing the machine, the empty combat suit—and that he wasn't wearing any clothes.

"This is ridiculous," the sergeant complained. "Why did they strip me?"

The question mollified Maddox a bit. "Who are 'they,' Sergeant? Quick. Tell me."

"Nerva Corp people, I suppose. You said this was Usan III. Sir," Riker said, with understanding lighting his eyes. "An android blew up outside the casino. Marines brought us in here. Spacers, sir, Spacers removed my clothes and hooked me to that infernal contraption."

"Right," Maddox said. "Now look over there, Sergeant. I see a pile of rags and some footwear. Maybe your garments lie there."

"And red bra and panties," Riker said, eyeing the pile dubiously. "I hope I wasn't wearing those."

Maddox didn't answer, as Riker had his senses back. The sergeant could take care of himself for a while. The captain concentrated on Meta as he brushed his wife's blonde head and made soothing sounds.

Riker had headed for the clothes. The sergeant stopped, surprise twisting his leathery features as he looked back at the captain. Perhaps Riker had never expected Maddox to make such sounds for anyone, not even his wife.

With a shrug as he muttered softly, Riker went to the pile, picking up smelly garments, making a face as he did. Soon enough, he began to don worn out garments.

"I need a weapon," Riker said.

"Look around for one," Maddox said.

The annoyance in his voice made Meta whimper, and she gripped him even more strongly than previously.

The captain found it hard to breathe. Meta was stronger than most men born on a regular G world. With care, he peeled her fierce grip from him, held her shoulders and peered intently into her eyes.

"Meta? Can you hear me?"

It took several seconds until she whispered, "Yes."

"I need you focused. Can you focus?"

"My head *hurts*," she complained.

"I know. You…you had an accident."

"Really?"

"That's right," Maddox said. "Once we're upstairs—"

"Where?" she asked, interrupting him.

"In orbit," he said. "We're on Usan III in the Nerva Corp Tower."

"Oh. Yes. I'm beginning to remember."

"That's good. Everything is going to be better soon. You have to focus first. I want you to focus."

Even more awareness came into Meta's green eyes. She glanced shyly at the hideous brain machine, shivered and looked up at him. "Maddox?"

"Don't think too much," he warned. "We have to get you dressed. Then we're leaving this place."

"What do you mean dressed?"

Maddox twisted around so she couldn't see the worry on his face. It was as he feared. A so-called Teacher on a New Man star cruiser had once altered Meta's thinking. It had left mental scars and may have made her more susceptible to these kinds of mind manipulations. Doctor Dana Rich had helped heal Meta that time. Might this experience cause a relapse? Maddox wanted to do everything he could to make sure that didn't happen.

They needed to get off Usan III fast. That meant getting out of Nerva Corp Tower.

"Riker," Maddox said.

The sergeant looked up from where he'd been searching.

"There should be weapons outside the room down the hall. You'll find two dead Spacers—"

Riker swore vilely, finishing with "*Spacers!*" Was the sergeant working himself into a rage?

"We don't have time for recriminations, Sergeant. We're on a timer. If we can't get out of here in time, everything we know is over."

That did the trick. "Sir?" Riker asked. "Isn't that a bit melodramatic?"

"Perhaps. Now get a move-on, Sergeant. We'll be out there shortly. Oh, and grab a projac for Meta, too."

Riker nodded, hurrying out of the chamber.

Maddox found Meta staring at the chairs where Riker and she had been hooked to the machine.

"Snap out of it, love," Maddox said gently.

Meta whirled around, and there was terror in her eyes.

Maddox had to clamp down on his own anger against the Spacers. They had messed with his wife. He was going to make them pay for that. He'd already made them pay by taking out two of their prime operatives on Usan III. Letting his anger loose now wasn't going to help, though.

"Are you ready?" he asked.

"I'm naked."

"Put those on." He pointed at the bra and panties and then shrugged off his jacket, handing it to her.

Meta stared at him and finally took a deep breath. She nodded, took the jacket and hurried to the pile. She slipped on the bright red bra and panties and then put on his jacket. It reached down to her mid-thighs like a dress but the sleeves were too long for her arms. She began rolling those up.

Maddox stepped to the empty armor suit. They might need it in case enemy guards showed up. As the captain slid into the suit, shoving his arms and legs into the right places, he wondered if he should have Meta and Riker climb into the other combat suits.

Even as Maddox thought that, he rejected the idea. They both seemed to have regained their wits. But could he be one hundred percent sure about their mental states? The short answer was no.

The locks snapped shut and he powered up the armor. Meta whirled around in terror.

"It's me," Maddox said.

She began shivering.

The faceplate whirred down. "Meta," he said. "It's me. It's me. It's okay."

She saw his face and nodded.

"Keep behind me," he said. "We're getting out of here."

"To go upstairs?" she asked.

"Right. Do you want a weapon?"

"Yes," she said, some of the old Meta surfacing at the idea.

They found Riker down the hall riffling the dead Spacers, their gory bodies on the floor. The sergeant gave Meta one of the projacs.

Her shoulders straightened and she grinned tightly up at Maddox.

"Listen," Maddox said. "I want you to keep those out of sight. Put them in a pocket. I'm going to herd you as if I'm a guard taking you somewhere. Maybe that way we can pass unnoticed. Meta, I'm going to have to close the visor."

She raised the projac. "I'm feeling better. That's okay."

He waited. She put hers in a jacket pocket. Riker hid his weapon too.

It proved to be a wasted ruse, however. Soon enough, Maddox in the suit herded them past uncaring Nerva Corp people. None of them even gave them a glance.

"What's wrong with them?" Meta finally asked.

"Maybe they all went under the same machine you did," Maddox said through a helmet speaker.

Meta cast him a worried look. Riker spat angrily on the floor.

"It doesn't matter," Maddox said. "They're zombies. They're going to leave us alone."

Meta visibly gulped but kept going.

Soon, they came to a set of stairs. That was what Maddox had been looking for. He wanted to get to the roof but no longer trusted the elevators.

"Kind of small for your marine suit," Riker said.

Maddox had come to the same conclusion and was already undoing the locks. In moments, he wriggled free of the armor, taking a heavy gun from a leg compartment for just these kinds of space marine emergencies. He rummaged around and found extra magazines.

Once sure the gun was loaded, he told the others, "This is a sprint. That means speed is critical. Sergeant, you will make sure that Meta keeps up with you."

"Who's going to make sure I keep up?" Riker muttered.

"That's the spirit," Maddox said. "I'll scout ahead. I expect the two of you to appear on the roof shortly. Don't disappoint me, Sergeant."

"I wouldn't think of it," Riker said.

"Maddox," Meta called fearfully.

He turned around, already five steps higher than the two of them.

"Don't leave me," Meta pleaded. "I'm frightened."

He didn't want to leave her, but he felt as if he didn't have a choice. "You're not really frightened," he said. "That's from the brain machine. The people here should be frightened of you."

She looked at him in a way that suggested disbelief.

"Keep up, darling. You must hurry."

"Maddox—"

He did not wait to listen anymore, but turned forward again and charged up the stairs at a blistering rate. Speed, he needed speed. And at a time like this, none of the other Star Watch agents could keep up with him. He bounded faster and faster, taking four and five steps at a time. The toll made him pant, but he refused to admit that he had a physical limit. The enemy had harmed his wife. The enemy had fiddled with the sergeant's mind.

"Focus," Maddox panted.

He was already on the fourth flight of stairs. Maddox wasn't sure why, but he had a terrible sense that he was already too late. The Spacers wouldn't go down that easily. He couldn't have slain all of them, right? If he had, the Nerva Corp people would likely wake up. They might prove dangerous as well.

Incredibly, Maddox bounded faster yet, reaching the last set of stairs. Maybe they should have headed for the spaceport and stolen a shuttle. Did he even know if there was an air-car parked up here on the tower landing-pad?

He didn't bother shaking his head, deciding to burn out negative thoughts. He was going to find out soon enough.

Maddox burst through the roof door, looking around wildly. Three people ran for the air-car parked at the center of the roof. The larger than normal air-car was already whining, obviously ready to take flight.

Without hesitation—in a rather brutal display of Star Watch Intelligence need—Maddox opened fire. The heavy gun kicked in his hand, the bullets taking down the three before any of them had a chance to surrender or fire back.

As the three pitched to the roof, Maddox noted their Nerva Corp uniforms and regular size. Those weren't Spacers. Could he have made a deal with them or learned more about the Spacers?

That was immaterial at this point.

Maddox sprinted for the air-car. Would it lift off? Would the pilot have seen what happened?

Maddox lowered his head so he could run faster, passing the dead Nerva Corp people. He almost sobbed with the effort. At last, he scrambled through the side-hatch, staring intently at the piloting seat with the gun ready to fire.

The seat was empty.

"Thank, God," he whispered.

Maddox hurried forward as sweat dripped from his face. He checked each compartment, and they were indeed empty. He also threw open a closet; no one hid there. Finally, he settled behind the piloting board. The air-car had a two-seater forward control area and six side-by-side seats in the passenger compartment.

Maddox checked controls, fuel, status—

He whirled around with an aimed gun, having heard a noise. Meta climbed aboard. Riker scrambled in next, closing the hatch behind him.

"We made it," Riker panted.

Maddox nodded, turning back to the controls. "Strap in," he called.

Meta slid in beside him in the navigator's spot, clicking the restraints. Riker sat in the passenger compartment, collapsing into a seat, but remembering to buckle in.

Maddox shifted the controls as the whining increased. The air-car responded smoothly as it lifted off the pad.

"What now?" Meta said.

"Up we go," Maddox said. He aimed the nose upward as they tilted back, and he gave the air-car more power. They began moving upward, gaining speed.

"Maddox," Meta shouted. "What's that blinking red light?"

Maddox leaned over toward her as he checked her panel. His shoulders deflated for just a moment.

"Is that a radar lock-on signal?" Meta asked him.

"Yes," Maddox said. "The spaceport's SAM site has a fix on us."

SAM stood for surface to air missile.

The comm squawked, and the spaceport operator demanded that Maddox identify himself.

The captain hesitated only a moment before switching on the small screen. He stared into the goggled face of yet another Spacer woman. He hadn't killed them all—yet. Had he been wrong about slaying both first class surveyors? Could this be Mako 21, or was this another ranking Spacer?

"I don't think so, Captain Maddox," the Spacer told him. "This time, you are not going to escape us."

-15-

"You must land immediately," the Spacer woman said, "or I shall launch an interceptor and destroy your craft."

She meant an *Interceptor*-class missile. From what Maddox had been able to discern regarding the air-car, he did not possess the weaponry or the electronics to stop or evade such a missile. Likely, the woman knew that just as well as he did. How could he use that?

"You leave me no other choice," Maddox said reflexively, having made his decision. "I am initiating the landing sequence."

He glanced at Meta, winking at her, hoping she understood.

Meta leaned forward, working her panel. She glanced sharply at him, nodding. She let him know by the nod that she understood and could do as he wished.

Maddox checked his board. The Spacer hadn't yet launched the interceptor. That meant the woman likely told the truth about wanting them to land. Good. This might work then.

Maddox did not intend to do what he had just said he would do. Instead, he banked sharply, turning the air-car away from the spaceport and the SAM installation. He did not intend to land anywhere that the enemy could capture them.

The reaction did not take long.

"What are you doing?" the Spacer demanded.

"Trying to land," Maddox told her. "Are you sabotaging my controls so I can't do that?"

"What?" the Spacer asked. "No. We are doing nothing to the air-car."

"Someone sure is," Maddox said. "If it's you, please admit it. I want to land."

"Captain Maddox, you are banking hard away from the spaceport. You're trying to escape."

"Untrue. I'm trying to land."

"This is official. I *order* you to land."

"Yes, yes," he shouted at the operator. "What do you think I'm trying to do? What's wrong with you? Don't you understand what I'm saying?"

"Captain—"

Maddox flipped a switch. Afterburners kicked in, pressing him against his seat. Meta also flattened against her seat as the air-car built up speed, roaring over the deck of the sandy surface. The craft began shaking from the strain.

"Keep this up and you'll clog the intakes," Meta shouted.

"Is this a not-so-subtle form of subterfuge?" the Spacer asked over the small comm screen. "If true, you will fail, Captain. I need merely launch the interceptor. It will easily demolish your air-car. You have no hope."

"Are you in line-of-sight yet?" Maddox asked Meta.

Meta shook her head.

"Line-of-sight, Captain?" the Spacer asked with a sneer. "Do you really think we came to Usan III as indigents and tramps? We are the Spacers. We have learned from our past mistakes. We are not like you territorial-bound humans who refuse to admit an error. We study and learn. That is how we have become so powerful in only a few hundred years."

"I stand in awe of your abilities," Maddox said.

"I have read your brief, Captain. I know about your predilections. You have been attempting to buy time while you line up for a long-range message burst to Starship *Victory*. Oh, yes, I am well aware of the starship's location behind Usan VI. What you don't know is that we are blanketing the planet with a jamming signal. You will send no messages to your Adok Death Vessel, haunted by a nefarious computer entity."

"Are you talking about the AI Galyan perhaps?" Maddox asked. He glanced questioningly at Meta.

"Got it," Meta whispered. She tapped the message screen and pressed a tab. A message pulse beamed toward *Victory*, leaving the air-car to travel halfway across the Usan System.

"How pathetic," the Spacer operator said over the comm line. "You do realize that the message failed to leave Usan III?"

Meta tapped the comm panel and looked up with alarm. "I think the Spacer is right," she whispered. "I detect heavy jamming. It's blanketing everything. I doubt the message-burst left orbit."

Maddox concentrated as the shaking air-car continued to skim the sands. This was bad. He didn't want to initiate Plan B until he knew more. He thought about this for several seconds and finally shouted at the comm screen, showing that he was overcome with rage.

"My, my," the operator said. "Are you attempting another subterfuge, Captain?"

"You have cloaked saucer ships in orbit, of course," Maddox said, seeming to try to control his seething emotions.

"The cloaked ships are coming, true enough," the operator said. "But—"

"The cloaked ships are here?" he blurted.

"Come now, Captain. If they were here, the ships would have sent shuttles down to pick up the crystals. No. The ships aren't here yet, but we control the orbital defensive satellite. It's so obvious that I'm surprised you failed to understand. I tell you this not because you have made me talkative through your emotional ruse, but because I want you to know that with the mere snap of my fingers, I can order the satellite to beam your air-car out of existence. You are in a hopeless position, Captain. You can die by missile or by beam. Surrender at once or you shall cease to exist."

"Will you give me a minute to think this through?" he asked.

"I am done waiting, Captain. Return to Capricorn. Land on Nerva Corp Tower. You have five seconds to decide. I will give you no more than that."

"You must be highly ranked indeed to be able to make such a decision on your own authority."

"You are still trying to stall, Captain, and you have lost three of your seconds doing so. I am about to press the launch button. Decide."

"Yes," Maddox said, sounding crestfallen, and he banked the air-car again, making a wide turn, climbing as he did so. In seconds, the air-car aimed for the town of Capricorn and the smudge of the Nerva Corp Tower in the far distance.

As Maddox did all that, he switched off an engine. The air-car sagged and slowed down.

"What are you attempting now?" the Spacer said.

"Meta was right earlier," he said. "Sand has clogged one of the intake valves. I've been forced to shut off an engine. I can turn it back on, but that might burn out—"

"No," the Spacer said. "You are heading in the correct direction. This might be a piece of subterfuge on your part, but it will gain you nothing. If you deviate from Nerva Corp Tower, a beam shall lance down from orbit and destroy you. I am allowing for no more deviations."

"I understand," Maddox said quietly. "We should be at the tower shortly."

"See that you are, Captain. I am monitoring your air-car, and now, so is the defensive satellite. Even if you land on the sand and attempt to flee, you will die. This time, Captain, there is no escape for you or your friends."

Maddox stared starkly at the comm screen. Finally, as if he could stand it no more, he turned his head. As he did, he blinked several times in quick succession at Meta.

She stared at him in surprise.

Maddox tapped his left index finger four times on a flight control.

Slowly, Meta reached for her panel. She made a few adjustments and then sent a single ultra-sonic, short-range pulse.

The Spacer operator on the comm line was alert. "What was that?" she demanded. "What treachery are attempting now?"

"That was me," Meta said in a dejected voice. "I...I was seeing if there was some way to pierce the jamming cloud."

"Do not try that again," the Spacer said. "Otherwise, I will assume you are planning a ploy. Land the air-car on the tower, Captain. Deviation of any kind will result in your destruction."

"Yeah, yeah," Maddox said in a surly tone.

The Spacer grinned at him tightly, triumphantly.

The captain sighed, and that was a genuine expression of emotion. He dearly hoped that Lieutenant Maker had heard the sonic pulse and knew how to interpret it. If the lieutenant hadn't…in that case, Maddox planned to transform the air-car into a kamikaze craft and take out the operator's SAM site before Meta, Riker and he perished in a fiery blast.

-16-

Lieutenant Keith Maker sailed weightlessly through the derelict-seeming torchship in orbit over Usan III.

Keith was a sandy-haired Scotsman with wiry, alert features. He loved all kinds of flying, the more dangerous the better. He considered himself the best pilot. He did not consider himself the best pilot in Star Watch or the best human pilot. He considered himself the best anywhere at any time, period, end of story.

He had many flying exploits to prove his claim. He had also played backup to Maddox for many of the captain's exotic missions.

Keith wasn't at his comm panel to receive or see Meta's single pulse. Neither was Keith's partner at his station.

The partner slept in a bunk, having grown increasingly inert the longer they had to wait up here in orbit doing nothing.

The torchship was ten times bigger than a Star Watch shuttle. It had an old-style reactor in back with huge cylindrical tanks attached to the central core. The life-support section was the small forward area, although the workers could use emergency shafts that went the length of the central rod of the ship. This torchship was an older model. It attained terribly slow speeds for a ship pretending to be an interstellar voyager that used Laumer Points to travel from one star system to another. A vessel of this sort was better served as an asteroid prospector's ship. It was slow, and for all its size, it lacked real cargo space.

The fakery of the ship was in the fuel cylinders attached to the central rod. In reality, only one cylinder had fuel. The rest had been enlarged into a hangar bay. Neither Keith nor his partner had gained any advantage by this. They had been in tight quarters for so long that the two men had learned to hate the sight and now the rancid smell of each other.

Inside the special hangar bay was a fold-fighter, a tin can in Star Watch lingo. It was an ugly little vessel that resembled a tin can with many antennas sprouting from it. The fold-fighter did have a few guns, and they would fire, although they would do minimal damage in a real space battle.

Sometimes, a fold-fighter carried a missile. If that was an antimatter missile, that gave the fighter some real hitting power. The other key to the fold-fighter was its ability to fold space, popping directly from one location to another, possibly a million kilometers away, in a split-second.

Needless to say, Keith had used the fold ability of the fighter to save the captain's bacon on many occasions.

As the small Scotsman sailed weightlessly through a corridor of the central torchship, a small device on his belt began beeping.

Keith heard it, and he snatched at it with great eagerness. Pressing his thumb against the device, he read a text that scrolled across the tiny screen.

The torchship's rather powerful computer had analyzed the sonic pulse. The ship's orbital location—that it was *in* the jamming area instead of outside it—and the nature of the pulse meant the signal had reached the torchship. With a teleoptic sensor, the computer had seen the air-car zooming over the sandy surface and added the factor of the defensive satellite's sudden jamming signals. The computer therefore gave it a forty-eight percent probability that Captain Maddox or one of the others had attempted to signal them for a fast pullout.

The sonic pulse had reached the torchship, not the actual message. In that sense, the jamming had worked.

In any case, Keith pressed a button twice and checked the time. The computer had received the message one hundred and eleven seconds ago.

A thrill of excitement swept through him. Keith wanted to get back to the barn, meaning Starship *Victory*, as soon as possible. Lieutenant Valerie Noonan and he had been having some arguments. They had had a thing between them for a time. Keith wanted to keep it that way, as he'd finally been getting somewhere with the Academy-trained beauty.

If this was Maddox sending a message, he could finally leave the torchship and not have to see his partner's ugly mug ever again. The man needed a hard pop on the nose, maybe several kicks in the ribs for added measure.

Keith did a summersault and twisted in the air. His feet struck a bulkhead as he bent his knees. Redirecting his path, Keith pushed off as hard as he could go.

He had to get to the fold-fighter, start the engines, locate the captain exactly, and figure out what he was going to do. Too many seconds had already passed for him to waste any time.

In these kinds of rescue operations, every bloody second counted.

He grabbed float rails, building up speed. If he hit his head against a bulkhead, that could easily dash him unconscious. But Keith wasn't worried. He was the best flier, even if that meant flying weightlessly through a torchship's corridors.

He judged the next corridor, grabbed a rail, pulled, readied his shoulder and grunted as he hit a padded wall, slightly changing his heading, aiming for a sealed hatch that seemed to speed at him like a bullet.

"Okay now, mate," Keith said. "Here we go. Seven-alpha-eight-tango-three-two-one, open baby."

There was an audible clack, and as Keith sped at the hatch, it opened. He grinned with delight.

Thirty more seconds, and he should be able to get the show on the road.

"Hang on, sir. Lieutenant Maker is coming to the rescue."

-17-

The seconds ticked away as the Nerva Corp air-car neared the tower. So far, there hadn't been any Lieutenant Maker appearing in the fold-fighter. According to Meta, the defensive satellite was tracking them, in addition to the SAM site near the spaceport.

"Even if Keith gets here," Meta said. "Where is he going to go to help us?"

"Are you tracking the torchship?" Maddox asked.

"Its engines have fired up," she said.

"That's the signal," Maddox said. "We have to be ready."

"Begging your pardon, sir," Riker said from the other compartment, "but how are we going to make the transfer? That is the plan, right, sir?"

"You already know how, Sergeant."

"You're not thinking about jumping out of a moving air-car, are you?"

"Bingo," Maddox said. His lips had thinned as he spoke. They had almost reached the tower. Even traveling as slowly as they had been, they were going to reach the tower too soon.

"Oh no," Meta said. "Do you see the reception committee?"

Maddox did. There were six blue-uniformed Spacers, provost guards by the looks of it, on the roof of the tower building.

At that instant, a fold-fighter shimmered into existence below them. The vessel was only several feet away and pacing them exactly. If it maintained that position, they should be able to jump down onto it.

"Thank you, Mr. Maker," Maddox shouted. "This is it." He began to unbuckle.

Even as the captain did so, a beam reached down from the sky and pierced a rear nozzle on the tin can. The fold-fighter wobbled, and might have veered away under a less experienced pilot.

"Hurry," Maddox shouted. "We don't have much time left."

"This is madness," Riker said.

Another beam struck, barely passing the air-car to strike the tin can. The fold-fighter was a larger vessel than the air-car.

The beam punched through the tin can's flimsy armor. This time, the aerodynamics fought the pilot's incredible skill. The craft veered away sharply, heading down hard for the sand.

"No," Meta whispered. "Keith—"

The tin can shimmered, and a third beam sliced down from the heavens. Just before that beam struck, the tin can vanished, disappearing from the situation.

The beam struck sand just outside the city limits, the beam turning the sand into slagged glass.

Maddox and Meta exchanged glances.

"There goes our ride," Riker said.

"Is the fold-fighter reappearing?" Maddox asked.

Meta studied her panel, soon shaking her head.

"What now, sir?" Riker asked. "Looks like our ride took off without us."

"Right," Maddox said. He reactivated the shutdown engine, giving the air-car greater power. He banked sharply, forgoing a blast from the anti-personnel cannons at the provost guards on the roof. Killing them wasn't going to change things. Either they escaped the SAM missiles and the defensive satellite or nothing else mattered. Unless they could get a message to *Victory*, all their twisting and turning was moot.

"Now they'll shoot us down for sure," Riker warned.

"We're not dead yet," Maddox said.

"If I might point out, sir—"

"You might shut up, Sergeant. I'm concentrating."

"Right, sir, shutting up I am."

Meta glanced back at Riker. The sergeant looked positively pale. Her husband looked grimmer than normal.

The air-car completed another turn, skimming over the sands as it built up speed leaving the city for the second time today.

"What are you hoping to achieve?" Meta whispered.

Maddox didn't answer. He was too busy watching the sensors. The comm light blinked. He refused to answer it, as he was done bandying words with the Spacer operator.

"They've launched," Meta said. "Make that two launches," she added.

"Hang on," Maddox said.

They all jerked forward as the air-car whined down at emergency speeds.

"How's that going to help us?" Riker pleaded.

"Shut up!" Meta shouted. "Let him think. We're all dead unless he comes up with something."

Ten seconds later, Maddox banged the air-car down onto the hot sands. They skidded, throwing sand everywhere, but they slowed down fast and came to a stop.

"Out!" Maddox roared. "Get out!"

Meta unstrapped and rushed for the opening exit. Riker leaped out the main hatch, disappearing from view.

Maddox remained in his seat, waiting.

Meta turned at the hatch. "Aren't you coming?"

"Soon," he said. "Go."

She obeyed, leaping from the door and disappearing.

Maddox immediately engaged the air-car, lifting. He manipulated the controls, unstrapped and rushed for the open hatch. He dove from the air-car, landing on the sands several feet down.

At almost the same time, the air-car increased speed. Seconds after that, the vehicle shot up into the sky, building up speed.

Maddox climbed to his feet. He shaded his eyes, watching the air-car. The first interceptor streaked like lightning across the sky, rapidly gaining on the air-car.

Maddox turned away at the last second. Even so, he saw the glow of the explosion against the desert sand.

Another interceptor roared through the skies, but it no longer had a target. The missile kept traveling, searching for something to destroy.

Maddox turned around. He could see Meta and Riker trudging across the sands toward him. The city was behind them. It amazed him how far from it they were already. Heat waves shimmered in front of Capricorn. It would take time to walk back into town.

Readjusting his wide-brimmed hunter's hat, Maddox began trudging toward the others. He'd had a dune buggy last time he went into the wastelands. This time, he had nothing but the clothes on his back. Not even a canteen or another jacket aside from the one he'd given Meta.

They wouldn't last long out here. Would the Spacers come to collect them? He had little doubt about that. He was sure the air-car stunt hadn't fooled anyone.

Maddox frowned. One thing bothered him. Why hadn't the defensive satellite beamed them with a heavy laser? It had taken the tin can out of action. Why not take out the air-car too?

Maddox increased his pace, feeling the heat of the sands radiating through the soles of his boots. The heat must be scorching his wife's bare legs. He had to get her out of the harsh starlight.

After all that had happened, were the damned Spacers going to defeat him?

Even as Maddox wondered, a shimmering began on the sands to his right, and to his amazement, the tin can appeared on the desert floor. The shot-up vessel did not move. It just sat there, perfectly folded onto the desert sand. There was no exhaust from the nozzles, no—

A port opened in the side. Keith stood there, with bright red blood on his shirt. Could that be *his* blood? At that moment, Keith toppled out of the tin can and struck the sandy ground outside.

-18-

Maddox reached Keith first. The others were running for the tin can. The pilot lay face-down on the hot sand.

Plowing down onto his knees, Maddox put his hands on the pilot's back.

Keith groaned.

"Are you badly injured?" Maddox asked.

Slowly, under his own power, Keith turned over onto his back. Blood stained his flight suit. There was a jagged hole in his chest, with blood seeping out.

Maddox tore off his shirt and pressed that against the wound. He could feel the heat beaming against his bare skin.

Keith groaned more.

"Hold it in place," Maddox ordered sternly.

Keith did so, pressing down with his hands. Good. The ace could still move his arms and work his digits.

"What happened?" Maddox asked. "Be quick about telling me."

Keith had grown pale with sweat streaming his face. "I'm sorry, mate. I failed you. I feel sick—"

"Belay that, Lieutenant. Give me a quick account. Is the fold-fighter still usable?"

"It has no motive power, sir."

"Damn it."

"But it can still make folds. That's the trick, sir. If you're smart—"

"We can fold out of here?" Maddox asked.

"That's what I'm saying, mate. You have to get us inside to do that, though, and only a small compartment is now sealed against space—if you know what I mean?"

Maddox did. But one thing bothered him. "What happened to the defensive satellite? Why isn't it beaming the tin can?"

Keith closed his eyes painfully. "Rogers, sir," he whispered. "The crazy-man dive-bombed the satellite with the torchship. He took out their main laser array. I imagine they're having an emergency up there right now. I doubt the entire satellite is going to blow, but they're not going to beam anyone for a time."

"Rogers crashed the torchship into the satellite?"

"That's right."

Maddox closed his eyes for a second. It sounded as if Rogers had killed himself in the process. That was a bitter loss, as Rogers belonged to Starship *Victory*.

Maddox wouldn't allow Rogers to sacrifice himself in vain. They had to leave before the Spacers arrived. The tin can's ability to maneuverer had been knocked down to folding, wherever that happened to be.

"Can you still pilot the fighter?" Maddox asked.

It took the lieutenant several breaths before he said, "It will be a piece of cake, sir. I could fly this baby dead. That means I'm in tiptop condition."

Maddox nodded. Riker and Meta could help Keith into the fold-fighter. He needed to investigate and get the fold mechanism started.

When he looked inside the craft—Maddox's eyes widened in astonishment. It was a junkyard in the fold-fighter. Smoke billowed from burned out instruments. How had the ace folded the tin can to exactly the correct spot on the sands? That was something of a miracle.

Gingerly, Maddox hoisted himself within. There were pieces lying everywhere. This thing should not be able to fold. Should he really risk his wife in his thing?

Maddox peered out of the hatch, seeing specks in the sky. Were those more interceptor missiles or air-cars?

It didn't matter. They had to get out of here or risk being captured and having their minds reprogrammed.

"No choice," Maddox muttered. He jumped out of the fighter and hurried to Keith.

"You're going to have get up and fold us out of here," the captain said. "I don't understand how this fighter is even here."

"Because I'm the best there is, sir."

"Agreed," Maddox said. "Can you remain conscious long enough to get us into orbit?"

"Don't know about that, mate. I think I've lost too much blood. But Hell, let's give it a go, right?"

"Right," Maddox said, putting his hands under Keith. "Are you ready?"

"Aye, mate. Let's get her done."

Maddox hoisted the pilot to his feet. Keith felt hot, and the blood continued to seep past the shirt the pilot pressed against his chest.

"Come on, now," Maddox said.

The two men climbed into the half-destroyed fold-fighter.

"Go the other way," Keith said.

Maddox peered back through the hatch. Those were air-cars, and they were coming fast. It would be close. Then, he noticed a rent in the compartment. He could see the rust-colored sky through it, which meant this particular compartment would not block the vacuum of space.

As the captain helped Keith through a short corridor, Meta and Riker climbed within.

"Air-cars are coming," Riker shouted.

"We know," Maddox said. "Shut the hatch and follow us. We have to find sealed compartments."

In seconds, Maddox helped Keith slide into the piloting chair. Keith was sweating heavily and panting.

"Are you sure you can fly us?" Maddox asked.

"Yeah," the ace whispered.

Meta shut the hatch to seal this piloting compartment. Riker found a spot on the floor.

"Get set…" Keith whispered. The pilot flipped switches, and the engine started, sounding labored, violently shaking the craft.

Maddox squatted on the floor.

Keith swore at something.

Maddox looked up at a screen. Air-cars were almost here. So were two streaking missiles that barreled from behind the air-cars, catching up fast. Maddox twisted around to stare at Meta.

She looked starkly at the screen.

"Meta."

She looked at him.

If he was going to say something, he lost the opportunity, as the suddenly roaring engine drowned out any possibility of speech. The fold-fighter shook even more violently than earlier. Smoke poured from somewhere, making Riker cough.

Keith let go of the bloody shirt, using two hands on the controls.

Maddox felt helpless, and he hated the feeling. The two missiles passed the air-cars, streaking down at them,

Abruptly, everything vanished. That seemed to last an eternity…until just as abruptly, stars appeared on the screen. In the distance was a rust-colored ball. It looked like the size of the Moon as seen from Earth.

"Is that Usan III?" Maddox asked.

There was no whine from the fighter. No engine noise at all. It was silent in here, although the smell of smoke was worse now.

"Keith?" Maddox asked.

The pilot had fallen unconscious, his head lolling to the side.

Maddox glanced back at Meta and Riker. Both of them stared back at him wide-eyed.

"We have some separation from the Spacers at least," Maddox said. "You two work on Keith. I'm going to see if I can contact *Victory*."

"What if Spacers show up in their saucer ships?" Riker asked.

"Let's do what we can," the captain said. "We'll worry about the worst when it happens. Until then, we keep on trying as hard as we can."

-19-

The fold-fighter continued to drift alone through space, about nine hundred thousand kilometers from Usan III.

No matter what they did, Riker and Maddox could not get the engine started. They used battery power to cycle air through the small compartment. Maddox had used an extinguisher to put out the fire that had kept pouring smoke. It didn't smell quite so electrical in here anymore.

So far, no one had needed to use the john, which was good. They did not have access to it.

They didn't even have a vacuum suit so they could explore other parts of the fighter. They were stuck in the tiny piloting compartment, with Meta working to keep Keith breathing.

Maddox had sent a message to *Victory*, which they could not see on the fighter's sensors. *Victory* was hiding behind the gas giant, but was supposed to have sensors orbiting on the star-side of the planet to pick up such messages. They could see rust-colored Usan III clearly enough, but hadn't used active sensors to study the damaged defensive satellite or the other spacecraft in orbit around the terrestrial world.

Maddox wanted to remain hidden out here for as long as possible.

As the captain waited, he made some calculations. Usan III was 7.1 light-minutes from the star. Usan VI, where Starship *Victory* hid, was 79.5 light-minutes from the star. That was almost the same distance that Saturn was from the Sun.

That meant the fold-fighter was approximately 72.4 light-minutes from the starship. He had sent the message an hour and a half ago, a little over 92 minutes.

Maddox had no idea yet if anyone on *Victory* had received the generalized-beamed message. Once the starship received the message, it would take 72.4 minutes for a return message to reach the fold-fighter.

It would take *Victory* quite a bit longer to travel here the conventional way. The vessel did have a star-drive jump, which could make shorter, intra-system hops if necessary.

So far, *Victory* hadn't appeared. That told Maddox Lieutenant Noonan had not received the message.

"Maybe we could signal one of the haulers," Riker suggested. "They could send a shuttle to rescue us."

"We certainly *could* do that," Maddox said. "My guess, though, is that the Spacers already have hidden vessels orbiting Usan III. Thus, if we hail the haulers…"

"I know what you're thinking," Riker said. "But being captured is better than dying from asphyxiation."

"Possibly," Maddox said.

Riker grunted, turning to stare at a bulkhead, maybe so he didn't have to look at the captain.

More time passed until Meta, Keith and Riker slept. The ace moaned occasionally. Meta made faces in her sleep, and twice, she cried out.

Maddox considered waking her, but finally decided against it. A bit later, he climbed into the pilot's chair and studied the screen.

The fighter used a simple teleoptic sensor—a passive device—to monitor the planet. Half an hour later, Maddox thought he detected movement. He tapped the board, using a zoom quality. Yes. The Nerva Corp Hauler, *Sulla 7*, was leaving orbit. It seemed to be accelerating, advancing to a hard burn, making it much more visible.

The hard burn indicated the hauler was in a hurry.

Maddox rubbed his chin. Might the Spacers have used Nerva Corp shuttles, rushing cargo up to the hauler, leaving with a load of crystals?

That seemed possible.

Just how big was the Spacer operation here?

If the Spacers were using the hauler, that would indicate that it was a smaller operation than he had first thought. If the Spacers had a fleet of cloaked ships, they wouldn't need to rush a hauler full of crystals anywhere. That they did rush the hauler indicated they lacked a fleet, maybe lacked any cloaked saucer ships in the system at all.

As Maddox pondered that, an image wavered halfway between the drifting fold-fighter and the planet. The wavering increased until a saucer-shaped ship appeared. It had dropped its cloaking.

Maddox frowned. The vessel picked up speed, as it headed toward the drifting fighter. The Spacer ship had obviously spotted them. A light flashed on the comm board, confirming that.

With a resigned sigh, Maddox tapped the screen. It shimmered until a Spacer woman appeared on the flat device.

"Captain Maddox," the woman said.

It looked like the spaceport's SAM site operator. She'd left the planet, then. Did that mean all the Spacers were leaving Usan III?

"That was cleverly done," the woman said, "escaping with your nearly useless fold-fighter. I congratulate you on being a worthy adversary."

She didn't talk like a mere operator, but someone important and possibly powerful.

"Are you Mako 21?" Maddox guessed.

"I am indeed," she said with a smirk.

Maddox forced his features to remain placid. He'd only slain *one* of the dangerous Spacers. There had been his chief mistake.

"I, of course, know how you know who I am. You spoke to my adjutant in the tower. Never fear, she has paid the penalty for her garrulous tongue."

"A real provost marshal went to the underground cell with his guards?" Maddox asked.

"Of course."

"Are you in charge of the Usan Operation?"

Instead of answering, Mako 21 said, "You are quite the slippery individual, Captain. Your title of *di-far* is well deserved. However, you have failed in the essential task."

"Which is?"

Her smirk became enigmatic. "I suspect that you will find out too late, Captain. I have a rendezvous to make. Otherwise, I would take you captive. Thus, I bid you—"

"Wait," Maddox said.

On the tiny comm screen, her head tilted. "Yes?" she asked.

"Did you kill the Strand clone?"

"Did I do so personally?" she asked, sounding surprised.

"Did you Spacers kill the clone?"

"That is an interesting question," she said, using a forefinger to tap her chin. "No, we did not kill the Strand abomination, although he died because we Spacers decreed we should not suffer a Methuselah Man of any stripe to live."

"You put a bounty out on him?"

Mako turned her head, presumably checking something off screen. She seemed satisfied with the thing and regarded Maddox again. "I bid you good-bye for now, Captain. Next time we meet, you will not be so fortunate."

Maddox thought fast. "Your words are in reference to the new Visionary? She's seen me in a future timeline?"

The Spacer had seemed ready to shut off the connection. With the new question, she re-regarded him. Her smile became strained. "If I thought it would do any good, I would warn you, Captain. You are a clever individual, after all. I believe you are capable of true learning. Unfortunately for you, your New Man heritage betrays you at every turn."

"Meaning what?" he asked.

"I understand. You're begging me for instruction. Yes. I will give it to you, even though I am wasting my breath." Mako 21 straightened and spoke in a deeper voice. "Beware of the Methuselah Man. He will attempt to lead you down a false path. If you take the path and succeed…you will bring fire and destruction upon humanity such as you cannot conceive."

"You forget your briefing regarding me," Maddox said. "I was in the Alpha Centauri System when the "A" star expanded to red star status. I have seen fire and destruction as I doubt *you* have ever seen."

"Ah. I see that my words sting. That is good, for the only words that ever truly sting are those spoken in truth."

Maddox scoffed. "You can't really expect me to believe that your new Visionary sees into the future."

"I do not *expect* it because you are too narrow-minded. Still, I'll ask this. Why do you think we returned to Usan III?"

"For the crystals," Maddox said.

"That is only partially correct."

"Are you going to say that you Spacers came here because of me?"

"There was a chance that we could have adjusted your…" Mako 21 stopped talking as she shook her head. "No. We tried—we tried," she said, sounding sad.

Maddox would have asked more, but before he could, Starship *Victory* slid into view, no doubt coming out of a star-drive jump. The vast and alien vessel came between the fold-fighter and the saucer ship.

"Finally," Mako 21 breathed, "it has begun." Her image abruptly vanished from the fold-fighter's comm screen.

At that point, several more saucer ships appeared, uncloaking, it would seem, five in all. Each Spacer saucer-ship was the same distance from *Victory* as the others, about three hundred thousand kilometers away.

As Maddox watched, he witnessed an ultra-white beam spear out of each saucer ship. The five beams struck *Victory*, no doubt attempting to pierce the heavy armor of the Adok starship so they could purge it from existence.

-20-

Lieutenant Valerie Noonan sat in the captain's chair aboard *Victory*. She had long brunette hair and astonishingly beautiful features behind her stern demeanor. In the captain's absence, Valerie was the commanding officer. She was known as a by-the-book commander. But she had also learned to bend now and again when the situation warranted it.

Valerie had studied Maddox and learned from him, although she did not try to copy his style. What worked for him did not necessarily work for her. That had taken her quite some time to learn.

She feared for Keith Maker's safety. That was part of the reason for her stern cast. They'd been having more intense arguments, and she wasn't sure that Keith was the right man for her. But she worried about him just the same. The fool didn't know when to throttle back. He thought he could fly any mission successfully no matter how stupid or dangerous it might be.

Given the situation, she also worried about Maddox, Meta and Riker, but not nearly as much as she worried about that hotheaded ace.

The ancient Adok starship that had thrust itself into the mix had two oval areas connected to each other. The vessel also had excellent heavy armor. Because the ship had just made a star-drive jump, the shields were down. That meant the five enemy beams struck the heavy armor, digging into the resistant substance as they attempted to achieve a burn-through.

Having just shaken off drug-smoothed Jump Lag, Valerie raised her head and balled her hands into fists on the chair's armrests. "Andros," she said in a stilted voice. "Where are my shields?"

She spoke to the short, stout older man who had thick fingers and unusually long gray hair. He was a Kai-Kaus Chief Technician. Maddox had saved the man and ten thousand other Kai-Kaus from a Builder Dyson Sphere a thousand light-years from Earth several years ago.

Andros, together with the AI Galyan's help, had detected strange gravity waves that had indicated cloaked Spacer vessels nearing the fold-fighter.

The attack against *Victory*, as such, did not come as a surprise. Valerie and the others had suspected it would happen like this. She was trusting to the starship's armor, and to Andros's quick action, to raise the—

"Shields," Valerie repeated, "I need those shields *now*."

"Chief Technician," said a holoimage of an Adok alien. The image possessed deep-set eyes in a strangely lined alien face. He was a deified alien AI, the last member of a lost race. "If you would engage the Bussard generator—"

"Of course," Andros said, interrupting Galyan. The Kai-Kaus's stubby fingers flew over a panel.

All the while, the five ultra-white beams continued to pound the starship. To make matters worse, missiles zoomed out of each saucer-shaped ship, racing toward the seemingly stunned *Victory*.

"I need those shields now," Valerie repeated.

"There," Andros said. "You should have them."

As the Chief Technician stopped talking, a shimmering electromagnetic shield snapped into existence outside of *Victory*. The ultra-white beams no longer struck the five spots on the starship. They hit the invisible shield some distance from the armored skin. Those five areas immediately began to turn red because the shield could not bleed off the excess energy fast enough. If too much energy struck the shield too fast, it would collapse.

Valerie snarled silently to herself before saying in a calm voice, "I want the disrupter cannon and the neutron cannon online as soon as possible. We're going to take out the Spacer ships one at a time."

The Spacer saucer vessels were each smaller than *Victory*. Together, the five had more mass, but not by much. It was like five angry hyenas facing a male lion that had just woken up from sleep. In the past, the starship had taken on six saucer ships and come out victorious. That meant they should be able to defeat these five now.

"Valerie," Galyan said. "We are in error concerning one particular. The Spacer missiles are not heading for us, but for the fold-fighter behind us. I believe the Spacers mean to destroy the fighter."

"What?" she said.

"I have already scanned the fold-fighter, Valerie. It is inert, motionless. I have also scanned the interior, detecting the captain, Meta, Riker and Keith."

"Roger that," Valerie said grimly. "Weapons, target the missiles first. We're going to take them out while we can."

The bridge crew started working smoothly as the last vestiges of Jump Lag slogged from the machines and the people. The ship's great antimatter engines began to thrum. Then, the deadly disrupter cannon beamed the first Spacer missile zooming around *Victory* toward the drifting fold-fighter. The deadly ray burned down one missile after another. It almost seemed as if the Spacers wanted them to do this.

"Lieutenant," Andros said from his board. "I'm detecting more gravity waves."

"Be more specific," Valerie said.

"The gravity waves are all around us," Andros said in astonishment. "I count…four more cloaked vessels. Nine saucer ships are enough to destroy us if we fight them head to head."

"I didn't ask for your recommendation," Valerie snapped. "I don't want you trying to slip your opinions in. I just want facts."

Andros nodded.

"Valerie," the holoimage said. "We cannot abandon the captain to the Spacers."

"Don't you start, Galyan," Valerie warned. "I know my job."

"I trust you to do the right thing, Valerie," Galyan said.

Lieutenant Noonan glanced at the little holoimage. He looked worried. Why did she keep forgetting that the alien AI had genuine emotions? Maddox, Meta, Riker and Keith were most of the holoimage's family.

"Don't fret, Galyan," she told him. "I have no intention of letting the Spacers kill the captain."

"Thank you, Valerie."

"No!" Andros said, as the Chief Technician studied his board. "This is bad. The enemy—"

"Are they using dampener rays against us?" the lieutenant asked.

"They are," Andros said. "The Spacers are making sure we can't jump out of danger. In my opinion, they mean to destroy us and are targeting the fold-fighter as a ploy."

Valerie bent her head in thought. Once more, Andros had given his unasked for opinion. She would deal with that at the proper time. But he had a point. She mentally juggled options and came to a swift conclusion. She would not let nine Spacer saucer ships defeat her or kill the captain, and Keith Maker.

"How many fold-fighters do we have in the hangar bay?" Valerie asked.

"Five," Galyan said.

"Right," Valerie said, her features becoming even sterner than before.

She decided to attempt a deadly tactic. It could work, but it could also backfire and possibly destroy *Victory*. She didn't see any other way of defeating nine saucer ships, though. They couldn't run. What other choice did she have? None that she could see.

"Galyan," Valerie said breathlessly, "instruct the pilots to arm with antimatter missiles."

"Antimatter?" asked Andros. "The enemy is only three hundred thousand kilometers away. We don't—do we *want* to launch antimatter missiles that close to us?"

Valerie slammed a fist against an armrest. "The Spacers want to fight. Okay. We'll fight nine of them at once, but we're going to play hardball. Do you have a better idea that has us winning, Chief Technician?"

Andros Crank turned pale, his lips moved soundlessly and finally, he shook his head.

"What about the captain, Valerie?" Galyan asked. "Do we leave him to his fate?"

She stared at Galyan. "No! One of the fold-fighters is going to collect the captain. Make it the last member of the squadron. He will not arm with an antimatter missile. Only after the pilot has returned the captain and others to *Victory*, will he arm with a missile and join in the attack. One way or another," she added, "we have to destroy nine Spacer ships."

On the main screen, the five visible saucer-shaped vessels continued to pound *Victory's* shield with their ultra-white beams. The ancient Adok starship lashed out with both the disrupter and older neutron beam. One after another, Spacer missiles heading toward the drifting fold-fighter blew up.

"Are any of the cloaked ships trying to work behind us for a shot at the captain?" Valerie asked.

"Two," Galyan said.

Valerie glanced at the weapons officer, a newer member of the team, a small young man with pinched features and dark hair. He looked nervous, not like Smith-Fowler who had been with them when they had gone into the deep Beyond. There was no doubt the new officer had a right to be nervous. This was a critical moment, his first under intense pressure. Galyan would be better at targeting, even if the captain didn't always like having the AI handle such key tasks. Even Maddox had Galyan fire sometimes. If she failed today, the captain, Keith and maybe everyone aboard *Victory* would die. This was a hardnosed moment, and she'd better make the right decision.

"Galyan," she said, "take over targeting and firing."

The weapons officer glanced at her sharply.

"You will only do so for the moment," Valerie added, deliberately not meeting the officer's dark gaze.

The holoimage nodded. "It is done, Valerie. I have control."

"Target the enemy ship nearest our crippled fold-fighter," she said. "Let's see if we can destroy one and chase away the other."

Precious seconds ticked away as nothing happened.

"Well?" Valerie demanded.

"Pinpointing the exact position of the cloaked ship is harder when targeting for a kill shot," Galyan said.

"Fire anyway," Valerie said.

"I wish to show the Spacers how exceedingly dangerous our starship is," Galyan explained. "I want to do so with a direct hit the first time. That will surely make the others nervous."

"I don't want excuses," Valerie said. "I want obedience."

Galyan glanced at her in surprise. "You are acting more like the captain every day, Valerie."

"Fire the damned beams," Valerie shouted, wondering if she'd made a mistake taking fire control away from the weapon's officer.

Galyan's features closed up.

Valerie couldn't believe this. The captain never seemed to have this kind of trouble. "I don't mean to yell at you, Galyan. I just want you to hurry before the captain dies."

"Yes, Valerie. I understand. I am firing…now."

On the main screen, a yellow disrupter beam flashed out at seemingly nothing. Suddenly, the beam struck a hidden object. The object shimmered and appeared—a Spacer saucer vessel with a shield already turning purple and heading for black.

"Nail them, Galyan," Valerie said, as she hunched forward.

The other saucer-shaped vessels de-cloaked, pouring more ultra-white beams at *Victory*. That did not help the one under attack, but it considerably weakened the starship's shield.

"Use the neutron beam as well," Valerie said. "Destroy it."

Seconds later, the purple neutron beam struck the same saucer-shaped vessel. Its shield turned black and suddenly collapsed.

The two beams from *Victory* struck the Spacer armor.

"That plating won't last long," Valerie said. It was something they had all learned from experience.

"*If* it is the same kind of plating as the last time we faced Spacers," Galyan said. "They may have improved their armor, although I am not detecting that."

Abruptly, the disrupter beam smashed through the armor and dug into the saucer ship's interior. It did deadly damage, destroying all sorts of systems and killing people. Other Spacers outside the direct beam or the nearby heat no doubt died from heavy radiation poisoning. Then, the disrupter beam struck the main engine. Four second later, the saucer-shaped ship blew apart, sending armor, innards, water vapor and people parts in all directions.

"Target the next ship," Valerie shouted, knowing she should speak calmly but unable to achieve it.

"Our shield is badly weakening," Andros warned her. "We can't withstand much more of this."

Valerie checked the readings. The shield did not have separate red areas anymore. With eight ultra-white beams striking, the entire shield had turned deep purple. Some areas had begun to turn black. If the Spacers were clever—

"The enemy missiles are changing heading," Galyan said.

Valerie ground her teeth together. The enemy was smart. "They're going to try to slip the missiles through our weakened shield," Valerie said, speaking before anyone could tell her. That was one way to keep the others from giving her unsolicited advice.

"You are correct," Galyan said.

Valerie was already biting a knuckle, worrying about the missiles. She'd gotten cocky. *Victory* could defeat six saucer ships coming at them normally, without Jump Lag given the enemy a head start. The five had gotten solid hits against the starship, and now there were eight enemy vessels. That was too many to defeat.

"Where are my fold-fighters?" she shouted.

Even as she asked, Andros tapped his board, saying, "If you'll look at Screen B, Lieutenant."

She did.

On the screen, four specks winked into view. The fold-fighter pilots had taken special injections, and they had each been selected partly because they could shake off Jump Lag faster than others.

Four antimatter missiles launched. The big missiles accelerated hard, zooming at nearby enemy vessels a mere three hundred thousand kilometers away and closing to *Victory*.

Two of the ultra-white beams stopped striking *Victory's* blackened shield and speared at the fold-fighters.

That was a mistake. They should have targeted the missiles. Each of the fold-fighters winked out, folding elsewhere. Those two beams thus speared into nothingness.

The antimatter missiles fanned out, heading in different directions as each one targeted a different enemy ship.

"Our shield will collapse in seconds," Andros said.

"Detonate the missiles now," Valerie said. "Wash the area with antimatter pulses."

"This close to *Victory?*" asked Andros.

Four enemy beams speared at the big antimatter missiles.

"Our shield won't protect us from the radiation wave," Andros said.

"Do it!" Valerie shouted.

The weapon's officer must have belatedly realized that he still had control of the missiles. The small man tapped his board.

Even as the enemy beams touched the missiles, four violent antimatter explosions ripped through nearby space. The warheads blasted hard radiation in all directions, sending out massive EMPs, heat and gamma and x-rays.

True to Andros's prediction, the gamma and x-rays struck *Victory's* blackened shield, overloading the gravely weakened electromagnetic defense. The entire shield collapsed. The x-rays, gamma rays and other radiation struck the heavy armor and the ablative foam behind it. Some ship systems went down immediately. Many people took heavy doses of radiation, some of them lethal levels that caused them to keel over dead.

On the bridge, some of the equipment burned out, flashed and smoked. Klaxons wailed and alerts blinked on and off.

"What's happening out there, Galyan?" Valerie asked. She swallowed an anti-radiation pill, hating the big thing. The bridge was a sealed area, one of the hardest to hit, but the readings showed they were not immune this time.

"I cannot tell yet," the holoimage said. "My sensors are only seeing white. The antimatter warheads ignited too close to us. If the Spacers recover first…"

Valerie's gut clenched. Surely, some of the Spacer ships had been destroyed. A few had been too close to the antimatter explosions to survive. A few farther away might have lost their shields. Others might have taken no damage.

She bit her lower lip with worry. She hadn't known what else to do. How else could *Victory* defeat nine enemy saucer vessels? Had she just doomed the starship? Believing that was possible was an awful feeling. What about Keith and the others? Had the designated fold-fighter rescued them before the antimatter blasts had washed through their area?

Valerie leaned forward, waiting, hating this part of space battle. The whiteout was already lessening. Once they could see again, what would they find?

-21-

Captain Maddox and the others, including a wounded Keith Maker, sat out the antimatter blasts inside a special container compartment in one of *Victory's* hangar bays.

The designated fold-fighter *had* reached them in time, bringing them back to a hangar bay. The fighter had *not* retrieved the drifting, almost destroyed fold-fighter, though. Even though that tin can had been the last to receive the already dissipating antimatter waves, they had been enough to shred the vessel into many different parts.

There were many emergency compartments throughout the starship. As Maddox waited in his, seething inside, he wondered how many of the crew had escaped the radiation poisoning.

Finally, an all-clear signal flashed over the hatch.

Maddox donned a radiation suit.

"Is it wise going out there so soon?" Meta asked from a steel bench.

"Yes," he said.

Maddox secured the helmet, went through the lock and stepped into the hangar bay. Some of the personnel who hadn't reached a container were sitting on the deck, gasping, looking pained; a few seemed to be in agony.

The captain clenched his jaw. He couldn't directly help the hurting right now, as he had other pressing business. Then, he saw radiation-suited medical people hurrying to the rad-poisoned.

Good.

Maddox spun on his heel and hurried for an exit. In moments, he broke into a sprint, his radiation suit crinkling as he ran.

He witnessed the effects of ship-wide radiation poisoning. Some of the most heavily saturated personnel lay gasping on their backs, seeming as if they would die. Maddox yearned to stop and help, but he was the captain. He was responsible for the entire ship, the entire crew. Were Spacers getting ready to board and capture his starship? Did he have *any* healthy space marines to help him repel boarders?

One thing surprised him, and he found it strange that it daunted him. Usually, Galyan would have appeared to greet him. That the holoimage hadn't done so told him the situation must be dire.

Finally, after a hard run that left him gasping and sweaty, Maddox entered the bridge.

Medical people were already giving injections against heavy rad poisoning. Presumably, the bridge crew had already taken their anti-radiation pills. Technicians under Andros's guidance were presently working on inoperative screens.

"Lieutenant Noonan," Maddox said through a helmet speaker. "Report."

The captain's chair swiveled around and a haggard-looking Valerie Noonan regarded him. "Captain?" she asked. "Is that you? Are you alive?"

Maddox twisted the helmet, taking it off, revealing his sweaty features.

"Captain," Galyan said. "It is good to see that you are alive."

"Yes," Valerie said. "How are the others, sir?"

"Keith should be fine," Maddox said dryly.

"Should, sir?" Valerie asked.

Although it went against the grain to explain anything at the moment, Maddox told her about Keith and that they had ridden out the antimatter blast in an emergency container.

"Thank you," Valerie said.

Maddox motioned abruptly, and Valerie scrambled out of his chair, making room for him.

"Galyan," he said. "Why aren't the Spacers boarding us?"

"I feel that I should make the report, sir," Valerie said.

Maddox did not look at her. He'd asked the AI. "Galyan," he said.

The holoimage glanced from Valerie to Maddox. "I believe the lieutenant made the correct tactical decision regarding the antimatter missiles."

"First," Maddox said. "I do not recall asking anything about that. Second, I will be the judge of that, not you. Simply give the report I asked for, Galyan."

"Yes, Captain," the AI said. "The Spacers are not boarding because they are no longer near the starship."

"None of them are?" asked Maddox.

"We destroyed one saucer ship under Valerie's direction," Galyan said. "The antimatter blasts appear to have destroyed two more. The rest are gone."

"Gone where?" Maddox asked.

"I have not yet been able to determine that, sir. It would appear they have cloaked or used a star-drive jump of their own devising to flee the Usan System."

Maddox frowned, and he swiveled the chair toward Valerie. "How many saucer ships did you face?"

"Nine, sir," Valerie said, standing at rigid attention.

"Nine?" Maddox asked.

Valerie nodded stiffly.

"Against nine…you did well to chase them off."

"Thank you, sir," Valerie said, staring off into the distance.

"Perhaps you made the best tactical decision possible, given the difficult circumstances."

Valerie said nothing.

"At ease, Lieutenant."

Valerie spread her feet and put her hands behind her back, her posture still rigid.

Maddox had a dilemma. It galled him to see so many dead and injured crewmembers. Those came from the antimatter explosions. However, under ordinary circumstances, the shield would have held against those blasts. That meant the eight enemy vessels had gravely weakened the shield. Without the antimatter explosions, however—

Maddox nodded as he regarded Valerie anew. "I appreciate your decision, Lieutenant. It must have been a hard one. I believe you saved us. Thank you."

Valerie opened her mouth in astonishment. She closed it quickly and looked forward again.

"Tell me exactly what happened," Maddox said.

Valerie began to speak, going over her decisions and the order of the events.

Maddox watched her and observed the others as Valerie spoke. Clearly, the weapons officer felt slighted, possibly demeaned by her decision to have Galyan do the targeting. He would have to think about that one. Otherwise, Valerie had done well. She could be so prickly at times. He noticed that she was under considerable strain and probably had taken too many rads.

Although he was disinclined to say more on the subject, he felt she probably needed to hear it.

"You saved my ship and my hide, Lieutenant. The antimatter attack was ballsy. At first blush, it seems like you went overboard. Upon further reflection…"

Everyone listened closely, including the techs working on the screens.

Maddox sighed inwardly even as he kept a calm outward demeanor. Perhaps this wasn't the time to damn with faint praise. He did not like to praise too easily or highly, as he felt people should earn it. What someone earned, someone appreciated. What someone got easily, that someone soon expected as her right.

"Upon further reflection, you did very well indeed, Lieutenant."

For the first time, Valerie smiled. She actually unbent, looking around. The captain had, for him, lavishly praised her in front of the bridge crew.

"Now get to Medical," Maddox said. "I want my second-in-command in tiptop shape. That's an order."

Valerie nodded, turning toward the exit. She stopped, and regarded the captain. "Thank you, sir."

That sounded heartfelt.

Maddox merely nodded. He wanted to get on with it already.

Valerie coughed several times, possibly from smoke, maybe from the strain, and she finally headed for the exit, leaving the bridge.

"Sir," Galyan said. "I have something to report."

Maddox glanced at the main screen. It was still down. Presumably, the AI had direct access to all workable sensors.

"Go head," Maddox said.

"I have been unable to detect any Spacer saucer ships or their signature gravity waves that reveal their cloaked position."

"You told me earlier the Spacers fled the system. Is that true or not?"

"That was and is my opinion, sir," Galyan said. "I hasten to add, that at this point it is merely an opinion and not substantiated fact."

"Understood," Maddox said.

"There is one other possible pressing matter."

"Yes?"

"The Nerva Corp Hauler *Sulla 7* is gone."

Maddox pinched his lower lip. "That's the hauler that used a hard burn to leave Usan III's orbit."

"That is correct, sir."

"And you say that hauler is gone?"

"Just like the Spacers are gone," Galyan said.

"You mean the *Sulla 7* has fled behind the planet?"

"I do not mean that, sir. I suggest that the hauler also had a star drive and employed it, leaving with the Spacers."

Maddox stared at Galyan even as gears worked in his mind. The hauler was gone. The Spacers were gone. The Spacers had attacked *Victory* as the hauler attempted to gain velocity.

"I see," Maddox said. "It appears the saucer ships attacked us in order to give cover for the *Sulla* to escape the star system."

"I give that an 83 percent probability."

"That low?" Maddox asked.

"Given the exchange rate for crystals and varth elixir on the open market and the Nerva Corp predilection for—"

"Never mind, Galyan," the captain said, interrupting. "Let us operate with the 83 percent probability. The *Sulla 7* is gone. And so, it appears, are the Spacer saucer ships. That would indicate the Spacers have pulled out of Usan III. Since we're not going to give chase…it's time to investigate the planet and see what we can discover about the Spacer operation that made it so important."

-22-

The captain did not necessarily believe that the Spacers would stay gone. Pretending to leave was an ancient Achaean trick as practiced against the Trojans, when Odysseus had left the wooden horse for the overjoyed besieged to find. Just like the Greeks of that time, the Spacers might come back, trying to catch them by surprise.

Victory took up a combat orbit around Usan III, sending several shuttles full of space marines to occupy the torchship-damaged defensive satellite. The takeover proved easy enough. An Intelligence sting quickly uncovered the personnel used by the Spacers. Brain scans did not turn up anything odd in those people; nor did the enemy agents have any coercive devices in their bodies. Might they have gone under the brain machine in Nerva Corp Tower? That seemed likely.

Maddox ordered the compromised personnel brought aboard *Victory*, putting them in the brig for the psych people to study.

Meanwhile, *Victory* repair teams worked overtime, getting the satellite back to combat-ready status within two days of their arrival.

During that time, Intelligence teams with space marine bodyguards swept through the remaining commercial and private orbital ships. There was some complaining by the ship owners and captains, and Maddox listened via screen for a time. Finally, the captain asked, "Would you rather stay in a brig aboard my starship?"

The complaining always ended there, if not the sore feelings over what some called, "Highhanded Star Watch actions."

The medical teams had their hands full aboard *Victory*. Nineteen people had died from radiation poisoning. Thirty-seven were on the critical list. One hundred and twelve listed themselves as sick but able for duty.

The damage repair teams were working harder and having less notable outcomes compared to the others. Realistically, the starship could use a week or two in a space dock. Even that might not prove enough.

Valerie drove the repair teams. The captain had given her the assignment, demanding she have *Victory* ready for regular duty in ten days.

Under normal circumstances, Maddox would have overseen the work himself. He was down on the planet, though, heading the Intelligence teams searching the corporate buildings, the casinos and the crystal mines dotting Usan III.

The brain machine that had been inside Nerva Corp Tower was gone, every piece of it. None of the teams found any Spacer corpses anywhere, although one team found traces of Spacer DNA in the underground cell and corridor where Maddox had shed Spacer blood.

"They were thorough," the captain told Riker in their planetary headquarters in the Star Light Casino. "But they weren't magicians. They left traces."

"Begging your pardon, sir, I don't understand how they cleaned up so well so fast. Did all the ship crews come down to help?"

That was a good question.

Maddox kept gnawing at the question like an angry dog with a meatless bone.

The breakthrough came when they put some of the Nerva Corp people under a psych probe. Until that point, the Nerva Corp people had sworn they had been doing their jobs like normal. None of them had seen any Spacers.

The story changed with the use of the probe. The problem was that four Nerva Corp people went into violent seizures after undergoing the probe. Two died, one sustained brain damage and the last slept for three days but otherwise seemed fine.

"We can't keep using the psych probe," Andros said. The Chief Technician was a master at the delicate machine. "I can't be responsible for killing more people, especially now that I know it could easily happen."

It seemed clear that the Spacers had set up triggers in selected people's minds. The Spacers had no doubt done so with the brain machine.

Because Andros was so adamant, Maddox let the Chief Technician sway him, although he wasn't one hundred percent sure that was a wise idea. So far, he'd learned that the Spacers had indeed mind manipulated everyone in the tower. Could they learn more about Spacer techniques if they kept probing? Most certainly. It would come at the cost of more Nerva Corp dead, though.

Maddox used a shuttle and went to the desert location where he'd originally found the Strand clone corpse. It was gone, every vestige of it. Had the planet and its denizens removed the corpse, or had the Spacers made a quick trip here and burned it or possibly taken it with them?

The crystal mines proved easier to crack in the sense of what exactly happened. The Spacers had taken tons of crystals with them, loading fast with Nerva Corp shuttles. Those shuttles had all gone to the *Sulla 7*. The hauler was gone, clearly, gone with the saucer ships.

A thorough search on the planetary varth market showed that the Spacers had bought or stolen the entire supply of the two-pronged elixir.

"It's hard to say, sir, which the Spacers wanted more," Riker said as they flew back to Capricorn in a shuttle.

The two men had spoken with Mount Carter, the chief varth hunter on Usan III. Carter represented the majority of the varth hunters, keeping their united supply hidden from all elixir thieves.

Carter admitted to Maddox that someone had secretly stolen the hoarded supply. Under normal circumstances, it would have meant Carter's head. The Star Watch Intelligence investigation was actually proving useful to him. He could point to the Spacers as the culprits.

That had made Mount Carter cooperative, something highly unusual for any of the secretive varth hunters.

"Elixir and crystals," Maddox said, piloting the shuttle. "The Spacers wanted both. Was this a one-time operation or do they plan to tap Usan III again?"

"Depends on if the Spacers are going to stick near Human Space or not," Riker said.

"That is one possible precondition, but not necessarily a needed one. I'd rather know how important the elixir and crystals are to their society."

Riker grunted agreement.

For a time, Maddox stared fixedly out of the front window. Mako 21 had suggested the Spacers had also come here to speak to him. How much credence could he place on that? If it was true, he needed to tell others. If it was a momentary statement meant to befuddle him, he needed to forget it.

What had the First Class Surveyor Senior said? She'd told him to beware—yes! She had told him to "Beware the Methuselah Man."

Maddox's grip tightened on the controls. By the Methuselah Man, had Mako 21 meant the Strand clone he'd found dead on the sands? Had she meant Strand the original as a prisoner of the Emperor of the New Men? Or could she have referred to Professor Ludendorff?

Maddox hadn't seen Ludendorff since the grim affair at Alpha Centauri during the Swarm invasion. The professor seemed to have held a grudge against him for what had happened there.

Maddox shrugged. Mako's cryptic comment likely meant nothing. Spacers liked to appear mystical. They were cultists—capable cultists who had developed a form of mind power through their technological modifications.

"Sir," Riker said, as he manipulated the comm panel. "There's an incoming call from *Victory*."

"Put it on the screen, Sergeant."

Riker tapped the panel.

Valerie's face filled the tiny screen. "News, sir," she said.

"Yes?" Maddox asked.

"Five ships have just dropped out of the nearest Laumer Point."

"Are they Spacers?" asked Maddox.

"No, sir," Valerie said. "It's a Star Watch flotilla headed by the *Moltke*."

"A *Bismarck*-class battleship?"

"Yes, sir," Valerie said. "Brigadier O'Hara is in charge of the flotilla."

"Really?" Maddox asked, surprised and delighted.

"And Professor Ludendorff is with her," Valerie said.

"What?"

"The Iron Lady wants to rendezvous with you right away," Valerie said. "She says it's a matter of interstellar importance. You're to head immediately to *Victory*. We'll star-drive jump to meet them."

"That seems like excessive haste," Maddox said.

"The Iron Lady was quite clear, sir."

"It's *Brigadier* O'Hara," Maddox said. "You will accord her the proper respect and not use her nickname on an open channel."

"Yes, sir," Valerie said. "I'm sorry—"

"No need for that," Maddox said, interrupting. "Just remember the proper form of address. If anyone would, it should be you, Lieutenant."

"Yes, sir."

"Please tell the brigadier that I'm on my way," Maddox said.

"I will."

"Maddox, out," he said.

The screen went back to its dull color.

"Ready, Sergeant?" the captain asked.

"What do you think this is about, sir?"

"I have no idea."

Riker glanced at him.

Maddox didn't like the way the sergeant did that, as it indicated that Riker understood that he—Maddox—was upset about something. He liked others to see him as calm and collected.

Beware the Methuselah Man. Maddox had a feeling that Mako 21 had been referring to Ludendorff. What was the professor up to this time? And maybe just as importantly, how had the Spacers known that Ludendorff was coming to the Usan System?

-23-

From the bridge of Starship *Victory*, Maddox studied the five-ship flotilla. It had come out of the Laumer Point near the first planet, a tiny rock world smaller than Mercury.

The flotilla had already moved to an area midway between the orbital locations of the system's first two terrestrial worlds. The captain noted the impressive bulk of the *Moltke*. It was the only battleship in the flotilla. He noticed with a start that only one other ship of the group was a Star Watch vessel—the *Defiant*, a missile cruiser.

The other three ships appeared to be armed freighters. They were almost the same size as the *Defiant* but lacked even its modest armor. The missile cruiser was a hit-and-run vessel, quite different from the *Moltke*. The battleship had stout armor and shields; the missile cruiser was under-protected in both areas. The *Defiant's* operational procedure called for unloading its missiles at a safe distance from any enemy and then running away to resupply. The missile cruiser had speed, but nothing extraordinary.

Why was the brigadier traveling so far from home in such an underpowered flotilla? Could one even call this a flotilla?

What was he missing here?

Maddox snapped his fingers. He should have seen it sooner. This had to do with Professor Ludendorff. The professor had been ultra-careful throughout the years at keeping out of the hands of Star Watch. The Methuselah Man had made an exception in the past with *Victory* and during parts of the Swarm invasion. That he traveled with O'Hara was nothing short of amazing. It meant something profound.

Would the professor have demanded an underpowered Star Watch presence as part of his "price" for agreeing to join the flotilla with the three freighters? Maddox was assuming those were his vessels.

To ask the question was to answer it. Ludendorff was one of the most paranoid people Maddox knew. Of course, hundreds of years of existence might make one so, especially as all the other Methuselah Men had been hunted down and slain with the exception of Strand.

"Galyan," Maddox said. "Scan the freighters. Tell me what's unusual about them."

The AI holoimage stood perfectly still with his closed eyelids twitching. Suddenly, he opened his eyes.

"I am detecting highly advanced shield generators," Galyan said. "Each of the freighters also has an exotic component. If those components, or their orifice originators, worked in synchrony—"

The AI abruptly stopped speaking.

"What is it, Galyan?"

"Sir, I believe the freighters working in synchrony might be considered as a single Q-ship."

"I have no idea what that is supposed to mean," Maddox said.

"A Q-ship, also known as a Q-boat, decoy vessel, special service ship or mystery ship, is a heavily-armed merchant ship with concealed weapons. The first known use of a Q-ship was in the 1670s on Earth, Pre-Space Age. The HMS *Kingfisher* was specially designed to counter the attack of Algerian corsairs or pirates in the Mediterranean by masquerading as a merchantman, hiding her armaments behind false bulkheads."

"I see," Maddox said.

"The most notable use of Q-ships occurred during World War I. Then, they were supposed to lure German submarines into making surface attacks. That gave a Q-ship the chance to open fire and sink them. In 1915—"

"Galyan!" Maddox said sharply.

"Sir?"

"If I wish to know more, I will let you know."

"Did I say too much, sir?"

"Far too much," Maddox said. "But you stopped when I asked you, so that was good."

"I am still learning tact, sir."

"Right," Maddox said. "Now, give me a moment."

Galyan fell silent.

Maddox drummed the fingers of his left hand on the armrest of his chair. Three freighters that could spring a powerful weapon when working in synchrony. That was good in case Spacers or others attacked the brigadier's battleship, but just how good were Ludendorff's freighters? He still assumed they belonged to the Methuselah Man.

"Galyan. Have you located the professor yet?"

"No, sir."

"Have you scanned the *Moltke* or the *Defiant* for him?"

"I have scanned all the ships, sir."

Maddox became thoughtful. "Do you suspect Ludendorff can cloak himself from you?"

"I give that a sixty-six percent probability."

"Are there jammers aboard the freighters?"

"Not that I can detect, sir. If you will remember, I was able to find the exotic equipment. That should mean I can locate the professor—but I cannot."

Maddox inhaled deeply through his nostrils. He was going to have to deal with Ludendorff again. He huffed out the breath. He and the professor had not parted on good terms after the victory over the Swarm invasion fleet. An evil spirit entity, the Ska, had also attacked back then. Star Watch had been powerless against it. A Builder from long ago had put the answer against the Ska deep into Ludendorff's subconscious for just such a time as they had then faced. Had the Methuselah Man by now learned to deal with the Builder programming embedded in him?

Since it was Ludendorff, Maddox suspected the answer was yes…and no. He recognized the utility in the last two Methuselah Men. But he did not care for either of them anymore. Strand was worse, but Ludendorff was no prize, either.

"What do you think this is about, sir?" Galyan asked.

"Spacers, perhaps."

"I suppose you could be right."

Maddox raised an eyebrow. "What's your analysis?"

The little holoimage froze again, his eyelids twitching. Finally, he looked up. "The Swarm, sir. They are still the greatest challenge for humanity."

"The Swarm are why the Spacers first fled Human Space."

"Exactly, sir," Galyan said. "So maybe you are correct and this is also about the Spacers."

"Right," Maddox said, as he pondered the problem. *Beware the Methuselah Man.* It was time to prepare for Ludendorff, which meant preparing for many conflicting eventualities.

-24-

A star-drive jump and a shuttle voyage later, Captain Maddox walked through a battleship door. As he did so, Brigadier O'Hara stood up behind her desk.

It was a spacious office deep inside the *Bismarck*-class Battleship *Moltke*. The desk was huge, impressive, constructed from oak.

Maddox was alarmed to note that O'Hara seemed smaller than he remembered. She almost seemed a tad shrunken. Was she getting old?

Obviously, she was older than the last time he'd seen her. That was always going to be the case. She seemed to show her age a little more than previously, though. Was that the ravages of time or the pressing weight of the responsibility of her position. Or did it have something to do with Ludendorff?

"It is good to see you, ma'am," Maddox said sincerely. He…cared deeply for the brigadier as a son would for his mother. He did not want to utter the word *love* about her even to himself. That was too raw an emotion for the captain concerning the woman who had done so much for him. He also sensed her concern for him, and that had always touched him.

"Captain," O'Hara said, coming around her desk, opening her arms wide.

Maddox saw the hug coming, and it almost seemed as if he had been waiting for it. Then, the brigadier hugged him, squeezing with affection.

He patted her back, and he even gave her a one-armed hug in return. He felt…strange doing that. He was Captain Maddox, the avenger. These softer emotions—

The brigadier released him, grabbing him by the arms and looking *way* up at him. "My," she said. "You look, look—I will say it, Captain. You are a handsome young man. How you must make the ladies swoon."

"I'm married to Meta, ma'am, remember?"

"Yes, yes, of course you are. Is Meta well?"

"Yes, ma'am."

"Excellent," the brigadier said, releasing him. "It's so good to see you my…my best agent," she finished lamely, as if she'd changed what she was going to say at the last second.

"I am glad to see you're well, ma'am."

"Yes, well, enough of that," she said, giving him a last slap on the arm. "Do sit down, Captain. I dislike peering up at you as if you're somewhere in the clouds."

Maddox sat in the nearest chair.

The brigadier returned behind her desk, putting her hands on the edge and gingerly sitting down. She seemed stiffer than he remembered.

Once she settled in, with her hands clasped on the desk, O'Hara regarded him. "Tell me what happened out here. We should get that out of the way before we begin."

Maddox gave a terse account of the past weeks. The brigadier did not interrupt. She took out a slate and stylus, jotting down notes.

"I have written a more thorough report," he said.

"No doubt," she said. "I will read it later, rest assured."

"Ma'am, there's one specific I left out of the report."

"Oh? I find that curious. Why did you leave it out?"

"You know I spoke with Mako 21, the First Class Surveyor Senior."

"From the sound of your verbal report just now, she made an impression on you."

"Yes, ma'am," Maddox said. There was no change in his demeanor, but he watched O'Hara more closely. "Mako 21 also told me to, 'Beware the Methuselah Man.'"

The brigadier stared at him, and she seemed to shrink inwardly as her facial features tightened.

"The phrase obviously means something to you, ma'am."

O'Hara didn't seem capable of speech just yet.

Maddox debated options, finally asking, "What has Ludendorff done this time?"

"Just a minute," the brigadier said hoarsely. She leaned down, opened a drawer and took out a small flask. She unscrewed the top and poured a tiny amount into a shot glass. Putting the flask away, the brigadier tipped back the shot glass and gulped the alcohol. She blanched afterward, made a half-coughing sound, and thrust out her neck. Finally, she put both hands on the desk and pushed herself back to a straight position.

"I needed that," O'Hara said.

"Do you believe Mako 21 spoke knowledgably?"

"No. That's nonsense," O'Hara said.

"Yet Ludendorff troubles you."

"Don't think I don't know what you're doing, Captain. You suspect Ludendorff of wrongdoing. I realize that's a natural reaction on your part, but you're wrong thinking he's been making trouble again. He has a list of new demands certainly… That's what has me…concerned for you."

"Concerned for me?"

O'Hara sighed. "You've been on the fringes too long, Captain. There are new developments taking place, terrible developments."

She told him about the Swarm "science team" invasions. One had hit the Commonwealth. One had hit the New Men in their Throne World System.

"Interesting," Maddox said.

"Is that all you can say? *Interesting?* It's a horrifying development."

"But not unforeseen."

"We're talking about the Swarm, Captain."

"I heard you the first time."

"Star Watch cannot defeat a dedicated Imperial invasion."

"We did before."

"You don't understand," O'Hara said. "The Lord High Admiral understands what this means. I do, too. I understand so well that…" She told him about her adventure to the Tau Ceti System.

Maddox sat impassively as she talked, soaking in the story. He understood the reason for her desperation, and Ludendorff's cunning. Yes. He could see all right.

"You never should have gone alone, ma'am. That was imprudent of you."

"I run Intelligence, Captain. I studied what little we know about the Imperium's gargantuan size and the…staggering number of ships they must possess. It boggles the imagination. A minor Imperial invasion fleet stretched the combined forces of Star Watch and the New Men to our breaking point last time. If you hadn't come up with your harebrained scheme of the Destroyers in the null zone, and if Ludendorff hadn't fashioned that awful soul weapon—with these two new science team invasions, I realized mankind had come to the end of its collective rope. So, yes, I took a risk, and it worked. Ludendorff had an answer. Isn't succeeding the important thing?"

"I suppose you're right," Maddox said, allowing the brigadier to appear to persuade him. He was going to have to take matters into his own hands after all. This could be tricky. "I still don't like your confrontation with two Strand agents."

"I can well understand that," O'Hara said. "We've dealt far too much with Strand lately. And that without actually meeting the original. That is all about to change, though."

Without showing it, Maddox grew more alert. "I don't understand what that means."

"I think you do, Captain. I believe you understand me perfectly. Star Watch, in conjunction with Professor Ludendorff, is going to break Strand out of his Throne World prison."

Maddox continued to sit impassively as the words washed over him. This was his worst suspicion come to life. Ludendorff or the Strand agents had turned the Iron Lady. The Strand agents might even have inserted wires into her brain.

Maddox had a grim certainty that he'd walked into a trap—a very elaborate trap—set either by Ludendorff or the Strand agents.

Meta had told him before how Ludendorff had come to see him in the hospital room after his final encounter with the Ska, and after using the strange soul weapon that Ludendorff had created. The professor had blamed him for what a Builder had done to his mind ages ago. Without the professor creating the soul weapon, Maddox would never have driven the Ska into Alpha Centauri "A" Star. Maddox would never have drained some of his own soul energy powering the weapon. He would never have been responsible for billions of people, and millions of Swarm, dying that day.

Maddox clenched his jaws. He refused to go back there in his thoughts. He had to escape this trap laid by Ludendorff or the Strand agents, and he had to take O'Hara with him and find a way to wrench her mind from their control.

"You look as if you're about to do something rash," O'Hara said.

"Not at all," Maddox said, squelching the obvious signs of tension and going into mission mode.

"Are you sure?" O'Hara asked doubtfully as she searched his face.

"Perfectly sure," he said, using all his skill to maintain an easy manner.

O'Hara finally nodded. "Good," she said, pressing a desk button.

It took everything the captain had within him to remain still as the door opened behind him. He tested the air... Maybe he couldn't smell it, but he knew. Ludendorff stood in the doorway behind him.

Maddox imagined a knife poised at his back. He glanced at the Iron Lady. She did not seem concerned. That could be the result of enemy mind control.

Maddox tensed imperceptibly. Space marines had taken his sidearm when he'd left the shuttle in the *Moltke* hangar bay. The marines had searched him, too, removing two other weapons. They had not found the one gun, though. Maddox whirled around in the chair and drew the hidden gun—on Professor Ludendorff in the flesh.

Yet that didn't seem right. The last time he'd seen Ludendorff, the Methuselah Man had aged. This Ludendorff looked like the one he'd been with for years. Could the professor have reversed the aging process? That didn't seem likely, but it also didn't seem impossible. The easier answer was that this was a Ludendorff clone or robot.

The professor scowled at the gun aimed at him. "I told you to take his weapons," he reprimanded O'Hara.

"I know you did," the brigadier said. "I was told the marines had done just that. I don't understand this."

"Well?" Ludendorff demanded of her. "Fix it."

O'Hara focused on Maddox. "Captain, put the gun away at once."

Maddox did no such thing. He rose to his feet, keeping the gun aimed at Ludendorff. By the distasteful twisting of the Methuselah Man's features, Maddox believed the professor lacked a personal force field; he'd once had a piece of alien tech to provide just that. The captain wasn't going to give Ludendorff the chance to activate one, just in case he had another alien device like the former one.

"Come inside, Professor," Maddox said in a cheery tone. Maybe this wasn't a clone or robot. "Close the door behind you. It's time we had a heart to heart, the three of us."

Ludendorff did not move.

"Step lively, Professor, or I'll shoot you where you stand and save us all a lot of trouble."

"Captain," O'Hara said sternly. "I order you to put down your weapon."

"Rest assured, I will, Brigadier," the captain said, "but not just yet. Inside, Ludendorff. It's time I find out what's really going on."

-25-

Maddox had dealt with the professor for years. He could tell when the Methuselah Man was thinking fast, searching for angles out of a mess.

"Three," Maddox said. "That's all the count I'll give you. Consider it a gift for old time's sake, for all the times you actually acted in our interest. Ready? No? Well, let's begin anyway, shall we? One!"

"See here, Captain," the brigadier said. "You can't just shoot the professor in cold blood."

"Two," Maddox said, and he shifted his position so he could watch both the brigadier and the professor at the same time. He…loved the old woman, he admitted to himself, but he didn't trust her right now. He was certain the professor had tampered with her mind.

"Fine," Maddox said. "Have it your way, Professor. Three—" he said, his trigger finger tightening.

"Wait, my boy," Ludendorff said, with perspiration dotting his broad forehead. "I'm entering the office. Look, I'm shutting the door behind me."

It closed with a snick.

Maddox eased some of the pressure from his trigger finger.

"I'm not going to approach you any closer," Ludendorff said, "as I'm unsure if you'll approve of such an action."

"Good choice, Professor," Maddox said. He used his boot and forcefully shoved a chair toward the Methuselah Man so it bumped against him.

Ludendorff automatically grabbed an armrest.

"Slide the chair around the brigadier's desk," Maddox said. "Put it at the corner, though. Brigadier, if you would be so kind, keep your hands off the desk and where I can see them."

"Captain," the brigadier complained. "This is an impossible situation."

"It's far from that, ma'am. Although it pains me to believe it, it is possible that you've been compromised."

"Are you mad?" she asked.

"Consider what I've heard," Maddox said. "You went alone to the orbital station in Tau Ceti. You were unconscious for quite some time. Your only companion was the professor. He showed you dead New Men with implants in their brains. That is well within his ability to stage."

Ludendorff had placed the chair in the ordered location and sat down. He also put his hands on his knees. Maddox wasn't sure, but the Methuselah Man might have been trembling the slightest bit. Was that suppressed rage or did the old goat realize he'd almost been shot dead?

"Ma'am, I must insist you follow my instructions," Maddox said. "The idea of using force against you—I find it repugnant. But I will use it if I have to, as I no longer believe you are in your right frame of mind."

"Well, I never, Captain," she said. "This is highly embarrassing—"

"Do you remember when an android impersonated you?" Maddox asked, interrupting her.

"How could I remember that?" O'Hara's lower lip had been quivering. That now ceased. She furrowed her brow and tilted her head at him. "But I see your meaning. You have not fired the gun. You wish to talk, it seems. You wish to ascertain the situation. Perhaps that isn't so bad." She turned to Ludendorff. "Captain Maddox is my best agent."

"He's a hotheaded fool," Ludendorff declared. "The only thing he has in his favor is greater than average *luck*."

"That's rot and nonsense," O'Hara said. "He's good. Why, he surprised me just now, and he surprised you. Admit it."

"He has his share of animal cunning," Ludendorff said. "Any lowbrow criminal has the same. That does not put him on my plane." The professor regarded Maddox. "What's the point of all this? Do you get your jollies by threatening your betters?"

Maddox made no reply. He watched impassively, analyzing behavior against past memories of the person. He also weighed options, wondering how to play this.

"Let's address the situation," Maddox said. "Perhaps we can come to a reasoned conclusion. The brigadier of Star Watch Intelligence has arrived at a fringe star system near the Beyond. She has traveled all the way from Tau Ceti in a single older-style battleship, accompanied by a missile cruiser, and that's it."

"You're forgetting about my three ships," Ludendorff said.

"Three freighters of dubious military worth," Maddox said.

"No!" the brigadier said. "They are potent vessels, I assure you of that, Captain."

Ludendorff exhaled with exasperation. "Brigadier, the captain is goading you. He wants you to reveal the properties of my privateers. I'd rather not oblige him."

"Why is that a problem?" O'Hara asked. "I think he should know."

"Know at my discretion," Ludendorff said. "I thought I had made that crystal clear to you."

"You did," O'Hara said. "But this—"

"The present situation changes nothing," Ludendorff said, interrupting her. "Captain Maddox is often overeager. In the past, a few of his indiscretions have worked for the greater good. Perhaps he even thinks he is doing well here. In the interests of our greater goal, I will put down this farce to his high spirits. In other words, if he puts away his gun I am willing to overlook the incident."

"That is good of you, Professor," the brigadier said, nodding.

Ludendorff made an offhand gesture.

"Perhaps the two of you could enlighten me about this *greater* goal," Maddox said.

"Do I have your permission?" the brigadier asked Ludendorff.

"He's still aiming the gun at me," Ludendorff said.

"Captain," the brigadier said.

"The gun will remain aimed at his chest," Maddox said. "Nothing said so far changes my original assessment of the situation."

"Bah," Ludendorff said. "You always were a monomaniac. You're far too impressed by yourself, Captain. I've never understood why the brigadier allows you such indiscretions. Yet, I'm tired of sitting here like a captive, and I seriously dislike having a gun aimed at me. Therefore—"

"You're mistaken, Professor," Maddox said, interrupting. "You are not *like* a captive. You *are* a captive."

Ludendorff's eyes narrowed. "I'm almost ready to walk out of here."

For the first time, Maddox smiled. It was a small thing, filled with deadly intent.

"Yes, Professor, go ahead. Get up and walk out."

"Would you shoot me in the back, my boy?"

With his free hand, Maddox snapped his fingers, with the deadly smile frozen on his face.

"I shall remember this," Ludendorff told Maddox.

If you live long enough, Maddox thought to himself.

"You're serious about continuing this charade, aren't you?" the brigadier asked the captain.

"Quite serious, ma'am. But it is no charade."

"I don't understand you," she said.

"Which proves that someone has tampered with your mind," the captain said.

"That does not necessarily hold," she said.

"You're the brigadier of Star Watch Intelligence," Maddox said. "You've read the reports about the professor during the last Swarm invasion, how he locked himself in his laboratory and developed the soul weapon—"

"No!" Ludendorff said huskily, pushing himself to his feet, growing pale. "I don't want to hear it. Stop! This is…this is too much." He was shaking his head. "You have no idea what it was like having the Builder program move my limbs and guide my thoughts. I abhorred the experience. I was a tool, *me*, Professor Ludendorff. It was unthinkable. The endless days and nights working to build that awful weapon—" Ludendorff stopped talking, staring at his hands.

"Your weapon won us the war," the brigadier said softly.

"By using *me*," Ludendorff shouted. He looked back and forth between the brigadier and Maddox. With an inarticulate shout, he sank into the chair, staring forward as he seemed to age before their eyes.

The brigadier glanced at Maddox.

The captain waited, watching the professor.

At last, the professor sucked down air, shuddering, seeming to recollect himself. He visibly took hold of himself, forcing the weakness and weariness away. It was an astonishing performance. Finally, the regular Professor Ludendorff seemed to have returned.

"Are you satisfied?" he asked Maddox.

"With what in particular?" the captain asked.

"We've relived my shame."

"No shame," the brigadier said. "You—"

"Please," Ludendorff said, interrupting. "I pride myself on my mental acumen, on being one of the few humans who can act in an independent manner. Instead, I find that I am a mere cog like everyone else. It is most upsetting and frankly, humiliating."

"You're still the professor," O'Hara said. "I came to you for help. You have the answer, the means for achieving humanity's salvation against the horrible Swarm Imperium. A mere cog, Professor? I don't think so."

Ludendorff was staring at her like a drowning man watching the one person with a rope. He nodded, and straightened a little more.

"You are correct," the professor said. "I am the essential man. It's hard to remember that sometimes. Having to relive such horrors—" Ludendorff scowled at Maddox. "Really, let's end this farce. Or tell us, at least, how we can convince you that we're both in our right state of mind."

Maddox nodded. "You can begin by telling me about the freighters—the Q-ships—and then tell me about your plan to save humanity, and why it needs Strand's dubious help."

Ludendorff glanced at the brigadier before studying Maddox. "First, put down your gun."

Maddox shook his head.

"Oh, very well," Ludendorff said. "If you must hold the gun as a phallic symbol of your virility, then suit yourself. I am the essential man. You shall see that soon enough."

"I'm sure that's true," Maddox said.

"Mock all you want," the professor said. "But here's the situation…"

-26-

Ludendorff settled himself more comfortably on his chair. He pursed his lips, eyed the gun for another second and then ignored it.

"It's interesting that you called my apparent freighters, Q-ships. That's rather accurate. I wouldn't have expected such historical insight from a man like you, a doer instead of a real thinker. But you're right."

"Q-ships?" the brigadier asked.

"A name merely," said Ludendorff. "It means a hidden warship. My freighters are not cargo haulers. They are science vessels after a fashion, although much more militarily powerful than the Swarm science ships. You see…" Ludendorff eyed the gun again before glancing at the brigadier. "I had decided a while ago that I no longer enjoyed surviving on the sufferance of others. Now, I have no desire to set up my own political system and thereby have the boring task of running a polity."

"You're too important to lead a large political organization?" the brigadier asked.

"Just so," Ludendorff said. "A president or even a dictator, for that matter, must attend to mundane matters on an almost continuous basis. That stifles the time for creativity and deep thinking. I am the most creative and the deepest thinker of all. Thus, I would be sinning against myself if I merely ran Human Space as its Lord Dictator. As you can well imagine, I am overqualified for the position and could have taken it upon myself long ago, if that had been to my taste."

"Your humility is astonishingly vast," Maddox said dryly.

"You mean that as mockery, I know. I am not humble, even though the experience with the *soul weapon*, as you say, left me…unsettled for a time. Once I recovered my equilibrium, I realized that I had been at the mercy of Star Watch and even the New Men for too long. It was time—if not to establish a polity—to arm myself with warships. Yet, I naturally realized that sovereign entities, such as the Commonwealth and the Windsor League, and even the Throne World, hate anyone powerful enough to commit violence. Sovereign entities with their warships desire to be the sole proprietors of war-making."

"You almost sound bitter," O'Hara said.

"Perhaps I am," Ludendorff said. "Perhaps, though, I am simply bitter at that aspect of human nature. My solution to the dilemma proved elegant indeed. Throughout human history, sovereign entities have allowed privateers, war-fighting ships with letters of Marque. A privateer acts like a pirate ship with a notable difference. A pirate is an outlaw, literally outside the law. A privateer has letters of marque from a sovereign entity, allowing him to commit violent acts under certain conditions."

"Are you attempting to so thoroughly bore me that I set down my gun in fatigue?" Maddox asked.

Ludendorff pretended not to have heard the comment. "My privateer Q-ships lack armor plating, such as even the missile cruiser possesses. They have powerful shield generators instead. When needed, they are able to defend themselves quite well indeed. Instead of arming them with laser or particle beam cannons, which any sensor officer could detect, they have a tri-system. When working in unity, the three vessels can produce a powerful Q-beam."

"And that is?" asked Maddox.

"Deadly," Ludendorff said. "I would say more, but I don't wish to bore you further."

A faint smile appeared on Maddox's face.

"I have recruited the crews," Ludendorff said. "They are loyal to me. I even have my own space marines."

"And you agreed to travel in the company of these Q-ships, ma'am?" Maddox asked.

"Of course she agreed," Ludendorff said. "She did it of her own free will. And the implication that she was foolish to bring a mere battleship and missile cruiser along is dead wrong."

"How is it wrong?" Maddox asked.

"We traveled incognito," Ludendorff said. "The *Moltke* and *Defiant* appeared to guard the so-called freighters. The two warships were too strong for pirates or even privateers to tackle but too small to cause any military fears from others."

"And if a Spacer Fleet had attacked your flotilla?" Maddox asked.

"No plan is perfect," Ludendorff said. "It's always a matter of good or bad odds. I should point out one other matter. Given your bigotry against me, I'm sure you'll find it unsettling."

Maddox inwardly tensed, although he continued to appear bland.

"The *Moltke* holds one of the Builder items you picked up last voyage. The item is no longer irradiated, either."

Maddox glanced at O'Hara in surprise.

"Yes, I have one of the items," O'Hara said. "The Lord High Admiral allowed me to take it with his blessing."

"What does the Builder artifact do?" Maddox asked Ludendorff.

The professor shrugged.

"No," Maddox said. "You need to do better than that."

The professor scoffed. "I can't tell you what I don't know."

"What do you think it does?"

"Ah," Ludendorff said, holding up a finger. "I have a suspicion, you are correct, but I'm not going to say under duress."

Maddox thought about that. In the end, he pulled the other chair to him, turned it around and sat down, all the while keeping the gun aimed at Ludendorff.

"No comment?" asked the professor.

"No, a question," Maddox said, "well, two questions. Why do you need Strand? How do you propose to spring him out of the Emperor's prison on the Throne World?"

"I'll answer the last question first," Ludendorff said. "*You* will go to the Throne World. With a little gold body paint, you could pass as a stunted New Man."

Once more, Maddox inwardly tensed.

If Ludendorff noticed, he appeared not to. "Armed with my insights and technological wizardry, you will free Strand and bring him to the edge of the Throne World System. There, your crew in *Victory* will pick the two of you up. From there, you will join me several star systems over."

"I cannot conceive of any reason why I would agree to such an insane act," Maddox said.

"Because I order it," the brigadier said. "You are a sworn officer of Star Watch. You can resign your commission, I suppose, but short of that, you will obey a lawful order or stand in contempt."

The faint smile returned to Maddox's lips.

"This is a serious matter," O'Hara said.

"First, ma'am, we must establish that you are not acting under Ludendorff's duress."

"This is ridiculous," O'Hara said. "I have just about had my fill of your insubordination. We have both participated in this farcical—"

"Ma'am," Maddox said, "anger proves nothing. A brain scan might help to convince me of your soundness."

"Do you wish to face a Board of Inquiry, Captain?" O'Hara asked.

"Not particularly."

"Then put down your gun," O'Hara said. "I am about to summon space marines, and I do not want them gunning you down for threatening a superior officer."

"Ma'am, you may summon them, of course. I won't stop you. However, I will kill Ludendorff the moment you do so."

"What?" Ludendorff said, sitting forward. "I most vigorously protest."

"That's insane," O'Hara told Maddox. "I am beginning to suspect *your* good intentions. The Spacers held you for a time. Maybe they tampered with your brain without you knowing it."

"What's this about Spacers?" Ludendorff growled, becoming alert.

"Someone named Mako 21 warned him about you," O'Hara said.

Maddox almost told her to remain silent, but he stopped himself. This could be interesting and insightful.

Ludendorff glanced at him sharply. "Mako 21," the professor said, as if tasting the words. "She must have been a First Class Surveyor, a highly ranked one. She must have possessed potent modifications, too. What was she doing on Usan III?"

O'Hara spoke up. "As I said, warning the captain. The Spacer told him to, 'Beware the Methuselah Man.'"

Ludendorff sat back, growing pale.

O'Hara's eyebrows rose. The professor's actions seemed to surprise her. "Does that mean something to you?" she asked the professor.

Ludendorff licked his lips as if he would speak, but he did not say anything more.

Maddox watched the interplay closely.

"The Spacers," Ludendorff finally said. "I cannot believe this. How could this Mako 21 know anything?" He frowned, rubbing his chin and regarding Maddox. "Tell me—what happened on Usan III?"

Maddox made a quick decision and told Ludendorff exactly what had happened.

"Oh, interesting, interesting indeed," Ludendorff said later. "The Spacers are wild fanatics, given to cultic fantasies. But they have delved into esoteric technologies and cannot be dismissed out of hand. This considerably complicates matters."

"Why?" asked Maddox.

"Clearly, it's possible Mako 21 knows our ultimate goal. The Spacers might try to thwart it."

"What is the goal?" asked Maddox. "It's time to tell me what this is about."

Ludendorff studied the captain, finally sighing. "Perhaps you're right. It's why we need Strand. You know as well as anyone that in numbers, the bugs dwarf the Human Race. Their Imperium is thousands possibly tens of thousands of times larger than the Commonwealth, New Men, all humanity combined. I have come to believe their Imperium lies in parts of three separate spiral arms. That is inconceivably vast, almost beyond comprehension for lesser minds. We barely defeated an invasion of eighty thousand Imperial warships. There is reason to believe that the original invasion was supposed to be even larger. If it had been one hundred and fifty thousand Imperial warships, say, we *would* have lost. Now, with these latest science-team invasions, we know that the Imperium is continuing its attempts to conquer us. We also know that they know how to use hyper-spatial tube technology as created by a Builder nexus."

"From what you said earlier," Maddox said, "the bugs used the hyper-spatial tubes poorly."

"For now, that's true," Ludendorff said. "What happens when the Imperium can use hyper-spatial tubes with precision? What happens when the Imperium launches three or more invasion fleets, each of them one hundred thousand warships strong?"

"It would be the end of us," Maddox said.

"Exactly," Ludendorff said. "Even you can see that."

"So…?" Maddox asked.

"So, we must remove their ability to create hyper-spatial tubes," Ludendorff said. "We cannot defeat them in straight battle, not with their mass against ours. Thus, we must avoid battle with them. I can see no other way to give us time to grow large enough to fight them."

"Grow large enough?" asked Maddox. "You just said they're in three different spiral arms."

"*Parts* of three different spiral arms," Ludendorff said.

"Either way," Maddox said. "We've barely begun to explore our local region of the Orion Arm. Thinking about expanding to other spiral arms when it would take—what, a million years to expand into our small spiral spur—"

"Don't be melodramatic," Ludendorff said. "It would take much less than a million years."

"Ten thousand years—"

"The *point*," Ludendorff said, interrupting, "is that we want to avoid a war with the Imperium now. We'll let the future take care of itself."

Maddox thought about that. "I imagine you're not worried, or worried to the same degree, about a Swarm invasion fleet traveling thousands of light-years through endless Laumer-

Points. From what we saw out there, a huge Chitin Empire stands between Human Space and the Swarm."

"In the Orion Arm, yes," Ludendorff said.

"Would Swarm fleets cross the vast empty space between the spiral arms to reach us?"

"You're still missing the main point," Ludendorff said.

Maddox frowned. "Oh. You already hinted at the answer. A Builder nexus creates a hyper-spatial tube."

"Ah," Ludendorff told O'Hara. "He begins to see."

"But... There's a way to destroy *all* the Builder nexuses at once?" Maddox asked.

"What?" Ludendorff asked. "That's madness. No, no, that's not the point. A Builder nexus creates and powers a hyper-spatial tube. *Victory* used such a tube and traveled over two thousand light-years. Such length takes more power than a shorter hyper-spatial tube. According to vigorous mathematical calculations, the theoretical limit of a safe hyper-spatial tube should be in the order of three thousand, nine hundred and sixteen light-years."

"That's precise," Maddox said. "What are the outer limits of an unsafe tube?"

Ludendorff shrugged. "Five or six thousand light-years."

"And how do you know all this to be true?" Maddox asked. "Theoretical means possible. Hard practical application is far more meaningful."

"Your point is well taken. We would be better served with accurate data. Yet, suppose the theories are accurate? In order to save ourselves, we would still have to overcome several tough problems. Firstly, how do we find all the possible nexuses capable of transporting Swarm fleets to or near Human Space? Are there five such nexuses, or fifty or five hundred? Secondly, how do we reach each nexus? Thirdly, how do we ensure that each nexus is destroyed? Fourthly—"

"Just a minute," Maddox said. "Who knows more about Builder nexuses and hyper-spatial tubes than anyone else?"

"Although it pains me to say it," Ludendorff replied, "the answer is, Strand."

"Which is why you want me to break him out of the Emperor's prison?"

"Exactly," the professor said.

Maddox thought a moment before turning to the brigadier, "And you agreed to this madness?"

O'Hara's face glistened brightly, probably due to the sweat on her face and the severe inner strain.

As Maddox opened his mouth to ask another question, he heard a heavy tread outside the closed door. Ah, he knew what must have happened. The brigadier must have stretched one of her feet to reach a hidden switch on the floor. Clearly, it hadn't been easy for her to press without him noticing, and maybe the act bothered her—hence the perspiration.

Maddox had a second where he understood what was going to happen. In that second, he wondered if Ludendorff was telling the truth. The Swarm Imperium was in at least parts of three different spiral arms. The extent of such an Imperium was mindboggling. Their warships—if they all came—would blot out the stars. Was it true that a nexus could only fashion a hyper-spatial tube five thousand light-years in length? That meant if they could destroy the nexuses in the Swarm's vicinity, within a perimeter of five thousand light-years in any direction, then the Imperial fleets could only come at them the old-fashioned, slow way—through one Laumer Point after another. That *could* mean the Swarm would tackle humans later instead of now, and that would give mankind time. In that second of rumination, Maddox supposed the brigadier *might* be in her right state of mind. The various possibilities stayed his trigger finger.

Abruptly, Maddox stood and set the gun on the desk. He would switch to Plan C and roll the dice of fate.

The next second, the door violently crashed open as a space marine in battle armor clanked into the room. A second marine followed on the first one's heels. They both interposed their armored bodies between Maddox and Ludendorff.

"Don't shoot!" O'Hara shouted. "Don't fire!"

The second marine's sleeve cannon was already aimed at Maddox. A round was in the chamber.

"Do you surrender?" O'Hara asked.

In response, Maddox held up his hands, palm forward.

A faceplate whirred down, and a hard-faced marine with a knife tattoo on his forehead regarded the captain.

"Should I kill him, Professor?" the marine asked.

Maddox glanced at O'Hara.

"These marines are his," she explained. "It's part of the deal."

"What deal?" Maddox asked.

"Put him in the brig," Ludendorff said.

"What deal?" Maddox asked the professor.

The second exoskeleton-powered marine grabbed Maddox in a crushing grip, lifting the captain off the floor. The marine turned toward the smashed door.

"Brigadier?" asked Maddox.

"I'm sorry," O'Hara said. "You'll have to ask the professor. He's officially in charge of the mission."

The last sight Maddox had in the brigadier's office was Ludendorff grinning in victory. Then, the marine marched out of the office, heading for the *Moltke's* brig.

-27-

Sergeant Riker grumbled to himself as he studied the *Moltke's* hangar bay from a spy-port in the shuttle that had brought Maddox to the battleship.

A squad of armored space marines surrounded the shuttle. Beyond the marines were various techs monitoring machines that kept a strict watch over the shuttle.

This was even worse than Maddox had originally suspected. After the captain had departed, a team of hard-faced men had scoured the interior of the shuttle, looking for any hidden compartments where a person could hide.

They hadn't found Riker's spot. He didn't know if they'd found Meta's compartment. The captain hadn't wanted his wife along. She had insisted, and she'd made solid arguments why she was the right person to do this. In the end, Maddox had agreed. He'd put aside his own desires for the greater good of the mission.

The boy was growing, Riker supposed.

The sergeant didn't know if the hard-faced, non-Star Watch personnel had found the captain's wife, because he didn't know where Meta had hidden. The captain had kept the various compartments secret. That way, the two of them couldn't give the other away.

"No," Riker whispered in alarm.

He saw Meta. The woman dropped down from a hidden cache under the shuttle. She hadn't even been *inside* the ship, but in some outer pod. Meta wore a regular Star Watch uniform, and she held a slate in hand, as she made notations. She was pretending to be part of the earlier search party.

"That ain't ever going work," Riker complained. They weren't dealing with stupid people, but clever sots that knew their business. Ludendorff always used the best, and from the feel of the hard-faced men, those had been the professor's people. They had reminded Riker of that bastard of a slarn trapper the professor used to keep around—Villars.

One of the techs at a monitoring machine shouted and waved his arm, pointing at Meta.

Two armored marines turned around. Likely, they both saw Meta at the same time.

She was a quick-thinking woman, and she showed her mettle now.

"Look out!" Meta shouted. "The shuttle is going to explode." She dropped her slate and sprinted away for apparent safety.

"What in the Hell?" muttered Riker.

At that moment, an explosion tore the underbelly of the shuttle. The blast lifted the entire vessel, surprising the sergeant inside, tossing him against a bulkhead and throwing him onto the deck. The shuttle crashed and tilted, and a fire began in a different interior compartment.

Scrambling off the deck where he lay, hearing the crackle of flames and smelling electrical smoke, Riker realized that must have been the captain's idea. Maddox must have anticipated incredibly tight security over here. Therefore, he must have decided to create a diversion.

Despite the fire and smoke, Riker went back to the spy-port, peering outside. An armored marine had caught Meta. She struggled, but not even her 2-G strength could prevail against exoskeleton power.

A siren blared outside, and regular damage control people raced in the shuttle's direction.

"I can't believe this," Riker complained. "He could have at least told me about the diversion."

Riker understood the cold-bloodedness of the captain's plan. He was sacrificing Meta's cover so his sergeant could slip off the shuttle as a damage control worker.

Riker examined his uniform. Nope. He'd better climb into a pair of overalls. Later, he'd need the uniform he was wearing. But he also needed the overalls to impersonate a damage control worker. It was time to get started.

***

Eight minutes later inside the shuttle, Riker passed a damage control worker wearing a rebreather and carrying a heavy extinguisher. The sergeant grabbed a rebreather of his own, put it on, waited for a chance and climbed down the shuttle ramp to the hangar-bay deck.

"We need a C line," he shouted from within the rebreather, waving an arm and pointing up into the shuttle.

Two other damage control people dragged a line, running up the ramp with it.

Riker followed them back inside the shuttle. He'd seen armored marines blocking the way free of the vessel. It looked like there was only going to be one way to do this. Riker hadn't wanted to do it, mainly because it was morally dubious. But wasn't that the nature of Intelligence work?

Hurrying to a different area of the smoky shuttle, looking around, making sure no one was going to surprise him, Riker tapped controls. A hidden bulkhead slipped open. He pressed a timer and moved into the armored slot, closing it behind him.

Five seconds later, more explosions lifted the shuttle, letting it slam down with a screeching crash. Riker was holding on tightly inside the padded closet. He knew that sections had flown off the hull, damaging areas of the hangar bay, maybe killing some of the people out there.

"Don't like doing this," Riker muttered. But he did his duty as per regulations. He opened the hidden compartment, closing it behind him and raced through the twisted maze of the half-destroyed shuttle. He found a badly injured person.

"You okay?" Riker shouted through his rebreather.

"My ribs," the man groaned, indicating his side where a small piece of metal had lodged.

"Let me help you."

Riker used his bionic arm to hoist the man to his feet. The man would have been too heavy otherwise. Then he slung one of the man's arms over his shoulder and began guiding him through the burning shuttle.

Klaxons wailed outside in the hangar bay. Some of the bulkheads there were torn. There were at least four armored marines lying on the deck, some of their armor dented, some torn open.

"We're killing good people," Riker whispered in dismay. "That's too much."

Despite his words, the sergeant helped his man past others waving them on. They reached a hatch, leaving the smoky, damaged hangar bay and the burning shuttle. A short way up the corridor, Riker passed the wounded man to medical people.

The man had fallen unconscious. That wasn't from the injuries but because Riker had injected him with a knockout drug.

"He's my best friend," Riker told the chief medic, forcing his eyes to turn moist with brimming tears.

"Go on," the medic said, jerking a thumb at the departing anti-gravity sled with the injured man lying on it.

"Thanks," Riker said with heartfelt gratitude, hurrying after the sled team. The sergeant began limping, and he veered off into a different corridor once the team had gained enough separation from him.

He looked around. He was out of the hangar bay and inside the *Moltke*. He shed the overalls in a closet and marched briskly in an MP Sergeant's uniform.

Since Maddox hadn't contacted them, this was Plan C. It meant the captain was likely dead or a prisoner. If he was dead—*no*. Riker didn't want to go there just yet in his mind. He couldn't believe Maddox was dead until he saw the corpse. Even then, he might doubt it. The other option was that Maddox had become a prisoner, and that likely meant the captain was in the brig.

It was time for some hardcore and exceedingly fast Intelligence work. "Damn if it don't always land on me to get the job done," Riker muttered.

The sergeant patted the stunner at his side. If Maddox was in the brig, did that mean Ludendorff was in charge here? That had been one of the captain's chief worries.

Riker didn't see how that could have happened on a Star Watch battleship. He didn't have Maddox's imagination. But he trusted the captain, and he knew that Ludendorff had to be one of the slipperiest and dirtiest players they'd ever met. Usually, the Methuselah Man was on their side—mostly, anyway. Whose side was Ludendorff on this time?

-28-

Maddox was in a large room near the brig, secured to a metal chair. Steel bands bound his ankles, wrists and neck to the metal construct. Strange machines waited around him in a horseshoe shape. At the open area of the machines, a strange trio of abnormally thin technicians in white smocks arranged ugly, scalpel-like tools on trays.

The three had bronze-colored skin and short red hair, with unusually thin noses.

Maddox didn't know their phenotype. They seemed altered from regular humans, not in a direct way, but maybe by living and evolving several generations on an alien planet. The alien world had changed them, first in subtle ways and now more overtly.

Two armored marines stood like statues by the back wall.

A hatch opened, and Professor Ludendorff moved briskly within. He came alone, and he seemed displeased. The professor wore dark garments, highlighting his thick white hair. He carried a computer slate in one hand. He also had a large bronze pendant hanging from his neck.

Was the pendant a mini-generator for a personal force field? The pendant had to do something—it wasn't just for looks. That was all Maddox knew for now.

The trio of abnormally thin medical personnel stepped aside for Ludendorff, each bowing his head as the professor passed him.

The professor halted in front of Maddox, staring at him in a challenging way.

"What have you done?" Ludendorff demanded.

"Made an operational error," Maddox replied. "In hindsight, I should have shot you when I had the opportunity in the brigadier's office."

"Bah!" Ludendorff said. "That's meaningless prattle. Without me, humanity dies to the Swarm. Is that what you want?"

"You're right. I don't want that."

"You're in no position to play games with me. Why, this could mean—" Ludendorff stopped abruptly and shook his head. "I forget myself. You're quite possibly the most egotistical man I know, half man, I mean. The other half is *New* Man."

Maddox said nothing as he strove to analyze his opponent.

"Does hearing that upset you?" Ludendorff asked.

"Some," Maddox admitted.

"Why is that, I wonder?"

"I haven't decided."

"I have."

"Oh?"

"But I'm not going to tell you," Ludendorff said. "I'll let you figure that one out on your own."

"That implies you're not going to—" It was Maddox's turn to abruptly stop talking.

"Do you fear to say it, Captain? Do you think the word will move me to act in that fashion?"

"I suppose I do."

"I'm not going to kill you," Ludendorff said. "I will, however, quite possibly have these seasoned neurosurgeons operate on your brain? Does the idea of mental adjustment bother you?"

Maddox waited before he spoke, trying to compose himself. He should have shot Ludendorff when he had the chance. But…he hadn't shot him. Thus, he must play the game as it stood. He must concentrate. It was possible he still had a card or two in play. That Ludendorff had come in angry likely meant Meta and Riker had begun Plan C.

"I dislike putting you at ease," the professor was saying. "But we're running out of time. We cannot allow the Imperium the time to send any more invasion fleets into Human Space. We must destroy their capacity to do so. That means finding and destroying the nexuses in their nearest border regions to us."

"You're serious about that, then?"

"That's a dull question. I wouldn't have spoken that way just now unless that was the case."

"True," Maddox said.

Ludendorff glanced back at the red-haired, bronze-colored neurosurgeons before studying Maddox.

"They are Bosks," the professor said. "Theirs is a small rocky world making for a precarious existence. For several centuries, they were alone, and they mutated accordingly as you can plainly see. Once the Laumer Points changed the space-traveling game, they learned exportable skills, becoming quite proficient in certain trades. Their time alone, however, gave them several unique features. One of those is a predilection for working in threes."

Maddox noticed something as Ludendorff explained. The dark eyes of the three Bosks focused avidly on the professor. They did not watch him like subservient workers might, but… They watched Ludendorff like scientists observing their experiment.

Maddox concentrated on what Ludendorff had just said. The Bosks had a predilection for working in threes.

"Three freighters," Maddox said sharply.

"Oh, you're perceptive as always, my boy," Ludendorff said. "The Q-beam is of Bosk design, as are the Q-ships. Yes. I recruited many of my technicians from their world. They are quite loyal, amazingly loyal, really. It is a pity the trio must permanently mark you."

"For the mission to rescue Strand?" asked Maddox.

Ludendorff nodded his head. "I did not lie about that. We desperately need Strand."

"Do *we,* Professor?"

"What are you implying?"

Maddox noticed that the trio no longer focused on Ludendorff, but on him. Were they in charge? If that was true... The captain wondered if he dared to use his greatest barb. Yes. He believed he did, as this might be one of his last opportunities to act.

"I have a theory," Maddox told Ludendorff. "But you're not going to like it."

"A theory," Ludendorff said. "Why would I care one way or another?"

"You don't want to free Strand."

The dark gazes of the trio intensified upon the captain.

Ludendorff chuckled. "I'm afraid I do want to free him, most urgently, in fact."

The trio glanced at each other, almost imperceptibly nodding before focusing on Ludendorff again.

"My theory is simple," Maddox said. How should he word this? "The Builders created the Methuselah Men. I doubt they wanted your breed to become extinct. Have you ever wondered why you and Strand haven't slain each other yet? You both claim to hate the other, is that not so?"

"I wouldn't go that far," Ludendorff said.

"I would. The answer is obvious. A Builder impulse put deep inside you long ago is driving you to attempt Strand's rescue, so the Methuselah Men don't die out."

Ludendorff turned pale and actually started trembling. He spoke in a low, outraged voice. "How dare you say a Builder impulse is driving me? How dare you imply that a Builder is once more in control of me? I am my own man, Captain. I decide my own fate. I have rid myself of *all* Builder programming."

Maddox made a scoffing sound.

Ludendorff's eyes bulged outward and he stepped nearer, slapping Maddox across the face. That made the professor red-faced, possibly in shame or shock at his deed. He shook a finger in the captain's face, and spittle flew from Ludendorff's mouth as he said, "I am my own man!"

The display surprised Maddox. He hadn't expected this. He glanced at the trio. The three studied the professor again like scientists gauging their experiment. The captain noticed other details he hadn't cataloged at first. The three stood unusually close to each other. Yes, they actually bumped against each other, and one of them lifted his fingers ever so slightly. That caused the other two to shift their gazes to that one.

Why had Ludendorff gone to that particular small rocky world? Had the trio done something to the professor? It certainly seemed as if that was the case.

Ludendorff turned his back on Maddox. The professor hunched his shoulders and breathed heavily as he clutched the computer slate he'd brought with him. Finally, the professor turned around. He was no longer red-faced, trembling or pale. He seemed to have regained his self-mastery.

"You have low animal cunning," Ludendorff said. "Some might even call that impressive. It is not true intellect, of course. You can achieve first-rate results in physical tasks and even do well in crafty dialogue. What you lack, however, is a true scientific mind that can comprehend technical marvels."

Maddox said nothing.

"I will not stoop to your level," Ludendorff said. "I will keep this at an exalted height."

Maddox still said nothing.

"My Bosks will alter you so you can move freely on the Throne World. It will be more than giving you a new skin hue. For a time, you will think better, move faster and…well, age at a precipitous rate."

"I will burn out?" asked Maddox.

"That's not bad," Ludendorff said. "Yes. It will be a form of burn out. The procedure will add decades to your apparent age, but not right away. First, you will go to the Throne World in secret as a practically real New Man. Once there, you will help to rescue Strand."

"And if I decline your offer?"

Ludendorff gave him a sinister smile. "You have fallen for my trap, Captain. Thinking yourself clever, you have given me the tool to coerce you."

Maddox waited, disliking the professor's glee.

"Notice," Ludendorff said. With both hands, he held up the slate. On it, a shuttle in a hangar bay exploded. A woman ran away from it, shouting a warning.

"That is your wife," Ludendorff said. "It was a clever ruse on your part, but it wasn't clever enough."

The professor tapped the slate. It showed the shuttle violently exploding, sending hull pieces against the bulkheads and causing the vessel to lift and crash against the deck.

"People lost their lives in that little episode, Captain."

Maddox did not watch the slate too closely. He didn't want to see Riker. He didn't want to appear too needy. Instead, he shrugged.

"What do I care?" Maddox asked. "You're killing me. I'm still killing some of yours."

Ludendorff's eyes glowed with hatred as he leaned near Maddox. "Just like you killed part of me with your…your *soul weapon*."

"Not me," Maddox said calmly, "but the ancient Builder who programmed your mind."

"No! Don't try to deny that it was your monomania…your monomania…"

The crazed look left Ludendorff's eyes. He blinked several times, rubbing his forehead.

Maddox noticed the trio of Bosks once more conferring together in their strange manner. What had really happened on the small rocky world? Did Ludendorff command them, or was there something more subtle at work?

It occurred to Maddox that maybe Strand's planning had gone much more deeply than they'd even believed last voyage.

"What's going on?" Ludendorff said. "Tell me what you're thinking."

"You don't seem like yourself, Professor. Even your regular speech patterns are off. Why is that?"

Ludendorff scowled.

The three Bosks stiffened. They definitely reached out, grabbing each other's hands and whispering with each other.

"How can you say such a thing?" Ludendorff demanded.

One of the Bosks cleared his throat. The professor's reaction was swift and surprising. He whirled around to face the Bosks.

"Sire," the speaker said. "You know the low animal cunning of Captain Maddox. He is a trickster who searches for a man's weak points."

"But I don't have any weak points," Ludendorff said.

The speaker bowed his head in a deferential manner. "Are you strong in *every* avenue of thought, Sire?"

The professor rubbed his jaw as if considering the question. "What are you suggesting?"

"We make no suggestions, Sire. We simply await your orders to alter him."

"Yes…yes…" Ludendorff said. "I will give that order. Yet, there was something I wanted to show him first. I wanted him to see…"

"His wife, perhaps, Sire?" the speaker said.

"Yes!" Ludendorff said, clapping his hands. "I wanted him to see the futility of trying to best the greatest man in the universe."

The professor spoke into a sleeve. "Bring the woman in."

A few seconds passed. Finally, a hatch opened. Meta entered. She wore a dancer's scanty garb, with bits of silk dangling from her lovely hips. She glared at Ludendorff, and jerked her shoulder at the guard who pushed her forward.

The guard wore a facemask and his uniform seemed rumpled and ill-fitting.

Maddox observed the pair, noting the looseness of the manacles around Meta's wrists. He noticed, too, that the guard had a bionic arm, just one, though, not both.

"Meta was once your good friend, Professor," Maddox said.

Ludendorff was grinning as he looked at Meta. "Eh?" the professor asked. "What's that? What did you say?"

"She was your friend on many missions," Maddox said.

"So?" Ludendorff asked. "I don't understand what you're getting at."

"It's nothing," Maddox said. "I made a miscalculation. I thought you were going to make her dance for us, and that made me angry."

Ludendorff peered at Maddox, and finally understanding donned. "Ah. You don't *want* the marines to watch her dance.

That's why you suggest she do so. You must know that I tend to order the opposite of whatever you desire. Yes, yes, I see what you're doing."

The professor whirled around to face the marines. "You two. Go! Get your friends. I want *all* of you to watch Meta do a strip tease for us while the captain is bound and helpless."

"No!" Maddox cried.

"Yes," Ludendorff said, rubbing his hands. "This is going to be a performance to remember."

-29-

The two armored marines clanked out of the hatch, closing it behind them.

Maddox tried to signal Riker, using his eyes to point out the professor's pendant. Would the sergeant realize Ludendorff had a personal force field on?

"I'm going to humiliate you, my boy," the professor said. "The marines are going to do more than just watch, you know?"

"What happened to you?" Maddox asked. "Where's Doctor Dana Rich?"

"Eh? What do you mean by that?"

"Have you forgotten about Dana, your love?"

The speaker of the three Bosks once more cleared his throat.

It took the professor longer to turn and regard the man again. "What is it this time?" Ludendorff asked.

"You look pale, Excellency," the speaker said. "Perhaps it is time…"

"Time, time, yes time for what?"

"For your injection, Excellency," the speaker said.

Ludendorff glanced at Maddox.

"Don't you see, Professor?" Maddox said, actually saying these things for Meta and Riker's benefit. "The Bosks are using you. They're your keepers. They must be Strand's agents. That's what driving you to these actions—these Bosk scientists. Kill them, Ludendorff, or you'll never be master of yourself again."

Ludendorff frowned. "No…that doesn't sound right."

"The captain is clever at using words to confuse his foes," the speaker said. "Ignore him."

"Listen to me," Maddox told Ludendorff. "I know your personal force field makes you believe you're invulnerable to any threat. But the Bosks are controlling you. Kill them, and you'll be free."

"The ravings of a madman will not sway his Excellency," the speaker told Maddox.

The other two Bosks jerked at the speaker's robe. He turned to them. One of the others glanced at the guard with Meta. The speaker also glanced at the guard.

"Kill those three now!" Maddox shouted.

"You're raving," Ludendorff said. "I'm not going to kill anyone."

Meta tore her wrists free of the manacles and charged the professor.

At the same time, the guard whirled around, facing the three Bosks. His drawn stunner spat three times in quick succession. Each shot struck a thin Bosk in the chest, causing each strange human to shriek and stumble backward, tangling his feet and tripping so he fell.

Meta veered away from a startled Ludendorff and charged the three fallen Bosks.

"Stop!" Ludendorff shouted. "I order you to stop what you're doing."

The guard—Riker—turned the stunner on Ludendorff, firing, but to no effect as blots of force appeared centimeters from the professor's clothes.

"Kill the three!" Maddox shouted. "That's the key to this."

Riker turned back to the Bosks, and he reset his stunner, likely to a higher setting.

"No," Ludendorff said. "Stop. I need them. I order you to stop."

"You don't need them," Maddox said, as calmly as he could. "They've done something to your mind, Professor. They're the ones forcing you to rescue Strand."

"That's not true," Ludendorff said.

Meta reached the Bosks. Riker had shot the speaker first. That one groaned as he pushed off the floor. Meta slid down, tackling him. She wrapped her arms around his head and twisted more violently than seemed natural or even possible.

Necks bones shattered loudly.

"No!" Ludendorff shouted.

Meta released the jerking, thrashing speaker, scrambling to the second Bosk.

Ludendorff pressed a button on his belt. A horrible subsonic sound caused Maddox to arch back in pain. The debilitating noise rose in pitch.

Maddox groaned.

Meta grabbed the second Bosk's head as she'd done the first, and she strove even as the noise struck her.

His neck bones cracked as well.

It was the last thing Maddox saw as the terrible noise emanating from Ludendorff's belt rendered him unconscious.

-30-

Professor Ludendorff stared at a bulkhead, his mind throbbing intensely. Images flashed before his inner eye, images he didn't want to remember. With a groan, Ludendorff tore his gaze from the bulkhead. He rubbed his forehead, turning back to the mayhem spread out before him.

Draegar 3, The Orator, was dead. Even more terrible, Draegar 1, The Primary, was also dead. Only Draegar 2, the Designer, lay groaning in pain, still alive but barely conscious as he lay on the floor.

The glorious Meta lay nearby, snoring softly, her scanty garments in delightful disarray. The masked guard—that was Treggason Riker, he believed, Maddox's trusty sergeant—was also unconscious, as was Maddox, still secured to the metal chair.

Ludendorff had purposefully overloaded their auditory senses, rendering them insensible. Draegar 2, the Designer, had been hurt, but not as badly as the others were.

Ludendorff took several lurching steps toward the infernal Captain Maddox. The half-breed might have just ruined everything. He should slay the captain and be done with it. He *would* slay him. He would…

Ludendorff bit his lower lip, pausing in his lurching advance. The captain had spoken a troubling name, a magic spell perhaps. Why else did his mind throb so painfully? Why did he see this woman of utter delight in his inner vision?

The professor stood motionless, trying to understand what had just happened. Draegar 1 and 3 were dead.

"Dead," Ludendorff said. That mattered, but he couldn't quite understand why.

The professor rubbed his jaw. He heard noise, a pounding at the hatch.

"Go away," he said.

That didn't help. The pounding continued.

Finally, a comm unit pulsed in his pocket. He dug it out, clicking it.

A hard-faced man with a dagger tattoo on his forehead regarded him. It was Jard the Commander, the leader of his space marines.

"Master," Jard growled. "You have locked the hatch. Your guards cannot reach you. Should they break in?"

Ludendorff stared at Jard.

"Master, are you—?"

"Do not question me," Ludendorff said, interrupting the commander.

Jard's eyes narrowed. "You are right," he said, although it didn't sound as if he meant it.

"I must…" Ludendorff grew wary. There was something wrong here. He couldn't pinpoint it, and that was amazing. He was the greatest man in the universe. Yet now he must use cunning, low animal cunning like the infernal Captain Maddox. Otherwise, something bad was going to happen to him.

"Commander Jard, are you concerned about me?" Ludendorff let his voice drip with mockery.

"You sent the guards away, Master. That was unusual."

"Yes, I sent them away to get others. Have they gathered the others?"

"Yes, Master. Will you let all of them rape the woman?"

"Do you wish for dibs, Commander?"

Jard's face seemed to glow with desire. "I have seen the woman. Yes."

"Yes?"

"Yes. I want her, Master."

"Then, you shall have her."

"I want her first. I do not wish for the others to mount her before I do."

"Then, order your men away."

Jard studied him closely. "Are you well, Master?"

"What did I say about questioning me?"

"Master, I want to—" Jard's features shifted. "May I speak to the Orator?"

"He is conferring with his brothers and they will speak with me. After we have completed our plan, you shall receive the woman and speak with the Orator."

Jard examined Ludendorff over the tiny comm screen. "Your eyes are bloodshot, Master."

"I will—"

Ludendorff remembered that he'd slept under a strange machine a day ago. Draegar 2, the Designer, had given him a pill at those times. The pill helped him sleep. While he slept—

"I must sleep soon," Ludendorff said. "The Orator says I must…nap in thirty-eight minutes."

At last, the suspicion left Jard's eyes. "Did the Orator suggest to you that I wanted the woman?"

"He did. It was why I locked the door."

"Is this another of your jokes, Master?"

"It is. Do you like it?"

"I do. And I want the woman."

"You will have her first."

The commander grinned hotly. "I anticipate the woman in…in thirty-five minutes. Jard out, Master."

"The hatch will be open then," Ludendorff said.

The tiny screen had already winked off. Thoughtfully, the professor pocketed the comm. He looked up and froze in shock as he found Maddox staring at him.

"What did you do this time, Professor? How did you get yourself in this fix?"

"Don't you dare question me. I'm the Master. I'm the greatest man in existence." Ludendorff rubbed his head. Why did it keep throbbing like this?

Maddox took in the dead and the unconscious, and he nodded within the confines of the neck shackle.

Ludendorff rubbed his head for a long moment before looking up. "You spoke about a woman earlier."

Maddox gave him a searching glance before the half-breed's features turned into the calm mask that Ludendorff envied at times.

"Do you know the woman's name?" Ludendorff asked.

"Doctor Dana Rich."

"Yes. Yes! I *know* that name. Who is she?"

"Your companion."

"What?"

"She was with you during the Swarm invasion."

"You lie," Ludendorff said, but without real conviction.

"Where did you go after leaving Earth?"

"Go?" Ludendorff asked.

"You talked about a small rocky world. You called the people Bosks. How did you find the world? Did you go directly to it after the Swarm invasion ended?"

Ludendorff frowned, the ache once more intensifying in his head. "I… I don't remember exactly."

"That's odd, isn't it?"

"Why is it odd?"

"Because you have the greatest memory in existence," Maddox said.

"That's true, that's true, I do, or I did. Why can't I remember the woman then?"

"Did the Bosks help you after the Swarm invasion?"

Ludendorff looked at Maddox blankly, finally nodding. "I think they did. I think that's what happened."

"Do you remember why you went there?"

The pain spiked between the professor's eyes. He clutched his head with both hands and cried out in pain. "I want it to stop," he said. "Make it stop."

"I can."

"Liar!"

"Stop thinking about the Bosks," Maddox said. "Stop thinking about Doctor Dana Rich, how beautiful she is and how much you enjoy making love to her."

Ludendorff's mouth opened as he looked up. "I made love to her?"

"You're the best in the universe at doing it. You trained Dana to match your sexual prowess."

Ludendorff blinked wildly, and he grew faint. "I do have sex, marvelous sex, intense and passionate like only a few have ever achieved. Yet…I haven't made love in, in—"

He looked up in astonishment. "I can't remember how long it's been."

"I do."

"How is that possible? You're my enemy."

"I'm not. I'm your friend. We've often worked together and achieved astounding results. Think about it carefully, Professor, and you'll realize I'm right."

A sly look stole over Ludendorff. "Why have I locked you in the chair then?"

"Because we feud sometimes," Maddox said. "This time, though…"

"What? Say it? Or are you afraid of what I'll do to you if you tell me the truth?"

"Clearly, the Bosks did something to your mind, and I'm beginning to suspect why and how that happened."

"That's impossible."

"There's that word again. It's not. I'm good at untangling mysteries. You know that."

"In a low sort of way, you are," Ludendorff insisted.

"True. But sex is often a lowbrow affair, is it not?"

"For your kind, perhaps, but not for me," Ludendorff said. "For me, it is a gloriously profound act."

"When was the last time you did it?"

"You claimed to know."

"I do know. It was before the Builder programming took over in your mind."

Ludendorff blinked and couldn't seem to stop.

"After the Ska died," Maddox said, "you wanted to kill me. Meta told me what happened. I don't think you've ever forgiven her for stopping you."

Ludendorff turned and looked at Meta lying unconscious on the floor. She was an incredibly beautiful woman, but not the right dusky color as his Dana.

"That's why you wanted to humiliate her with the space marines," Maddox said. "You were going to let the…where did you find your space marines?"

Ludendorff winced with pain, rubbing his forehead as he if could rub out a spot there.

"It doesn't matter," Maddox said. "I think you went to the small rocky world and spoke to the Bosks. There, in some manner, they persuaded you that they could ease your mental anguish. I don't know if those three were Strand's agents or if they had their own agenda. But they've been using you, manipulating you. It would never have happened if—"

Ludendorff cried out in horror as he clutched his head. He continued to cry out, squeezing his head, finally moaning and sinking to his knees.

"What have I done?" Ludendorff whispered. "Dana, Dana, what did the Bosks do to you? What happened?"

"What did the Bosks do to *you*, Professor?"

From on his knees, Ludendorff looked up at Maddox. Anguish twisted the Methuselah Man's features.

"Break their conditioning," Maddox said. "Prove to all of us that you are the Methuselah Man. Look. Two of the Bosks lie dead."

"They are the Draegar," Ludendorff whispered.

Maddox almost said more, but he saw something on the professor's face that stopped him.

"Draegar 1 is the Primary," Ludendorff recited. "Draegar 2 is the Designer. Draegar 3 is the Orator. They are in symbiosis with one another. Together, their united brains are stunning in outlook and ability. They…they helped me purge any remaining Builder programming within me. I am my own man now."

"Could the Draegars—"

"No! Together, they are the Draegar."

Maddox nodded even if he didn't fully understand. "While the Draegar helped you, could he have inserted his own programming into your mind?"

"That's impossible," Ludendorff whispered. "I took every safeguard."

"The Draegar might have eased some of your mental anguish," Maddox said. "Clearly, one of the costs was the ability to make love to Dana. Or maybe Dana's love was thwarting their progress with you."

Ludendorff swallowed heavily as he hunched his shoulders.

"The marines are going to be coming soon," Maddox said.

"You overheard the conversation?"

"The leader of the marines wants to rape Meta first."

"He is Jard the Commander. He is a bondsman of the Draegar, a creature of the vats."

"The Bosk space marines belong to Draegar?" Maddox asked.

Ludendorff nodded.

"Did Draegar manipulate O'Hara's mind as well?"

"It's possible," Ludendorff said. "He was alone with her for a time on the station."

"The Tau Ceti Station?"

Ludendorff nodded.

"Is Draegar one of Strand's agents?"

"Maybe. I…I seem to remember that Strand—" Ludendorff groaned. "I remember now. It's like a veil lifting from my thoughts. Strand created the Draegar and the vat-born. I was desperate after the Swarm invasion. With Strand a prisoner, I believed I could control the Draegar. Somehow, I made a mistake while there."

"You were distraught after the invasion," Maddox said.

"Yes."

"The Builder program had sapped you of your normal brilliance."

Ludendorff swallowed. "What are we going to do? Jard is coming. He might come with one or two others. He can summon the rest of the vat marines and kill us all."

"Unlock me, Professor."

Ludendorff stared at him and finally shook his head. "I cannot."

"It's the only way you're going to find Dana again."

Ludendorff began blinking. Maybe he was too distraught to notice Meta rising from the floor. She picked up a computer slate, tiptoeing toward the professor, no doubt intending to bash him over the head with it.

"Free me," Maddox told Ludendorff.

A sudden look swept over the professor. He whirled around from on his knees. Meta swung. The computer slate struck the force field, stopping centimeters from Ludendorff's face.

"Treachery," Ludendorff declared.

At that point, the half-conscious Draegar 2, the Designer, removed a small device from his smock. From on the floor, he aimed it at Ludendorff, and a narrow beam flashed past any protective force field and struck Ludendorff in the shoulder.

The professor howled in agony, and who knew if he would have died if the ray kept beaming. Riker also stirred on the floor. He saw what was happening, used his stunner and blasted Draegar 2, the Designer, until the bronze-colored human collapsed. The device tumbled from the Designer's twitching fingers.

Meta raced to it, snatching it from the floor. She did it just as Ludendorff recovered his poise, pawing at his belt device.

"Don't do it, Professor," Meta warned.

Ludendorff looked at her, stricken.

"Remove the pendant and take off your belt," Meta said. "If you don't do it this instant, I'll kill you."

Ludendorff considered his options, and at last, he did as Meta bid. He found a numbing patch and put it on his bloody shoulder, adjusting his garments as best he could to hide the burn. Then he composed himself, waiting for everything to come crashing down.

-31-

Meta freed Maddox. Maddox took the pendant, the belt device and one of the three identical palm-weapons off the Draegar.

Meta kept Draegar 2's palm-gun, and Riker took the last one.

Ludendorff sat cross-legged in a far corner. He seemed resigned to whatever fate offered him. The patch had numbed his shoulder, so he likely didn't feel any pain from the shot.

Riker had trussed up Draegar 2, the Designer. The strange human glared at the sergeant but never uttered a word.

"Can the man speak?" Maddox asked Ludendorff.

The professor looked up, considering the question. "Can your mind speak?" he finally asked.

"A quick yes or no answer would be more helpful."

"Draegar 2, the Designer, is a mind not a man," Ludendorff said. "You see him in humanoid form, but that is an illusion."

"If I kick him in the shins, will the illusion scream?"

"I realize you think of yourself as clever," Ludendorff said. He cocked his head. "And yet, that is an interesting question. I don't know. Maybe we should try it."

With sudden swiftness, Ludendorff scrambled to his feet, rushing toward the bound man.

Maddox intercepted him, holding the professor back. "I much prefer this to resignation. But let's wait for a more opportune time to torment the man."

"He's not a man, exactly."

"It doesn't matter," Maddox said. "Now, tell me. Are you going to try to interfere against us?"

Ludendorff glared at Maddox before shaking his head. "I have some deep thinking to do. Then, I must find Dana."

"Maybe she's aboard one of the Q-ships."

Ludendorff paled. "If they've done anything to her…"

"I have an idea," Maddox said. "We have Draegar 2. Maybe we can exchange him for Dana—if she's over there."

"Yes!" Ludendorff said. "That's a splendid idea. I wonder why I didn't think of it first."

"You're not yourself," Maddox said. "Otherwise, I'm sure you would have already seen it."

"Don't patronize me. I find that more insulting than anything else you could do."

"Right," Maddox said. "Maybe your full recovery isn't that far off after all."

"Someone is coming, sir," Riker said from the partly opened hatch where he had been peeking out. "It sounds like armored marines."

"How many?" asked Maddox.

"By the footsteps, three," Riker said.

Maddox nodded. He'd tested a palm-gun earlier. It was an incredible little device. The Draegar must have used the lowest setting for shooting Ludendorff. At the highest setting, the thing was like a hotshotted laser.

If combat armor had one true vulnerability, it was the visor. That was almost-always the easiest place to achieve a burn-through.

"Get back," Maddox said.

After closing the hatch, Riker retreated behind the metal chair. He rested his shooting arm on the piece of furniture, no doubt to steady his shots.

Meta was to the right and back five meters from the hatch. She held a dead Draegar in front of her, using the corpse as a body shield. Maddox was to the left the same distance from the hatch, doing the same with the other dead Bosk.

He hoped the vat-born space marines would hesitate to murder a Draegar. Of course, these two were already dead, but the marines didn't know that.

"One, two—now," said Riker, who had been silently counting cadence.

The unlocked hatch opened, and a marine in combat armor walked in.

Meta beamed the marine in the visor, tracking him as he walked deeper into the room. Riker did the same to the second marine that had followed the first.

The last armored marine looked in. Maddox shot the visor—but the marine pulled back, clanking away.

Meta and Riker each achieved a burn-through. One of the face-shot marines crashed to his knees, raised his arms as if to fire and fell to the side. The other marine staggered backward, slamming against a bulkhead before clanging onto the floor.

Maddox had already dropped his Draegar and sprinted after the third marine, passing the dead or dying ones. He supposed the last of the three was Jard the Commander. Combat armor increased a man's speed, but not enough for Jard to pull away from Maddox. The confines of the ship's corridor prohibited Jard from using the full benefit of his exoskeleton-powered suit.

As the captain sprinted down the corridor, catching up, he beamed the back of the helmet. The armor was thicker in back than the visor was. He held the beam to the spot until the armor began to melt.

The marine whirled around. The arms lifted, the cannons fired—Maddox had already ducked back into a side corridor.

The firing stopped, and a loud clang told Maddox the suit had crashed onto the floor.

Suspecting a trap, Maddox peeked around the corner. The armor was on the floor. The suit cracked open along a seam, and a beefy marine wriggled out much as Maddox had done on Usan III.

Maddox pocketed his palm-gun and hurried toward the vat-born marine.

"I should have known," Jard said, climbing to his feet. He was a big man, just as tall as Maddox, but likely a hundred pounds heavier. He had a wide face and a muscled jawline. A knife tattoo adorned his forehead. He had dark hair and stark white skin. The man bulged with muscles, likely a combination of steroids and intense power lifting.

"Is Draegar dead?" Jard asked with a strange intensity.

"Why did you slip out of your suit?"

"You already know why. It shorted out. Now, answer the question." The man's intensity increased. "Is Draegar dead?"

Maddox wasn't sure what was going on, but he found it fascinating. "Two of them are," he said.

Jard frowned as if the captain had spoken gibberish. "I don't understand you."

"My words are simple enough. Two of the Draegar are dead."

"There is only one Draegar aboard the *Moltke*. Why then do you say two are dead?"

"Draegar has three…images, right?"

"Images?" asked Jard.

"Three…personas?"

"There is only one Draegar," Jard said.

"Fine. But he's made of three…components, right?"

"Do you mean three personalities?"

"There you go. Two of his personalities are dead."

Jard snarled as he began to shake his head back and forth. He gnashed his teeth and flexed his thick fingers.

"Why does that bother you?" Maddox asked.

Jard's eyes bulged outward, and the muscles along his neck became like steel cords. He howled like a lost soul and charged madly like a beast.

Maddox had intended to fight Jard man to man. He wanted to feel the man's bones break under his fists, as Jard had wanted to rape his wife. Maddox had felt a primal desire to beat the man—if not to death, at least into bloody submission. Now, with this madman going berserk—Maddox sidestepped the wild rush, ducking the initial blows. He drew the palm-gun, turned and drilled Jard in the face as the commander whirled around for a second charge.

Before Jard could reach him, the vat-grown marine thudded dead onto the corridor floor.

Maddox stopped beaming, feeling soiled. What had just happened? Who were the Bosks? Who were the Draegar, and why were vat-grown men so brutal and elemental? Before he tried to clear the *Moltke* of the rest of these men and before he bargained with the Q-ships, he believed it would be wise to know who and what he was dealing with.

-32-

Maddox eyed Draegar 2, the Designer. The man—the *personality*, whatever that meant exactly—sat miserably on the floor, with his hands tied behind his back.

Riker had removed the other two…personalities, Draegar 1 and 3, depositing them in a ship's storage closet. Meta had sopped up some of the blood and covered the areas with capes and jackets, including the dead marines. The corpses in the armor suits made big mounds.

Ludendorff sat brooding in the large metal chair, tapping his lower lip from time to time. The Methuselah Man kept shaking his head, saying, "No. No. That's not going to work."

"We don't have much time," Riker said quietly.

"Please don't talk," Maddox said. "I'm thinking."

"Why don't we race to a hangar bay and take a shuttle?" Riker asked. "Seems like the sooner we're back on *Victory,* the sooner we can clean up this mess."

Maddox raised his head, eyeing the older man. "Brigadier O'Hara is stuck in their web."

"Whose web?" Riker asked.

"That's one of the particulars I'm trying to determine. Now please shut up, Sergeant. I can't think if you're annoying me."

Riker glanced at Meta. She shrugged, clearly trying to be sympathetic to both of them.

Maddox clasped his hands behind his back. He'd been thinking while hurrying back to the chamber. He'd also been trying to think as Riker and Meta cleaned up the chamber.

The captain eyed Draegar 2 sidelong. Did he really believe the man couldn't talk? No. Still, he'd seen many strange creatures and strange humans in his time. Why not this three-in-one man? Why not yet another weird group of humans?

What did these altered and vat-grown humans ultimately want?

Maddox mentally examined what he already knew, starting with the brigadier's story. There had been two New Men on the Tau Ceti Station. Later, Ludendorff had shown O'Hara two New Men corpses with wires in their brains. That had convinced the brigadier she had been dealing with Strand agents. And yet...according to what Maddox had learned some time ago, there hadn't been any more free New-Men Strand agents after the Methuselah Man's imprisonment on the Throne World.

Maddox quit pacing and glanced at Ludendorff.

The professor noticed. "You've thought of something, my boy?"

"A possibility," Maddox admitted.

"Well? What is it?"

"Do you remember the Strand New Men agents you showed O'Hara?"

Ludendorff nodded.

"Did you really kill them?"

The professor opened his mouth to answer and then shut his mouth with a snap. "I believe I did. But I'm beginning to wonder if some of my thoughts are manufactured memories. I'm no longer certain of many of the things I've *seen* in the past year."

"Undoubtedly," Maddox said, "the answers lie aboard the Q-ships. Why are you traveling aboard the *Moltke* instead of staying in one of your privateers?"

"I had thought in order to keep an eye on O'Hara," Ludendorff replied.

"And now?"

"Maybe it's as you're suspecting—I'm here in order to keep me off the Q-ships."

"If we can clear the Bosks from the *Moltke* and establish our authority here, we'll have a battleship, a missile cruiser and

Victory. They'll have three Q-ships. I wonder how long the Q-ships will do nothing until whoever is over there acts."

"'Acts,' as in attacks us?"

"Precisely," Maddox said.

"No!" Ludendorff said. "We must never allow that. I don't know it as fact, but I believe Dana is aboard one of the Q-ships. I will certainly not allow a battle to take place that could jeopardize her life."

Maddox raised his eyebrows and then resumed his pacing. Something was off here. According to Ludendorff, long ago in the past Strand had created the Draegar, the vat-grown marines—

The captain halted and closed his eyes as if in pain, shaking his head. "I've been a fool. It is obvious."

"Not to me, my boy," Ludendorff said. "What have you determined?"

"It ain't obvious to me, neither," Riker complained.

"The place you went—the small rocky world—holds genetically modified people," Maddox explained. "That's like Meta's world and what happened to me. Think about it. A place like that with superior beings and advanced technology would have been in the mix for control of Human Space a long time ago."

"Perhaps this is their first testing, their dipping their toes in the water, so to speak," Ludendorff said.

"That's a minor possibility," Maddox said. "The more reasonable answer is that they're part of the same groups we've been seeing all along, but with a new twist."

"Spit it out, my boy," Ludendorff said. "You're not making sense yet."

Maddox shook his head in disbelief. "The answer was right there from the beginning. Two New Men greeted O'Hara on the Tau Ceti Station. Think about it. After many years of sparring and with some help, the brigadier bested the Throne World's Intelligence efforts on Earth. I imagine that has stuck in their prideful craw for some time now."

"You're forgetting something," Ludendorff said. "Those two were Strand's New Men."

"No, they were not. They were regular New Men renewing the Throne World's Intelligence efforts against the Commonwealth. This whole scheme has their heightened brilliance stamped all over it. Yes…" Maddox said. "The New Men have been far too quiet lately. According to you, a vast Swarm science team invaded their Throne World System. They destroyed the Swarm, but… I imagine the sudden attack must have worried them. They likely interrogated Strand during and after their victory. They saw their future vulnerability to more and greater hyper-spatial tube attacks. Wouldn't the New Men have come to a Strand-like conclusion: destroy the Builder nexuses so the Swarm could no longer use hyper-spatial tubes? Maybe the New Men are gathering the people and devices that thwarted them in the beginning in order to use them to halt the Swarm menace, at least for the foreseeable future."

"You mean regular New Men ensnared me in their web?" Ludendorff asked.

"The New Men must have broken Strand, learned about the Bosks and set up a sting operation there," Maddox said. "They not only collected you, but Mary O'Hara, Starship *Victory*—"

"And *you*," Meta said sharply, interrupting. "The New Men want you as well, husband."

Maddox glanced at his wife, nodding. "That means we only have a little time left. If I'm correct about the New Men being behind this—we must remember that they move with incredible swiftness."

"Begging your pardon, Captain," Riker said. "But would the New Men really break the treaty like this? I doubt they want another war with us. If the rest of us humans team up, we can beat them. Heck! Admiral Fletcher was getting ready not so long ago to find and storm their Throne World."

"You have a point," Maddox admitted.

"It could be we're dealing with a *faction* of New Men," Ludendorff said. "Theirs is not a monolithic society as many believe. The Emperor rules the Throne World, but he balances his authority as the strongest Dominant among many."

"Whatever the case," Maddox said, "we have to purge the *Moltke* of Bosks, establish regular authority here, contact

Victory and maneuver into the superior position against the Q-ships."

"I'm too tired to do all that, my boy. My head is a cauldron of conflicting emotions and ideas. Part of me loathes you and your wife. Part of me yearns to destroy anyone who has tampered with my mind. I thought you were the hated culprit. But you're right. The Builder invaded my mind long ago. I was wro—"

Ludendorff turned away sharply.

"No one is asking for any sort of apology," Maddox said, "least of all me. That was then. This is now."

"Yes," Ludendorff said in a hoarse voice. "Well said. I concur with the feeling of letting bygones be bygones. I detest making…well, you know."

"The key is the vat-grown space marines," Maddox said. "It's time we rounded them up and let the regular Star Watch officers run *Moltke*. That will be phase one."

"Do you have any idea how to achieve this?" Ludendorff asked

Maddox did, and he began to tell them.

-33-

Stage 1 of freeing the *Moltke* of the Bosk space marines proved relatively quick and painless.

Ludendorff donned his pendant and belt and hurried to their special quarters. The quarters were off-limits to the regular Star Watch crew. The Bosk marines were not wearing armor in their quarters. Thus, Ludendorff simply walked among them and knocked them unconscious with sub-sonic blasts. Maddox, Riker and Meta entered afterward and secured the fallen with plastic ties, leaving the Bosk marines trussed up in their rooms.

Stage 2 was trickier.

With his personal comm unit, Ludendorff called on-duty marine section leaders. Three times, the under-commander wanted to know why Jard hadn't called. Ludendorff used the same excuse each time, and it worked. The under-commander brought his marines to Ludendorff on the double.

The place was an ambush site. There, Ludendorff used a jamming device so the marines could not summon aid or warn others.

Because Maddox had not been able to figure out a different way, he, Meta and Riker used the deadly palm-guns and beamed the marines through the visors, killing them to a man.

It was ugly and brutal, but losing to the Bosks and then the New Men was worse. They also got lucky. The terrible palm-guns lasted long enough to do the killing, and they refined their techniques. The one time the ambush went south, they'd already worked out the kinks and reacted faster than the Bosks and slew them anyway.

The *Moltke's* regular crew started getting anxious with all these space marines clanking everywhere. Twice, O'Hara called Ludendorff, asking him if something was wrong. Some of her people were getting nervous, asking her.

Ludendorff made sympathetic noises and gave O'Hara BS explanations. After the second call, Maddox pointed out that the explanations would never have worked if O'Hara had been in her normal state of mind.

Soon thereafter, Ludendorff led Maddox, Riker and Meta to the Bosk techs. They used the sub-sonic blasts and plastic ties on them. Twice, quicker-witted techs attempted to contact one of the Q-ships. They might have succeeded, but Riker stunned the callers before that could happen.

Maddox, Meta and Riker had inserted special earplugs to resist Ludendorff's device.

In the end, two hundred and ninety-eight Bosks were hogtied in their quarters. The rest were dead, stashed in various off-limits locations.

Soon, O'Hara called a third time, demanding to see Ludendorff.

"Certainly," the professor said, giving her his present location.

Despite the mind manipulation having dulled her, O'Hara practiced a deception. She came with a squad of regular *Moltke* MPs. Maybe she planned to arrest the professor or maybe she'd heard too many strange reports. In the end, it made no difference. O'Hara and her MPs dropped to the sub-sonic blasts.

Meta and Riker secured the MPs with plastic ties. Maddox carried O'Hara, and placed the brigadier on Jard's cot. The Bosk commander had possessed a room to himself.

The captain shook her shoulder. After a time, O'Hara awoke groggily.

Even though Maddox and then Ludendorff explained the real situation to her, O'Hara refused to believe it.

"I know what I saw," she said. She referred to the New Men corpses on the Tau Ceti Station, their sawn-open skulls and the wires sticking out of their brains. "I don't know what the captain has done to you, Professor, but it is desperately wrong."

Maddox pulled Ludendorff aside. "Why isn't she accepting the truth? You did?"

"I should have foreseen it," Ludendorff said. "It's my superiority at work. Her mind simply isn't as strong or as complex as mine. Consider. Once reality stares me in the face, my superior intellect overcomes whatever fallacies are binding me. I adjust. I even adjust against intense programming because in a mental sense, my mind has herculean powers."

"Either that," Maddox said, "or your love for Dana broke through the webs they overlaid on your mind."

"I just told you why I overcame their mind manipulations. Do not attempt to belittle my lofty achievement."

"Of course not," Maddox said. "I stand corrected."

Ludendorff eyed him, shaking his head afterward. "You don't really believe what you just said. You're far too smug, Captain. Sometimes—"

"Let's concentrate on liking and cooperating with each other," Maddox said. "Whether we realize it or not, the two of us have produced remarkable achievements over the years. I doubt either of us could have done as much alone."

Ludendorff tugged at his lower lip. "Perhaps you have a point," he said quietly. "Brains and brawn—it is a good combination."

"We can't keep O'Hara locked up for long," Maddox said. "Nor can I just take over the *Moltke* by giving an order."

"Those are problems," the professor admitted. "Perhaps the two of us can convince the commodore of the real situation."

"I doubt she'll have the imagination to accept the truth," Maddox said. "She'll think we're trying to mutiny."

"Perhaps if we sabotage the battleship's engines," Ludendorff said. *"Victory* could face the Q-ships on its own."

"It will be better for our bargaining position—to gain Dana's release—if we can present the Q-ships with overpowering force."

Ludendorff tugged at his lower lip again. "You do realize that much of what we believe to be true is mere supposition.

Hmm, you desire a strong bargaining position… I know. Several quick disrupter shots at the main shield generators would cripple the Q-ships' defenses, as they would not be able to raise their shields for some time. That would leave them at *Victory's* mercy, giving you a powerful hand."

"Right," Maddox said. "And that way, we won't have to sabotage the *Moltke's* engines. It's also probable that given enough time, the commodore will side with *Victory*, a fellow Star Watch vessel. O'Hara is conditioned, not the commodore or the other Star Watch officers. Good thinking, Professor."

Ludendorff nodded. "The trick is in contacting *Victory* without having the Q-ships intercepting the message."

Maddox grinned.

"What is it, my boy?"

"Follow me," Maddox said. "I know exactly what to do."

-34-

On the bridge of Starship *Victory*, as Valerie sat in the command chair, she listened closely as Galyan explained everything the captain had told him.

Maddox had sent a secret signal fifteen minutes ago. It had been a short burst of extremely low frequency. It had meant one thing.

The deified AI could project his holoimage for an appreciable distance. The *Moltke* had been just inside the outer limit of that range, allowing Galyan to appear where Maddox hid on the battleship. Now, the little AI finished telling Valerie the precise message.

"You're sure about all this?" the lieutenant asked.

"Yes, Valerie, I am one hundred percent positive."

"It's a wild story."

"The captain thought you might have trouble believing me. Under those conditions, he told me to ask you if any of Strand's or the New Men's plots had ever been simple?"

The lieutenant studied Galyan. "Did the captain seem to be under any duress?"

"No, Valerie."

"Was Ludendorff with him?"

"He was."

"Riker and Meta, too?"

"They were all there."

"O'Hara?"

"No. She was not there, as this procedure would be unnecessary if the brigadier had been present."

Valerie frowned. "At least you're not suggesting I fire on the *Moltke*."

"Excuse me, Valerie. I have not made any suggestions. These are the captain's orders. He expects you to obey on the double."

Valerie looked up at the main screen. The "flotilla" had stopped accelerating some time ago. They all moved on velocity alone toward Usan III. The three Q-ships were behind *Moltke* in relation to *Victory*. The *Defiant* was farther behind as befitted a missile cruiser. It would take a little maneuvering for the Q-ships to be in *Victory's* direct line of fire.

"Weapons?" Valerie asked. "Can you pinpoint the location of the shield generators on the three Q-ships?"

The man's fingers blurred over his board. "I have the locations from our original scan. I am not presently targeting the Q-ships, though."

"Will you need to do a sensor lock to destroy them?" Valerie asked.

"That would up our odds for precisely hitting the targets."

"Valerie," Galyan said, "I can do the shooting."

"Not this time," she said. "That's Mr. Stimson's job. Figure out a firing sequence," she told the weapons officer, Sublieutenant Brian Stimson.

"Yes, sir," he said, and went to work.

"You are going to comply with the captain's orders?" Galyan asked.

"What do you think about all this, Andros?" Valerie asked.

The Kai-Kaus Chief Technician shrugged.

Valerie frowned, realizing she shouldn't have asked him. But since she had, Andros could at least have said something. Was he smarting over last time when she's told him to keep his opinions to himself?

She wished Keith was on the bridge at Helm. She would rather have had him do the targeting, too. Truth be told, she wanted to give Galyan the task. But she had to let the sublieutenant do his job sometime. Was this the right moment?

Should she really attack on Galyan's word? No. That was the wrong question. She had no reason to doubt the AI. What had happened over there aboard the *Moltke?* This all sounded complicated and convoluted.

"I have the targeting parameters set," Stimson said.

"Thank you, Mr. Stimson. Await my orders. Helm," Valerie said. And she proceeded to give the orders that would slow the mighty starship just enough that in eight minutes, all three Q-ships would be in direct line of sight of the disrupter cannon, as the *Moltke* would no longer be in the way.

Helm made the adjustments. The ancient Adok warship shed some of its velocity. It began to move slower in relation to the other ships of the flotilla.

Valerie waited, her palms turning moist and her mouth drying out. This was crazy. Why was she so nervous? It wasn't as if she was firing on official Star Watch vessels. These were auxiliary ships, privateers according to Galyan. Officially, they were under Professor Ludendorff's command. But Ludendorff had been with Maddox and had given Galyan the go-ahead.

"Lieutenant," the comm officer said. "One of the Q-ships is hailing us."

"Put them on the main screen."

A moment later, a hard-faced man with a knife tattoo on his forehead regarded her.

"This is Captain Nard of the *Bernard Shaw*. Are you Captain Maddox?"

"I'm Lieutenant Valerie Noonan in acting command," she said. "The captain is aboard the *Moltke*."

"I want to speak with your captain."

"I'm afraid I can't help you then," she said. "I haven't spoken to the captain since he landed over there. I imagine he's in deep conversation with the brigadier."

"This is an emergency," Nard said.

"Do you need assistance? I can help you."

"I can't speak to you about the emergency. I must speak to your captain."

"Then, I suggest you contact the *Moltke*. I can't help you at present."

The man stared into her eyes. Then, he rudely checked her out. It was obvious and insulting. Captain Nard almost licked his lips.

"What was your name?" he asked.

"Lieutenant Noonan."

"Why has your ship slowed down, Lieutenant?"

She sat up straighter. "I am not in the habit of explaining myself…to anyone but the captain. Can I help you with anything else?"

"I'd like to meet you."

"But I don't want to meet you, Captain. Don't take this the wrong way, but it's personal."

Instead of frowning, Captain Nard grinned. One could almost call it a leer. "Now I desire to meet you more than ever. Good-bye, woman. We will meet again soon, never fear."

The screen went blank. In its place, the ships reappeared.

"Valerie," Galyan said. "The Q-ships' shield generators have come online."

"Mr. Stimson?" she asked.

"I can fire at the first Q-ship's generator," the sub-lieutenant said.

"Fire when ready," Valerie said. "Helm, give us some extra speed. I want the other two Q-ships in a direct line of sight yesterday."

Victory's mighty antimatter engines purred with power as the disrupter cannon heated up. It had been pre-warmed, so the process was faster than normal. At the same time, the starship's shields rose to full strength.

At his weapons board, Stimson pressed a switch.

The yellow disrupter beam flashed, spearing out at the nearest Q-ship. The shield generator was online, but the shield wasn't up yet. The beam smashed through the seemingly paper-thin hull, roaring through equally useless bulkheads until it struck and devoured the shield generator.

In three seconds, Stimson tapped his board. The beam quit raying.

"Acquiring the second target," Stimson said, his voice only slightly shaky. Once more, he pressed a switch.

The powerful disrupter beam flashed for a second time. The second Q-ship's force field had flickered into place, but not quite fast enough. The yellow beam smashed aside the paltry shield, and once more battered through hull and bulkheads before devouring the vessel's main shield generator.

"Valerie," Galyan said. "The Q-ships are powering up their main weapon."

"Knock down the last Q-ship's shield generator," she told Stimson.

"The *Moltke's* commodore is hailing us," the comm officer said.

"Ignore her for now," Valerie said.

"The commodore is ordering you to stop firing. She says she'll have to fire on you if you continue to attack flotilla vessels."

"I'd like to see her try," Valerie snapped. "Where's that beam, Stimson? I don't see it."

The weapons officer tapped his board. For the third time, the disrupter beam lashed out. This time, it struck a powerful shield. The shield held against the deadly disruptor beam.

"Add the neutron beam," Valerie said. "Smash down the shield."

"The *Moltke* is warming up its heavy cannons," the comm officer said.

Valerie leaned forward on her chair, watching the Q-ship's amazing shield take the full brunt of the disruptor and neutron beams. That was more than a mere privateer. The shield hadn't even turned red yet.

"Valerie," Galyan said. "I have analyzed the Q-ships' weapon. I believe the vessels work in tandem. I think it is a killing weapon. Do not let it strike us."

"I can't smash down the last shield," she said.

"The *Moltke's* commodore has given us his final warning," the comm officer said.

Valerie bit her lower lip. The last Q-ship's shield still wasn't going down. If Galyan was right—

"Stimson," she said, "target the first Q-ship."

"Lieutenant?" the man asked.

"Fire at it, Stimson. Take it out."

"The first Q-ship doesn't have a shield," he said.

Valerie stood up. "Take out that Q-ship. Fire!"

Sub-lieutenant Stimson tapped his board. The disrupter and neutron beams no longer hit the last Q-ship's shield. Instead, they both fired on the original Q-ship. The beams licked through the hull and swept through the vessel, smashing down living quarters, storage areas, engine compartments and the special coils making up the tri-weapon Galyan had detected. Something about those coils erupted with violent force. They exploded, beginning a chain-reaction throughout the Q-ship.

At that point, the freighter-like ship blew apart in a titanic blast. The blast shredded the sister Q-ship beside it, destroying the vessel. It did so without starting another chain-reaction blast, though. The first wave explosion struck the powerful shield of the last Q-ship.

The shield went red, brown, black, and barely held on.

The strange blast-wave reached the Missile Cruiser *Defiant*, destroying it as the sleek vessel simply crumpled under the assault.

The *Moltke's* shield had just shimmered into existence. The shield took the brunt of the wave-blast, going down in the end, but absorbing enough that the heavy armor stopped any further damage to the battleship and its crew inside.

Victory's shields proved more powerful, which surprised no one.

Valerie had slumped back into the command chair. She couldn't believe what had just happened. Under her orders, two Q-ships and a Star Watch missile cruiser had ceased to exist. She would be court-martialed for this. Without knowing it, she groaned, feeling sick at heart.

"Lieutenant," Andros said.

Valerie was blinking in disbelief at the main screen.

"Lieutenant," Andros said again.

Turning slowly as if her neck was rusted, she looked at the Chief Technician. He was worried. "What is it now?" she asked.

"The Laumer Point," he said. "I'm detecting gravity waves where none were before."

"Meaning what?" she said, sounding groggy.

"I suspect cloaked vessels have just come out of the Laumer Point," Andros said. "They wouldn't have arrived cloaked, of course, due to Jump Lag, but we must not have noticed them appearing. They're cloaked now. I'm counting twelve separate gravity fields."

"He means Spacer saucer ships have arrived, Valerie," Galyan said.

"Where are they?" she asked Andros.

"I just said," Andros told her. "They've come out of the nearby Laumer Point. That's near the system's first planet."

Valerie stared at the main screen. She'd just destroyed three friendly vessels, ruining her career and killing however many innocent people. And now the Spacers were back, with twelve cloaked saucer ships? Could these twelve take out a Q-ship, the *Moltke* and *Victory?*

"Galyan," Valerie said. "I need to talk to the captain."

-35-

Maddox had decided on a bold move. During the short battle, he, Ludendorff, Riker and Meta had rushed through the battleship's corridors. Maddox and Ludendorff guided an anti-gravity sled with a suited and subdued O'Hara on it. Riker and Meta guided a second sled with a bound and gagged Draegar 2 on it.

The four of them wore medical garb, complete with surgical masks. They hurried toward a hangar bay, a special one, which according to Ludendorff held two *Moltke* fold-fighters.

The combat klaxons no longer sounded in the corridors. The commodore had come on the intra-ship comm system, explaining to the crew what had just occurred.

"If anyone has spotted Captain Maddox or Professor Ludendorff, contact the bridge at once," the commodore added. "Consider the two dangerous. If anyone knows the whereabouts of Commander Jard, I want to know immediately. Commander, if you're hearing this message, please report to the bridge at once."

Commodore Tam Tancred said more, but nothing further pertaining to Maddox and his team.

The commodore was a relatively young woman according to the brief Maddox had read on her before arriving on the *Moltke*. She was an up and coming star, the reason she had become a commodore at such a young age and why she commanded a battleship, even if it was an older *Bismarck*-class.

The four of them continued to race down the corridors, passing various people. None of the crew gave them an extra glance. The disguises were doing their job. The *Moltke* had just been in battle. It made sense that people were hurt, possibly dying, needing medical attention.

"Here comes the hard part," Maddox said, as they approached the hangar-bay hatch. "Let me do the talking," he told professor.

Ludendorff had taken to brooding again, and did not answer or acknowledge that he'd heard the captain.

"If you want to see Dana again…" Maddox said.

Ludendorff looked up sharply. "We may have just killed Dana. Two Q-ships no longer exist. The odds are that Dana was aboard one of the two."

"Maybe," Maddox said. "Maybe she wasn't aboard any of the Q-ships. As you pointed out before, much of what we believe is speculation."

Ludendorff grunted, and he didn't seem quite as distraught as he had seconds before.

The hatch slid open as they reached it, and the four of them pushed their anti-gravity sleds through toward one of the fold-fighters. Incredibly, only a few personnel were in the special hangar-bay. None of them were MPs or Star Watch marines.

"Can you fly a fold-fighter?" Maddox asked.

"If I must," the Methuselah Man said.

"Let's do this," Maddox said.

The four of them brought their sleds to the nearest tin can. Maddox punched in a code, but the hatch remained shut.

"You there," the captain shouted at a man. "Come here."

A tech came running.

"Open this," Maddox told him.

The thin man stepped back in alarm.

Maddox drew a gun and poked the tech in the stomach. "I can kill you if you want to display your patriotism and bravery for everyone. It's all the same to me. One of your fellows can do the smart deed for me. You'll be my example."

"No," the tech whispered. "Don't shoot me. I'll open the fighter."

Maddox indicated the hatch.

With a few swift taps, the tech complied.

As the hatch slid open, Maddox used the handle of his gun and struck the tech a sharp blow on the back and base of his neck. The poor sod crumbled to the deck.

"Was that really necessary?" Meta asked.

"It wasn't for us," Maddox said, "but for him. Now, he can point to the bruise and show he stood up to us."

"You should have struck him on the forward part of his body then," Ludendorff said. "A brave man has scars on his chest and face. A coward has scars on his back and neck."

"Climb aboard," Maddox said dryly. "We can debate the ethics of my actions later."

They hurried in, securing the prisoners in a side compartment. The rest of them piled into the small piloting chamber.

"What if they don't open the main hangar-bay hatch?" Ludendorff said.

"Why would that matter?" Maddox asked. "We have a fold-fighter. We're not even going to lift-off, but fold directly to *Victory*."

Ludendorff stiffened. "May I point out that *Victory* likely has its shields up? The shields will have to come down before I can do that."

Maddox snapped his fingers. "Piece of cake."

Ludendorff frowned and began shaking his head. "I am not a daredevil like your fool of an ace. If I perform such a maneuver, I will have shown that my skills are superior. I do not think you wish me to crush his ego like that."

"If you can't do it," Maddox said. "Tell me now."

"Of course I can *do* it."

"Then lay in the coordinates."

"But I have a few reservations," Ludendorff added. "A single miscalculation could see us fold into *Victory's* hull."

"Don't miscalculate," Maddox said.

"Might I suggest we simply fly to the starship?"

Maddox ruminated a moment, and nodded. "Maybe that would be wiser. Fold out of here and appear behind *Victory* in relation to the rest of the flotilla."

"You mean the *Moltke?*"

"That will work," Maddox said.

"This way, you don't have call *Victory* and give away our position to the commodore or the last Q-ship."

"Can the last Q-ship hurt us anymore?" Maddox asked. "They just had the tri-gun, right?"

"Wrong," Ludendorff said. "The Q-beam was their deadliest weapon. The last ship is far from powerless, especially in relation to a fold-fighter."

"I hate to interrupt the jawing," Riker said. "But we have company coming. I suggest whatever we're going to do, we do it now."

Maddox and Ludendorff looked up at Riker's side screen. *Moltke* MPs raced into the hangar bay. Others followed dragging a portable flamer.

"Any time you're ready, Professor," Maddox said.

Ludendorff manipulated his board. The tin can's engines purred as the small vessel began to shake.

"Better hurry," Riker said. "According to my sensor, the *Moltke's* shield generators have just come online. If the shield comes up—"

"Blast it!" Ludendorff said, hitting the piloting board. "Someone is using an override code. I'm not going to be able to fold. This is insufferable. Someone is outthinking me."

Maddox figured it must be this Tam Tancred. She would have the override code readily available on the bridge. He'd hoped to move so fast that she wouldn't have thought of it in time.

"Right," the captain said. "Now we do this the hard way."

Riker looked at him abashed. "The four of us are going to storm the bridge?"

"What?" Maddox asked. "Don't be ridiculous. No. I have something else in mind, a distasteful procedure." He shook his head sharply like a lion shaking water off its paw.

"The portable flamer is almost ready," Riker said, staring at his side screen. "They'll burn us if we try to come out and charge them."

Maddox gulped air, holding it and letting it out slowly. Then he stood and hurried toward the hatch.

-36-

Forty-five minutes later, Maddox finished his explanation as he stood on the bridge of the *Moltke*. Five burly military police guarded him, with drawn guns aimed at his back. He'd traded the fold-fighter's safe passage to *Victory* by giving himself into the commodore's custody.

Commodore Tam Tancred eyed him curiously from her command chair. She'd been absorbing the tale without objections or comments but with lively interest.

The commodore was a small woman with a buzz cut and a hawk-like stare. She made swift movements when she jerked her hand or turned her head. Otherwise, she held herself motionless. She now slid out of her chair and circled Maddox and the MPs. She had a shapely ass, indicating hours on a treadmill and possibly doing lunges or weighted squats. Her features were too pinched to be called good-looking, but she was slender like a rapier and her uniform was sharply creased and so clean it was shiny.

After completing a circuit, she stopped before the captain, although a ways from him. She must have never dealt with a New Man before. Maddox was only half New Man, but he still had astonishing reflexes and speed. He could attack, and probably grab and turn her before any of the MPs fired their guns. But she clearly didn't know that, surely thinking her distance from him was enough for her safety.

"This fantastic tale you spout—"

"Is the truth," Maddox said, interrupting her. "Brigadier O'Hara has been brainwashed. I believe by the bronze-colored Bosk now in *Victory's* custody."

"I know you killed the other two," she said. "We found their corpses where your people hid them. You broke their necks. That strikes me as a passionate killing. Yet, you do not seem like the demonstrative sort. From everything I've heard about you, you're supposed to be the ultimate realist, which indicates little emotion. Thus, you did not personally kill the other two."

That seemed like false logic, but the commodore might be more amenable to him if he pretended to be impressed with her deductive skills.

"Meta killed them," Maddox said.

"Meta is your wife?"

Maddox nodded.

"You may be interested to know that the last Q-ship's captain called," Tam said. "He demanded the return of the Draegar. If he hadn't called before you made your offer, I wouldn't even be talking with you. He did not request this, you understand, but demanded it quite insistently."

"You've never heard of the Draegar before this?"

"I've seen the three people you and the Q-ship's captain call the Draegar. That I've never heard those three supposed techs called that before and now discover their importance…"

"That proves my testimony," Maddox said.

"Indeed it does not," Tam said. "But it lends credence to the idea that I have not been informed of all the facts. Ludendorff fled with your people. You also took O'Hara without my realizing it. I am aware that she went to the Tau Ceti Station alone, as I commanded the *Moltke* then, too. I admit that I'm stunned to discover you've amazingly subdued all the Bosk space marines on my battleship, and without any of us noticing. That was a skilled feat."

The commodore frowned, which put a vertical line between her eyes, and she spoke with a new, complaining tone. "I never liked having the Bosks here. I never understood why my regular marines had to go aboard their Q-ships. Now, most of my marines are dead, killed by your people's savage attack. I suppose my remaining marines have already gone under the Bosk mind conditioning on the last Q-ship, if what you've been saying is true."

"Commodore, how familiar are you with the Methuselah Men?"

"What's your point?"

"Strand and Ludendorff are cagy, slippery, brilliant and fantastically egotistical. Whenever they're involved in a problem, it leads to a convoluted situation. Our present dilemma is nothing compared to some earlier adventures. You're a straightforward Star Watch officer. I respect that. Intelligence operations that include Methuselah Men and New Men..." Maddox shook his head. "They're *always* messy."

"I've yet to see direct evidence that New Men are involved in any of this," the commodore said. "It is true that to a degree you have their physiology."

Maddox stiffened.

She noticed, cataloging that. "What do you suggest I do now?"

"Essentially what you're already doing," Maddox said. "Regain control of your battleship by keeping the Bosk marines and techs under guard and preferably in the brig."

"There are too many of them for the brig."

"Whatever you do, keep them secured, tied up if you have to. Events are going to shake themselves loose soon enough. Spacers are out there. New Men might be hiding in the last Q-ship. It's possible Doctor Dana Rich—"

"Who?"

"She's the professor's woman."

The commodore nodded thoughtfully.

"Work with me," Maddox said. "Maybe we can free your last space marines. Maybe, if they've undergone conditioning, we can break the enemy's hold over their minds."

"If my last space marines are brainwashed, I would be foolish to give them freedom of movement on the *Moltke*."

"Agreed," Maddox said.

"Or," Tam said, "I could put you in the brig or trade you for Brigadier O'Hara. I didn't realize you had her when I agreed to your terms. In that sense, you were not forthcoming with me."

"I admit to some desperation earlier."

"You deceived me."

"I wouldn't go that far."

"But I would," Tam said, "and I'm holding the ace card—you, the leader for your side. Once I exchange you for O'Hara, I can go home and report to the Lord High Admiral."

"Maybe," Maddox said. "But suppose everything I've said is true, especially that the brigadier has been brainwashed. Once she returns here, she might countermand your orders and make you do something foolish again."

Tam turned away.

"The brigadier already made you exchange your marines for Bosk marines," Maddox said, slipping in his argument like a knifeman putting a blade between his foe's ribs.

Tam regarded him coldly. *"Victory* destroyed two allied Q-ships and a Star Watch missile cruiser. That is the real crime here. I demand O'Hara and the officer responsible for firing on the Q-ship. Once I have them, you shall go free."

"Forget it," Maddox said.

Tam's features twitched as if the captain had slapped her across the face. She took a step toward him.

The MPs grew more alert.

"I will not negotiate regarding Brigadier O'Hara," the commodore said. "I demand you return her at once. If you refuse, the military police will take you to the brig. There…there you can rot until we return to Earth."

"I can give you the brigadier, I suppose."

"That's more like it. I also want the officer responsible for firing on the Q-ship and thus, in effect, destroying the *Defiant*."

"I'll trade the brigadier for me," Maddox said. "But under no circumstances will I hand over one of my people to you."

"You most certainly will if you hope to regain your freedom."

"My honor means more to me," Maddox said.

"What are you even saying?"

"The officer in question acted under my direct orders. I need no scapegoat nor do I make any apologies for what she did. After all of this is over, I'll explain what happened to the Lord High Admiral and accept whatever punishment he deems fit."

The faintest of frowns touched the commodore's lips. "They say you're a notorious liar."

"They also say I'm a strict man of my word."

"That's what a liar would say."

"Commodore Tancred, the Swarm have begun their second round of invasions into Human Space. Soon, hundreds of thousands of Imperial warships will be here. They will crush humanity out of existence and burn our planets to the bedrock. That is a fact. You know I fought to stop them before. You know I've done more than anyone else to give humanity a fighting chance against the bugs."

"Modest, aren't we?"

"Are you modest?"

"Ouch," the commodore said. "Did I touch an exposed nerve?"

Maddox came to ramrod attention, facing forward, playing the part of a rules stickler.

"The Admiralty Board chose you because you're loyal to the Commonwealth and to Star Watch," he said. "They also chose you because you're better than the rest. You're trained to obey, and you're also trained to use your head."

Tam watched him, but said nothing.

"Has Brigadier O'Hara been giving you reasonable orders?" Maddox asked.

Tam still said nothing.

"Was it reasonable to empty the *Moltke* of its trained space marines, putting obvious thugs in their place?"

"I obeyed the Iron Lady," Tam said in a clipped voice.

"I know. I'm not asking you if you know how to obey. I'm begging you to use your mind and reason like you've been doing while listening to me. This is a crazy situation. You said so yourself. Wasn't it also crazy for the brigadier to go alone to the Tau Ceti Station? That's why this is happening. New Men caught her there. They adjusted her thinking. Brigadier O'Hara has been compromised, and you now realize that. If you follow her commands again, you're as good as following the New

Men, which means you'll be acting against Star Watch. I know that is against your oath."

The commodore had been listening raptly. She now began to slowly shake her head as she addressed the MPs. "I can't believe I'm saying this, but put away your guns."

No one moved, least of all the five MPs.

"Did you hear me?" she demanded of the military police. "Put up your guns."

Two of the MPs kept their guns trained on Maddox. The other three advanced around him, aiming at the commodore.

"It is time," the burliest of them said in a rote manner.

"I gave you an order, Mister," Tam said.

"I am giving a new order," the burly MP said. "It is time."

"Time for what?" asked Maddox.

The burly MP turned toward the captain. The MP's features twisted and tears were in his eyes, almost as if he was fighting an inner compulsion. By jerks and starts, he began to raise his gun—

Maddox moved faster, pressing the button on his belt buckle—the belt Ludendorff had lent him before he exited the fold-fighter. As the captain did so, he also pressed the pendant dangling from his neck, another loan from the professor. A soft hum only Maddox could hear indicated the thing had snapped on its force field.

The MP fired, and the bullet plowed against the personal force field enveloping Maddox. The bullet halted and dropped at the captain's feet.

At that point, Maddox pressed the sub-sonic switch.

The MPs cried out, three of them covering their ears. The last two fired their guns, trying to kill the captain.

It made no difference.

The commodore collapsed. Then the five MPs sank to the floor, unconscious.

Maddox continued to press the stud. He watched the rest of the bridge-crew fall unconscious to the floor. Only then did he cease radiating the incapacitating noise.

He hadn't expected this last ploy. In fact—

Maddox lunged for the commodore's command chair. If these five MPs were brainwashed stooges, were the rest of the military police likewise under the enemy's control?

He'd better find out fast, and if so, stop them from freeing the Bosk space marines.

-37-

Maddox hesitated as he stood beside the command chair. What was he going to do, tell the other MPs this was Captain Maddox speaking? If they were brainwashed, that wouldn't make any difference. If they had their own minds...

The last any of the military police had heard, the last anyone aboard the *Moltke* had heard, was that Maddox was wanted for questioning. The others would know the five had taken him to the bridge. Thus, if he spoke and they demanded to speak to the commodore, to anyone else on the bridge, for that matter, and he told them the others couldn't speak because they were unconscious—

That would ensure the remaining MPs stormed the bridge. The main hatch was locked, but that wouldn't stop them for long.

Leaving the command chair, Maddox hurried to the other fallen bridge officers, going to the men. He examined them, where they had fallen, and finally chose a heavy individual. He pulled out the man's wallet, opening and inspecting it.

This was Lieutenant Samuel E. Clarke, the Communications Officer.

Maddox drummed his fingers on the lieutenant's panel, slid into the chair and opened a channel with ship security.

"Lieutenant Masters here," a man answered.

"The commodore said to cease the investigation," Maddox said.

"What?"

"Stop what you're doing."

"The commodore said to stop searching the rest of the ship?"

"For now," Maddox said.

"Why? She said the search was top priority."

"I know. There are new developments."

"What about the space marines?" Masters asked. "Why have they vanished? Why haven't any of us seen them?"

"Do you want to ask the commodore regarding the new orders?"

"Yes!" Master said.

Maddox paused, thinking fast. Then he added a little more time to the wait. Finally he spoke, "As soon as she's done interrogating Captain Maddox, she will give you new orders."

"Who is this?" Master said.

"Lieutenant Clarke, the Communications Officer," Maddox said.

"Do you have a cold, Lieutenant?"

That sounded like a trick question. "What are you talking about?" Maddox asked.

Masters hesitated before saying, "Nothin'. I'll tell the others to wait before they continue searching. You happen to know what's going on?"

"I would say more, but the commodore is worried. That's why she's interrogating the captain."

"Then, we should be searching the ship."

"Even if one of your men trips a nuclear device?" Maddox asked.

"Is that what this is about?" Masters asked in a hollow voice.

"I can't say, and you heard nothing from me. Do you understand?"

"We'll wait. I didn't realize. We'll wait. Masters out."

Maddox sagged against his chair. That could have gone a whole lot differently. He leapt up and hurried to the commander's seat. From it, he opened communications with *Victory* and said as little as possible.

Seconds later, Galyan appeared on the *Moltke's* bridge. The AI holoimage noticed the fallen and the five trussed up unconscious MPs on the floor.

"Good work, sir," Galyan said, "impressively fast work from a weak position."

"Have you been observing the last Q-ship?" Maddox asked.

"Yes."

"Notice anything unusual?"

"Their sensors are sweeping the other Q-ships' wreckage."

"Anything else besides that?"

Galyan's eyelids fluttered. "Sir, when the fold-fighter appeared behind *Victory* in relation to the battleship, I detected a low frequency beam. It originated from the last Q-ship and went to the *Moltke*. I did not know what it meant at the time. Now, I give the event a 78 percent probability that it activated the MPs presently lying on the floor."

"I think you're right. Excellent deduction, Galyan."

"Thank you, sir," the holoimage said, squaring his thin shoulders.

"What is the Q-ship doing now, other than making its sensor sweeps?"

"Waiting," Galyan said. "It has not accelerated or decelerated, but has retained its shield and is scanning the debris as I told you. Maybe its captain is afraid to break away from us."

Maddox sat in the command chair, studying the battleship's main screen. "Are the Spacers heading toward us?"

"Negative," Galyan said. "They also appear to be waiting."

"Waiting for what?" Maddox asked.

"One of the other players to make a move, I suppose," Galyan said.

Maddox squinted at the main screen. The Spacers had come back, if this was the same group that had left a while ago. Why would they have come back? He didn't know. It could be for a variety of reasons, most of them bad.

The captain slid off the seat and crouched beside Commodore Tancred. He shook her right shoulder and kept on shaking until she groaned.

"My head hurts," she said from the floor.

"Better get up, Commodore. We have work to do."

The small woman groaned again as she slowly worked up to a sitting position. "My head is throbbing. What happened?"

"The captain used a sub-sonic blast against you," Galyan said.

The commodore's head swiveled around until she spied the little Adok. She yelped and scrambled to her feet, lunging to her chair, opening a hidden slot and grabbing a gun. She fired, and the beam passed harmlessly through the holoimage.

"By all the saints," Tam Tancred whispered, turning pale. "What's going on?" she asked Maddox. "Is that a ghost?"

"No. It's a holoimage," Maddox said.

Her features tightened until understanding changed her demeanor. She aimed the gun at Maddox. "Hands ups, Captain. I'm retaking control of my ship."

"Not just yet," he said.

She fired, the beam striking his personal force field. She continued to fire even as he advanced upon her. Abruptly, she stopped, letting her gun swing down beside her right thigh.

Maddox deactivated the field and tore the gun from her grasp. "Sit down, Commodore. Listen to me for a while. We have to work together if we're going to stop whatever's going on."

"What is going on?" she asked.

"That's what I'm trying to determine."

The commodore studied his face, glanced at Galyan, let her shoulders slump and slid back into her chair. "Go head," she said. "I'm listening, and this had better be good."

-38-

When Maddox finished telling the commodore the situation, he returned the beamer to her and agreed to let medical personnel onto the bridge to check the fallen.

Soon, new and suspicious MPs stood on the bridge, watching him, although they kept their weapons holstered. Backup officers were at the bridge stations, making checks. More than a few of the new people glanced at the alien holoimage in amazement.

"Commodore," the new comm officer said. "The Q-ship captain is demanding to speak to you."

"He is, is he?" Tam said. "No. I'm not speaking to that pig now. Tell him he can call back later."

Her reaction surprised Maddox, although he didn't show it.

The commodore eyed him. "I'll agree to one of your…requests. The Bosk quarters will remain off-limits for a time. We'll leave the Bosks captive for now."

"That works," Maddox said. "I'm interested in the Q-ship captain."

Tam frowned.

"I'd like to see a recording of your last conversation with him."

"Whatever for?" she asked.

"I have a theory, but I need to confirm it first."

The commodore shrugged after a moment. "You can watch it over there."

Maddox stepped beside a female officer as she tapped her panel. On the screen appeared a leering Captain Nard. Maddox saw the resemblance instantly, and had no need to listen to the conversation. He glanced thoughtfully at the commodore.

Tam had been pretending not to watch him, but noticed the scrutiny. "Well?" she demanded. "Did you confirm your theory?"

"I did, and I'm curious. Did you ever speak to the commander of the Bosk space marines?"

"I imagine you mean the Bosk marine commander on the *Moltke*. Of course, I saw him. Why do you…?" She frowned as she reexamined the side screen. "By the saints," she whispered. "He's the marine commander's twin."

"Triplet," Maddox said.

"What?"

"It appears all the Bosks operate in threes," Maddox said. "Well, maybe just the higher-ranked ones. I'd thought the condition was just in relation to the Draegars. But it seems more universal. Two identical Bosks named Jard and Nard implies there is a third."

"Three clones, then?"

"Vat-creatures," Maddox said. "That doesn't necessarily mean clones, but vat or culture grown people."

"Why would they do something like that?" Tam asked with a tinge of horror.

"Why do we do the things we do? Because that's how we were raised."

"There has to be a logical explanation for the practice to have started."

"Maybe," Maddox said. "But that isn't germane to our problem. Look at his face. It could be the Bosk marine commander. The Bosks operate in threes. The Draegar had three personalities in three different people. You knew nothing about this until I told you."

"Fine," Tam said. "You're making a point, I see. What is it?"

"The oddity of the Bosks confirms that I've been telling you the truth. In other words, you can trust what I've said."

Tam grew thoughtful and finally nodded. "Your story is becoming more believable. The MPs' action earlier also shows that. Let's say I believe you. What should we do next?"

"What is the Q-ship doing?" Maddox asked Galyan.

"I have already told you, sir. It is scanning the debris fields."

"The wreckages of the Q-ships?" asked Maddox.

"Yes."

"Start scanning the debris. I want to know why Nard is scanning it."

Galyan turned toward the *Bernard Shaw*.

"This is incredible," Tam said. "Your holoimage can personally scan the debris?"

"No," Maddox said. "He's doing it through *Victory's* scanners. Galyan is the ship's AI, an ancient deified Adok personality several thousand years old."

Tam shook her head in disbelief before straightening in her chair. "Barnes," she told the sensor officer. "Start scanning the debris fields."

"What am I searching for, Commodore?" the man asked.

Tam glanced at Maddox.

"Something unusual," the captain said.

Tam turned to the officer.

"I heard that," the man said. "Something unusual. That should be easy." He sounded sarcastic.

"Captain Nard is after something," Maddox said. "We want to beat him to whatever it is."

"It would help if we had *some* idea," Tam said.

Maddox bent his head in thought before sharply looking up. "People," he said. Then he snapped his fingers. "New Men! See if you can spot any New Men."

"Dead or alive?" Warrant Officer Barnes asked.

"Most certainly alive," Maddox said. "That means wearing a vacuum suit or in an escape pod."

"Alive after the explosions that wrecked his Q-ship?" Tam asked dubiously.

"That's why I'm betting it's a New Man," Maddox said. "They can act astonishingly fast and make critical decisions in seconds. With only a few seconds warning, a New Man might have realized the need to reach an escape pod and have made it there."

"I have to admit that I'm more than doubtful," Tam said.

"Have you faced New Men before?"

The commodore shook her head.

"It's hard to explain if you haven't seen them in action before."

Maddox fell silent as he waited. The others did likewise.

The three ships—the *Bernard Shaw*, the *Moltke* and *Victory*—scanned the scattered and widening debris of the two destroyed Q-ships.

A little over three minutes later, Warrant Officer Barnes said, "I may have something. It's definitely human occupied. I don't know how I'm supposed to tell the difference between a regular man and a New Man. Whoever is out there is alive. He's in some kind of containment shell. According to my readings, his oxygen is running low. He's not going to last much longer."

Maddox faced the commodore. "You need to make a decision. Trust me and work together…"

"Or?" Tam said.

"I don't want to give you an 'or' because I dislike making threats," Maddox said.

"You're threatening me?" Tam asked in surprise.

"What did I just say? I'm *not* threatening anyone."

"I'm in charge here," Tam said, "not you. If I… Oh," she said. "You still have your advanced tech on your person. You're threatening me with another sonic blast."

"Commodore, I have made no threats."

"No, but you've implied them. You're good, Captain. You're slick." She nodded. "Fine. Here's the deal. I'll let you go. You can even collect your New Man out there if you want to. I want the brigadier back, though."

"Even with all you know?"

"The Lord High Admiral personally told me to protect Mary O'Hara. I'm Cook's protégé. I owe him everything. The last thing I want to do is to let the Lord High Admiral down."

"I owe Mary O'Hara my life," Maddox said.

"Then, you understand my situation."

"No," Maddox said. "Because I always do what I must to succeed. Sometimes that means going against the one I owe everything to."

Tam shook her head. "I don't operate like that, Captain. I'm loyal, probably to a fault."

Maddox eyed the commodore. She and the brigadier outranked him. But he wasn't going to let that stand in his way. There was someone out there, likely a New Man, and he had the last Draegar aboard *Victory*. Yet if there was one person that he was intent on saving, it was the Iron Lady.

"I'll agree to your deal," Maddox said, "on one condition."

"I'll have to hear it first."

"My people will transfer your captive Bosk space marines and techs onto *Victory*. That way, the brigadier can't order you to release them."

"The brigadier might order *you* to release them."

"She might," Maddox agreed.

"But you're not going to listen to the legal authority of our flotilla?"

"I haven't said that."

"Will you obey the brigadier if she gives you an order?" Tam asked.

"Will you agree to my condition?"

"First, I want to know—"

"Commodore, I plan to save the Commonwealth any way I can. I plan to restore the brigadier's full mental faculties to her. The Q-ship out there likely holds the people—or those who can tell us—who modified the brigadier and Ludendorff. We also have twelve Spacer ships possibly waiting to pounce on us. We have the *Moltke* and *Victory*, two powerful ships, but still just two. It's imperative that we work together, as that way we're likely to succeed."

"Nice speech," Tam said. "Very well, I'll agree to your condition. But I don't have your freedom of action. I have to obey the legal authority over me. If I don't, in the end, we have nothing."

"Galyan," Maddox said. "This is what I want you to tell Valerie." He gave the holoimage his instructions.

"Commodore," Warrant Officer Barnes said. "The Q-ship is moving toward the debris with the container."

Tam looked searchingly at Maddox. The look implicitly gave him the deciding authority.

"Right," Maddox said. "Now, it gets interesting."

-39-

The *Moltke* and *Victory* maneuvered toward the container drifting in the debris. If a New Man was inside and aware of the situation, he did not attempt to signal anyone, not even Captain Nard of the *Bernard Shaw*.

Once more, Nard hailed the *Moltke*. This time, Tam took his call, speaking to him via the main screen. The Bosk captain complained about her interference. He told her to stay away from the wreckage as he attempted to rescue what survivors he could.

"I can't do that," she said.

"I insist that you—"

"I'm under orders," she said.

Nard shook his head. "I will repeat myself. Do not interfere with my rescue attempt to—"

"Captain Nard, I have given you my answer. Accept it, as there is nothing you can do to stop me."

Nard scowled at her to such a degree that it seemed like an unspoken promise: *I'll remember this until the day you die.*

Shortly thereafter, two shuttles launched from the Q-ship. One of the shuttles rushed toward the life-support container. The other shuttle set up an over-watch position, arming its weapons.

Victory launched several strikes fighters. They were many times faster than the shuttles. Half the strike fighters blocked the first shuttle's path. It attempted to maneuver around them. They opened fire across the shuttle's bow. It maneuvered wildly, trying to weave through the shells and then heading resolutely toward the drifting container.

As Maddox made the transit to *Victory* on a *Moltke* shuttle, he gave the order. The strike fighters fired a second time, destroying the Bosk shuttle and killing everyone aboard.

The second Bosk shuttle made a hurried turning maneuver, fleeing back to the *Bernard Shaw*.

Soon, Maddox landed on *Victory* and marched through familiar corridors, reaching the starship's bridge. He settled into the command chair just in time for Captain Nard's latest threat.

"Put him on the main screen," Maddox said.

Captain Nard appeared. He looked just like the space marine commander that Maddox had face-shot on the *Moltke*. The head was just as wide and the forehead held the same knife tattoo.

"Where's Lieutenant Noonan?" Nard demanded. "I want to talk to her not you."

"I want immortality," Maddox said.

"What does that have to do with *my* wants?"

Maddox said nothing to that.

"Are you deaf?" Nard demanded.

"I killed your triplet," Maddox said.

The Bosk's eyes narrowed. "You mean Commander Jard of the *Moltke's* space marines?"

"Yes, that one," Maddox said.

"In that case, we're blood foes."

"Sounds about right to me."

Nard opened his mouth and then closed it. "Bring her here," he said to someone off-screen. "It's time."

Soon, a muscled Bosk marine manhandled Doctor Dana Rich into view. She was dusky skinned with long dark hair and exotically beautiful features. Dana wore a dancer's garb, silks for the most part, that hid little of her pleasing form. She appeared to be drugged; her eyes didn't focus and she didn't seem to recognize Maddox.

The captain sat back as his heart began to beat faster. Dana Rich was his friend. She'd been part of *Victory* for a long time. She was family. As he sat back, Maddox examined the bridge with his peripheral vision. Ludendorff was nowhere to be found. That was good. He didn't need the professor's interference right now.

"You know this woman," Nard was saying. "I know very well that Professor Ludendorff knows her. Tell the professor what I will personally do to her if you do not give me the Draegar."

"Are you suggesting we make an exchange?" Maddox asked.

"No exchange," Nard said. "Send the Draegar to me or I shall publically abuse the woman."

"Tell me again how giving you the Draegar helps me."

"By doing so, it delays her raping."

"I need more than that," Maddox said. "I want to save her from your touch."

"Then you must exchange yourself for her," Nard said, his dark eyes aglow with cunning.

"And if I decline your offer?"

"Then I will rape her now before your eyes."

"I see." Maddox said. "Well, if you do that, I will kill the Draegar. Furthermore, I will then destroy your vessel. Are you ready to die, Nard?"

"I am Captain Nard to you."

"You are my blood foe, remember? Thus, I do not recognize your rank."

Nard stared for a moment before laughing harshly. "You should have been a Bosk, Captain. You understand our ways. I shall enjoy breaking your skull in the vise. I will sing as you scream in final agony, listening to your bones creak and crack."

"I will repeatedly kick you in the balls as you grovel before me," Maddox said.

"A challenge!" Nard said. "Let us meet, you and I. Let us fight hand to hand. The winner takes all."

Maddox eyed the Bosk captain. The big man played the brutish character well. Yet, that was a clever challenge, as Nard had nothing to lose at this point. The man was clearly in the inferior position. All he had was Dana Rich and the *Moltke's* remaining space marines.

How could he use the challenge against Nard? First, he mustn't display any kind of weakness. The Bosk would pounce on it.

"A fight..." Maddox said, as if thinking about it. "What weapons would we use?"

"None but our hands and feet," Nard said, "as I need no weapons to crush you. Are you man enough to meet me in the challenge ring?"

"More than man enough," Maddox said, sitting sharply forward as if stung.

"Ha!" Nard laughed. "Maybe you are man enough. Let us fight."

Maddox glanced to the side before regarding Nard. "First, I must gain permission."

"What? You're not the starship's commander? But I thought—"

"I'll call you back," Maddox said, "But I will never fight if you can only trade me soiled goods."

"Ha! You obviously care for the woman. Gain this permission soon, Captain. I am eager to test the professor's woman. I will do so after I have crushed the last breath from your feeble lungs."

"As I am eager to torture the Draegar after I urinate on your cold corpse," Maddox said.

Captain Nard turned pale, and with a shaking hand, he cut the connection.

Dana Rich was on the *Bernard Shaw*. Had the Bosks treated her ill?

"Captain," Valerie said from her panel. "The life-support container is coming aboard. I have medical personnel waiting to—"

Maddox stood. "You have the captain's chair, Lieutenant. I'm heading to the hangar bay. At last, we may be getting some answers as to who is really behind all this."

-40-

Maddox wasn't taking any chances with a possible New Man. Who was in the container? If it was a New Man…

He and his team wore combat armor, surrounding a heavily shielded container on the "A" hangar-bay deck. The container's peculiar shielding had made finding the man inside harder than otherwise, explaining why it had taken so long to discover him. That length of time had made Captain Nard's search noticeable. If the shielding had been to disguise the person's escape, it had done the opposite this time.

A special tractor-beaming strike fighter had dragged the container here while the others kept watch over the Q-ship.

"Captain," Valerie said, speaking via a comm in his helmet. "The professor has, ah, communicated his desire… Well, sir, he's asking for your permission to—"

"Now, see here, my boy," Ludendorff said, interrupting. "You need me there at a time like this. I don't know why you didn't tell me what was going on."

Maddox scowled inside his helmet.

"We're all in this together," Ludendorff added.

"Of course you're right about that," Maddox said.

"Excellent," Ludendorff said. "I'm on my way."

"Not so fast," Maddox said, as he kept watch of the container. Did the person inside see them out here? Was the person waiting for them to act?

"You just said I'm right," Ludendorff said.

"That we're all in this together," Maddox said. "I'll handle it from here."

"Nonsense, my boy, you're likely dealing with a New Man—"

"Precisely," Maddox said. "It's why I'm handling it."

"Now see here—"

"If I'm right about all this," Maddox said, "this New Man—if it is a New Man—had a hand in tricking and possibly modifying you. I don't want a possible Trojan horse beside me right now."

"I find your words insulting."

"Give it a rest, Professor."

"Confound it," Ludendorff said. "I resent your automatic arrogance—"

"I'm signing off," Maddox said.

"Just a minute, now," the professor said. "Is there any word regarding Dana?"

Maddox made a swift calculation. Ludendorff wasn't supposed to be on the bridge. Yet, someone had let him on. Valerie should know that ship-to-ship communications between *Victory* and the *Bernard Shaw* was strictly off-limits to—

Maddox grunted to himself, ending his musings. Ludendorff knew about Dana. The captain didn't know that for certain, but—

"We'll discuss Dana after I'm finished with the New Man," Maddox said.

"Then Dana is on the Q-ship?" Ludendorff asked.

"She is," Maddox admitted, deciding it was foolish to lie about it.

"This is preposterous," Ludendorff declared. "When were you going to tell me?"

"I wanted it to be a surprise," Maddox said, "as in, here is your companion; we've already saved her for you."

"I don't believe that for a minute."

Maddox scowled again. That was almost tantamount to insulting him on his bridge. He'd had enough of this. He hated others questioning his orders. It was time to concentrate on the New Man.

"Lieutenant," Maddox said sharply

"Here, sir," Valerie said.

"Escort the professor off the bridge. Summon Sergeant Riker—"

"Bah!" Ludendorff said, interrupting. "If I'm not wanted here, I will go elsewhere. Good day to you, sir."

"Lieutenant," Maddox said.

"Here, sir," Valerie said again.

"Under no circumstances is Professor Ludendorff allowed to be by himself or in any restricted areas on the ship."

"Now see here—" Ludendorff said.

"I want Galyan to join Riker," Maddox said, speaking over the professor. "If anything unusual or even halfway suspicious happens to or by the professor, Galyan must immediately come and tell me no matter what I'm doing."

"It sounds as if you don't trust me," Ludendorff said.

"We're all in this together," Maddox said smoothly. "I need your expertise, but it's possible there is a glitch or two in your thinking."

"If you're referring to the enemy's former manipulation—"

"Exactly," Maddox said.

"You already know that I've overcome it."

"True. But there might be a glitch or two waiting to happen. I can't risk that with a New Man here. Surely, you can see the logic of my position."

Ludendorff grumbled.

"No one is more dangerous than you," Maddox said. "Thus, my need for extreme caution in dealing with you."

Several seconds passed.

"Er, well, yes," the professor said. "I can understand *that*. I am highly dangerous because of my superior intellect. Since you recognize that, and are willing to tell it to me straight, I will cooperate with you. I'm leaving the bridge, Captain."

"Leaving with Sergeant Riker and Galyan in tow," Maddox said.

"If you insist," Ludendorff grumbled.

"I most certainly do. Maddox out."

One of the armored marines was motioning to him. Maddox nodded in his suit, and raised his arm cannons at the container. The other marines did likewise.

The container's sole hatch had opened a fraction. A spy device had slid out, the tip moving one way and then another, as if it was an eye, and then it zipped back in.

Before anyone could comment on that, the hatch slammed down onto the deck. Three spherical objects rolled out fast.

Maddox's left arm-cannon roared. A second later, three other designated marines opened fire. The shells obliterated the three rolling objects before they could activate—if that had been their purpose.

"Go," Maddox said.

Two marines clanked toward the container, the first stepping onto the downed hatch and ducking his head through the entrance. An electrical discharge sizzled from the interior of the container, the blue lines zigzagging over the marine's combat armor and that of the man following him. The two suits fell backward onto the deck, immobilized.

The container glowed, and many electrical lines zigzagged from it, catching the various marine suits, immobilizing one after another as they began to topple.

"Fire!" Maddox said.

Unfortunately, his order did not reach any of the other marines, as his helmet comm no longer operated.

Seven shells left the captain's arm cannon, each of them striking the container's nose cone, doing so in the same spot. The fifth shell smashed through the dented armor. The sixth and seventh ricocheted inside the container, causing the glow to stop. That killed the electrical discharges, which gradually faded away before stopping altogether.

Maddox had toppled in his suit, frozen like the others. Yet, even as the armor clanged sideways onto the deck, it began auto-unlocking.

Maddox had anticipated something like this. Thus, each marine had set his suit for auto-opening the instant it lacked power. As the exoskeleton-powered suits clanged onto the floor, each opened like a clamshell, allowing the marine inside to wriggle out.

Some of the marines were already pulling out the weapon each had stashed inside with him.

At the same time, a golden-skinned New Man exploded out of the container. He wore a silver-colored one-piece and gripped a pistol. He moved fast, like a leopard, firing as he ran.

An un-armored marine crumpled to the deck, his head a gory ruin. A second rained blood from his chest, stumbling backward until he crashed down.

Two marines fired back, sending heavy black capsules at the New Man. With uncanny reflexes, he dodged each capsule so it sailed harmlessly past him.

Maddox cursed inwardly. This was costing him *Victory* marines. He'd forgotten about the lethal speed and cunning of New Men. The starship had grabbed a tiger by the tail, and the New Man was slaughtering them, the normals.

Gritting his teeth while lying on the deck—he'd slid out of his armor suit—Maddox aimed his shotgun-like weapon from a prone position and fired one capsule after another.

The New Man killed three more marines and dodged four more capsules before he sidestepped the wrong way. One of the captain's cunningly placed capsules touched the New Man's left arm. Immediately, tangle webs sprouted from it. Several stuck to the New Man's skin, tightening, pulling the other strands onto him.

The golden-skinned superman tried to keep his gun hand free. But not even he was divine. Another capsule fired by a marine tangled his legs. The New Man hopped with both feet tangled, showing amazing balance. He got off another shot, but missed this time, only wounding a marine in the arm.

Finally, four capsules hit the superman at once, the black tangle webs enswathing him, and the New Man thudded onto the deck.

"Watch out for his gun," Maddox said.

The captain vaulted himself onto his feet and rushed the fallen New Man. He found the golden-skinned superman lying on the deck, straining to bring the gun around.

Maddox kicked it, but the New Man held on with incredible strength. It felt as if something snapped inside Maddox's head. The captain stomped on the golden wrist three times, finally hearing bones break. He kicked the gun again, and it tumbled out of the New Man's weakened grip.

The superman stared up at him. Instead of glaring with pain or rage, the New Man looked at him calmly, hiding any agony from the broken wrist.

"Captain Maddox," the New Man said in a conversational tone. "Release me at once if you want to save your subhumans."

"Are you bound to the Emperor?" Maddox asked, striving for the same calm manner.

"You have heard my words. I am not in the habit of giving a warning twice. Now, you must act on my words before it is too late."

"Are we going to have to do this the hard way?" Maddox asked.

The New Man studied him two second longer before looking away. The muscles on his neck tightened and strained with effort.

Maddox realized the prisoner was trying to break the tangle strands through sheer willpower. The New Man kept straining, and the black tangle strands actually shifted. Incredibly, two strands broke.

Maddox had never seen that happen before.

"Quick," he told a marine. "Give me a hypo."

The New Man exhaled as droplets of sweat dotted his face. "Release me. It's the only hope. You're dooming everyone if you don't do exactly as I say."

Maddox accepted a hypo from a marine. He knelt beside the bound New Man.

"This is your final warning," the New Man said.

Without commenting, Maddox pressed the hypo against the golden skin, listening as compressed air shot a knockout drug into the superman's bloodstream.

It took longer than it should have. Finally, the New Man's eyelids fluttered and he fell unconscious. It was time to do this the hard way.

-41-

The problem was that the hard way took time—time to inject the New Man with the right drug, not too much and not too little. Then, the questioning started.

After two hours of grueling almost useless work, Maddox realized this was going to take far longer than he expected. He called in Riker, explained the situation and had the sergeant take over.

Stepping outside, Maddox thought furiously. He had several problems that all needed his immediate attention. He had to break down the New Man, rescue Dana and the *Moltke's* space marines from Captain Nard and all the while keep the brigadier from interfering.

The New Man was going to take time. Riker knew interrogation techniques, but against a superior New Man, the sergeant would likely come up short.

Maybe he could use Ludendorff on a limited basis. The professor would have the mental agility to ask the right questions and to know how to handle a New Man. Maddox would have to keep Intelligence operatives in the chamber while Ludendorff interrogated in order to keep an eye on the Methuselah Man. That might hinder some of the professor's trickery.

Whatever he did, it would be a risk using Ludendorff.

Maddox rubbed his jaw. He had too many irons in the fire. He needed help; he couldn't manage them all himself in a short amount of time.

He decided he would use the professor on this limited, provisional basis. He would trust that the Methuselah Man had regained his full senses, but he would also watch him carefully, using a variety of people, including Galyan.

Now, what about Captain Nard and Dana?

Maddox rubbed his jaw some more.

If Nard was like Jard, his triplet, he was brutal, but knew how to obey commands. Would Nard go berserk like Jard had in the corridor when he believed the Draegar was dead?

That seemed probable.

Well, he had to keep the deaths of Draegar 1 and 3 secret, then. He didn't want Nard going crazy. There was no telling what the Bosks would do under that condition. Dana might never recover from any brutality at their hands.

Now, it was true that Captain Nard had kept Dana a prisoner for a long time. But it would seem—

Maddox's gaze tightened. A New Man had been floating in the stellar debris. That obviously meant that at least one New Man had been aboard the Q-ships. Where there's smoke there's fire. Did that mean then that if one New Man—?

"There are more of them," Maddox said quietly. It was the logical deduction. Now, it made better sense why Nard had tried to set up a fight. A New Man might have shown up instead of the captain. The New Man would assume he could defeat Captain Maddox, and thereby hold him hostage and gain the release of the *Bernard Shaw*.

Maddox had thought he'd been playing Nard, but it was possible the Bosk captain had been playing him. If there were at least one more New Man in the mix, would the *Bernard Shaw* draw other New-Man-crewed vessels here?

Maddox eyed the hatch to the Interrogation Chamber. He needed to get back there and break this New Man fast. He had to find out what they were dealing with. Not only might more New Men show up, but Spacer ships were still orbiting Usan I, waiting for something.

"Galyan," Maddox said.

The holoimage appeared.

Maddox relayed some of his thinking to the AI. Then, he said, "I'm giving you and Valerie the Nard problem."

"Captain?" asked Galyan.

"I still want you to watch Ludendorff. But you need to figure out a way of freeing Dana from Captain Nard."

"How?"

"That's your problem now," Maddox said. "Do it. Have Valerie help you. Know, though, that more New Men could be aboard the *Bernard Shaw*."

"That seems obvious," Galyan said. "We found the one among the debris and therefore—"

"Get to work," Maddox said. "We no longer have the luxury of excess time."

"I understand, sir. You can count on me." With that, Galyan disappeared.

That left the brigadier. Maddox frowned. He had a method of internment, but he didn't want to use it on the Iron Lady. He would have medical personnel examine her while keeping her under sedation for…how long?

They could start with one day, no more than three, though. Maddox exhaled. It was a crude method, and he would have to answer to her later. But he didn't see what else he could do.

Maddox made a call and gave instructions. By that time, he'd become antsy. He was wasting time out here when he should be interrogating the New Man.

Could the others do their jobs?

He couldn't worry about that now. He had to break the New Man.

Maddox headed for the hatch, half-believing that he could hear the ticking of the clock as time wound down on the Human Race.

-42-

Tars Womack the Dominant resisted the interrogation with cunning, stubbornness and fierce pride. Womack began with lies and switched to half-truths as the serum befuddled his superior intellect and as exhaustion robbed him of his energetic defense.

Maddox asked questions for hours on end. Ludendorff took over in the company of two Intelligence operatives and uncovered more in a shorter amount of time than the captain had been able to achieve. Riker tried his hand a second time after the professor left the room, panting. Unfortunately, the sergeant got absolutely nowhere with Womack. Riker did keep the New Man occupied, however, giving the superman no time to rest and regain his equilibrium.

In a real sense, they besieged his mind, hammering it with serum, questions and exhaustion. A few times, they shocked him with electricity. That retarded the process, as Womack derived strength from the pain.

"The pain restores his senses," Ludendorff replied in another room as they strategized. "We must forgo it."

After that, they relied on the truth serum alone. They gave Womack repeated injections over the next three days. The New Man resisted, but his strength began to ebb after the second day. After debating it with himself, Maddox gave a new order. They would keep the New Man awake until he broke or died from exhaustion.

"It is inhumane treatment," Galyan said in a side room.

The AI had been giving a report on the progress with Captain Nard. Unfortunately, there was little. Nard had grown increasingly insistent, bringing Dana to the screen and slapping her in front of Valerie.

The lieutenant had given orders to destroy the *Bernard Shaw*. It was only as the disrupter cannon glowed with power that Nard backed down.

According to Galyan, Valerie would have shattered the shield and blown the generators in the ship.

"She might have caused the ship's destruction," Maddox said.

"Naturally, I pointed that out to her," Galyan said. "Valerie was seething with rage. She feels that Dana has been abused far too much. She wants to kill her tormenters, fixating on Captain Nard."

"On no account is Valerie to do that again," Maddox said. "If you can't free Dana, at least keep Nard occupied. Once Womack breaks, we'll know more about life aboard the Q-ship and how to rescue Dana."

"Breaks, sir?" Galyan asked.

Maddox explained his plan, which was how Galyan had come to learn about the order of breaking Womack or killing him in the process.

"Your plan is inhumane," the AI repeated.

"You're looking at this the wrong way," Maddox told Galyan. "Soon, the Swarm will figure out exactly how to use the nexuses. Once they do, and they send their invasion fleets, it will mean the death of the Human Race. Given such circumstances, Womack won't get any mercy from me. Remember, he's holding back. He can stop this at any time by telling us what we need to know."

"We are not barbarians," Galyan said, "but civilized beings."

"That may be," Maddox said. "But we're desperate. I know you remember the last time the Swarm invaded. We barely won. Next time, they'll use even more warships. Given double or triple the warships, they'll wipe us out."

"Why do you believe Womack has the answers to stop such a vast assault?" Galyan asked.

"That was the Q-ships' objective when Ludendorff acted as their cat's paw. They wanted *Victory* and...something else in order to complete the mission. I need to know what that something else was."

"Suppose you are right. You should immediately inform the Lord High Admiral about the situation. Admiral Cook can then confer with the Emperor of the New Men. Together, the two can arrive at a solution, and likely faster than we can."

Maddox examined the yellow-colored drink in his hand. It was a stimulant so he could renew his interrogation. He was so tired his bones ached. He couldn't understand how Womack kept resisting their efforts. *He* wouldn't have lasted this long if their roles had been reversed. The idea that New Men were that far superior...

Maddox looked up. "First, I don't believe the Lord High Admiral and the Emperor would do better."

"That could be a vain conceit on your part, sir."

Maddox shook his head. "We're about to face Swarm numbers on such a gargantuan scale that normal ways aren't going to work against them. We beat them last time because a few people had the right answers and we followed those answers ruthlessly."

"Do you mean the Destroyers you uncovered?"

"That was part of it, certainly, but I mean Ludendorff with the soul weapon. This isn't a matter of mankind, new and old, all pushing together in the same direction. We can't out-produce the Swarm industrially or outfight them with our limited numbers. In fact, there is no way we can face the Imperium on equal footing, setting our society against theirs, and hope to win."

Galyan stood silently as if computing the statements. Finally, he said, "I loathe the Swarm, as I have more reason to hate them than anyone. They obliterated my species, leaving me alone in the universe."

"I know."

"But if we have to resort to such heinous techniques to survive—killing a man by remorseless questioning—do we even deserve to survive?"

"Of course we do," Maddox said.

"You said that without thinking about it."

"There's nothing to contemplate. It's them or us. I'm for us, no matter if it means wiping out all the Swarm in the universe."

"That is an illogical argument, as you are not now seeking the Imperium's demise, just a way to foil them from using the hyper-spatial tubes to reach us."

Once more, Maddox examined the drink before regarding Galyan. It surprised him, but he found squeezing the truth out of Womack to be a demoralizing process. It was an ugly, barbaric method as Galyan had suggested. Yet, what else could he do? He would not stop looking for a way to save humanity until he was dead.

"You never made your real point as to why we are engaging in this ugly process," Galyan said.

"No, I suppose I didn't," Maddox said. He drained the yellow liquid, waiting for the stimulant to begin its work.

"I would like to hear your reason," Galyan said.

Maddox inhaled as he set down the glass. "We beat the Swarm last time because we had a few people with the right answers."

"They were geniuses?" asked Galyan.

"That's one name for them. I call them Strand and Ludendorff and the Builders behind them. The Methuselah Men created the New Men. The Methuselah Men also gave humanity many of its technologies that allowed us to fight the Swarm. Most importantly, the Builders through Ludendorff gave us the soul weapon that drove the Ska into a star. The expanding star destroyed enough Swarm vessels that we could defeat the tiny remnant afterward. One man with the right answer was the critical difference."

"Your gaining the Destroyers also critically helped."

"Without the soul weapon, not even the Destroyers would have been enough."

Once more, Galyan stood still, no doubt computing the argument. Finally, "You speak about the Builders—the first cause. They also built the androids that have threatened the Commonwealth for years."

"Yes," Maddox said.

Galyan's eyelids fluttered before he said, "I am also a product of their advanced technologies."

Maddox nodded. Thousands of years ago, a Builder had aided the Adoks against the Swarm. Galyan's people had lost in the end, but Galyan had gained immortality of sorts, and humanity had gained Starship *Victory*.

"Here's the answer for my ruthlessness against the New Man," Maddox said, wondering if he was explaining it to himself. "I believe Womack holds critical information. Does his information originate with Strand? I think that's possible."

"If you are correct," Galyan said, "that would be yet another Builder-derived first cause."

"Yes."

"There is something I do not understand. If the New Men—in Womack—could destroy or block various Swarm nexuses, why have they bothered here with us? Why haven't they already begun the great task?"

With a surge, Maddox stood. He felt the stimulant working as the fog lifted from his mind. "I don't know the answer to that, but I sure as Hell aim to find out."

"Thank you for your explanation," Galyan said. "Now, I would like to reiterate our problem with Nard. You have given us instructions regarding the Bosk captain, but the tension between us is tightening to an intense degree. I do not know how much longer Valerie can occupy the Bosk."

The stimulant quickened Maddox's thinking. "Don't occupy him, then. Solve the problem by rescuing Dana."

"That could result in Dana's death. Besides, you told me that Womack would give us—"

"Forget about Womack. Take the right risk and free Dana. Get it done, Galyan."

"Remember how I said the pressure is getting to Valerie?"

"She can handle it," Maddox said.

Galyan eyed the captain and pondered the statement. "I understand, and I only have one other comment to make. The Spacer ships are still in orbit around Usan I. They have not attempted to communicate with us, but they're scanning us constantly as if waiting for a sign."

Maddox's eyes glittered. It felt as if a noose tightened around his throat. There were too many problems at once.

"The first one who finds what he's looking for will have the edge," the captain said. "The Spacers are waiting for something, a sign perhaps, as you suggest. That's partly what's driving me. I have to discover Womack's truth before the Spacers get what they want and make their move against us."

"You believe more Spacer ships are en route to the Usan System?" Galyan asked.

"I don't discount it," Maddox said. "Now, get out of my way. I have a job to do."

-43-

One hundred and twenty-seven million kilometers away from *Victory*, twelve, cloaked Spacer vessels maintained an orbit high above Usan I, a small, hot, rocky Mercury-like planet.

Inside the *Scarlet Tulip,* the saucer-shaped flotilla flagship, in a highly charged and sealed chamber, Mako 21 floated naked in a sensory deprivation casket. She'd been floating in the sluggish liquid for 53 hours already, attempting one of the most unique experiences a modified Spacer could achieve.

Through the chamber's Wi-Fi connection, the casket and thus Mako were linked to an immense Meditation Machine. The machine had many peculiar features, including a carefully calibrated set of Usan III crystals and a half-alive cyborg computer, with the human brain tissues soaked in a prince's ransom's worth of varth elixir. The cost of such a Cy-computer and machine was astronomical. To date, since the uncanny invention of the Meditation Machine, twenty-eight had been built. Only twenty-six still remained, with one more presently under construction.

The Meditation Machine—the concept and production of them—was a Spacer secret. It had several functions and one great purpose. Mako 21 presently attempted to utilize that purpose.

With her interior modifications amplified by the chamber's Wi-Fi connections, she engaged the Cy-computer, this one named *Harmonious Benevolence.* This augmented her mental strength and transduction projection ability. Using the newfound force, Mako emitted her thoughts through the Usan III crystals.

It was like an atom charging through a circular accelerator, building up speed.

Such a process took energy, infinitely more than Mako could give and much more than a single saucer-ship could supply. The Spacers had developed *radiant energy*—RE for short. Radiant energy was unique, taking many individually modified Spacers distilling their combined electrical projections through a RE amplifier.

Each flotilla saucer ship generated RE and beamed it at the *Scarlet Tulip*. RE did not store well, having an incredibly short half-life. Thus, the other eleven vessels continued to beam RE at Mako's ship in order to supply her with the needed power.

An ethereal glow soon enveloped the *Scarlet Tulip* to such a degree that it seemed as if Mako's ship shifted into a different reality, as if it was no longer fully there.

That wasn't altogether an illusion, even if it wasn't exactly what occurred.

Supercharged with RE, Mako's thoughts intensified and strengthened, building power as she groaned inside the casket.

She could not see, hear, smell, taste or feel anything other than herself as she floated in the sluggish liquid. Like Shu 15 years ago, Mako had been surgically blinded in order for her to more fully integrate with her modifications. She could see, after a fashion, when she wore the customary Spacer goggles. In any case, the deprivation in here was the point. Her body—her gross physicality—no longer bound her thoughts or emotions. She was thus free to cast her mental energies into the Cy-computer, Harmonious Benevolence. Together, they projected their combined thoughts through the Usan III crystals, speeding up and using yet more radiant energy.

The first ten hours in the casket had been to purge herself. The second ten she had balanced her mind. The last thirty-three hours had been a grueling effort to build up the needed processes to commit the great and wonderful act.

Mako's body floated in the sensory deprivation casket. Her mind—her thoughts and consciousness, in reality—left the *Scarlet Tulip* in what the Spacers termed an astral journey.

In a momentary flash of awareness, she saw all twelve Spacer vessels in high orbit of Usan I. She could feel the pulsating thoughts of Maddox and his people in the three vessels one hundred and twenty-seven million kilometers away. She sensed the living souls on Usan III.

But she did not have time for any of them. She had a more important objective. She had done this only twice before in her life, only once successfully. It was why she was Mako 21 instead of Mako 20.

Her consciousness zoomed beyond the Usan System. She saw comets, asteroids, planets and stars. They were hard matter, and in her new astral state, did not count for much. There were rivers of something, undercurrents in the universe that coursed with strange eddies. Among them was a darkness, a thing emanating from far away. Mako avoided that, as the dark wriggly thing pulsated with hateful energy.

There! Mako sensed a wonderful being of translucent light far ahead. She sped in that direction, questing across the cosmos with her amplified mind. She did not see, hear, feel, smell or taste anything during this journey. She sensed, in a mental or astral manner, awed at the beauty in the stellar distance.

She increased speed, using the RE supplied by the other vessels in her flotilla. She soared. She roared at incandescent speeds, an astral beam of light.

Then: *Contact!*

In the sensory deprivation casket aboard the *Scarlet Tulip*, Mako stirred, and she smiled.

Her consciousness had connected with another Spacer who was also in a dark casket aboard a similar saucer-shaped ship powered by others in its flotilla. That one had already connected to three other Spacers scattered several hundred light-years in various directions. The other connected Spacers were using other Meditation Machines to achieve this spectacular feat, meeting at a point equidistant from one another.

The five, which now included Mako, had gained union. They needed just one more to bring a multi-mind consciousness-entity into existence.

That one joined several minutes later. It was the new Visionary of the Spacers, their new leader since the old Visionary had perished in the Ska's Destroyer during the expansion of the Alpha Centauri "A" star.

With the new Visionary's joining, the six wrapped their thoughts around each other. They knew supreme closeness that brought sublime unity. It was glorious and loving, fulfilling and intimately belonging to a singular group of likeminded beings.

In the casket aboard the *Scarlet Tulip* in the Usan System, Mako 21 murmured softly, feeling wonderful and complete. She had union with others like herself, and with the *di-far* of *di-fars*—the Great One, the new Visionary—who could see into the future.

Then an odd event occurred, at least, it seemed off to Mako. An eddy from the undercurrents of the universe detached from the dark thing she'd tried to avoid before. It joined them, but it did so softly. Even so, Mako felt a jolt she did not like.

"It does not matter," the Visionary said. "It is a pulse of energy I use at times to aid in my visions."

That was disturbing news to Mako. She was certain the pulse from the dark thing was bad, not helpful energy.

Then, the multi-mind consciousness-entity began to examine Mako's progress. She forgot about the dark thing with its dreamy quality. Mako was with the others as they judged her. She had failed to capture and hold Captain Maddox on Usan III. Before starting out on her mission, Mako had been so certain that she could achieve such a feat.

The Visionary, who was in charge of the multi-mind consciousness-entity, now showed Mako the predictions regarding said event. That caused the dreamy dark thing to perk up, radiating something…

Mako tried to understand the dark radiating thought—yes, it was a thought from—

This was bewildering, not the dark thing, no, what the Visionary was telling her.

"You knew I would fail to hold the captain?" Mako asked.

"There was only a slight probability you could hold him for long," the Visionary said.

"But why did you...?" Mako let her question fade away before she could finish it.

"The wheels of fate are turning," the Visionary said through the multi-mind consciousness-entity, the joining of some of the strongest minds in the Spacer Nation. "Methuselah Man Strand has become a tool. He has tried to twist in the hand of his user, but he fashioned the New Men too well. They have bottled him and drained his brain of its greatest secret."

"How...?" Mako spoke the single word before also letting that question fade.

"Poor dear," the Visionary said. "You strive so hard but you fail so often. In reality, I foresaw your last two failures. New Men in their improved star cruisers ambushed and captured the *Sulla 7*. They stole the prize you had worked so hard to fill with Usan crystals and varth elixir, the prize you fought for and sacrificed ships so it could escape from Captain Maddox."

"You *knew* star cruisers would lie in wait for the *Sulla 7?*" Mako asked in amazement.

"Your questions hold a barb for me," the Visionary said. "If I knew about the star cruisers, why did I allow the *Sulla 7* to travel its projected route? Ah, Mako, if only it were that simple."

"Please, teach me," Mako said. "I would like to know. I have failed twice in quick succession. The failures burn in me."

"In reality, you have failed three times in quick succession," the Visionary said.

The words hurt, but Mako held her tongue, waiting for enlightenment.

"That is the first lesson," the Visionary said. "Learning when to wait. Learning when to stop speaking. But you want more, do you not?"

"I want to grow," Mako said. "I would be like you, if it were possible."

The other four murmured, their sounds praising Mako.

"You are strong for one so young," the Visionary said. "You seek to grasp the great rung, even though your latest exploits led to bitter failure."

"Teach me to do better," Mako pleaded.

"You do not yet truly understand," the Visionary said. "What does 'better' mean? Are your failures bad?"

"I don't understand. Help me to know what you mean."

"Mako, Mako, Mako," the Visionary said. "Knowing is a precise word, a hard and definite word. I am the Seer, the one who looks into the darkness."

The words jolted Mako once again. Could the Visionary be referring to the dark thing that had joined them?

"That darkness is the future that unfolds in strange and often contradictory ways," the Visionary said. "What I saw with the *Sulla 7*... Let me see if I can explain. I *perceive* many but not all strands of possibilities. I assign the possibilities I see a probability number as I travel down many ifs and might-bes. Some are good. Most are evil. But some of the evil ones lead to glorious possibilities that stagger my imagination. Oh, listen, little one, the antimatter explosions from the battle around Usan III irradiated the crystals and varth elixir aboard the *Sulla 7*. You did not know it, but the cargo was contaminated. That was your third failure."

"What? But I made certain that—"

"Do not interrupt me, little one. That is the second great lesson you must take to heart."

The rebuke stung to such a degree that Mako felt herself parting the slightest bit from the multi-mind consciousness. The even *slight* loss of union was awful. The love of the others tearing away from her *hurt*.

"I am ashamed," Mako said. "I am irredeemably flawed."

"That is not true," the Visionary said. "Come, rejoin us, Mako. Be one with us again."

The other four hummed with encouragement, while the dark strand seemed to watch her intently.

Despite the undercurrent with them, Mako found the strength of heart to rejoin them. It felt so good to belong again.

"Now listen, Mako, and do not interrupt me. I am going to tell you hard truths. If you would be even a little like me, you must accept these bitter dregs in order that you might grow."

Mako almost told the Visionary that she would listen. At the last second, she held her thoughts in abeyance.

"Oh, good, that is good," the Visionary said. "Now, it is certainly true that you are deeply flawed. That does not make you useless, just that you haven't yet learned the truly deep lessons. In these last instances, I was able to turn your flaws so they furthered the Great Plan. I knew Captain Maddox would defeat you and I foresaw the strange transformation of the Usan III crystals as the antimatter radiation struck them. The New Men captured the *Sulla 7*. But they will only find misery in using the crystals. The varth elixir is another matter. They can still use it despite the radiation. By the time they understand why the crystals harm them, though, certain future ventures of theirs will have failed. Because of your flaws combined with my foresight, we have hammered yet another nail into the New Man coffin. In time, the horrible New Men will no longer sully our future paths as their Throne World lies in smoldering ruins. You aided in that."

"You wanted me to fail?" Mako asked in bewilderment.

"It wasn't a matter of wanting. It was a matter of using the most likely probabilities in the best combination I could find."

"The lost *Sulla 7* will cause that much harm to the New Men?"

"Mako, I will accept failures from you, but I detest any slow-witted questions. Continue on such a course, and you will risk dropping from 21 to 20 or maybe even to 19. If that were to happen, you would lose some of your dearest modifications."

Mako's boosted consciousness shivered in horror at the threat. That horror sharpened her senses, however, as she struggled to maintain her wits.

"Forget about the New Men and the cargo," the Visionary said. "The capture happened for a reason that you will learn soon enough."

"I...I didn't realize."

"Of course you didn't," the Visionary said. "That was why you were the perfect tool, Mako."

Tool? She was a tool? In the casket aboard the *Scarlet Tulip*, Mako frowned within the darkness and utter solitude.

"Am I only useful as a failure?" Mako asked.

"You are useful when you are useful," the Visionary said. "Is that not enough?"

Mako sensed the other parts of the multi-mind consciousness-entity turning against her, as they seemed to pull away. That caused the dark undercurrent to express emotion, evil laughter. She quailed at its and their hostility, made a thousand times worse because she had felt the glorious love and unity of the multi-mind only seconds before. She had been lifted up to this great Spacer mystery only a year and a half ago. She did not want to lose this glorious privilege. Nothing in normal life was like soaring among the stars and joining her sisters in astral union.

"I am useful," Mako said, striving to radiate love and willingness, as a good Spacer should.

"You do not fool us," the Visionary said. "You are upset and you seek to deceive. That is wrong. You are flawed. So far, you achieved the needed results by failing each time. Do not add lies to your other flaws."

At that point, Mako caught a tiny glimpse of what awaited her. It was paralyzing and horrifying, and she realized the future paths were partly fueled by the dark undercurrent.

"Stop peeking into my mind," the Visionary said.

Mako wanted to stop, but she could not. The horror of her fate drove her to want to know more. All her life, she had striven to be a good Spacer. She had climbed the ladder of ambition, entering the sisterhood of bodily modifications. She had delved into the deep secrets, sensing more than seeing a glorious future for the unique Spacer Nation. Now…now *this* awaited her?

"I knew you would not be able to stop yourself," the Visionary said. "It is your nature. You strive and struggle even when you know it isn't good for you. That is your fate, Mako. Unless you can—"

"No!" Mako said, the horror of her future tearing words from her that she had hoped to keep quiet. She wanted to belong—but *this*. "You mean to destroy my mind and personality. You mean to enslave us to an alien monster of inhuman desires. How is this good for the Spacer Nation?"

"You spoke too soon," the Visionary said. "You saw one possibility. There are others."

"But—"

"Wait, Mako. Do not speak too soon again."

Mako found it almost impossible, but she waited.

"The Methuselah Men think they are the chief wonder of the Builders for the Human Race," the Visionary said. "But that is false. *We* are the prize creation of the Builders. We serve them, as others cannot conceive. The hard ones—the New Men—will corrupt the goodness given humanity by the Builders."

"But the Swarm—"

"Do not name humanity's doom, little one. It will only upset you. Sisters, are you ready? We must infuse Mako with resolve and purpose. She has looked into a future she cannot fathom because she has failed to understand the true nature of the Spacer Nation."

"We are humans!" Mako cried.

The dark undercurrent that had joined the multi-mind entity pulsed with power. It seemed to darken the others, but it added power to the Visionary.

"We are the *egg* of the new Builders," the Visionary said. "We search the cosmos for the right sperm that will generate something much greater and more glorious than mere *Homo sapiens*."

"No," Mako wept. "What I saw was awful. It waits for us."

More dreamy power flowed into the dark undercurrent that had joined them. It was ancient and willful, and utterly domineering.

"Hurry, Sisters," the Visionary cried. "This is the moment and the reason we have joined today. Teach Mako the lessons she so desperately seeks. Mold her into the Spacer that will alter the cosmos in our favor. This is a pregnant moment of true destiny. We have waited an eon for this moment. Finally, the fates and possibilities have rushed together. If we are strong enough, if we are resolute enough, we can turn Mako into the egg of Tomorrow."

"No!" Mako screamed. "Please don't do this to me. I'm human. I want to remain human. I want to be a Spacer—"

The others struck, buoyed up by the Visionary's words and powered by the ancient thing with an adamant and inhuman will. They molded Mako's naked consciousness in ways that would never have been possible otherwise. She was a waif in their dark-powered consciousness. The process was heartless and savage. It was stunning, almost poetic in a way.

The Sisters of Meditation used the dark rawness of the undercurrents of the universe to add to, and take away from, the personality of her once known as Mako 21. The Visionary guided them, as her dark visions of many futures drove her to this consummating act. Like a madwoman with a meat cleaver, she hacked out this and ripped out that. It was brutal, and it left Mako gasping like a prey animal gripped by wild beasts.

Then, with Mako a raw wound before them in the stars—and with the dark thing driving them without their knowledge, the five rebuilt the little one at the Visionary's beckoning. The guiding star of the Spacer Nation shoved this and that into the new budding personality. The little one would still be known as Mako 21, but she was becoming a thing to behold, a fury with willpower and toxic might, a woman with extra consciousness to complete a deed no ordinary human could even conceive, let alone bring to fruition.

"Now," the Visionary whispered to her Sisters of mayhem and wild fate, to the making of a new one to lead the Spacer Nation to heights never foreseen by mortal man.

The one called Mako 21 shrieked and could not stop herself as she tore her consciousness from the others and from the dark will that originated somewhere in the Sagittarius Spiral Arm. Mako ripped herself from the Cy-computer, Harmonious Benevolence, aboard the *Scarlet Tulip*.

That upset many delicate balances. The continued RE flowing from the other saucer ships built up too fast in the Cy-computer. It was Harmonious Benevolence's task to channel the RE into the right places. The Cy-computer had fed Mako the RE in order to project her astral consciousness through the cosmos. Mako had torn herself from that in an instant. That meant the incoming RE had nowhere to go. Like a mountain avalanche that blocks a stream, Mako's abrupt tearing-free meant a rising buildup of RE. The bubbling, deepening radiant energy drove the cyborg brain tissues mad, which in turn closed valves and conduits in the computer parts, burning them out with sizzling power as the RE dissipated in awful surges.

The great Cy-computer burned out in an orgy of agony as the varth elixir bubbled into froth. That might have permanently brain-damaged Mako, but she slid out of the Wi-Fi connection just in time.

Even so, inside the sensory deprivation casket, Mako screamed. She thrashed and kicked wildly. Sensors detected her activity. Klaxons blared outside.

In less than a minute, two Spacer acolytes raised the lid, helping a weeping Mako from the sluggish liquid.

The new Mako could sense their stares, and she knew she was going to have to answer hard questions about the dead Cy-computer. Then it struck her, what she *would* do.

The changes to her consciousness now rearranged her physical brain. It made her wince, stiffen and begin to shake.

"Mako?" one of the acolytes said. "Hang on, Mako."

Mako's face had frozen into a hideous mask. Just as swiftly as the transformation occurred, it was over. Mako sighed and relaxed even as her facial muscles lost their rigidity.

She recalled her fear of questions. Now, she didn't care. She would say what she would say. They would obey. She knew that. She knew that she had become something more, something impregnated with fate and power.

She accepted in that moment the dark future that the Visionary strove to achieve. It was glorious indeed. The Visionary had chosen her as the instrument of elevation. Oh, yes, she would strive for this with all the cunning and willpower that she possessed in new, superhuman abundance.

"Are you well, Mako?" asked the same acolyte as before.

"Take me to the bridge," Mako said.

"The bridge? You must decompress first."

In the shadowy chamber of Wi-Fi connection, Mako's blind eyes narrowed. Yes. She must follow the norms for a little longer. She must practice careful deceit. If the others discovered what had happened during the union…

I don't have much time, Mako realized. She almost laughed. *Neither do any of them.*

Then, she let the two guide her to the decompression chamber. Soon now, she would begin the next phase in her glorious transformation into something completely different.

-44-

One hundred and twenty-seven million kilometers away aboard Starship *Victory*, Maddox walked around Tars Womack in the interrogation chamber.

The New Man was strapped down onto a table with an intravenous tube in his left arm. Medical machines to the side monitored the prisoner's condition. Several techs watched other machines, one that included his biorhythms. Toward the back, two marines stood guard. Three Star Watch Intelligence operatives were always on duty. Vid cameras recorded everything.

Ludendorff had complained twice already about the number of people in the chamber. That only affirmed the captain's wisdom in this approach.

A haggard-looking Sergeant Riker had stumbled out of the chamber. He'd been questioning Womack for two and a half hours this time around.

Maddox cleared his throat as he finished speed-reading a transcript of Riker's questions and Womack's answers.

A picture was developing. Like a puzzle with thousands of pieces, they inserted one more piece at a time.

Strand had modified and refashioned the Bosk culture maybe sixty years ago, from what Maddox had found. It had been a lost colony from the earliest space flights. His ultimate development had been the Draegar. The trio of bronze-skinned thinkers had an outlandish IQ. That amazing and united intellect had been focused upon the Builders, trying to understand them and their nexuses better.

Every Builder artifact Strand could find or steal, every Builder fact was fed as data to the Draegar. Strand had also attempted to understand what the Builders had done to the Methuselah Men to make them what they had become.

Then, Maddox had captured Strand and given him to Darius. Darius had taken the Methuselah Man to the Emperor. There, Strand remained a prisoner, infrequently questioned on a matter or two. So far—and that included during and after the science-team Swarm invasion—the Methuselah Man's internment had been mild.

During Riker's questions, the sergeant appeared to have stumbled onto a name, a well-known name.

"Lord Drakos," Maddox now told Womack. "On the Throne World, you claimed that Lord Drakos had access to Strand."

They knew Drakos because he had arrived with the New Man Fleet during the First Swarm Invasion. He had been shorter than the average New Man, with broader shoulders. He had disliked humans and Captain Maddox in particular. According to what they knew, Drakos lacked or appeared to lack some of the latest New Man genetic purity. Perhaps because of that, as psychological compensation, Drakos insisted on genetic excellence.

While lying on the interrogation table, Womack twisted his head from side to side. He clearly struggled with himself, maybe trying to resist the truth serum. Finally, he nodded.

"Lord Drakos interrogated Strand?" Maddox asked.

"No," Womack said in a hoarse voice.

"Did Drakos question the Methuselah Man?"

"Spoke to," Womack said.

"Ah," Maddox said, "spoke to. What did they speak about?"

Womack began to recite a long litany of useless subjects: the weather, time, food, comfort, anything but the key issues. The New Man had practiced the same trick earlier. Sometimes, it took him hours to recite a list before the critical piece of information fell out.

"Did Drakos ever ask Strand about Ludendorff?" asked Maddox.

Womack froze. The New Man licked his lips before closing his eyes. He began moving his head from side to side again.

"What did Strand tell Drakos about Ludendorff?" Maddox asked.

Womack's eyes blazed open. He turned and stared at Maddox. "Don't you see?" he whispered. "Don't you understand yet? Ludendorff is the key. You shouldn't have let him interrogate me. He knows. He knows. He has to know."

"Know what?" Maddox asked, wondering if this was a rabbit trail or something truly important.

"No!" Womack said. "Not knows. Conditioned."

"You conditioned Ludendorff against…what?"

Womack arched back, straining against his bonds. He began to laugh in a loud and ugly manner. "Fool! You blind half-breed fool! They say you're smart. They say you're cunning. But you're a slow-witted ass like all the subhumans. It's so obvious. Why can't you ask the right questions? What makes you so dense?"

Maddox recoiled at the accusations until he remembered there were others in the chamber with him. He strove to regain his composure.

Womack continued laughing. "Lord Drakos was right. He has a handle on the situation. The Emperor should listen to him. But no…Drakos is a throwback to ruder times, before we become such ultimate specimens. That is so shortsighted because Drakos has the right mindset. It's why we listen to him. It's why this will work, should have worked, but you ruined everything, Maddox. You who think you're so clever. This time, you fell for it. This time, you can't see. If you don't free me soon, it will be too late."

"He's raving," a tech said.

Maddox ignored the technician. Of course, Womack was raving, but he also might be finally—

"Wait," Maddox said. "You're not talking about Ludendorff being conditioned. Lord Drakos conditioned *you!*"

251

Womack stared at him with wide eyes. The New Man strove to answer. His eyes seemed to plead that Maddox ask him something else.

"What's wrong?" Maddox asked.

Womack threw back his head and howled like a lost soul. He continued screaming and screaming.

Maddox leapt to him, grabbing Womack's shoulders. They felt like iron, the muscles were so rigid.

"Fight the compulsion," Maddox said.

Womack's face was bathed with sweat. "Tell me…tell me…"

"Yes, tell you what?" Maddox asked.

"For…for…"

"Forget!" Maddox said, finally understanding. "Forget the question."

Tars Womack collapsed against the table even as he began to shiver.

"Sir!" a med tech said. "He's on the verge of a severe heart attack. You need to…" the man's voice droned off as he looked up at the sleeping New Man.

"Heart attack?" asked Maddox.

"The readings," the tech said. "You barely averted his death."

Methuselah Man Strand had often conditioned or mind-manipulated New Men he'd captured. Clearly, Drakos had conditioned or had had Womack conditioned in some way. That hadn't been about Ludendorff just now, but Womack.

Maddox found a seat and collapsed onto it. What did this mean? If he were to guess, it meant that Drakos had drained Strand of his gruesome strategies and tactics. The Methuselah Man had given his secrets and methods to a ruthless New Man willing to practice the same horrors that Strand had.

Strand had been the creator of the New Men, their father, as it were. Drakos was one of them, their brother. And Drakos would rather Womack die than anyone else learn his secrets.

Maddox touched his jaw. Had Lord Drakos drained Strand of his knowledge? Or had Strand deceived Drakos into doing his dirty work? Had Strand "confessed" things to Drakos in order to move the New Man by hints and by fostering Drakos' blind ambitions?

What did any of that mean here and now? Maddox pondered the implications…until his head snapped up.

"Galyan."

Nothing happened.

"Galyan," Maddox said more loudly.

An instant later, the holoimage appeared.

"What's Ludendorff doing?" Maddox asked.

Galyan looked surprised. "I don't know, sir."

"You're supposed to be watching him."

"But you countermanded the order."

"I most certainly did not."

"I clearly remember that you did," Galyan said. "You suggested I shouldn't try to do two things at once. I should concentrate on the Captain Nard Situation. Do you not remember? We were in the professor's quarters—"

Maddox groaned aloud, shaking his head.

"What is wrong, sir?" Galyan asked.

"Ludendorff tricked you."

"I do not see how."

"Find him *now*," Maddox said. "Tell me where he is."

The little holoimage stood perfectly still, his eyelids twitching, twitching, twitching— "I cannot find him," Galyan said.

Maddox stood. "We have to find Ludendorff. We have to find him this second."

-45-

Professor Ludendorff wasn't on Starship *Victory* because he had snuck over to the *Moltke* in one of the shuttles ferrying the captured Bosk space marines and techs to the starship. Each shuttle had gone back and forth several times.

It had been easy to sneak aboard, as none of the shuttle personnel expected one of *Victory's* crew to hide in an empty taxi to get onto the battleship.

Once on the *Moltke*, Ludendorff moved inconspicuously through the battleship's corridors. He wore the simple disguise of a Star Watch uniform, a wig and plasti-flesh as used by vid stars. No one recognized him.

Finally, he reached a restricted area.

"Sir," a marine said, stepping from a hidden alcove. "Do you have pass to be here?"

"I do, I do, my boy," Ludendorff said, looking up in surprise. "Let me see. Where did I put it?"

The professor began to rummage through his uniform.

The marine became suspicious, drawing a gun and pointing it at Ludendorff.

"Hands up, please," the marine said.

Ludendorff looked up again, with his hands in his pockets. "I have my pass," he said. "May I pull it out?"

"Very slowly," the suspicious marine said.

Ludendorff complied, drawing out a black leather wallet by increments.

The marine held out a hand, as he used the other to aim the gun at Ludendorff.

Meekly, the professor handed over the wallet.

"It's sticky," the marine complained, as he accepted the wallet.

"Candy was in the same pocket," Ludendorff said, backing away.

"Halt," the marine said.

Ludendorff halted and put up his hands. "If you'll check the pass, you'll see that I'm cleared."

The marine blinked several times, frowned at Ludendorff and concentrated on the wallet. With exaggerated slowness, he opened it. Because of that, the gun was no longer aimed at the professor.

At that point, the drug smeared on the wallet completed its work, and the marine toppled onto the floor, unconscious, the wallet sliding away until it came to rest at Ludendorff's right foot.

"Well, well, well," the professor said. He drew a handkerchief from his pocket, used it to pick up the wallet and stuffed both away in a jacket pocket. Then Ludendorff grabbed the man's wrists and dragged him out of the away.

It was time to get the Builder item and activate it before anyone could stop him.

***

The Builder item did not look alien. It resembled a marble polygonal block the size of a man's head.

Professor Ludendorff was in a high-security chamber that looked like the inside of a polished metal cube. There were hidden cameras. Ludendorff had deactivated all of them. There were no chairs, no table, no…nothing but for himself, the safe he'd opened, and the white polygonal shape inside it.

He reached into the safe and dragged the Builder item closer. It was damn heavy, and therefore dangerous just from that perspective—if he did this wrong, he might smash one of his feet.

The professor was panting by the time he had tugged the block to the safe's edge. It was a three-foot drop to the floor.

"I'm not as young as I used to be," Ludendorff muttered to himself.

He shook his head a moment later. It was time to get serious.

The universe was a nasty, ruthless realm. Humanity needed to be smarter, faster, tougher and more ruthless than any other species. Otherwise, mankind might face extinction sooner rather than later.

The Swarm was out there. Given the chance, the Swarm would swamp humanity with hundreds of thousands of warships. There was no beating the bugs at this point in time. The Imperium knew about humans. That was thanks to Commander Thrax Ti Ix, which in part was thanks to the last Builder in the Orion Arm of the Galaxy.

The Swarm Hive Masters had learned about the existence of hyper-spatial tubes through Thrax's data. Swarm science teams had gone out, at least two of them, unlocking the nexuses' secret and prematurely launching two weak assaults. Given a little more time—an unknown span—and real Swarm invasion fleets would enter Human Space.

Could humanity outfight hundreds of thousands of Swarm warships coming at them in wave after wave after wave?

Ludendorff shook his head.

With trembling hands, he grabbed hold of the Builder rock and made the final tug. The thing shifted, tilted, and... He barely danced out of the way as the rock crashed onto the metal floor.

The professor took out a clean handkerchief and blotted his sweaty face. The perspiration hadn't come from the exertion, but from fear. Yes, he was afraid, deeply, soul-shatteringly afraid.

He blotted his face again before stuffing the hanky away.

Ludendorff feared that he was still compromised. A deep Builder compulsion had driven him to build a horrific soul weapon two years ago. It had propelled his limbs by controlling his mind.

The professor made a sour face. No one was going to control his thoughts again.

He dragged his right wrist across his lips. He'd gone to the Bosk world, thinking some professional help might cleanse his mind from that awful episode. That had been a ghastly mistake. It had been a trap, a trap that had ensnared his mind a second time.

Womack suggested Lord Drakos had broken Strand, and taken the Methuselah Man's itinerary lock stock and barrel. The child had ensnared the father. It had been like Zeus castrating his father Cronus—the original king of the gods—and taking over the divine realm.

A fierce look twisted the professor's face. This Cronus was coming back, baby. He was sewing his balls back on and becoming a man again. That meant freeing Dana, his lover, his woman.

"No!" Ludendorff snarled. "I will not be your patsy, Strand. I fell for one of your tricks, but now…"

The professor licked his lips as he regarded the polygonal white Builder stone sitting on the floor.

He had a good idea what the artifact did. He'd had that idea when he'd chosen which Builder item O'Hara should tease from the Lord High Admiral.

It still surprised the Methuselah Man that Cook had given her the item.

Ludendorff cocked his head. Was that really the case? Maybe O'Hara had lied to the Lord High Admiral. Maybe the Draegar—the combined entity 1, 2 and 3—had fed him that line in order to foster his illusion.

Here in this room, that didn't matter. He'd slipped off *Victory* and slipped here. So far, the others hadn't found him. If he could garner the courage, he could get on with this and do what he had to.

Ludendorff stood over the rock and cracked his knuckles. Slowly, he lowered himself to the floor and sat down cross-legged beside the rock. He rotated his head, hearing neck bones crack. Finally, he reached out with both hands, wriggling his fingers over the ancient item.

This might hurt. This might rip a few illusions from his mind. This could open avenues in his brain that he didn't care to travel. This might reveal other Builder compulsions buried deep in him.

"No more," Ludendorff mouthed.

He knew what it felt like to be used. He knew the sensation of sitting back in his own head and having someone else run his body.

"Begin the process, old boy," he told himself.

His hands hovered just barely above the rock, and still, he could not quite get himself to do it.

What if Maddox opened the door and found him like this? What if he started now, and minutes later, right when he was about to find the great truth, the others dragged him away.

It might bring madness. It could drive him crazy with curiosity.

The professor arched his head back and breathed deeply in and out, attempting to compose himself. This might be the great test of his character.

"So be it," he whispered.

Ludendorff brought his head forward and touched the stone with his fingertips. It was cool. With slow motions, he began to caress one side in an ancient pattern.

To his horror, the rock began to hum audibly. Worse, a thousand times worse, the rock seemed to magnetize, to pull his hands onto it so they could not tear free. It magnetized his flesh. The rock also turned warm as it hummed.

"What am I doing?" the professor whispered.

A facet of the polygonal rock grew clear.

Ludendorff shivered, because something in his mind warned him that this was the first time in fifteen thousand years that this rock had activated.

Ludendorff almost hunched his shoulders in a valiant effort to rip his magnetized hands free.

"Knowledge," he whispered. "This should bring fantastic knowledge. I am the professor. I seek knowledge. This is the great boon."

He knew that he was telling himself this so he could screw up his courage. In order for Cronus to sew his balls back on and take charge again—

"Yes," he said. "I must be in charge. Too long, I have stepped aside for others."

Thus, Ludendorff clenched his jaws, gripped the polygonal stone fiercely and stared into the clear side of the stone.

It was a frightening sensation of falling, falling and falling into a horrendous abyss of the mind. He felt as if his mind plummeted toward a—

Ludendorff's head arched back as if he'd been electrified. The professor's mouth opened as he tried to scream. His eyes bulged outward. The process...the process...it felt as if his brain was on fire. He heard popping and crackling, he saw a Builder, he saw old Methuselah Men—a riot of images began flashing faster and faster before his inner eye. He delved into the past. He saw the Builder of old programming his mind...

Ludendorff was on an assembly line of some sort. There were hundreds like him, some human, some not so human. It chilled the professor seeing this. He had always believed that he was unique, a special specimen of the master race of aliens.

"No," he whimpered. "I am only one cog among thousands."

The images kept flashing in his inner eye. He saw hundreds of Methuselah Men die appalling deaths. They fell like wheat at harvest. They were rooted up like weeds.

Slowly, it dawned on Ludendorff that he *was* special. But his uniqueness did not come from his creation, but from his long life. He had been fashioned like thousands, perhaps even millions of others—if one included alien Methuselah Beings—but only a handful of them had survived for as long as he and Strand had done.

Now began a laborious process that taxed Ludendorff to his limit. His hands remained glued to the stone as it became hot. He sweated until his garments were soaked with perspiration.

A dim part of him realized that he might be killing himself, or the process was killing him. It wasn't the heat against his hands, but the sizzling throughout his heightened intellect.

He saw, he probed, reasoned, rationalized and computed things that he had long forgotten. He—

The hatch to the chamber opened. Captain Maddox charged within, although Ludendorff wasn't aware of the intrusion.

"Don't," someone said. "It's dangerous to touch him."

Foam, a torrent of foam, gushed against Ludendorff. It blasted against his face, went down his mouth so he began to choke. It blasted against his hands and cooled the heated rock that he could not release.

The foam continued to churn, cooling the stone, cooling— Ludendorff ripped his hands free, toppling backward. Maddox tackled him and dragged him through the foam away from the still-pulsating stone.

"What…?" Ludendorff said. It was his last question before falling unconscious.

-46-

Captain Maddox brooded as he stood before an observation deck on *Victory*. He wasn't sure what his next move should be. He had several dilemmas and too many questions with too few answers. To help him think, he studied stars. He had his hands clasped behind his back. The Usan star was the brightest object out there. Near the star, he knew, waited twelve cloaked Spacer ships.

A day ago, one of the ships had uncloaked, glowing eerily. Galyan was still studying the data, trying to determine what, exactly, that meant.

Maddox shook his head. He wasn't overly worried about the Spacers. He had other problems that needed his immediate attention.

The first was Captain Nard and the *Bernard Shaw*. Despite Valerie and Galyan's best efforts, they were no closer to a solution to freeing Dana Rich. Nor did they know if more New Men were on the Q-ship.

The second problem was Ludendorff. The Builder stone was aboard *Victory* now, in a special safe. The captain had overruled Commodore Tancred, whisking the Methuselah Man and the stone from the *Moltke*. The professor was still unconscious with burned palms. The man was barely breathing. What had the stone done to him?

The third issue was Tars Womack the Dominant. Womack claimed he could help Ludendorff. Womack also suggested they summon backup, and annihilate the Spacer ships and storm the *Bernard Shaw*. According to Womack, there were no more New Men. He had been alone on the Q-ships.

Maddox had the distinct impression that Womack wanted him to use the Laumer Points that would head inward toward the center of the Commonwealth. Would *Victory* jump into an ambush if he did that?

That seemed more than likely.

Womack claimed he wanted to help, that he was sick of Lord Drakos having used him. The last straw had been Womack's near death during the questioning, so he said.

Finally, the last and most important problem was the nexuses that needed destroying. Should he take *Victory* into the Deep Beyond this instant, searching for the nexuses? How did one go about finding them?

Yes. If he broke into a nexus and knew how to manipulate it, the thing should bring up a map of other nearby nexuses…

Yet, how could one lone starship—?

"Sir."

Maddox swung around as his right hand dropped to his holstered side.

"I am sorry, sir," Galyan said. "Did I startle you?"

"How many times have I told you not to come in behind me like that?" Maddox said.

"Three hundred and fifteen times so far," Galyan said.

"That was a rhetorical question."

"Oh. Yes. That makes sense. I shall add new parameters to my matrix in order to—"

"Galyan," Maddox said, interrupting. "Why are you here?"

"The professor, sir," Galyan said. "He is awake and he is asking for you. He said it is urgent."

"Right," Maddox said. "Maybe now we can find out what the professor was doing with the Builder artifact."

"And what the artifact does, sir."

"That's what I just said."

"Not precisely," Galyan said. "In point of fact, you just—"

"Galyan," Maddox interrupted.

"Ah. I realize what happened. I was too garrulous. Besides, the professor said immediately. Shall I tell him you are on the way?"

"No," Maddox said, as he headed for the hatch.

"Should I join you, sir?"

"No, Galyan. Keep watch of the *Bernard Shaw* for me."

"For what in particular am I watching?"

"You'll know when it happens," Maddox said, exiting the observation deck and hurrying for medical.

-47-

Ludendorff was propped up in bed when Maddox entered the medical chamber. The professor's burned hands were bandaged and he had tubes in his arms. His white hair was in disarray, all things the captain had expected. What he hadn't expected was the large smile on the professor's face.

The Methuselah Man did not look like someone demanding immediate action or everything would go south.

"I'm glad you're here, my boy. We must strike now before time runs out on us."

Maddox stood motionless for a moment.

"Did you hear me?" Ludendorff asked.

"I did."

"Well?"

"Why are you smiling?"

"What? Oh," the professor said, nodding. "Yes. I quite understand. The dichotomy has flustered you, and well it might, well it might. Now, look here, first things first, right?"

"Professor, what happened? You wouldn't release the rock even though it was burning your hands."

"Yes, yes, that's perfectly obvious. By the way, thank you for your quick thinking. How did you know to bring an extinguisher?"

"I didn't. Galyan suggested it. He popped in on you and popped out as I ran to…to help you."

"Stop me is what you mean," the professor said.

Maddox and Ludendorff stared at each other.

"Yes," the captain said. "I came to stop you, possibly kill you."

"Ah. Good. You're going to tell the truth. That will save us time. We don't have much left, you know?"

"Are you referring to the nexuses?"

"Soon enough, my boy," the professor said. "At this point, I'm referring to the star cruisers undoubtedly racing to intercept us."

"You saw that with the stone?"

"Eh? Saw it? What do you mean 'saw it'?"

"Like the Builder Scanner at Pluto," Maddox said.

Ludendorff shook his head. "No, no, no, that's not it at all. The rock isn't a scanner."

"What is it then?"

Ludendorff opened his mouth, possibly to answer, and then he closed his mouth with a click of his teeth. "You don't know what it does, do you?"

"Are we going to play twenty questions?" Maddox asked.

Ludendorff's nostrils flared, the smile lost most of its power and he abruptly shook his head. "No. As much as I'd like to make you squirm, this time, you and I have to work in tandem. You may not see it, but trust me, you desperately need me this voyage."

Maddox waited.

"Oh, this is most unfortunate," Ludendorff complained. "I finally have the upper hand and I must relinquish it because otherwise the Human Race dies. Why do I always have to save humanity from destruction? No," the professor said, raising one of his bandaged hands, rustling the plastic tube attached to his arm. "I know the answer to that. It was the reason why I was formed, and the reason why I have survived the centuries. It is my duty. It is my obligation—but not an obligation to the Human Race, as such. Rather, I am obligated to—"

"Professor, what in the world are you talking about? You're not making sense."

Ludendorff carefully lowered his bandaged hand, until it rested on his blanketed lap. He sighed, looking down at his hands, and then looking up at Maddox, studying him.

"You are the last person I truly wish to confide in, you know," Ludendorff said. "Your arrogance—let me rephrase. I've wanted to wipe away your knowing smirk for so long, my boy, so very long. You always come out on top, and that has been very trying on me these past few years."

Maddox said nothing, wondering where the Methuselah Man was going with this.

"You're a—oh, never mind," Ludendorff said. "I had a crisis of soul, you could say. I despise anyone controlling me and especially controlling my superlative mind."

Maddox nodded briskly, wishing the old coot would get on with it.

"Creating the soul weapon truly taxed me," Ludendorff said. "I fled to the Bosk world, and there…there…"

The professor's features tightened until they had turned into quiet rage. "Strand's people got hold of my mind. You know all that. I haven't decided yet if Lord Drakos got the better of Strand or if it was the other way around. One thing I do know: Womack is a deadly danger to us. We must beware everything he says."

Maddox did not respond.

"I know, I know," Ludendorff said. "You believe—" He stopped talking and decisively shook his head. "No! I don't have time to indulge in theatrics. Drakos or Strand, it doesn't matter to us now. What matters is that Womack is their creature. I believe there are other New Men in striking distance of this star system. It is the rational explanation for what we've witnessed."

"Professor, what does any of this have to do with the Builder stone?"

"That's a good question, an astute question. I went to the stone because I divined some of its properties beforehand. It is an ancient device, once used by Builders all the time."

"It wasn't made for human hands?"

Ludendorff snorted. "On no account, my boy. The process nearly killed me. I do believe I would have died if you hadn't happened by with your foam. You likely saved my life."

"Galyan had a hand in that."

"Even though this is hard to say, thank you, my boy, thank you. I appreciate your timely aid."

The words shocked Maddox. It took him a second before he said, "You're welcome, Professor. I was glad to do it."

Ludendorff nodded, inhaled and stared at Maddox. "The stone is an ancient device that linked with a Builder mind. It augmented his reasoning capacity. It added computing power—if one wants to use a mechanical explanation as to what the stone did."

"Why did it burn your hands, then?"

"A simple process of heat transfer," Ludendorff said. "That occurred because of the electrical connection with my brain's neurons. The connection gave me greater thinking power. With the added capacity, I carefully thought through several problems. I also studied my memories, searching for clues. I did a self-diagnostic, you could say. I found one or two other compulsions or hypnotic commands inserted into me on the Bosk world, and I eliminated them. I purged my brain of foreign control so that I once more was fully Professor Ludendorff."

"Oh," Maddox said.

"Luckily, I was able to free myself quite early in the process," the professor continued. "That allowed me time to study various problems, coming to logical conclusions. Naturally, pure logic cannot always succeed in a world of emotive creatures like men. I did teach myself how to use the nexuses with greater clarity."

"What?" Maddox said. "That sounds impossible."

"To an ordinary monkey brain such as ordinary people possess, yes, I would agree. We're talking about an advanced Methuselah Man mind already enlarged by the original Builder modifiers. My mind was fashioned or shaped so I could use an input augmenter. You see, it's easy, really. I simply used my memories of the time I've been in a nexus. I looked at the controls in my memories and used storage data in the augmenter and taught myself to remember the correct methods of usage."

"You're saying—"

"My boy," Ludendorff interrupted. "I now know more about nexuses than my esteemed college, Strand. If you can get me inside a nexus, I can figure out what you need to know to detonate it and use it to find other nearby nexuses."

"Did Womack know about the augmenter?" Maddox asked, suspiciously.

"He might have known through Strand," Ludendorff said.

Maddox shook his head. "That doesn't make sense then. When Womack was in charge of the expedition, why didn't he reroute the *Moltke*, board the battleship and take the Builder artifact—"

"Listen," Ludendorff said, interrupting. "Can you listen to me for a moment?"

Maddox nodded.

"We lack time," the professor said. "We should have already gone to the first nexus—"

"Professor," Maddox said.

"What? Oh, yes, quite, quite, you want me to get on with it. I must confess, it is quite stimulating having one's intellect enlarged as I've just experienced. I am the true genius due to the augmenter. According to my calculations—"

"Professor, get to the point. You're driving me crazy."

Ludendorff cocked his head and frowned a moment before nodding. "We must storm the *Bernard Shaw* at once. We must save Dana and the *Moltke's* marines—"

"That's out of the question. As soon as we storm the Q-ship, Captain Nard will kill Dana at best."

The good will evaporated from the professor's features as a sinister intelligence radiated from the Methuselah Man's face.

"Listen here, my boy. This is what I suggest you do if you want to storm the *Bernard Shaw* the easy way."

Ludendorff began telling him, and Maddox found the plan intriguing…

-48-

Saving Doctor Dana Rich and one-third of the *Moltke's* marines proved technologically provocative. Maddox had expected a daring rescue or possibly having Ludendorff build a stasis field, such as Strand used to employ. The rescue problems were legion; the stasis field seemed like the only way to go.

Ludendorff had a different idea. It helped that he remembered everything about the Q-ships that the Draegar had instructed him to forget.

"The beauty of the plan comes down to their extreme paranoia," Ludendorff lectured. "The Bosks owe that paranoia to their evolutionary modifier, Strand. He really cannot trust anyone. It is his great failing."

Maddox found it frustrating listening to all this. He constantly prodded the professor to hurry up.

In the end, Galyan was the main instrument of liberation, although Maddox paved the way for the holoimage's insertion onto the *Bernard Shaw*.

"Now see here, Captain," Maddox said from *Victory's* bridge. "How do I know the doctor is well enough to trade?"

Captain Nard leered at him from the screen. "Take my word for it. She's well."

Maddox smiled grimly while shaking his head. "But I don't and won't take your word for it. I must see for myself or have a representative of mine see before I can agree to a swap."

The leer slipped away as Nard become angry. "Have a care how you speak to me, *half*-breed."

The insult caused a twitch in Maddox's right cheek. But he suppressed it and analyzed the words. Why would Nard say such a thing? The most reasonable explanation was that he'd heard someone else say it. The logical someone would be a New Man. That raised the odds that at least one New Man was aboard the *Bernard Shaw*. The raised odds gave Maddox greater confidence in Ludendorff's strange plan, as the professor had predicted more New Men.

"I need confirmation on the doctor's mental and physical state," Maddox said evenly.

"Then I want confirmation that the Dominant is well."

"Fine," Maddox said. "Send someone over to check him out."

Nard's eyes narrowed suspiciously. "This is a trick," he said. "I don't know how, but it is."

"It's hardly a trick," Maddox said. "It's a fair offer, tit for tat."

"You're suggesting we exchange officers?"

"No. I'm sending my holoimage aboard your vessel."

Nard's head swayed back. "Your holoimage? No. That's out of the question."

"I don't see why," Maddox said reasonably. "A holoimage is as harmless as they come. It's an image, a projection. The instant you raise your shield, you'll cut the projection ray and the holoimage will disappear from your vessel."

"That's the point," Nard said. "I will not lower my shield."

"Your paranoia does you no credit, sir," Maddox said. "A highly suspicious man is usually that way because he knows himself, and he knows that he practices deceit. Your suspicion of us causes me to think you're planning a deception against us."

"This has nothing to do with me. Our shield is our chief protection. I will not unilaterally drop it."

"I understand your reluctance," Maddox said. "But come now, it isn't fully rational. You can watch my starship and battleship with your sensors. They will show inert cannons. At the first sign the cannons are energizing, you simply raise your shield. I expect you to keep your shield generators online—that's only rational. Besides, you can always detonate your vessel, killing our friends. We want to avoid that. I can clearly destroy your ship anytime I want. But I don't want, and that's why we're talking instead of having you die like you deserve."

The big Bosk captain grew scarlet-faced as his features hardened. He clearly ground his teeth, but he also struggled to contain his anger. Finally, as his normal color returned, Nard hunched forward on his chair. "You're…not being truthful. You desire the woman, as she is important to you." The Bosk's eyes narrowed as he sat back. "Very well. I demand the Dominant and the Draegar in exchange for her."

"The doctor *and* the marines," Maddox countered.

Nard obviously worked to keep the surprise off his brutal face even as he hunched forward again. "You will agree to the exchange?" he asked.

Maddox nodded. "First, though, I need to assess the doctor and the marines, seeing that they are unharmed and worthy of trade."

The surprise faded as Nard stared at him. "I will let you know if this examination is acceptable within the hour."

"Fine," Maddox said.

It didn't take an hour. Captain Nard reappeared thirty-four minutes later.

"Yes," the huge Bosk captain said. "I agree. Send your holoimage. Let it inspect the people. They are unharmed. Afterward, we can make the exchange."

"Do you wish to send over an officer to exam the Dominant and the Draegar?" Maddox asked.

"No."

"When will you be ready to receive the holoimage?"

"When will you be ready to send it?" Nard countered.

"Ten minutes."

"So be it," Nard said. "But know, Captain, that if you attempted any trickery, I shall detonate my ship, taking everybody with me."

"I understand," Maddox said. "In ten minutes, we shall send our holoimage."

***

Galyan was uneasy as the minutes ticked down. He stood on the bridge near the captain, with Professor Ludendorff sitting at a panel specially installed for the Methuselah Man.

"This is highly unusual," Galyan said for the umpteenth time.

"Now, now," Ludendorff said from his location on the bridge. "There is absolutely nothing to worry about. You have always been able to speak, projecting sound from your holoimage. Maybe you don't realize how unusual that is. I have merely modified you so you can do more than just speak. In fact, you have two new functions. One is to act as an emitter. The other—"

Ludendorff chuckled nastily.

"If this does not work…" Galyan said.

"I don't understand how you can possibly be worried," Valerie said. "It's a brilliant idea."

Ludendorff nodded.

"I admit that I am happy to oblige by saving Dana," Galyan said. "I am just unsure if any of this will work. What happens to me if they raise their shield?"

"You'll disappear," Ludendorff said, "as that will cut off the signal."

"I understand *that*," Galyan said. "What I mean is—"

"Enough," Maddox said, already agitated. "They've dropped their shield."

"They can raise it before we can warm up our disrupter cannon to fire," Andros said.

"Noted," Maddox said. "Good luck, Galyan. Let's see if this works."

"Oh my," Galyan said, as he fidgeted nervously. Abruptly, the alien holoimage disappeared—and reappeared on the bridge of the *Bernard Shaw*.

Galyan looked around. Huge Captain Nard with his knife tattoo sat in his captain's chair. The Bosk kept his hand on the handle of a holstered gun as he eyed the holoimage.

Other unsavory Bosk personnel sat at their stations, watching him, many with curled lips as if he was a contagious disease. Two giant Bosk marines aimed weapons at him, but that was senseless. Their beams would pass harmlessly through him. Surely, they knew that.

"You're the holoimage?" Nard demanded harshly.

Galyan dipped his Adok head. "That is correct, Captain Nard. I am Driving Force Galyan, the former Commander of Starship—"

"I'm not interested in your title," Nard said, cutting him off while nodding toward one of his men. "You're going to go with him and see the people. Do you understand that?"

"I do, Captain, and I appreciate—"

"That's enough," Nard said. "Get off my bridge. You're...strange."

Galyan did not agree, but he wasn't here to argue. He turned to the officer Nard had pointed out. The man headed for the hatch. Galyan floated after him.

As Galyan left the bridge, he heard Nard muttering to himself in an almost superstitious manner.

That was quite odd. Galyan had not believed the Bosks a superstitious race. Surely, Methuselah Man Strand would have bred that out of them.

In any case, Galyan followed the officer down a ship corridor—and abruptly disappeared. The holoimage reappeared in a special chamber with many monitors. Ludendorff had remembered the Q-ship's layout, and told him where this place would be. Two golden-skinned New Men sat behind the monitors. They were both tall and wearing silver suits, and neither turned around to peer at him as his appearance had been utterly silent.

So far, everything was happening as the professor had predicted it would.

"The holoimage is gone," one of the New Men said.

"Gone where?" the other asked.

"I don't know. Just gone."

"That is against our accepted protocol. Find him at once."

The searcher leaned forward and manipulated his board.

At that point, Galyan cleared his throat. He did not need to clear it, as it wasn't blocked, but he had watched several vid shows the last few days and had seen the hero do that many times.

The two New Men whirled around, drawing holstered beamers.

Galyan activated the special feature that Ludendorff had installed in his holoimage through working on the central unit aboard *Victory*. For a millisecond, Galyan buzzed. Then, instead of sound emitting from his mouth, a deadly electrical discharge blew from him. The discharge struck both New Men at the same instant. It did not simply shock the individuals, but sizzled them with high voltage electricity.

Each New Man flopped backward, dead and burned, striking the deck at almost the same instant.

Seconds later, a floating Galyan used his other new feature. He sent comm signals through his holoimage to switches on the panels. Those special switches activated interior ship systems.

Throughout the *Bernard Shaw*, hidden gas capsules began to hiss. No one on the Q-ship was immune to the odorless and colorless gas. Men and women fell unconscious in the Engineering Sections, in sleep quarters, in cargo holds, in fighter bays, on the bridge, in the brigs—everywhere on the *Bernard Shaw*, except in the monitoring room where Galyan floated, observing the situation.

As Galyan confirmed the successful completion of his mission, he moved his ropy arms. This was fascinating indeed. The professor had given him an ability to directly influence reality. He could do more than just talk and see. He could now eject killing volts of electricity and emit the right kind of comm signals that—

"Galyan."

That was Captain Maddox hailing him. It was time to leave the *Bernard Shaw*.

In an instant, the little holoimage disappeared. He reappeared on *Victory's* bridge, giving his report.

Before he was through, the captain ordered strike fighters and shuttles to launch and head for the Q-ship.

It was just in time, too.

"Sir," Valerie said from her board.

Everyone, including Galyan, turned toward her. She'd become pale and had spoken the single word forcefully.

"Report," Maddox told her.

"Star cruisers, sir," Valerie said, while staring at her panel. "They're appearing near the third planet. If I were to guess, they used star-drive jumps to reach there."

"A-ha!" Ludendorff cried. "I *knew* more New Men would show up. It looks like the real threat is finally beginning."

"Sir," Valerie said. "The Spacer ships have begun accelerating. They're heading toward us. Oh. Sir, someone calling herself Mako 21 wishes to talk to you."

Galyan turned to the captain.

Maddox seemed to be brooding. Finally, though, the captain straightened. "Put her on the main screen, Lieutenant. Let's see what the Spacer has to say."

-49-

Mako 21 appeared on the main bridge screen aboard *Victory*. She seemed much like before, a small Spacer with petite features and the round goggles they all wore. She sat more stiffly than Maddox remembered, and there was something else that he couldn't quite define. She seemed more...*aware*, although how he could tell that Maddox could not have explained. She sat differently, he supposed, and there was an air about her... She almost seemed...alien in a way. Yet, how did that make sense?

"Captain Maddox," Mako said.

Their ships were over one hundred million kilometers apart, making a severe time delay between them.

"Surveyor Mako," he said.

Minutes passed.

"I must warn you about the star cruisers," she said. "They are hostile, wishing you harm. I believe you hold something of value to them, something they intend to get."

Maddox glanced at Valerie before regarding the Spacer again. "Why would you care if they're hostile to us?" he asked.

It took several minutes again until Mako 21 gave him a predatory flash of teeth. "The star cruisers attacked a Spacer convoy earlier."

"Indeed," Maddox said. "Could the Spacer convoy have held the *Sulla 7* or been composed solely of the stolen Nerva hauler?"

"That is immaterial to my warning."

Maddox drummed his fingers on an armrest. "Do the New Men have the *Sulla 7* in their custody?" If so, maybe he could get it back.

After the normal time delay, Mako said, "You must forget about the hauler, as it is already quite far from here. You will not see it again."

"I can't forget it," Maddox said. "You stole Usan crystals and varth elixir. You slaughtered innocent people and manipulated minds. If nothing else, you owe the people of Usan III a great deal of compensation. Before we continue our discussion, I want to know when and how you're going to pay them for your crimes."

Minutes passed.

"Captain," Mako said, while continuing to hold her motionless pose. "I haven't contacted you to discuss such mundane matters. The star cruisers are hostile to you. On all accounts, you mustn't allow them to destroy your ship."

That was interesting. Why would the Spacer care what happened to *Victory?*

"What's going on here?" Maddox asked the others.

"She has a hidden motive," Ludendorff said.

Maddox already knew that. "Any idea what it is?" he asked.

The professor shook his head.

"Hmm…" Maddox pressed the comm button. "How do you know what the New Men desire?"

"That, also, is immaterial," Mako said later. "I know. Let us leave it at that. These New Men have attacked a Spacer convoy. I wish to teach them a hard lesson, as I was the convoy leader. My desire to teach them—we have a common cause, Captain. That is the thing. Will you accept Spacer aid?"

Maddox shrugged before pressing the comm button. "I will indeed. Now, you must excuse me. The New Men are hailing me."

Mako vanished from the main screen. A New Man appeared. He sat in a different sort of chair. He was tall, dark-haired and golden-skinned with a haughty manner and a half sneer on his lips. Like many New Men, he wore a silver garment. This one had a Star Nebula pinned at his left pectoral.

The star cruiser—there were five of them all told—was much closer to *Victory* than the Spacer vessel. There was almost no time delay between the transmissions.

"I recognize you," the New Man said in a proud voice. "You are Captain Maddox of Starship *Victory*. I am Don Del Franco of the *Resolute*. I have monitored the *Bernard Shaw*. It is in distress. I am officially informing you that the Bosk homeworld is presently under Lord Drakos's protection. We are his kinsmen and thus extend our protection to the Bosks and thus the *Bernard Shaw*."

"You will be happy to learn then that Professor Ludendorff had gained letters of Marque from the Commonwealth," Maddox said. "The *Bernard Shaw* is an official Q-ship in a Star Watch flotilla. Thus, the vessel is under my protection and authority."

"You lead the flotilla?" Del Franco asked.

"I am its spokesman."

"I want to address the flotilla leader."

"You can speak to me," Maddox said.

"No. You are an inferior. I want to speak to your superior."

Maddox stiffened at the words.

"I am not referring to your genetic status," Del Franco said. "I am referring to your inferior status within the flotilla hierarchy. Thus, you do not need to take any offense at my words, although reasonably you should not, as I have only spoken the truth regarding both your genetic and official ranking."

"It is my misfortune to inform you—"

"Captain Maddox," Del Franco said, interrupting. "Put Brigadier O'Hara on or let me address Commodore Tancred. What I have to say is too important for mere underlings."

"He is trying to bait you, sir," Galyan said.

Maddox nodded. Of course, the New Man was trying to bait him. Maddox was attempting to use that in order to manipulate the conversation. "Let me make this plain to you," he told the New Man.

"I have spoken," Del Franco said, his voice hardening. "That means you will now—"

The New Man's image vanished from the main screen.

The others stared in surprise at Maddox, as he had cut the connection with a click of a button on his armrest.

Several seconds passed in silence.

Valerie broke it by saying, "The star cruisers have begun accelerating toward us, sir. There are five altogether. According to my scans, the five have improved shields and disrupter cannons. I'm unsure *Victory* and the *Moltke* can defeat five improved star cruisers."

"They won't attack just yet," Ludendorff said, as he eyed Maddox. "They're trying to rattle our esteemed captain with aggressive maneuvering."

Maddox pressed his fingertips against each other as he tapped his index fingers against his chin. "At this point, do we really need the *Bernard Shaw* anymore?"

"*Victory's* shuttles have launched from the Q-ship," Galyan said. "They hold Dana and many of the rescued *Moltke* marines."

"Have all our shuttles launched from the *Bernard Shaw?*" Maddox asked.

"The last two are getting ready to leave the Q-ship," Galyan said.

Maddox turned to Valerie. "Order the last shuttles to take the corpses of the New Men, but couch the message in code."

"Smart move," Ludendorff said. "This Del Franco will undoubtedly intercept the messages. But what's the point, my boy? The kinsmen will demand Tars Womack, the two dead New Men and likely the Draegar as well. If we give them corpses—"

Maddox snapped his fingers as his features hardened, as if he'd tasted something unpleasant. "We're going to give them the *Bernard Shaw*. This isn't a picnic. We're agreed on that, right?"

"What are you planning?" Ludendorff asked.

"To give them a poison pill," Maddox said. "We've delayed in the Usan System too long. We know our assignment, and yet, we aren't getting any closer to achieving it. These New Men mean to capture my vessel. Maybe the Spacers are going to help them do that."

"You don't trust Mako?" Ludendorff asked, "or accept any of her explanations?"

"I do not," Maddox said. "Five improved star cruisers and twelve saucer-shaped ships. The odds are heavily stacked against us if they attack us in concert. Normally, I would use the star drive and leave. But I can't abandon the *Moltke*. It lacks a star drive. No. We're going to play this down and dirty, clearing the board as much as we can. Afterward…let's see what's left and we can make our decisions then."

-50-

Sometime later, the five star cruisers decelerated as the *Moltke* and *Victory* drifted away from the *Bernard Shaw*.

At the same time, the twelve Spacer ships popped out of view, reappearing near the Q-ship. Each of the saucer-shaped vessels had used their star drive to jump directly into the fray.

"That should make this interesting," Valarie said.

A few minutes later, she added, "I'm detecting a flurry of messages between the Spacers and the New Men. I can't hack into the comm streams, though, so I don't know what they're saying."

"You don't need to," Ludendorff said. "I imagine Del Franco is threatening Mako. Maybe she's threatening him back."

"Or this is a ruse on both their parts," Maddox said.

"Eh?" asked Ludendorff. "You really think the two of them are working together against us?"

"It's a possibility we can't discount," Maddox said.

Ludendorff cocked his head, as he no doubt assessed the idea. "No... I don't think so. This is something else, but damned if I can figure out what that something is."

"Sir," a comm tech said. "There's an incoming message from the New Man."

Maddox nodded.

Don Del Franco appeared on the main screen, eying the captain in a superior way. "You're making a wise choice surrendering the *Bernard Shaw*, Captain. We have the stronger force, although it was always possible that you might have damaged one of our vessels if we fought."

Maddox had already decided on his ploy against the egotistical New Man. He would act the part of a sullen and sulking commander, as that would be what Franco expected from him. He thus stared tight-faced at the New Man.

"Come now, Captain," Del Franco said in a paternalistic way. "You're acting like a subhuman. You're superior to such stunted stock to indulge in this emotionalism. You must not brood like a cretin, but learn to accept reality as it is. According to my brief on you, you are usually more sanguine. Can my truthful comments about you earlier have upset you to such a degree?"

Maddox shook his head sharply.

Del Franco laughed. "You're so transparent, Captain. You wish to ape your betters. That is clear and perfectly understandable. Or maybe I'm reading this wrong. Could you be seething because you're only ranked third in such a small flotilla? Perhaps you understand that your genetic heritage is far superior to the sub-men set above you."

"You have something of mine," Maddox said.

"Oh?"

"The *Sulla 7,*" Maddox snapped.

Del Franco lofted dark eyebrows. "What does that even mean?"

"Don't lie," Maddox said. "I know you captured the Nerva hauler from the Spacers. They stole it from us, filled with Usan crystals and varth elixir."

"Captain, your logic is flawed. We took nothing from you."

"I didn't say *you* took it from us. I said it *is* ours."

"Don't you know the fundamental rule of the universe?" Del Franco asked. "Possession is nine-tenths of the law."

"Meaning?"

"Quite simply, when we encountered the Spacers, they possessed the *Sulla 7*. We took it from them, using a basic axiom of life. The predator takes from the prey. If you wish for compensation regarding the *Sulla 7*, you must take it up with the foolhardy Spacers—providing they survive their unaccustomed daring in nearing us as they're doing."

"So you don't deny—"

"Captain!" Del Franco said. "I grow weary of your insulting tone. But that is a secondary issue. I wish to know why no one aboard the *Bernard Shaw* is answering our hails."

"It isn't my ship anymore," Maddox said sullenly. "Thus, I have no idea."

Don Del Franco's dark eyes glittered with malice. "Have a care, Captain. I am not a subhuman who takes well to having anything thrown in my teeth. There are supposed to be Dominants aboard the vessel. I demand an immediate explanation as to their whereabouts."

"I'm already giving you the ship," Maddox said. "Isn't that enough?"

"Giving us the ship was due to fear, reasonable fear, as we possess the superior vessels. You were and are acting in your own enlightened self-interest. I suggest you continue doing so before I become angry with you. Where are the Dominants?"

"I don't know," Maddox grumbled.

Del Franco shook his head. "I do not wish to activate my disrupter cannons. But if you maintain this mulish—"

"The Dominants are asleep on the Q-ship," Maddox said.

Suspicion grew on Del Franco's golden features. "Why are they asleep?"

"Because we used their paranoia against them," Maddox said. "They held Doctor Dana Rich, and we wanted her back."

Del Franco stared through the main screen at Maddox. "That does not make sense. Are you suggesting that you *outthought* Dominants?"

"Yes."

After a moment, Del Franco began to nod, as if he'd figured something out. "You're being coy with me, Captain. You're trying to maintain airs. I know you have succeeded several times against Throne World Dominants—"

"You and I are supposed to be allies," Maddox said, interrupting. "But you haven't treated us as allies. Know, sir, that I am recording this and will bring it up for arbitration."

Del Franco scoffed. "Don't you understand that I'm not a signer of that ridiculous accord? That means I'm not bound by the unholy agreement between the Commonwealth and the Throne World."

"That isn't what Tars Womack told me."

Del Franco stiffened.

Maddox grinned at the New Man as if he'd scored a point in a complex game.

"Womack is on your ship?" Del Franco demanded.

"He's my captive," Maddox boasted.

Del Franco turned to someone off screen on his bridge.

"Now," Maddox said.

Valerie stared at a control on her panel. She raised a trembling hand. With a swift move, she brought her hand down and tapped the control.

That sent a pulse from *Victory* to the *Bernard Shaw*. The Q-ship presently drifted between the five star cruisers, meaning it was much closer to them than to *Victory* or the *Moltke*.

On the main screen, Del Franco turned to Maddox. "What just happened? Why did you send an impulse to the—"

At that moment, the stacked antimatter warheads crammed aboard the *Bernard Shaw* detonated in one fantastic explosion. The detonation vaporized the Q-ship and all the sleeping Bosks aboard. There hadn't been enough time to take them off. Thus, the Bosks perished just as the vessel itself ceased to exist.

The antimatter explosion grew as heat and x-rays and gamma rays, along with a giant EMP, radiated in every direction. The combined destructive force hit the five star cruisers. The powerful shields winked out against the incandescent fury of the incredible antimatter annihilation. The heavy armor proved just as effective as the shields—melting and vaporizing to nothingness. That left the bulkheads, the water coils, engines, storage compartments, people and other sundry items aboard each vessel. They were destroyed or dead in seconds. There were no survivors, although there were particles of debris that spewed outward at high velocity.

It was a brutal sneak attack committed with underhanded deception. The Bosks and New Men alike perished.

Maddox derived no joy from the annihilation. He had seen it as the logical answer, however. He had to get on with the mission and destroy Swarm nexuses. If he didn't get to it quickly enough, nothing was going to matter.

Extreme need had brought about extreme action.

Victory and the *Moltke* had maneuvered beforehand in such a way as to put more distance between the star cruisers and them. At this point, the Spacer ships were closer to the detonated Q-ship than the Star Watch vessels were.

The annihilating blast dissipated in strength as it continued to expand. That blast now hit the Spacer shields, darkening each of them. The distance was just enough that none of the twelve shields went down.

The shields of *Victory* and *Moltke* also darkened, although not to the same degree as the saucer-shaped vessels, which had had been closer to the original detonation site.

"Accelerate," Maddox told Helm. "Warm up the disrupter and neutron cannons," he told Weapons. "Valerie, tell Tancred to ram down the Spacers' throats. We're going to take them out before their shields can dissipate the energies blackening them."

Amid the aftermath of the cruel antimatter blast, the two Star Watch vessels began accelerating at the twelve weaker Spacer ships. The sensors on all the warships showed whiteout. It would take time for the sensors to "see" again. During that time, Maddox and Tancred drove at the known locations of the Spacer ships.

"Are we sure the Spacers were going to help the New Men?" Valerie asked.

"We've been over that," Maddox said. "We can't be one hundred percent sure what they were trying to do. But this is the wrong time to worry about niceties. We should have already started on our mission, yet here we are in the Usan System. That's going to end now."

"I know all that," Valerie said.

"Then do your task," Maddox said, sternly. "Leave the thinking to me."

An unpleasant silence filled the bridge.

Maddox brooded on his command chair. He'd murdered innocent Bosks. He knew that, and it bothered him. The New Men—they were Lord Drakos's kinsmen. Maybe he'd struck with an under-the-belt blow against them, but all was fair in love and war.

So why did he feel guilty?

Maddox shook his head. As he did, he happened to notice a tight-lipped Lieutenant Noonan. Maddox sighed. Maybe he shouldn't have been so rough with her a moment ago. He used to be that way all the time, but he'd changed his manner, at least to a degree, in order for smoother functioning. It hadn't really been that much of a rebuke, but—

Damnit. He hated this sort of thing. Still, it was good for him to bend occasionally if it helped crew morale. It didn't help, however, that he hated doing this.

"Lieutenant," Maddox said in a gruff voice.

Valerie barely looked up at him.

"I shouldn't have said what I did a second ago," Maddox told her. "I'm…I'm sorry."

Valerie nodded, and she looked at him.

He gave her a nod, and he tried to tell her with that nod that he really was sorry he'd said what he had in the tone he'd used.

"I'm fine, sir," Valerie said, her voice telling him that she really was. "We're in the middle of battle. I understand."

Maddox nodded again, in appreciation. He'd made the correct morale decision. That was good. Maybe it was even wise.

The captain sat up, looked at the main screen, saw that the whiteout was dissipating, and knew it was time to kill the Spacers.

-51-

The *Bismarck*-class battleship and *Victory* hit the twelve saucer-shaped vessels head-on. The *Moltke* was an older vessel, but it had been designed and constructed for exactly this type of fight. It had heavy shields, heavy armor and upgraded cannons. It was made to slug it out with similar kinds of warships.

Each saucer-shaped vessel had a bulbous core and a thin outer ring like the planet Saturn. They had much weaker hull armor and shields of maybe half the strength of *Moltke's*. Those shields were still black and slowly turning purple in areas as the dissipating process began.

The same was true for *Victory* and the *Moltke's* shields, that they slowly dissipated the horrible blocked energies. Their shields were quite a bit stronger, however. They hadn't gone as dark, and thus dissipated more easily and more rapidly. The two Star Watch vessels were heavier and stronger, the Spacer ships were quicker and more nimble.

As Maddox leaned forward on his command chair, he wondered about the Spacer plan, why they'd jumped near the *Bernard Shaw*. The only thing that made sense was that Mako and Del Franco had been in collusion against him.

"When have Spacers and New Men ever acted in concert?" Ludendorff was asking. "I can't think of a time. They are like cats and dogs, natural enemies."

"That's not true," Valerie said. "In Detroit, my dad had a pit bull and a Siamese cat that loved each other, Hank and

Daisy Mae. You couldn't tear them apart, not even at suppertime."

"That's an unnatural exception," Ludendorff said, not missing a beat. "But exceptions often prove the point. You remember the strangeness of the affair because you recognized even then that cat and dogs should hate each other."

"I've never thought that," Valerie said, stubbornly.

Ludendorff waved his right hand. "My point remains the same: Spacers and New Men have seldom to never mixed. Can anyone think of a time they've done so?"

"I can," Maddox said.

"Where?" asked Ludendorff.

"Here in the Usan System."

"No, no," Ludendorff said. "You're missing my point. We don't really know *why* the Spacers jumped so near the Q-ship."

"What if they wanted payback against the New Men?" Valerie asked.

"Yes, that's my point," Ludendorff said. "Don Del Franco as much as admitted to us earlier that Mako was right. The New Men had taken the Nerva hauler."

"That actually proves *my* point," Maddox said, as the two Star Watch warships remorselessly closed to pointblank range against the Spacers. "They were acting together against us."

"My boy, you're thinking with your emotions, as Del Franco suggested. You seldom do so—"

"Galyan," Maddox said, interrupting. "Target Mako's ship first."

"I am picking up strange readings, sir," Galyan said. "It is from Mako's ship. She appears to have unique equipment aboard her vessel."

"Captain," Ludendorff said. "Perhaps we can bargain with the Spacers."

"There's no more time for that," Maddox said. "The Spacers robbed Usan III and abused people with mind control. I'm putting a stop to that once and for all."

"But if you're mistaken about their intent—"

"Fire," Maddox said, speaking over Ludendorff.

Galyan looked at the captain in a questioning way.

"Fire!" Maddox repeated, as he pounded his armrest.

The starship's antimatter engines purred with power, and a yellow disrupter beam shot out of the terrible cannon. A second later, the neutron beam lashed out at a secondary target.

Commodore Tancred followed the captain's example as the *Moltke's* heavy beams began to churn.

Now began a true slaughter only minutes after the annihilation of the five star cruisers. The Spacer shields were weak and went down at almost the first touch of the Star Watch beams.

"Why aren't they firing back?" Ludendorff wondered aloud.

"Keep firing, Galyan," Maddox said. "We're striking while the iron's hot."

Finally, a different saucer-shaped ship winked away as its star drive mechanism engaged. Another followed the first.

"Don't let any more get away," Maddox said.

Five saucer-shaped vessels had already become molten debris. There had been two heavy explosions. With others, chunks and plates of broken metal hull and bulkheads drifted aimlessly in the stellar darkness.

The other Spacer ships engaged their star drives as the *Moltke* and *Victory* continued to lash out with their heavy beams. Two more enemy vessels crumbled under the intense assault, breaking apart as interior explosions ripped through the expanding debris.

During that time, the rest of the Spacer vessels winked away, each using a star-drive jump to flee the carnage.

Galyan scanned a widening area, but none of the Spacer ships appeared in the zones. It was more than likely they had made light-year jumps, getting far away from the murderous Star Watch warships.

Maddox sank back, relieved. The burden of command and the risk of all these lives under him had kept him tense throughout the proceedings. He'd risked everything against the New Men, hoping to trick them with the *Bernard Shaw's* detonation, and it had worked.

The Spacers had thrown a wrinkle into his plan. But by doing so, they'd handed him a golden opportunity. He'd exploited the opportunity ruthlessly, destroying seven enemy saucer-ships. He hadn't expected that.

Five had gotten away, but he'd nailed seven of the troublemakers.

"That was too easy," Ludendorff said from his panel.

"Easy?" Maddox asked, stung by the words. "That wasn't easy."

The captain stopped talking as his gut churned. He'd murdered innocents today in order to win. He'd done so because he *had* to win. He had the answer to the Swarm problem, which meant he had to save his people so he could save Human Space.

"I smell a rat," Ludendorff declared. "The Spacer move… It had a hidden motive that we're not seeing."

Maddox refused to respond.

"I am picking up a distress beacon," Galyan said.

Maddox couldn't help himself. He traded glances with the professor. Ludendorff gave him a look that said, "Here it is, the hidden motive."

"Where's the signal coming from?" Maddox asked.

"From the debris of Mako's flagship," Galyan said. "I am detecting a life-pod, sir."

"I tell you," Ludendorff said, "that was far too easy. The Spacer vessels had no reason to jump so near the *Bernard Shaw*."

"What do you suggest I do?" Maddox asked, beginning to wonder if the professor was right.

Ludendorff thought about it before looking up. "Under no circumstances should you rescue the life-pod."

"Are you suggesting the Spacers *knew* we would attack them?" Maddox asked. "No. It would have to be more than that. Do you think they knew we would detonate the Q-ship and thus came close enough so their shields took a near overload? The idea seems farfetched—why would Mako allow seven of her ships to perish?"

"I'm making no such assumptions," Ludendorff said. "I'm simply acknowledging that this easy slaughter, these back to back amazingly stunning victories, are against the odds to a stark degree."

"The two victories derived from the same *Bernard Shaw* detonation," Galyan pointed out.

"I know all that," Ludendorff said. "I'm suspicious. I'm sensing…a hidden hand attempting to maneuver us in ways we don't understand. I cannot give you a concrete reason as to why I feel this, but the life-pod definitely proves my point."

Maddox recalled his meetings with the old Visionary years ago. The ancient woman had claimed to possess the ability to see into the future. Could Spacers really see into the future, at least some of the time? If they could, could they have set up a diabolical plan to plant Mako on their starship? Instead of having a hidden android, they would have a hidden Spacer, as it were.

"Should I hail the life-pod?" Valerie asked.

Maddox eyed Ludendorff. The Methuselah Man had gained fantastic insights by using the Builder artifact. Might the professor have a point about this two-stage battle being far too easy? He'd seldom won so handily before.

Why had the Spacers jumped so near the *Bernard Shaw*? Now that he thought about it—

"No," Maddox told Valerie. "You will not hail the life-pod. We're leaving it."

"Someone's in there," the lieutenant said. "Look. We've killed a lot of people today—"

Maddox cleared his throat, interrupting her, and he gave Valerie a significant glance. In the past, he would have told her to obey orders, not to question him. Today, he gave her an opportunity to reach the conclusion…maybe not quietly but without another rebuke.

"Yes, sir," Valerie said. She looked troubled, but she said no more.

Was he making the right decision? Maddox wasn't sure. But one thing he did know. It was time to reach the first Swarm nexus. The question was…how were they going to go about doing that?

-52-

"Trust me, my boy," the professor said. "This is the only way to ensure her full revival in an acceptable amount of time."

Ludendorff stood with Maddox in a medical chamber, with Brigadier O'Hara lying on a med-cot. She was still under sedation, as per the captain's orders, with monitors constantly assessing her condition.

The professor noted the way Maddox looked at the old lady. It was interesting. Maddox almost seemed like a son worried about his mother. What was the real connection between these two?

Ludendorff shrugged inwardly. It hardly mattered to him one way or another. It was time to fix the old woman and get on with it. He was eager to attempt this, wondering if he could achieve a miracle cure.

"It seems foolish to use the stone again," Maddox said.

"Nonsense," the professor said. "I won't be using it as I did before. This will be a controlled situation, as you'll be here, watching me."

"I can't watch your mind," Maddox said.

"A tree is known by its fruit, isn't that so?"

Maddox eyed him before replying, "It's been said."

"Come now, I know you read the Good Book. Thus, I know you're familiar with the concept."

"Fine," Maddox said, "a fruit and a tree and all that."

Ludendorff raised an eyebrow. "You've been under tremendous strain lately. Is it finally getting to you?"

Maddox turned a cool eye upon him, saying nothing.

Once more, Ludendorff shrugged inwardly. The truth was that he felt wonderful. Using the stone the first time had changed so much for him. His mind felt invigorated. He almost felt young again, as if he could dare any challenge. The universe hadn't seen him like this for centuries.

The professor rubbed his newly healed hands. The quick healing had come about through an advanced procedure. Ah. This would be the challenge of a lifetime. He wasn't thinking about the brigadier as the great challenge, but halting the expected Swarm expansion into Human Space. Still, he needed to concentrate on the brigadier right now. First things first.

"You're sure this won't harm her?" Maddox asked.

"I'm not a god that I can predict the future. Certainly, it *might* harm her, but I doubt it will."

"Can you do it quickly?" Maddox said. "I want to be away—"

"My boy, unless I do it quickly, the process will kill me."

"And the brigadier?"

"Dead as well, I'm afraid."

Maddox studied him.

"But if we delay and the—"

"Right," Maddox said, interrupting. "Do it."

"It will take time to set up—"

"I said, do it. Let's get this done and be on our way."

***

Ninety minutes passed before the professor was ready. He stood beside the groggy, supine brigadier, with the Builder polygonal stone on a stand beside him. Maddox stood in the background with several extinguishers lined up at his feet. Galyan stood beside the captain, ready to record the ordeal.

"Do you realize what we're attempting to do?" Ludendorff asked the half-revived O'Hara."

"It sounds like black magic to me," she complained. "But I'm sick of being under sedation because I'm untrustworthy. I want myself back. I want what the Draegar or possibly you stole from me at the Tau Ceti station."

"I did nothing untoward to you," Ludendorff said. "Believe me when I say that this is the handiwork of the Draegar, all of him, 1, 2 and 3."

"I don't understand their unity, their three-in-one personality," O'Hara said.

"It is strange," Ludendorff agreed. "But it produced fantastic results. It's no wonder Strand continued the experiment."

The grogginess departed O'Hara's face as she perked up. "What does that mean, Professor?"

"Nothing right now," he assured her. "It's time to begin." He glanced back at Maddox. "I believe the captain is itching to leave the Usan System. He wants this over and done with before we go."

O'Hara also looked at Maddox. The captain shuffled his feet as if feeling guilty. Oh, yes, Ludendorff realized. The captain must feel bad for keeping her under sedation all this time.

The professor cleared his throat.

O'Hara jerked her head back around, staring at him as fear billowed into her eyes.

"Relax, my dear," the professor said. "This should take but a moment."

In truth, he didn't know that. This was a test, a risk, a possibility. He wanted to practice on the brigadier so he would know what he was doing later on his darling Dana. His love was back, and she was in terrible condition. He desperately wanted to cure her of the obvious tampering the Bosks had done to her. He also needed to erase some evil memories from her mind. He wished Captain Nard were still alive so he could torture the dreadful ruffian.

Ludendorff inhaled through his nostrils, raised his hands, and with a sudden lunge, clamped them onto the white Builder stone.

He was ready for the process this time. He knew what to expect. Even more importantly, he was one hundred percent in charge of his mind now, with its improved qualities.

Actually, he was surprised the captain was allowing this. Repeated use of the stone should enlarge his intellect more each time. If he had one fear of doing this, it was that he would become so smart that he would no longer have anything in common with regular humans. He might literally turn into a super-genius thousands of years in evolutionary advance of modern man.

Would being the hyper-advanced super-genius be an even lonelier existence than previously? Should he allow himself such mastery of mind? What would happen to him?

Ludendorff grunted as the stone activated, beginning to heat up against his hands.

This time, the linkage between the stone and his brain's neurons happened faster and more smoothly. It was possible the stone was becoming used to him. That was both interesting and…hmmm…ominous?

He might want to practice a bit of caution today. This could all too easily be like the Sorcerer's Apprentice where he opened doors too wide to control. Yes. He would be cautious. Therefore, he began to block certain linkages.

It was like letting a small stream of raw energy into his mind instead of the raging torrent that was possible.

"Now," he whispered.

Maddox had moved forward. With shaking hands, the captain grabbed one of the brigadier's hands and set it against the Builder stone.

O'Hara screamed in a high, thin voice. It was a pitiful sound.

The stone reached out, using Wi-Fi-like connectives, linking her brain to it.

Ludendorff used that, mentally routing through the stone to join the brigadier.

"How is this possible?" the brigadier asked through direct mind transference. Her brain literally spoke through electronic synapses to the professor's brain.

"Listen closely, Brigadier," Ludendorff said, using the same procedure. "We have mere seconds to do this."

"Seconds?" O'Hara mentally asked.

"It won't seem that way, but it's really only a few seconds of time."

In those seconds, Ludendorff guided her thoughts. He did it gently. Together, they roved through her memories, finding the times the Draegar had mind-manipulated her and the times she went under the hypnotizer.

"I didn't realize," she mentally said.

"I know," the professor said directly into her mind. "Let's undo the damage, shall we?"

"Can we?"

"You can't," he said. "But I can if you'll let me. Will you let me?"

O'Hara hesitated.

"I can leave the mind manipulations in place, if you like," he told her.

"What will happen to me then?"

"I must report to the captain truthfully. You will have to resign your post, as you will be mentally compromised."

"Yes," O'Hara said. "I can see the logic of that. Yes!" she said, with determination. "Let's wipe my mind clean of their tampering."

Ludendorff struck instantly. He did not do anything nefarious to her mind. He simply rerouted the patterns overlaid upon her brain. He hated mental control upon himself. The brigadier was a friend. He thus hated the idea that Strand—through his tools—would control the brigadier of Star Watch Intelligence.

O'Hara moaned.

Ludendorff worked fast because he could. She followed in her mind, watching him, although she could not have watched everything.

Then, it was done. He'd cured her. But now, his mind was falling deeper into the Builder stone.

"Now," Ludendorff managed to croak.

It seemed to take forever, but Captain Maddox pressed a trigger and foam poured over the stone, cooling it and breaking certain mental linkages.

It was hard, but Ludendorff yanked the brigadier's mind free of the Wi-Fi-like connection even as he did the same for himself. He tore his hands from the hot stone, felt the foam cascading over him, and collapsed onto the deck, unconscious and exhausted from the ordeal.

-53-

The Spacer once known as Mako 21 waited in the life-pod drifting in the darkness of the Usan System.

She'd performed her duties to the letter, leading her command to slaughter. It hadn't particularly bothered her, as *she* had purpose for existing. She had been shown what awaited her, and it was glorious beyond reckoning.

Mako 21—called Surveyor Mako by other Spacers, all of them ignorant of her true calling—cautiously manipulated the control panel of her tiny capsule. According to the readings, the two Star Watch vessels were already accelerating toward two different points in the star system.

Seventeen lonely hours had passed since the end of the murderous space battle against Star Watch.

"No," Mako whispered to herself, as she realized with finality that the captain would not pick her up as he was supposed to have done. His failure to act within the accepted future was unexplainable and incalculable.

She'd sacrificed her ships, knowing that she would survive in the life-pod. Some of the saucer-shaped ships had also escaped, as foreseen. That had all been part of a process that would help bring the great Spacer dream to fruition. A curious Captain Maddox was to have rescued her, and she would have become a prisoner aboard *Victory*, traveling with them into the Deep Beyond…and the glory that awaited her there.

Yet, inconceivably, the two Star Watch vessels were going their separate ways and doing so without her. The battleship headed for a Laumer Point that would take it to Earth if it kept journeying in the same direction. The ancient Adok starship headed for a completely different Laumer Point that would take it into the Beyond. Clearly, *Victory* would travel to the nexus that the New Men had used these past few years, as the Xerxes System nexus no longer existed.

"Come back," Mako said pitifully. "You're supposed to do your part, Captain. You have...you have betrayed..."

Mako closed her eyes and pressed her forehead against the small control panel. She knew what must have happened to destroy fate. It was obvious, now that she thought about it. Captain Maddox was *di-far*. That meant he could lift destiny from the rails and set it on a new track.

Oh, this was awful.

By not picking her up, Maddox might have just destroyed everything she'd worked all her life to achieve. The leap into the dark, the joining with the multi-mind, the transformation into the "egg" she had become... Maddox had stolen all that from her by not picking her up. He'd foiled the great Spacer plan. He had—

No. Wait. That wasn't the *only* way.

Mako scrunched her petite brow. There was a secondary path. She'd never studied it in depth because... She remembered why now. It was a torturous path and fraught with peril for her, for Maddox and...and... Mako's brow scrunched even more as she remembered the few glimpses of the torturous alternate-future path she'd seen during her astral travel, within the union and the multi-mind entity.

Oh, this was going to get complicated. If she followed the secondary route...yes, she would still *use* Maddox, but he could possibly prove to be as slippery then as he had been today.

Mako was curious. What process had Maddox the *di-far* used that had allowed him to foil the more certain fate? Maybe figuring out *how* the *di-far* had been able to derail her optimal destiny this time would be as important as her transformation into...into—

Mako groaned as she raised her forehead from the panel. Even though there was the possible secondary path, she felt adrift. Seventeen hours ago, everything had been set. She'd known how events would proceed. But the Visionary and the multi-mind entity had forgotten what it meant that Captain Maddox was *di-far*. The Visionary had foreseen Maddox's power to perform his necessary deed. She had not been able to see that this very strength gave him the possibility of changing the Spacer future.

Yet, if events weren't foreordained as Mako had believed them to be...

"I must strive to achieve the great goal knowing that there is a possibility of losing," Mako whispered.

That was a daunting thought. She needed to gather strength.

Mako pushed off and floated across the tiny life-pod, coming to rest on the sole seat, reclining the back until it, and she, lay flat. She laid her hands across her diaphragm and practiced deep breathing as she composed herself. She thought about options. She—

Behind her goggles, Mako's blind eyes flew open. She sat up, pushed off and floated to the control panel. With practiced ease, her slender fingers roved over the controls, manipulating switches.

She cataloged *Victory*. She studied and stored information—Mako laughed once. It came out as more of a shriek, which was odd. The shrieking laugh wasn't caused by worry. Instead, as she studied the secondary way, she saw a path, a new method that could intercept the old pattern so events brought her to the same glorious future as previously envisioned. If she could make that happen, she too would have become *di-far*. She had choices, and her choices might yet lift fate off the rails and set it back onto the true path. That true path would be the great beginning of the Spacer Nation. It would bring about a glorious outpouring of—

Mako's head jerked back as a chronometer caught her attention.

Much more time had passed than she'd realized. The *Moltke* had vanished as it entered the Laumer Point near the Usan Star. Was Brigadier O'Hara on the *Bismarck*-class battleship? Earlier, when the two great vessels had been near each other, a shuttle had left *Victory*, gone to the *Moltke* and remained there.

In the life-pod, Mako shrugged. It didn't really matter where O'Hara was. *A curiosity, nothing more,* she mused dismissively.

That wisp of curiosity vanished as Mako scanned a tiny screen in her panel. A huge Nerva hauler was headed toward her. With a shock, she realized it was the *Sulla 7*. But…but the New Men had pirated the hauler from her. Why then would the *Sulla 7* come back to the Usan System, and how had it been able to do so without her seeing it come through a Laumer Point?

She must have been asleep when it had come through a jump gate. Yet, the New Men should have sent the hauler to the Bosk homeworld. Instead, it was here and heading toward her.

Mako scratched her head.

What *will* guided the ship toward her? What new player had entered the mix to change the equation even more? According to the Visionary, antimatter radiation had altered the Usan crystals and the varth elixir in the *Sulla 7's* cargo holds. That meant the crystals and elixir could no longer prove useful, didn't it?

The hours passed as Mako waited until the *Sulla 7* began to decelerate. Finally, the mighty vessel moved through the recent battle debris near her life-pod.

Starship *Victory* was no longer in the Usan System. Captain Maddox had left, heading toward his strange destiny. If a few events had changed, certainly the broad outline had not. Of course, it depended on what the *Sulla 7* might do now to destroy her future. If she could twist the hauler into her plans, Maddox would not like the fate awaiting him.

As Mako watched, an armored shuttle left one of the *Sulla's* hangar bays. What would this hidden one want from her? How could he or she know that Mako was so critically important as to send a mighty hauler to pick her up?

Mako nodded to herself as she realized this amazing truth. In this part of the Orion Arm, she had become the most important being in existence.

A new thought process began as the time passed. Captain Maddox would never have been able to trick Don Del Franco if fate hadn't already blinded the New Man. Del Franco hadn't understood that he'd faced more than Maddox, but also the undercurrents of the Spacer Nation as it sought the great prize. This was so because the new Visionary and multi-mind entity with their extraordinary power had been seeding possibilities and probabilities everywhere.

Mako checked again. The armored shuttle, more than one and a half times the size of a Star Watch shuttle, gently braked. Soon, it parked beside the life-pod, dwarfing it.

An underbelly port opened and a mechanical arm unfolded. Hook-like grippers clutched the life-pod, slowly drawing it to the armored shuttle. As that happened, the shuttle rotated. Finally, the arm drew the life-pod and Mako into the shuttle bay and the port closed. Exhaust fumes billowed as the vessel headed back toward the *Sulla 7*, picking up speed as it did so.

Shortly, the shuttle braked again and entered the hauler via the same hangar bay it had left. A massive bay door slid closed, sealing the shuttle inside. The hauler's mighty engines engaged and, majestically, the *Sulla 7* headed in the same direction that *Victory* had taken.

All the while, Mako waited within the life-pod, wondering who was going to greet her when its outer hatch opened.

-54-

Mako felt a gentle push against her right shoulder. She awoke with a start, having fallen asleep in her life-pod.

Despite her best efforts to probe the outer surroundings with her Spacer transduction modification, nothing had worked. That had astounded her until she'd found an intricate force field surrounding her pod like a bubble. At that point, she'd known that someone with Spacer understanding and tech had captured her. Instead of worrying endlessly, Mako had concentrated on survival and gone to sleep, conserving her energies.

Now, she had awakened with a start as a—she yelped in surprise. A robot gently pushed her right shoulder. She scrambled away from its touch and struck the robot with her transduction, finding the thing's controls and shutting it down.

The metal construct crashed onto the deck, its various lights going dark.

Galvanized into action, Mako stood, gingerly stepping over the thing. The life-pod had normal gravity. She lurched forward and passed through the open hatch, entering a small cargo bay with many strange machines surrounding her life-pod.

She tried to use transduction against them, and realized the machines generated the force field that had kept her mods at bay.

Walking faster, she physically pushed through the force field. Good. The field was only meant to keep out Spacer transduction, not a physical body.

A small cry of glee escaped her, but she refrained from running. Instead, she stopped and took stock of the situation, slowly scanning around.

A hatch to her left was open. Had the robot come through there? Mako headed in that direction.

Should she use her transduction to scan ahead? Mako decided against that. If her adversaries were aware of Spacer tech, they might be monitoring for that. Maybe it would be smartest to simply use her senses to assess the hauler.

Mako passed through the hatch into an empty corridor. Her stomach rumbled. She was hungry, but she ignored that. Her legs felt rubbery because she'd been trapped in the life-pod for too long. Shaking her head, refusing to let that bother her, she broke into a trot.

Soon enough, she reached another hatch, tried to manually open it, and found it locked. Now, she used her transduction, manipulating the interior energies. A lock clicked, and the hatch slid up.

Mako stepped through, and she stopped in shock. She had stepped onto a balcony overlooking a huge hangar bay. On the deck below were several Spacer saucer-shaped ships in special cradles fabricated to hold the bulbous centers.

Mako blinked in bewilderment. Spacer ships? Hadn't the New Men captured the *Sulla 7?* Why then were Spacer ships docked down there? Why weren't there vast quantities of Usan crystals?

Before Mako could use her mods to study the ships, she heard the scrape of shoes behind her.

"Impressive, eh?" a man asked.

Mako whirled around and squeaked in terror. A small, wizened man in black clothes regarded her. He had wrinkled features and jet black eyes that radiated menace. He wore a bronze pendant on his chest. It maintained a force field around him. He also gripped a pistol aimed at her.

"Strand?" she whispered.

"A clone merely," he said.

"But…"

"Yes, you killed me on Usan III, isn't that right?"

"Me?"

"You ordered me killed. I know that much."

Mako nodded woodenly. A Strand clone had come to Usan III. At her orders, a Spacer operative had slain the clone. Well, the operative had reported to her that he'd completed the mission.

"The operative lied to me," Mako said, understanding what must have happened.

"Yes," the clone said.

"How did he…? Why did…? I don't understand."

The Strand clone chuckled nastily. "You will understand eventually. Now," he said, waving the small pistol, "move along. It's time you woke up to reality."

Mako frowned more deeply. "Maddox found a dead Strand clone in the desert with two varths waiting for him."

"That wasn't me, of course," the clone said. "It was a simulacrum of me, good enough to fool the half-breed."

Mako rubbed her forehead. "How can you be here? Why did my operative lie to me? Did you brainwash the operative?"

"Dear girl," the clone said. "You will move along. You'll have all your answers in a moment. It is going to surprise you, believe you me."

Mako swallowed and she felt faint. She hadn't foreseen Strand in any of her futures. Did that mean she no longer had a path, or was Strand able to hide himself in the future paths that Spacers could travel?

She didn't see how that could be possible.

Numbly, Mako passed the clone of a Methuselah Man and walked down a long and empty corridor.

"Tell me this," she said once.

"No talking," the clone said. "This is a surprise. It's going to help you."

"Why would a Methuselah Man help a Spacer?" she asked.

"That's a good question. It's a…" Strand fell silent.

Mako looked back over her shoulder. The clone seemed troubled. That made no sense.

"What's going on here?" she asked.

"Shut up," he said in an ugly tone. "Just do as you're told, you stupid wench. Can't you get anything right?"

Mako's lips firmed as she decided to remain silent. Time passed as they marched. She grew faint as her stomach rumbled.

"It's not much farther," the clone said, sounding like himself again.

Finally, the clone directed her to a hatch. Mako steeled herself and headed toward it. Something blocked her transduction from scanning what lay beyond the entrance.

The hatch slid up. She went through, and a provost marshal clicked a device while other marshals grabbed her, yanking her to the side. Then, yet more provost marshals grabbed the clone. Apparently, the marshal clicking the device had shut down the clone's pendant-generated force field. A different marshal ripped the pistol out of Strand's hand.

"You could have just asked for it," the clone complained.

Mako couldn't believe this. Spacers were in charge of the hauler—or had Spacers invaded the Nerva ship while Strand had gloated over her?

"Mako," a familiar voice said. "Do close your mouth. It's time for the next step in your training."

Mako looked around, but couldn't see who had said that.

Then, an entire bulkhead slid up. Behind it sat the new Visionary on a great white throne. She wore a polar bear fur and gripped a staff with a sparkling gem on the end. Around the throne were armed provost marshals with drawn guns. Everyone wore the customary Spacer goggles.

"Visionary?" Mako asked.

"It is I," the Visionary said lightly.

Mako turned to Strand. The small clone was in the grip of two provost marshals. The Strand clone seemed quite unhappy about it.

The Visionary chuckled. "Yes, you're amazed. But enough of that. It's time for you to learn a secret, dear one. Come, Mako, come and sit down at the foot of my throne. I'm going to tell you what happens from here."

-55-

Starship *Victory* hurtled through the Beyond, using Laumer Points and the star drive when it helped expedite matters. The navigators used star charts gained throughout the years by Patrol surveys, with the professor filling in the blank spaces.

Brigadier O'Hara had left some time ago, joining Commodore Tancred on the *Moltke* when it had headed out of the Usan System.

Ludendorff had healed from the second ordeal with the Builder stone. He'd wanted to free Dana from her mind conditioning, but Maddox had told the Methuselah Man to wait for several days. The professor had argued until the captain had become insistent.

"Give me one good reason why I should wait," Ludendorff demanded as they argued in an observation bubble.

"I watched you during the brigadier's therapy," Maddox said. "While using the stone you turned unbelievably pale, whiter than I've seen anyone become. And there was something about you then that troubled me."

"Please be more specific," Ludendorff said icily.

Maddox nodded. "You didn't quite seem human anymore."

"What?"

"Professor, I've seen beings change. Last voyage…" Maddox shook his head. "It is a terrifying thing you're doing. You're linking your mind to an ancient Builder tool. How can you be certain the tool isn't changing you as you use it?"

"Don't be foolish," Ludendorff said. "I'm in total control of the situation."

"Ah. I see. That's why I have to spray you with foam each time. That's why we have to pry you from the linkage. Because you can disengage from it any time you want."

Instead of becoming angry, the professor became thoughtful. "You may have a point," he finally said.

Maddox raised his eyebrows. That did not sound like the Ludendorff he knew.

"What's wrong now?" Ludendorff asked.

"Your reasonableness," Maddox said.

"Are you trying to insult me?"

"The opposite," Maddox said. "This is visible proof that you're changing. We'd better think long and hard before you risk the stone again. You don't want to transform into an alien entity."

Ludendorff blinked repeatedly, finally sitting down in a chair. "Do you have any water?"

Maddox went to a small bar, grabbed something and pitched the professor a water bottle.

The professor unscrewed the top and guzzled the contents, gasping afterward. "Yes. I see what you mean. We've run across strange things in our journeys. We've seen Swarm viruses and a Builder device controlling a Destroyer. Maybe the linkage *is* a subtle trap. It's hard to fathom that because I feel so much stronger and in charge of myself. Yet, I've already wondered if I might become too intelligent with repeated uses."

Maddox said nothing.

"In such a case, I would develop beyond humanity. I would transcend normality and become… I don't know what I would become. I'm not sure I'm ready to evolve into something else. I like myself just as I am. No. This could be a sweetened trap as you've suggested. Who doesn't want to become even smarter and wiser, knowing more and more?"

"What will we do with Dana then?" Maddox said.

"You're asking me?"

"Professor, I've never found you to be this reasonable. I would like to reward it, encourage it. Yes. I want to restore

Dana. Surely, with your heightened intellect, you can come up with another method of restoration."

"Hmm…" Ludendorff said, as he drummed his fingers on a side desk. "I think Draegar 2 might have a better idea."

"I'm sure of that," Maddox agreed. "How do we get Draegar 2 to talk, if he can talk?"

"If I could link with his mind—no, I've already rejected that route. This is harder than I realized. By linking with the Builder stone, I can solve many complicated problems. Yet, if I link up with it, the thing may subtly change me until I'm something different."

"We have to get the Draegar to communicate with us," Maddox said. "Wasn't one of his functions to figure out more regarding nexuses?"

"I suppose that's true," Ludendorff said. "Now, Captain, let's change tracks for a moment. We're heading for the New Man nexus. We should arrive there in a week. It's the only local nexus whose location I know. Unfortunately, there might be star cruisers guarding it. What do we do in that instance?"

"I haven't decided yet. It will depend upon if it's a Throne World star cruiser or one of Lord Drakos's groups."

"Let's consider a hostile group first."

"In that case, it would depend on how many star cruisers are blocking our path," Maddox said.

"Surely, you've come up with contingency plans."

Maddox shook his head.

"Hmm…" the professor said. "The New Man nexus, for lack of a better term, isn't like the Xerxes System's nexus. That was a haunted star system. This one is devoid of any unusual structures or legends."

"Or anything that might drive you to distraction?" asked Maddox.

Ludendorff waved that aside. "I'm not the same as I was in those days. Remember, the old compulsions were still buried in me then. Now, I am my own Methuselah Man."

Maddox turned sharply to peer at Ludendorff.

"Did I say something foolish?" the professor asked.

"Strand likely has deep compulsions."

"I suppose that's true. What's your point?"

"Could those ancient compulsions have driven you two into your...traitorous acts?"

"Hardly traitorous—" Ludendorff shook his head as he stopped speaking "That's an interesting speculation, my boy. I don't know. I'll have to think about that. Whatever the case, we have to ready ourselves for the worst. Once we use the nexus, the hyper-spatial tube will launch us far into the Deep Beyond. It will be like last time we went out there. The pressures of the Deep Beyond will mount. Can your current crew take it as well as the crew that went deep before?"

"We'll make it work."

"You're missing my point," Ludendorff said. "We have a week to prepare. A week to save Dana. A week to make Draegar 2 talk or to find a way to communicate with him. We—and you as the captain—should do everything in our power to ready the crew to excel in the Deep Beyond as we face... What are we going to face? I suspect we will face new dangers, marvelous and deadly beyond anything we've seen so far."

"Maybe we'll face three hundred thousand Swarm vessels guarding a nexus," Maddox said.

"That's a real possibility we shouldn't discount."

Maddox nodded solemnly. "You raise excellent points. I'll have to call a meeting and light a fire under my chief people. You're right. This is a time to get ready. Once we're in it... The Deep Beyond...it was a terrifying journey last time we went out so far."

"I think we're a stronger ship than before," Ludendorff said. "I'm stronger. You're more humane. The others have faced perilous tests. This time...the Swarm Imperium, we're going to take on one of the strongest, if not the strongest, political entity in our galaxy. That's food for thought, eh? *Victory* truly is a one-of-a-kind vessel to attempt this."

"Right," Maddox said. "We need Dana. So, before we part and get started on our separate tasks, let's decide on a preliminary way to begin to restore the doctor the hard way. If we can find a better way, well and good, but maybe we're just going to have to muddle through this. What do you suggest, Professor?"

Ludendorff gave it serious thought. Then, he began to tell the captain what they should do.

-56-

The week racing through Laumer Points and jumping with the star drive propelled the ancient Adok starship through the near Beyond and into what Patrol people called the mid Beyond.

Ludendorff did not give the navigators the Throne World System's position. Instead, he gave them enough data so *Victory* unknowingly skirted around the fabled system as it headed farther out to the waiting nexus.

They traveled inward along the Orion Spiral Arm, meaning that if they continued in this direction over time—a long, long time—they would reach the galactic core.

Twice, Valerie detected star cruisers in the distance.

Each time, Maddox ordered evasive maneuvers.

Not once did the star cruisers attempt to chase or hail them.

"Are they under orders to ignore us, do you suppose?" Valerie asked the captain on the bridge.

"What about that, Professor?" Maddox asked.

"Their behavior was strange to be sure," Ludendorff agreed. "This deep into the Beyond…I would have thought the New Men would challenge our presence. Perhaps the latest Swarm attack has caused them to change their protocols. Yes. That is undoubtedly the answer."

They continued to race through mid-Beyond star systems.

During the seven days of endless jumping, the professor worked with Dana and a psych team. She was under constant watch and evaluation.

"It's difficult not using the stone," Ludendorff admitted to Maddox one day. "I believe I could cure her like that."

The professor snapped his fingers.

Maddox continued to counsel patience, and reluctantly, the professor agreed.

They had no more luck with Draegar 2. The bronze-skinned Bosk spent his time in silent contemplation, often staring at a bulkhead or restlessly playing chess against himself.

At the professor's suggestion, they gave the Bosk access to online books. Draegar 2 read voraciously, devouring thick volumes in a matter of hours.

One evening ship-time on the fifth day from the Usan System, Maddox and Ludendorff studied a video of Draegar 2 hunched over a reading screen, flipping a page every few seconds.

"You're telling me he's ingesting the text's meaning, reading like that?" Maddox asked.

"Absolutely," Ludendorff said.

"What's his IQ?"

"I'm beginning to wonder if it's higher than mine."

Maddox did a double take.

"Believe me," Ludendorff muttered, "I'm also astounded at the idea."

"Forgive me, Professor, but I'm more astounded that you would admit to such a thing. It's out of character."

Ludendorff frowned as he side-glanced at Maddox. "Are you attempting to goad me?"

"No. I'm…surprised. Draegar 2 is truly smarter than you even after your using of the Builder stone?"

"That does seem preposterous the more I consider the idea," Ludendorff said. "Yet, I cannot read like that. And yet…you defeated the combined Draegar. He can't be *that* intelligent then. But…he soundly tricked me." The professor shook his head. "I don't know what to suggest. The only way we can link with him—"

"Out of the question," Maddox said.

"You didn't even hear my idea."

"I don't have to. You want to mind meld with Draegar 2 using the Builder stone. That would be insanely dangerous."

"Nonsense," Ludendorff said. "Look how we restored the brigadier."

"O'Hara wasn't your mental superior," Maddox said.

Ludendorff blushed. "Now see here, Captain. I'm not going to submit to this badgering. We must study his reading list."

"Galyan," Maddox said.

The holoimage popped beside them as the two men faced a computer screen.

"Have you analyzed Draegar 2's reading list?" Maddox asked.

"Yes, Captain," Galyan said. "The list is fifteen percent stellar data, fifteen percent medical with a high concentration on human anatomy, twenty-five percent on ancient galactic legends, fifteen percent on android, bionic processes and thirty percent on robotics of all forms."

"What does that suggest to you?" Maddox asked Galyan.

"I have insufficient data to guess," Galyan said.

Maddox hid his surprise. He had an idea, a sinister one in which Draegar 2 helped fashion an android alien. "Professor?" he asked.

"I'm not sure," Ludendorff said, giving the captain another side-glance. "You're hinting at something."

Maddox nodded. "I don't trust the Builder stone. I wonder if it's more than an intelligence enhancer."

"What do you think it is?" Ludendorff asked.

"A Builder's brain-core perhaps," Maddox said, as he watched Ludendorff closely.

The professor noticed the scrutiny and finally nodded. "Yes. Your last voyage would undoubtedly cause you to suspect such a thing. I learned about your last mission through my own channels. You're wondering if the Builder stone will try to fashion a new body and insert itself into the thing's braincase."

"The thought has crossed my mind," Maddox said.

"What else?" Ludendorff asked. "Clearly, you suspect more."

"I do," Maddox said. "I wonder if the Builder core has ever truly shut down. Maybe it's still linked to you, and linked now to Draegar 2. It's using his mind and eyes to read data on what it wants to know."

"What a wonderful imagination you have, Captain," Ludendorff said. "But I have a question. If what you suspect is true, wouldn't the stone have infiltrated Galyan and possibly already gained control of the ship?"

"Possibly," Maddox said.

"Is that why you're wearing my force-field pendant and keeping a Draegar pistol ready? Will you shoot me to save your ship?"

Maddox did not respond.

"I hate to disappoint you," Ludendorff said. "But I am very much in charge of myself. The Builder amplifier is exactly that. It is not a secret Builder brain-core or a storage unit that can insert a Builder personality into a machine man. You have led yourself down a false trail."

"Have I really?" Maddox asked.

"Draegar 2 is an evolutionary marvel, upgraded, no doubt, by Strand's genius. My recognition of his genius does nothing to belittle my own achievements. Whether you believe it or not, the process with the Builder stone helped erase a few…malfunctions that had crept into my personality over time. I truly freed the brigadier. I think the only way I'm going to free Dana is by using the stone."

"Suppose you're right. Suppose you use the stone on Draegar 2 next, and he proves more cunning than you suspect."

"You mean Draegar 2 twists the stone's process and somehow gains mastery over me?" the professor asked.

"Exactly," Maddox said.

Ludendorff studied the Bosk on the screen. The professor bit his lower lip. "I cannot fathom such a thing. Yet, as I watch him read, I marvel at how quickly he absorbs information. It shows a leap in human intelligence."

"Could this Draegar have been smarter than his two brothers?" Maddox asked.

"I suspect only Strand could tell you that."

"Galyan?" Maddox asked.

"The professor is telling the truth," the holoimage said, "at least as he conceives of the truth."

"Here, now," Ludendorff said, looking at Galyan and Maddox in turn. "What's this? What is the AI saying? No, no, don't tell me. It's obvious. He was monitoring me, acting like a living lie detector."

"That is correct," Galyan said.

Ludendorff eyed Maddox. "You really are a suspicious man, aren't you? You don't trust anyone."

"I had to be sure," Maddox said.

Ludendorff made a face before turning thoughtful. "Well, I suppose the man who would draw a gun on his superior officer and hold her hostage while he interrogates me would also pull this kind of trick. I can't say I approve. But, given the nature of our task, I'll let it pass. Do you finally trust me then?"

"Yes," Maddox said.

Ludendorff laughed. "You only say yes to try to put me at ease. We are a pair of scoundrels, Captain. Maybe we're just the thing humanity needs to save it from the Swarm."

The professor glanced at Draegar 2 on the screen before regarding Maddox. "Is there anything else, then?"

"As a matter of fact," Maddox said. "There is."

"Well…?"

"I do want you to use the stone again."

"Eh?"

"On Tars Womack," Maddox said. "I've been thinking about what you said concerning contingency plans regarding the New Man nexus. We've questioned Womack extensively, and he's proven highly resistant to regular Star Watch methods. For a while, I thought he would come around, as someone had conditioned his mind—Lord Drakos, possibly—and that seemed to anger Womack. I've since come to believe that that was false, fakery on Womack's part. He's tried hard to pit you and me against each other. He's hiding something critical, possibly about the nexus or maybe about our hidden foe. At the very least, a powerful mind scan with the stone could let us know what to expect at the nexus so we can prepare accordingly."

"If we're going to use the stone one more time," Ludendorff said. "I'd rather save Dana."

"There will be plenty of time to save Dana," Maddox said, "providing we can destroy the Swarm nexuses. If we can't destroy them, saving her isn't going to matter."

Ludendorff scowled as he rubbed his throat. "There's a risk to me using the stone again."

"Granted," Maddox said.

"You're unconcerned with risking my brain, are you?"

"No, as we'll need your brilliance to win. But if we can never get there to get started, none of that is going to matter."

Ludendorff exhaled. "I hate your bottom-line thinking. It's hard to argue against, though. Very well. I'll agree to this. Tars Womack is our next target."

-57-

Thirty-one hours later, even after Maddox explained the direness of the situation, Tars Womack protested against any form of mind probing.

The captain understood that the New Man would not allow himself to be intimidated into freely giving them vital information. Thus, they moved on to the original option.

Soon, marines in power armor struggled against the thrashing prisoner as they set him onto a table with metal bands for his ankles and wrists. Tars Womack's muscles stood up in stark relief as he grunted and growled. Finally, the exoskeleton-powered suits won out, the manacles snapping into place. The Dominant immediately went limp, no longer struggling but breathing like a bellows as sweat poured from his golden skin. Every muscle seemed to relax as he closed his eyes, no doubt planning his next move.

The chamber stank of exertion. It held the table, with medical monitors arrayed around it. A stand to the side carried the white polygonal Builder stone.

Maddox had watched the Builder artifact throughout the proceedings. He still didn't trust that it wasn't an incubator for a long-lost Builder mind. Galyan monitored the thing's temperature. The AI would tell of him of the slightest change. Even so, the captain stepped up and gave the stone a quick touch. He did not feel any shock or connection with it. The stone also felt the same temperature as the last time he'd done this.

One thing did happen, however. Womack's eyes flew open as he examined Maddox.

"You're making a mistake," Womack said, his breathing already under control.

"You've had plenty of time to talk," Maddox replied. "You only have yourself to thank for the treatment."

"I'm not an animal."

"Neither am I," Maddox said.

Womack appeared puzzled. "I never said you were an animal."

Maddox ignored that, as he added, "Neither were all those women animals, the ones you kidnapped during the Throne World invasion of "C" Quadrant."

"What do they have to do with anything?"

"You kidnapped hundreds of thousands of young, Commonwealth women, taking them into the Beyond, no doubt to your breeding stations, forcing them to mate with you."

"Breeding with us is an honor."

"Is it?" Maddox said, unable to conceal his anger.

From the table, Womack reexamined the captain. At first, the New Man appeared puzzled by the emotion. Then, understanding lit in his dark eyes. Finally, malice tinged with cunning ignited there.

"Your so-called calm is actually emotional armor," Womack said, much as a psychologist might. "It shields you from hard truths. This apparent disgust at our methods is a sham, a clear sham. I know why you need it—in order to hold on to a pristine sexual view of your mother."

Maddox's eyes narrowed.

Womack tested his manacles, finding them solid. He contemplated a moment before sneering at Maddox. "Before the mission, I was privy to your Intelligence file. It held interesting data, to be sure. I happened to notice an addendum, a file about your mother. It turns out she was something of a whore, enjoying the sexual congress at the breeding facility to an intense degree, begging for others to mount her so she could feel continued orgasms."

The words hit Maddox like repeated shocks in his brain. Finally, rage welled up in him, although he held himself perfectly still.

Womack laughed harshly, no doubt noting the effect.

The noise acted as a lash against Maddox, making him twitch. Still, another, utterly analytical part of him wondered about something else. If this New Man Intelligence file held an addendum about his mother, might there have been a second addendum about his unknown father?

The analytical part in Maddox wondered how to tease such data from Womack. The emotional half assured him that if Womack lied about his mother, the New Man would also lie about his father.

"It's difficult to accept harsh realities," Womack was saying, almost sounding conciliatory. "Hmm... Maybe this will help. Her file was color-coded. By the colors, I discovered that many of the old guard bred your mother because she strove so hard to please each one of them."

Maddox angrily stepped toward Womack as his rational half strove to master his rage. He even analyzed the words. *Many of the old guard*—that indicated Womack had no idea of their identities. The New Man merely knew that Maddox loved his mother and that taunts could irrationally prick him. As a Star Watch Intelligence officer, he recognized the ironclad logic of his analysis. As a son, he yearned to know his father's—

Maddox halted. What was Womack hoping to achieve by this? The New Man knew himself fatally trapped. Surely, Womack recognized the Builder stone as an alien device. Could the New Man desire a quick death in order to conceal any critical hidden knowledge he held?

"In fact..." Womack said slyly.

Like a strongman struggling to heft a heavy weight over his head, Maddox heaved it up with a final surge of willpower. He mastered his rage, locking it behind an icy resolve.

The captain smiled coldly at Womack. As he did, the logic of the situation strengthened his resolve. That put a hint of superiority into his smile.

Incredibly, that reversed the polarity of the psychological attack, acting like a slap to Tars Womack's inner identity.

"No!" the New Man said. "You're inferior to me."

"Clearly that's the case," Maddox said. "Indeed, that's why you're *my* prisoner and not the other way around."

"Luck proves nothing," Womack said.

"Ah, proverbial luck," Maddox said.

Before the captain could continue, the hatch slid up and Ludendorff entered the chamber. The Methuselah Man cocked an eyebrow at the scene but continued to saunter toward the stone without speaking.

The two armored marines had moved to the back wall, their motors purring as they maintained a careful watch over the bound New Man.

Once reaching the stone, Ludendorff halted and turned to Maddox. "There's a problem. How are you going to push his hand against the stone? He's likely too strong for any of us except the marines with their armor. I'm not sure what will happen to a marine if he's touching Womack's skin while the New Man touches the stone."

"Problem solved," Maddox said. "We'll set the stone—*you'll* set the stone on Womack's bare stomach."

"It's a heavy stone," Ludendorff said.

"Womack has powerful abs," Maddox said, as he glanced at the New Man.

"True," Ludendorff said. "But is that really the reason for putting it on his stomach? Are you, in fact, indulging in cruelty?"

"He spoke badly about my…" Maddox trailed off before he said more.

Womack's self-assurance had returned as he barked a harsh laugh. "If you must know, I spoke badly about his whorish mother. It wilts the brave captain to hear that I spit on her foul memory. If he were a real man, he would remove the insult by fighting me hand to hand."

"I see," Ludendorff said. "This is my counsel, Captain. Ignore him."

"Don't worry about me," Maddox said.

"My boy—"

"You know what was the most interesting thing of all?" Womack asked, interrupting. "The threesomes and even the foursomes—"

The captain's icy control vanished as he shouted, stepped forward, drawing a Draegar pistol and shoving the barrel against Womack's forehead.

The New Man's eyes gleamed.

Ludendorff opened his mouth, but said nothing. Slowly, he closed his mouth, waiting.

Maddox's gun hand shook as his trigger finger tightened. He understood what Womack was doing. He understood and yet he'd always hated what the arrogant supermen had done to his mother. The idea that she had gone to a breeding facility like millions of other women—

At the last second, Maddox eased tension from the trigger. If he gave in to murderous rage, he would do so again, and again, and again. Soon, he would no longer be Captain Maddox, the best Intelligence officer in Star Watch. Yes. Emotions were imperative, doubly so if under the control of an iron will. As an unchecked source, wild emotions would lead him into a lifetime of increasing misery.

As if at a firing range, Maddox holstered the Draegar palm-pistol.

A deep red mark showed on Womack's forehead. The New Man closed his eyes, perhaps uncertain at the end if he'd truly wanted to die.

Maddox breathed deeply, silently counting to ten.

"Let's get started," the captain said quietly.

"You're still sure about this?" asked Ludendorff.

Maddox didn't say a word, although he nodded.

"Very well," the professor said. "But be ready for highly unusual results. One can never be sure with a New Man."

-58-

Ludendorff began the process much like before. He touched the polygonal Builder stone and felt the connection faster than ever. He had become tuned to the stone and his mind slid into the neural connections as if he did this every day.

He rethought the captain's suspicions of a day ago about the stone holding a sleeping Builder intellect. With greater awareness, the professor studied the ancient object. He could well understand why the captain suspected such a thing, but Ludendorff soon saw that this couldn't be the case here for several reasons. For one thing, there was nothing biological about the stone. For another, there weren't even mechanical processes that imitated some of the processes the last Builders had used.

That was a relief, as Ludendorff didn't want a repeat of what had happened aboard *Victory* last voyage.

Now, using the stone and understanding his own body better than ever, Ludendorff began an interior chemical process that gave him greater strength. With it, he hefted the stone with both hands. The rock was becoming warmer, but he still had a full half-minute before the stone began to cook his palms.

"No!" Womack shouted from the table. "Don't let it touch me. This is evil. You are evil. You helped make us. Why, then, are you doing this to me?"

Ludendorff ignored the words, placing the stone beside the squirming New Man and pushing the rock against Womack's bare right arm.

The stone touched Womack's skin. The New Man arched back and howled as he attempted to thrash away from the contact.

Ludendorff understood the artifact so much better now. He mentally moved with lightning speed, as Womack's superior brain neurons had already linked to the amazing Builder stone. The Methuselah Man froze the New Man, and he struck with his mind, probing Womack's memories, striving to understand if the New Man knew what would be waiting for them at the nexus.

After a moment of horror, Womack fought back like a savage beast trying to tear its leg free of a sprung trap. Ludendorff almost felt sympathy for him.

Then, because the professor couldn't help it, he probed the memories about what Womack had done to him at Tau Ceti and even earlier at the Bosk homeworld. The scenes flooded back with flickering speed. Womack had been in charge of the 'Trick the Professor Operation.' Ludendorff saw how Draegar 1, 2 and 3 had invaded and twisted his mind. Reliving the process through Womack's memories angered Ludendorff. Seeing himself a prisoner, much as the New Man was a prisoner here—

"No," the professor wheezed.

"Yes," Womack hissed, and in that moment, he attempted to use the stone and turn the process against the professor.

The two struggled for supremacy, using the Builder stone as a battlefield. Mind was pitted against mind. One was old and cunning. The other was young and strong with a belief in himself and his superior people's destiny.

It was as if they lay cheek to jowl, their foul breaths fogging over each other's face. They pitted mind against mind, will against will and energy against energy. Like two giant snakes entwined and tightening one against the other, each trying to choke his foe to death, Ludendorff and Womack mentally warred.

The Methuselah Man knew more about the stone's processes, having used it longer. The New Man had fantastic iron will, a desire to win that was almost beyond Ludendorff's understanding. Womack had grown up in a fiercely competitive society. Winning was all. Losing meant intense shame. In that society, Womack had gained high rank. He was just under Lord Drakos in authority.

"You ran the deception against me," Ludendorff said in their mind-to-mind contact.

"I am the leader. Yes. I made the decisions. I will yet defeat you, old man."

"Did Drakos send you to the Bosk homeworld or was that Strand's order?"

"Defend yourself," Womack hissed.

For a time, Ludendorff did exactly that. He studied the New Man's tactics and methods, saw how Womack liked to strike suddenly and pile all his strength into the second blow, using the first as a deception.

"Knowing that won't help you," Womack hissed.

"Perhaps," Ludendorff said.

Finally, the New Man's intense mental assault slackened as Womack assessed what to do next.

"Was Strand in charge of the operation?" Ludendorff asked.

"Strand is a prisoner, old man."

"I recognize that. Yet, Strand spoke with Drakos on the Throne World. Who uses whom?"

Womack laughed. "You're too foolish to know the answer. You're too old fashioned to recognize true brilliance when you see it."

Ludendorff heard Strand in those words, and it made him certain that Methuselah Man Strand had tricked Lord Drakos in some nefarious fashion.

"But that's just what I want you to think, old man," Womack said.

"Are there more Strand clones around?" Ludendorff asked.

"Maybe there are Ludendorff clones. Did you ever think of that?"

Finally, the Methuselah Man struck as the words prodded him into action. If Strand or Lord Drakos had fashioned Ludendorff clones, he would make them suffer for an eternity. He was Ludendorff. He was one, himself. He did not want Ludendorff clones in the world. He would rather have sons and daughters made the old-fashioned way through loving and lying with a woman.

"You truly are stuck in the past, old man," Womack said. "I can see your thoughts. You're pathetic."

"I am old indeed," Ludendorff mentally said, striving now with fierce will. He'd lived for centuries, guiding and helping ungrateful humanity. Once, Strand had been his partner. They had done so much together. Then, a sickness of mind had invaded his brother's mind.

"Brother?" Womack asked.

Ludendorff struck, using all his cunning, all the mastery of the stone gained from the last two times—

Womack's defenses fell with bewildering speed. Like a proverbial house of cards blown by the wind, they toppled and fluttered in the mind-to-mind contest.

Too late, Ludendorff realized that something in Womack's mind had pricked him into this fierce assault. At the same instant, a hidden control in Womack caused the New Man to utterly drop his mental defenses, exposing himself to annihilation.

Ludendorff tore apart enemy brain cells and neural connectives. With all his might, the professor reversed course and strove to repair the damage and return the memories as they dribbled from the dying New Man's mind.

"I tricked you, old man," Womack mentally jeered. "You lose yet again."

"Someone is using you," Ludendorff said, desperately trying to keep Womack alive. "Help me against them. Give me a clue as to who wants you dead."

"A clue?"

"You're almost gone, Tars Womack. Who has used you like this and made you his pawn?"

A thought began in Womack's mind, and something controlling in the mind killed the memory even as it began to take shape.

At that moment, Ludendorff released Womack's mind, lest he be caught in the death throes and begin a chain reaction process in his own mind. The Builder stone did have a tricky property. It could heighten certain thoughts, amplifying them with dreadful power. Thus, in dying, a dying man's mind could pull down his linked foe with him, causing the other brain to kill itself in mimicry of the real death.

"Help," Ludendorff managed to say.

It was barely enough, but it was enough. Cool foam hit the Builder stone, and that allowed Ludendorff the advantage he needed to once more make his escape from the ancient marvel.

-59-

Maddox paced back and forth, as medics worked to revive the newly dead Tars Womack.

The New Man's body jerked at times, his arms flopping. The zapping electrode sounds were hideous…and ineffective. Finally, the chief medical officer stepped back from the body on the table, and shook his head.

"Dead for good?" asked Maddox.

"Yes, sir," the medical officer said.

Maddox clenched his jaws so the muscles hinging them bulged outward. The captain merely nodded afterward, moving away.

Why was everyone dying on them?

"Sir?"

Maddox whirled around, reaching for his holstered sidearm.

Galyan dipped his head. "I did it again. I'm sorry, sir. I should have cleared my throat first before just—"

"What is it?" Maddox said.

"The professor is groggy, but he's awake. He's asking for you."

Maddox nodded sharply to indicate he'd heard the words. Then his long legs ate up the distance as he exited the chamber and strode to Ludendorff's cubicle. Medics had rushed the Methuselah Man there ten minutes ago.

Ludendorff was sitting up, rubbing the back of his neck. Meta stood nearby, holding a cup of water for him.

"Thank you," Ludendorff told her.

Meta and Maddox exchanged glances as the professor noisily slurped his water.

"How's Dana doing?" Maddox asked quietly. He figured that was what Meta wanted him to ask.

"You're pushing the professor too hard," Meta whispered. "Look at him. He's like death warmed over."

Ludendorff did look bad, his face a mass of wrinkles, baggy eyes and sheer exhaustion.

"How's Dana?" Maddox whispered again.

Meta shook her head. "She's in bad shape. I've never—you should let him use the stone on her. Nothing else is going to work."

Maddox let his features fall into a blank mask. Maybe Meta was right. Maybe Ludendorff should fix his woman before the stone destroyed the Methuselah Man. But maybe his first idea had been right. If they won, Ludendorff could fix his lover then.

"That was an interesting experience," Ludendorff said, as he set the cup down.

The captain faced the old man.

"You should rest, Professor," Meta said.

"I will, my dear. First, your husband wants his report."

"Surely, that can wait," Meta said.

Both Meta and Ludendorff looked at Maddox.

"A quick rundown is all I want," Maddox said. "Why did Womack die?"

The professor winced as if someone had punched him in the gut. "That wasn't by design, well, by my design."

"Meaning?" asked Maddox.

With halting words, Ludendorff told them what had happened during the mental connection, how Womack or something in Womack had tricked him. The New Men had wanted to die at the end to conceal something.

Maddox was nodding before the Methuselah Man had finished speaking. "Then we're right back where we started, knowing nothing."

"I don't agree with that," Ludendorff said.

Maddox waited for the professor to expound on the idea.

"Right there at the end, I saw our nemesis, a memory picture," Ludendorff said. "He was tall for a man, but short for a New Man, and his skin tone wasn't as golden as it could be."

"Lord Drakos?" asked Maddox.

"None other, my boy, it was the Devil himself."

"Does that tell us if Drakos issued the orders or if Strand is using Drakos to issue the orders?"

"Through Womack's memories, I saw some of the operations on the Bosk homeworld and on the Tau Ceti station. I witnessed…hmm, certain *crudities* of approach that Strand would never have ordered or tolerated."

"That tells us nothing," Maddox said. "Drakos simply could have made mistakes in the translation of Strand's orders."

"No, you're wrong, as the crudities concerned the Draegar and me. Womack oversaw much of the process. He…seemed to fumble at times, which confused the Draegar. If Strand had given commands regarding the Draegar and me, he would have been quite precise. Rather, I saw an operation being run by a man who had half knowledge and was smart enough to guess many of the other components but not all of them."

"Meaning what?" asked Maddox. "You're just saying what I did, but in a different way."

"No. I most certainly am not. Perhaps you can't understand the differences. They're subtle. Strand would have insisted Drakos get key matters correct, as he would know their importance. But if Drakos had pried information from Strand, the New Man would undoubtedly miss a few key factors because the Methuselah Man would do everything in his power to hold something critical back to screw the man screwing him. *How* Drakos achieved this prying, I do not know. From Womack's memories, I received the impression of a man trying to revive a system he only half-understood. If you think about it," Ludendorff added, "it makes better sense considering what we've been seeing."

"For instance?" asked Maddox, still dubious about the professor's point.

"Why didn't Womack or the Draegar attempt to use the Builder stone when it was theoretically in their possession?"

"When they ran the Star Watch flotilla through you, you mean?"

"Exactly," Ludendorff said. "Why not have me take the Builder object from the *Moltke* and bring it to the *Bernard Shaw?*"

"They had you ask for the stone. That's why O'Hara talked the Lord High Admiral into releasing the artifact into her custody."

"True," Ludendorff said, "but that proves my point. They didn't know *why* they asked for it. They had learned they needed the object, but not the deep reason for it."

Maddox finally nodded. Maybe the professor was onto something. "Let's run with this," the captain said. "Tell me why they went to such lengths to try to capture *Victory*."

"I have a theory, no more."

Maddox waited for it.

"I'm beginning to believe that they combined two or even three planned *future* missions into one," Ludendorff said. "This fits with my idea that Drakos stole or forced the information from Strand. The Methuselah Man revealed his greater strategy. But instead of Drakos seeing that Strand had a step-by-step plan, that there were distinct stages that needed to be achieved before they tried more, Drakos attempted to do everything in one giant mission. For instance, I suspect Strand did not desire or need *Victory* to attempt Swarm nexus destruction. He had the Q-ships for that. Strand's plan for you, *Victory* and the brigadier would be to help him infiltrate his agents into Star Watch."

Meta, who had been listening, laughed with disbelief. "I get it. Lord Drakos and his people shouldn't have bothered with us—with *Victory* and Maddox—but should have already attempted to destroy the Swarm nexuses."

"Exactly," Ludendorff said. "That's what Strand would have done if he had been in charge. The Q-ships, the Builder item and I would have been enough to try stopping more immediate Swarm invasions."

"So the others—Lord Drakos and Womack—made a mistake in forcing his people to try to capture *Victory* now," Meta said.

"Clearly," Ludendorff said, as he glanced at Maddox. "Lord Drakos attempted to do too much in too short of a time. From the little I know of the man, that fits his pattern. He often acts rashly or too soon. There is another thing. It is in the nature of a New Man to attack too hard rather than to wait too long. I have long argued with Strand that that was our greatest mistake concerning the New Men. We put a spur in their genetic makeup. They are all amped up and jumpy, wanting to move and act rather than contemplate a situation."

Maddox nodded absently, not noticing Meta examining him carefully. She opened her mouth, likely to make another comment.

Ludendorff noticed her and gently cleared his throat.

Meta glanced at the professor. He barely shook his head. Her eyebrows rose. He shook his head again. Meta closed her mouth.

Would that comment have been about how Maddox seemed to have a spur in his makeup, prodding him to act, sometimes before thinking things through?

Maddox inhaled, looking at the professor. "So now we know that Lord Drakos is behind the Draegar and the—"

"Just a minute," Ludendorff said. "That's not what I said. Lord Drakos took control of the operation. Strand still conceived it. Like many great ideas, if the genius that made the plan no longer runs it, it likely no longer runs in the way it was meant to."

"That sounds convoluted," Meta said.

"Yes," Ludendorff said.

"Fine," Maddox said, as he considered the implications. "Ah. If Throne World New Men are at the local nexus, we can tell them about the co-opted Strand Operation and implicate Lord Drakos."

"Maybe," Ludendorff said.

"We'll trade them the information for access to the local nexus," Maddox said.

"And if Drakos' people are at the local nexus in strength?" Ludendorff asked.

"If they're there in strength…" Maddox said. "We'll have to retreat, as I doubt I can use the same antimatter-loaded Q-ship trick twice."

"Our main problem still remains," Ludendorff said. "We don't know what's waiting for us at the local nexus."

"Don't kick yourself, Professor," the captain said. "We've learned that Strand is still a Throne World captive. If we succeed in our greater mission, it will be much easier to rid ourselves of Lord Drakos than it would be to rid ourselves yet again of Strand."

"That's an excellent point, my boy. Yes. We're farther along than we were before mind-probing Tars Womack."

"Without a doubt," the captain said.

"And we know one other thing," Ludendorff said.

Maddox waited for it.

Ludendorff looked at him intently. "I need to use the stone to heal Dana's mind."

Before Maddox could comment, he heard Meta step up behind him. She clutched his right triceps, squeezing. He understood this signal. What was the right choice? Would Ludendorff fight harder for humanity if his woman were healed? Of course, he would.

"Maybe you're right," Maddox told the professor. "But first, you need to rest. Afterward…yes. We need Dana. We need everyone if we're going to stop the Swarm invasions."

Meta squeezed his triceps a last time, her way of saying thank you.

The wide smile on Ludendorff's face confirmed Maddox's decision. If they could use the local nexus, they were heading into the Deep Beyond. More than anything else, they would need high morale to fight the awful pressures awaiting them.

They barely made it back from the Deep Beyond last time. This time it would probably be even worse.

-60-

Many hundreds of light-years away in the Nerva Hauler *Sulla 7*, Mako 21 awoke from a long, deathlike sleep.

She rubbed her aching head, unable to assess her surroundings because it was pitch black in here. Her mouth felt dry, her body drained, from ordeals she could not remember.

What had the Visionary been doing to her? Why couldn't she remember?

Mako looked around in the blackness, but she could tell nothing. No...that wasn't exactly right. She felt the *thrum* of the mighty hauler. That was important somehow... Yes. They were racing to a critical place, but she couldn't remember how she knew that.

Mako refrained from trying to get up because she didn't know if it was safe to move in here.

With pursed lips, she rethought that. She was a Surveyor First-Class. No! She was even more than that. She refused to let fear dictate her actions.

She attempted to swing her legs off the bed. That failed miserably, however, as her legs would not budge. Mako was determined to know why, and attempted to sit up. That did not happen, either. She tried to move an arm, but found that straps held the arm down. She tried the other arm. It had also been tightly secured by straps.

I'm trapped, Mako realized.

Yet...she'd rubbed her head earlier. How could her arms be trapped now?

In the darkness, Mako frowned. It was time to discover the causes to her problems. First, her head ached because…because…ah. She knew. Her head ached because she'd been inside the Educator many times. This last time had been the longest.

The Educator had taught her many things while she'd slept in its belly. The Educator was a Spacer invention, and acolytes had slid her into the center of the huge machine like an old-fashioned CAT scanner. Normally, the Educator was reserved for language lessons. She had learned…otherwise, as the Educator had been dialed to its highest setting.

Mako felt a little better because she knew why her head ached and why she'd been in darkness. The Educator worked best in the dark as it massaged the mind with electronic impulses.

Why did her body ache, though? What was the cause of that?

In the darkness, Mako scrunched her brow—

Oh. That was simple. Her body ached because she'd received two new bodily modifications during the trip. One of the modifications involved anti-gravity mesh inserted inside her feet, her upper back and in her forearms.

She had trained—no, she had not trained in the normal sense. In her sleep, the Educator had simulated extended dream-flights. If she was free of the restraints, she could no doubt fly as well as any anti-gravity-mesh-assisted human could do. The last modification—

My left index finger, she realized. It could act like a beam weapon, charged by the power supply under her ribcage near her heart.

Two new inner modifications indicated further work for her as a Surveyor/Spacer-Intelligence operative.

That still did not explain how earlier she'd rubbed her forehead while strapped down on a table.

Mako turned her head wildly, trying to see. Was someone in the dark here with her? Had that person rubbed her head?

Hmm… That did not make logical sense. She'd rubbed her head as she thought about it. No one could time it like that…unless the other read her mind. Yet, Mako did not believe mindreading likely. She doubted anyone aboard the hauler could read her mind. Her modifications were too powerful to allow something like that.

Then—

I did it, Mako realized. *The Educator taught me to use my other modifications in new manner.*

Yes, she could now move matter in subtle ways as her brainwaves stimulated her modifications that could move her skin, scratch her back and—

The straps holding down her legs, torso and arms unlatched and lifted off, moved by her new tech-driven telekinesis.

Mako sat up on a bed of sorts. She had no idea how high off the ground she might be. She thus used her modifications to search the darkness. It took effort and concentration—

Click.

Light flooded the chamber.

Since Mako had effected that, she'd been ready for the blinding light, having covered her goggles with both hands. Slowly, she began to let a little light between her fingers.

Soon, she removed her hands from her goggles and perceived—Mako slid off the bed and examined the chamber. A vast machine filled the room. She would have slid into a hole in the middle of the machine, as this was the Educator.

As Mako stood studying the machine, an outer hatch slid open and two provost marshals entered. Each aimed a beamer at her.

Mako concentrated.

The marshals cried out, each releasing his suddenly hot weapon so both clattered onto the floor. The men looked up at her, and charged in unison.

Before Mako could stop herself, she reached out with the power of her modifications, searched their interior bodies and snipped a critical artery inside each. Both marshals collapsed onto the floor, twitching in their death throes.

Mako might have walked out of the chamber, but she stopped in horror, looking at the two dead men. She couldn't believe that she'd so casually murdered two provost marshals.

"It happened too fast," she said weakly.

A cold chuckle was the only reply.

Mako's head snapped up as she searched— "Visionary," she said.

"Yes, Mako," a reply came out of a wall-speaker.

"You've been watching me."

"All the time," the Visionary said.

"You're changing me, aren't you?"

"Oh, indeed," the Visionary said.

"Why are you doing this?"

"That is the question of the ages, Mako, but you already know the answer."

Mako cocked her head. Was that true? Did she know the…? She had an answer, but it was incomplete.

To test her belief, Mako asked, "I am the Spacer egg?"

"Yes," the Visionary said.

Mako thought about that, finally asking, "What good is an answer that you don't understand?"

"You tell me."

"Ah," Mako said. "My incomplete knowledge is a signpost. It tells me in what direction I'll find my answer if I'm willing to keep looking."

"Very good, Mako," the Visionary said.

"*What* is the Spacer egg?" Mako asked.

"You are," the Visionary said.

"I would like greater clarification."

"I know."

"Are you trying to test my patience?"

"Mako," the Visionary chided. "There is really very little that I can teach you from here. Most of it you will have to learn on your own. The problem is that you aren't using your abilities to their fullest. As the first step, you must start thinking, really and truly thinking."

Mako did just that, engaging her intellect upon the problem of the Spacer egg. After a time, her head came up sharply.

"You're talking about an evolutionary step," Mako said.

"And?" the Visionary prodded.

Mako's brow furrowed as she considered— "Not just an evolutionary step," she said, "but a *guided* evolutionary step."

"I have a question for you."

"Ask," Mako said.

"If we were to speak together—I mean in the same room—would you try to kill me for what I've done to you?"

Mako found that a shocking question until she considered the two dead provost marshals. She'd become a living weapon. The Visionary wisely feared her.

"Would my word that I wouldn't harm you mean anything to you?" Mako asked.

"Let's find out," the Visionary said. "Will you give me your word?"

"I will. You are safe with me until the journey ends."

"I will have to ask for clarification. Do you mean the end of the journey aboard the *Sulla 7?*"

"That," Mako said.

"Then I accept," the Visionary said. "I have a few questions for you, and I suspect you'll have a few as well for me. This is a gravid voyage, you know?"

Mako mentally tested herself, scanning her body. "I'm not pregnant."

"I would kill the Strand clone if you were," the Visionary said. "No. You're going to impregnate something."

"I'm female, so how is that possible?"

"You're right," the Visionary said, "you are female. But you are also the Spacer…well, egg wouldn't be the right term exactly, but it will suffice for now."

"You've…changed me so I can perform a specific mission?"

"A mission of galactic importance," the Visionary said. "After you complete the mission…the universe will never be the same."

"I'm intrigued," Mako said. "Tell me more."

"Good and yes," the Visionary said. "I'll be there in a few minutes."

-61-

As Mako learned her next lesson aboard the Spacer-recaptured Nerva hauler, Starship *Victory* exited a Laumer Point, arriving at its middle-Beyond destination.

Lieutenant Noonan perked up from a mild form of Jump Lag and began to scan the star system. She stiffened almost immediately.

The main hatch opened and Maddox strode within.

"Sir," Valerie said, while swiveling around in her seat. "We've reached the system with the New Man nexus."

Maddox rubbed his hands in anticipation as he approached the main screen.

"The system has a G-class star," Valerie reported, reading from her panel. "It's 1.21 percent the mass of the Sun. There are three inner terrestrial planets, an Asteroid Belt and four outer gas giants with a greater Oort Cloud beyond."

Maddox nodded while mentally ingesting the data.

"I'm not finding any planetary or orbital settlements," Valerie said. "There are three star cruisers. They're orbiting the nexus, sir, at the discreet distance of one million kilometers. The nexus appears inert without any appreciable radiation around it."

Valerie tapped her panel.

On the main screen appeared a dot for the nexus, with three red dots farther out representing the star cruisers. The giant Builder artifact was in the system's Asteroid Belt. The nearest object to the nexus was an asteroid fourteen kilometers wide, presently 32 million kilometers from the Builder pyramid.

"The New Men have failed to fortify the star system?" Maddox asked the professor.

The Methuselah Man sat at his station. "I would have told you if they'd done so," Ludendorff said.

"Which isn't an answer," Maddox pointed out.

"No fortifications, my boy," Ludendorff said. "There's your answer."

"Have the star cruisers attempted to hail us?" Maddox asked Valerie.

The lieutenant shook her head.

Maddox turned and walked to his chair, sitting, thinking about the situation. "Plot a heading to the nexus," he told Keith.

"Aye, aye, sir," the ace said, tapping his board. "Course laid in, sir."

"Engage, Mr. Maker," Maddox said.

Keith manipulated his piloting board. Seconds later, *Victory* began to accelerate toward the distant Builder object.

***

It took eleven hours before the star cruisers gave any indication that they noticed the Star Watch vessel closing in on the nexus.

A New Man hailed *Victory*. Valerie tapped her board, opening channels.

"You are illegally entering Throne World territory," the New Man said via comm on the bridge loudspeaker. He did not show his face on the main screen even though Valerie had made it possible for him to do so if he'd wished.

Valerie now informed the captain, who was in his quarters sleeping.

Maddox slipped out of bed, yawned and met Meta coming out of the shower. He inspected his gloriously naked wife. This was the right way to wake up.

He embraced Meta and kissed her lingeringly.

"You're feeling better," Meta said archly.

"According to Valerie, the New Men are warning us. I take that as a good sign."

Soon enough, Maddox appeared on the bridge in his uniform, finishing a cup of coffee, his hair only slightly damp as he sat down in his command chair.

Valerie informed him of a second warning that had come ninety seconds ago.

"What's the tactical situation?" Maddox asked.

"We're ten million kilometers from the nexus and closing fast," Valerie said. "The three star cruisers have maneuvered into a blocking position. We're at much greater velocity than they and can still break off if we do it soon."

"Noted," Maddox said, while fingering his chin. "Mr. Maker."

"Aye, sir," Keith said.

"Reduce our velocity to one quarter of our present speed."

Keith waited a second and then manipulated his board.

"Open channels with the originally hailing star cruiser," Maddox told Valerie.

She did so, looking at him afterward.

Maddox faced the blank main screen. He was giving them video. They hadn't yet done likewise. Some might consider that rude, but he was going to ignore the slight.

"This is Captain Maddox of Starship *Victory*," he began. "I'm on an urgent mission of critical importance to the Throne World and the Commonwealth alike. We're aware of the recent Swarm invasion into the Throne World System, and of your defeat of the invading force. Likely, you're also aware that Admiral Fletcher of the Grand Fleet annihilated a second Swarm invasion into the Hydras System.

"It is Star Watch's belief that we must stop further invasions before the Swarm Imperium floods our systems with several hundred thousand warships. We have a plan that will halt the Swarm assaults for the foreseeable future."

Maddox waited for a reply.

Victory had reduced its velocity, but it was still moving toward the nexus. The distance between the ancient Adok vessel and the three star cruisers was minimal in terms of communication lag.

Maddox forced himself to remain erect and poised. Was he dealing with one of Lord Drakos's groups or were these Throne World New Men? If the star cruisers warmed up their cannons, he would fight regardless of their designation. *Victory* had a fighting chance against three.

"Sir," Valerie said.

The lieutenant did not need to say more, as a New Man appeared on the main screen. He was standing—quite tall and even stately in manner. There was something different about him, even though he wore a common silver uniform. He had an extraordinarily intense gaze and radiated strength and determination.

"I know you," Maddox said, recognizing the New Man.

The other nodded.

"You are Golden Ural."

"That is correct," the other said. "I am the Emperor's troubleshooter, and I find it puzzling that you are so far from home."

"Did you receive my message concerning the Swarm?" Maddox asked.

"I would not be talking to you otherwise, Captain."

Maddox nodded. "We're here because we have need of the nexus."

"It is ours," Golden Ural said softly.

Maddox found that it was difficult to sit while the other stood. That was odd, wasn't it? There was another thing. He felt a strange liking for Golden Ural, and he didn't know why. Maybe it was the other's stately presence. The New Man seemed regal rather than arrogant in ways none of the others he'd met so far had.

The captain stood up and squared his shoulders.

"You have quite the reputation, Captain Maddox. It would be a feather in my cap to capture your starship and present it to the Emperor as a gift."

Maddox ignored the comment. He felt it hadn't been spoken as a threat, but as something else. "You and I fought together against the original Swarm invasion," he said. "We beat an Imperial Fleet once."

Golden Ural studied him for a time, finally saying, "That is true."

"It would be a shame if we fought amongst ourselves while our worlds were under Swarm threat."

Golden Ural spoke sooner this time. "Perhaps you are correct in your thesis, Captain."

"We must destroy the nearest nexuses in Swarm space," Maddox said. "According to Professor Ludendorff, a nexus can only create a hyper-spatial tube four thousand light-years in length. If we destroy the local Swarm nexuses, the Imperium will have a harder time invading Human Space—and Throne World territory as well."

"That is logical," Golden Ural said.

"That is our mission—my mission…sir," Maddox said.

Golden Ural's eyes seemed to gleam and an odd smile crept upon his majestic face. Maddox could not understand the smile's significance.

The New Man looked away, but it didn't seem as if he looked to anyone else off screen. Finally, Golden Ural regarded him again.

"The professor is at fault," the New Man said. "The precise distance of a regular hyper-spatial tube is five thousand light-years. A nexus can create even longer ones, although they become more unstable the longer they project."

"I assume Methuselah Man Strand told you all this."

It almost seemed as if Golden Ural would answer the statement. Finally, he shrugged.

"If Strand told you all this," Maddox said, "you should recall that I captured the Methuselah Man and sent him to your Emperor as a gift."

"That is true. You did."

"I did it as a gesture of goodwill."

Golden Ural nodded as if Maddox had scored a point in a long and intricate debate. "We allied with Star Watch in order to face the first Swarm invasion partly because of that gesture. In other words, it was well paid for."

"That is true," Maddox said, mimicking the other's style.

Once more, the New Man smiled faintly, and he took a visible breath. "Captain, I am going to commit a possibly treasonous act. I find that I like your grit. I applaud your daring, and you have shown yourself to be a resourceful man. I also fear that humanity is fast nearing extinction."

"Do you include yourself in the last statement?"

"I do not. We...*superiors* shall survive, as we have already made the first move in that regard. There is another thing. We have already stymied the Imperium regarding further assaults upon the Throne World."

"Ah," Ludendorff said from his station.

Maddox turned to the professor.

Ludendorff said, "He's telling you the Emperor sent a strike force against the Swarm nexus that launched the invasion against the Throne World."

"Is that Professor Ludendorff I hear?" Golden Ural asked.

Maddox faced the screen again. "It is."

"Tell the Methuselah Man that he is correct," Golden Ural said. "In order to stifle your simian curiosity, Captain, I will relate certain facts. The Emperor and I together with Methuselah Man Strand arrived at the same strategy as you seem to have reached. We must destroy nearby enemy nexuses. By his arcane means, Strand calculated that the Deneb System was the launch point against the Throne World. That is where we sent our strike force."

Maddox could hear Ludendorff tapping his board, possibly looking up data on the Deneb System.

"I won't say how many star cruisers departed on the mission," Golden Ural said. "None have returned yet. The Emperor is loath to send more ships, especially given certain parameters."

"What are those parameters?" Maddox asked.

Golden Ural smiled faintly. "I am not at liberty to say. Nor do I think the Emperor will forgive me if I tell you more. Hmmm... I will point out that if the Swarm continues to attack, they will likely hit the Commonwealth first. That is obviously because the Swarm can no longer use the Deneb System nexus to reach the Throne World. Your defense will give us long enough to relocate into a safer part of the galaxy."

Maddox blinked several times. "Relocate?" he asked. "That sounds an awful lot like fleeing like wet hens."

Golden Ural's eyes seemed to gleam. "Some among us would agree with you, Captain. I am not one of them, however. Survival is paramount."

"You…you would need normal men to join you in your flight," Maddox said. "Otherwise, you would only bear sons, never women. Within a generation, New Men would be no more."

A hard look appeared on Golden Ural's face. Maddox thought he might have said too much.

"Will you attempt to bar us from using your nexus?" Maddox asked. "If so, I'm willing to exchange data concerning Lord Drakos's manipulation of Strand, which has allowed Drakos to suborn some of Strand's former plans and people."

The fierce look departed the New Man's stately features. "Lord Drakos did what?"

Maddox told Golden Ural their suspicions about the short, broad-shouldered New Man and how he'd used the Bosk homeworld and their people.

"How did you happen to uncover all this?" Golden Ural asked.

Maddox hesitated. If he told the Emperor's troubleshooter about the Builder stone, might Golden Ural try to take it? For some reason, Maddox thought not. Despite his normal dislike of New Men, he told Golden Ural how they'd learned their truths.

"A web of deceit all around," Golden Ural said when Maddox had finished. "This time, Lord Drakos has gone too far. The Emperor will want to hear this. Yes. That is a worthy exchange."

The tall New Man inhaled deeply, nodding after a time. "You have the incomparable Professor Ludendorff with you. He will likely uncover the same facts that Strand found within the nexus. Will that help you to complete your mission? It is difficult to see how, even with your remarkable Builder stone. Still, our strike force has likely destroyed several Swarm-controlled nexuses. It appears more must vanish in order to give allied humanity more time, a century perhaps, before the Swarm finds a new way to attack all of us."

"*If* your strike force succeeded," Maddox said.

"Yes, if," the New Man said.

Maddox wanted to ask, "Well?" but he waited.

"You have poise," Golden Ural finally said. "I admit that I am disinclined to let you throw away your life on a suicidal mission. It also pains me to let this Builder stone fall into enemy hands."

Maddox frowned, not understanding the New Man's apparent concern for him. The part about the Builder stone made more sense. Perhaps he shouldn't have told Golden Ural about it.

"I admire daring," the New Man continued. "But even more, I admire the man that found the answer to defeating the Swarm last time. Maybe it's time for you to let another Star Watch operative make the suicidal mission."

"I'm here," Maddox said. "I have the right tools for the job, and I've done it before. This is too important a mission to let an inexperienced man do it."

Golden Ural nodded. "Perhaps you're right. I wish you luck, Captain. May you succeed beyond your wildest dreams."

It was strange, but Maddox felt an odd lump in his throat; and for the life of him, he couldn't explain it. "Thank you, sir," he said. "I appreciate it."

The screen went blank before anyone could say more.

Maddox's head swayed back and he smiled. "He's likeable…for a New Man, I mean." Adding the last because Ludendorff gave him an odd scrutiny.

"The star cruisers are veering off," Valerie said. "Golden Ural is keeping his word," she told Maddox. "They're moving out of our way."

"Right," Maddox said. "Reduce velocity again, Mr. Maker, and set a slow course to bring us within eight kilometers of the nexus."

"Aye, aye, mate," Keith said.

Maddox glanced at the Scotsman.

"I mean, sir," the ace muttered, as he began to make his manipulations.

-62-

Several hours later, the starship drifted in slow orbit around the giant silver pyramid in space. Just like all the others they'd seen, the ancient Builder structure dwarfed *Victory*.

The pyramid was an amazing sight, as if someone had once poured a molten river of silver into shape here and it had cracked over the ages. There did not appear to be any rhyme or reason why the Builders had picked *this* star system and this location in the Asteroid Belt. But the nexus was here. That was enough.

"How does it look to you?" Maddox asked the professor over a view-screen.

"I'm not ready to make a judgment, my boy. Now, are you sure you're not coming with us?"

"Quite sure," Maddox said. "I appreciate Golden Ural's gesture, but I'm not ready to fully trust any New Man, especially as he has three star cruisers at his disposal."

"The three ships have moved well off," Ludendorff said.

"That's just the thing a New Man readying a trap would do," Maddox said.

"You're a suspicious man." On the screen, the professor glanced at Meta sitting beside him. She would be the only one joining him in the nexus, as she was one of the few who had been inside one before, this one in particular. That had been many years ago already while in the company of an altered man named Kane.

"Guard the barn, then, if you would," Ludendorff said. "I hope to be back in two hours."

"As fast as that?" asked Maddox, surprised.

"One can hope," Ludendorff said, "but I suppose you're right. It will likely take longer."

"Good luck," Maddox said. "And take good care of my wife."

"Never fear, never fear, she's in good hands."

"Watch him," Maddox told his wife. "He's pulled fast ones before. Don't let him do it again."

"I'll watch him," Meta said, as she glanced at Ludendorff.

The professor was already checking his board, pretending he hadn't heard that.

Maddox stared longingly at his wife. He didn't like Meta going, not one bit.

"I'm the best candidate for the task," Meta said. Maybe she'd seen his concern. "I've been in there already."

"Watch out," Maddox said, wanting to tell her that he loved her, but unable to do so while others were listening.

"Any last minute suggestions, sir?" asked Keith. He was piloting the shuttle.

"Same as Meta," Maddox said. "Watch the professor."

"Aye," the pilot said. "I have my eye on the old man."

"Enough," Ludendorff said testily, looking up from his panel. "Time is dribbling away. Let's do this while we still can."

Did the Methuselah Man seem nervous? Maddox couldn't say he blamed him. The nexuses always made *him* nervous.

"Good luck," the captain said.

The scene wobbled, and the three passengers disappeared from the screen. In their place appeared the shuttle as it lifted from the hangar-bay deck and headed for the giant opening into space.

They'd really made it to the nexus. They were finally doing this.

***

Twenty-eight minutes later from the bridge, Maddox, Valerie and Galyan watched the shuttle slow serenely into a parking orbit beside the giant nexus.

"It is strange," Galyan said in a faraway voice. "But the longer I study the nexus, the more akin I feel to it."

"What's that?" Valerie asked, bemused. "You feel kinship with the pyramid?"

"Why is that surprising?" Galyan asked. "It is old. I am old."

"It's supposed to be a lot older than you are," Valerie said.

"Compared to each other that is so," Galyan said. "I am comparing the pyramid and me to you short-lived beings."

"Okay…" Valerie said.

"There are other similarities between the pyramid and me," Galyan said. "The Builders fashioned the nexus. Builder technology helped to fashion me, a deified AI."

"You're becoming sentimental in your old age," Valerie said.

"Of course," Galyan said. "That should not surprise you. I have emotions. They were built into the AI programming."

"Are you monitoring their passage?" Maddox asked Valerie.

The lieutenant straightened and turned to her board. "Yes, sir," she said, tapping the screen. A second later, "The shuttle's bay door has opened. Ludendorff and Meta are using a sled to head the final distance."

Maddox nodded sharply.

"Is something wrong?" Galyan asked.

Maddox did not answer.

"Did you hear me, sir?" Galyan asked.

"I did," Maddox said.

"This is interesting," Galyan said. "According to my psychological program, you are exhibiting worry. Are you concerned about Meta?"

Maddox glanced at the holoimage but said nothing.

"Sir," Galyan said. "The psychology program indicates heightened worry in you. This is unwarranted. Meta is more than competent. She is a highly rated Intelligence operative."

"Galyan," Valerie said, shaking her head. "Leave him alone."

"The captain is being too quiet, Valerie. That is unhealthy. He should trust Meta—"

"Galyan," Maddox said.

"Sir?"

"Go check on the Builder stone," the captain said.

The holoimage's eyelids fluttered. "The stone is in the safe."

"Go check on it," Maddox said.

"I understand, sir," Galyan said. "You do not want to admit that—"

"Galyan," Maddox said with force. "Go. And. Check. The. Stone."

The holoimage disappeared.

Valerie cleared her throat.

Maddox ignored her.

"He was only trying to help," Valerie said.

"I'm aware of that," Maddox said.

"Meta can handle herself."

Maddox stared at the lieutenant, although he did not say anything.

Galyan popped into existence. "Captain, the stone appears to be there. Yet, I detected a flaw in its nature. On further analysis, I found that it was a fake. Someone has taken the real Builder stone and replaced it with an inferior replica."

"Dammit," Maddox said, as he smacked a fist into his other palm. "I knew the professor was acting strangely. I figured it had to be nerves. I…I can't believe I trusted him even a little. Ludendorff knows he wasn't supposed to take it over there. How did he pull the switch and pass the inspection?"

Maddox shook his head. It didn't really matter how he'd done it, just that he had. Ludendorff had pulled another fast one, and this time while Meta was the only person with him. What was that egotistical maniacal Methuselah Man thinking? The Builder stone would likely activate something horrible inside the nexus. Why couldn't Ludendorff follow orders for once?

"He tricked me, sir," Galyan said, crestfallen. "Sergeant Riker and I inspected the luggage, the shuttle and the space-sled."

Maddox turned to Valerie.

The lieutenant swiveled around and faced him, shaking her head. "I don't know why or how, but something is jamming our communication. I can't even contact Keith now."

Maddox faced the main screen, watching the small sled near the giant nexus. Ludendorff had taken the stone with him. There was no telling what was going to happen next.

-63-

Ludendorff sat astride the space-sled as if it were a huge motorcycle, piloting them toward the ancient silver structure. Both Meta and he wore spacesuits, as the sled did not have a canopy or an enclosed compartment.

He wished Dana were behind him, not Meta. He'd worked on Dana's mind two days ago. It had been a harrowing experience. He knew Dana too well. That was the reason it had been so difficult for him. Still, he'd fixed what he could in her mind, restoring her independence of will. He'd also deadened a few of the worst memories.

Once this was all over, Ludendorff had plans for the overly aggressive Bosks. He was going to make their entire world pay for their crimes. He would make sure that no Bosk ruffian ever had a chance to do something like that to anyone else.

Meta tapped his left shoulder from behind.

Ludendorff twisted around to stare at her. All he saw was his reflection against her mirrored visor. Naturally, Meta must be worried, as they had lost communication with Keith in the shuttle and with *Victory*. That was by his design, of course. He could not have the captain telling him to abort the mission because he'd taken the Builder stone along.

With a gloved hand, Meta held up a jack.

Ludendorff nodded his helmet.

Meta snapped the jack into one of his spacesuit's slots.

"Professor," she said in his earphones, with the cable connected. "We've lost communication with Keith and with *Victory*."

"No matter," he said in a pseudo-cheery voice. "We will prevail despite all odds."

"Did you expect that to happen?" she asked.

Ludendorff grew alert. He heard the accusation in her voice. He had to be careful with Meta. Yes. It would be wise to remember that Meta was very strong and could prove a difficult opponent. He needed to mollify her suspicions. It was good the captain hadn't joined them. He'd dreaded that, which was why he'd asked Maddox to come, using reverse psychology.

"I feared this could happen to us, yes," Ludendorff told Meta. "I'm unsure if it's a New Man trick, but we can't discount that. It could, however, simply be a reflexive move from the nexus."

"Maybe we should go back and try again after analyzing this."

"No, no, my dear," he said. "That would be entirely the wrong move. We should forge ahead and make the hyper-spatial tube. We might not get another opportunity to do so, especially if this is a New Man trick. On all accounts, we must reach a Swarm-territory nexus."

Meta was silent a moment. "Maybe you're right," she said. "But I'm also wondering if you caused the jamming. It is how you've operated in the past."

"My dear," he said in a scoffing voice. "You have entirely the wrong idea about—"

"Do you feel that, Professor?" Meta asked, interrupting him.

He felt the barrel of a beamer poke against his space-suited back. "Why yes," he said. "I do feel that."

"It's a beamer. It's saying, 'Don't double-cross us. If you do, I'll kill you.'"

Ludendorff knew they all expected him to complain about such treatment. If he failed to do that, it would likely arouse her suspicions even more.

"Really, my dear, this is quite unwarranted. I've thrown in my lot with Star Watch. I'm risking my life to save humanity. The least you could do is—"

"Don't take this personally," Meta said, cutting him off. "I'm worried like you. I know what Maddox would want me to do, and I don't intend on letting him down."

"How wonderful," he said.

She removed the beamer from his back. His manner must have worked, mollifying her suspicions just enough, at least. He'd better remember to lock Meta out before he began the great test. Otherwise, he might have to shoot and possibly kill her. If he did that, he would have to kill Maddox in order to remain alive. Why did everything have to be so difficult?

***

Meta sat behind Ludendorff on the space-sled. The vast Builder pyramid frightened and awed her. She felt the greatness and power that literally radiated from the unbelievably ancient structure.

She was a gnat compared to it. Humanity was nothing but a flea in the universe. The Swarm supposedly covered much of the galaxy. How were they really going to stop the bug Imperium from destroying mankind? It seemed like a vain hope.

Why am I so pessimistic? That wasn't like her. Did the nexus radiate pessimism at her?

Meta tightened her grip on the beamer that she kept in her lap. Maddox had told her to watch the Methuselah Man. Was Ludendorff planning another piece of treachery? Why would he do that now? Dana was back aboard *Victory*. The professor loved Dana. He'd used the stone on her mind. The doctor had been asking for Ludendorff before they left. Surely, the professor would do nothing to jeopardize his ability to be with her.

Within the helmet, Meta scowled. It was time to concentrate on the giant structure. If she remembered correctly, the professor was heading for a different area of the pyramid than the last time she'd been here.

Kane had—he hadn't headed for the apex up near the top. The professor did, though.

Would it look different this time inside the ancient structure? It had been seriously weird the last time, with Kane.

Meta gulped, and kept telling herself to keep her wits about her. Maddox should have come, but he'd sent her. She wouldn't let her husband down, not for anything. The fate of humanity might rest on what she did or didn't do.

I'm not going to let you trick me, Professor. This time, you're going to follow orders to the letter.

-64-

Ludendorff brought the space-sled to a stop near the pinnacle of the pyramid. He visually searched for a sign on the prehistoric surface.

He and Strand had been to this nexus many times during the years they'd manipulated the Thomas Moore Society people, turning them into the New Man Defenders. The two of them had gone inside several times, exploring the ancient structure. Strand had always had a better grasp of the Builder mind and had thus figured out so much more concerning the nexus.

This time, however, Ludendorff believed that *he* was going to know more. He'd brought back-up in the form of the Builder stone. Using the stone should work, meaning without triggering some primeval switch because they were inside the giant pyramid.

But what if I'm wrong about the stone? What if the Builders put a trigger in the nexus?

No, no, Ludendorff told himself. He wasn't wrong. He was right. He—

There!

The professor frowned. That was odd. It was almost as if something had spoken in his mind as his gaze passed over a certain location on the apex. He probed himself, seeking another inner-voice confirmation, but none came. He must have imagined the inner voice, although he couldn't completely convince himself of that.

That brought doubt, and he despised doubt at a time like this.

He cocked his head, waiting for an inner voice to agree with him. Again, none came. He'd tried to trick whatever had spoken in his mind the first time.

The professor contemplated possibilities. He didn't like the obvious conclusion. The stone might have misled him. The primeval artifact could be even subtler than he was.

Ludendorff slowly turned in his seat to stare at Meta's visor. The jack still linked them. He made a final calculation and realized he was going to do it despite the clear risk that the stone had compromised his mind. If the stone thought it had fooled him…the artifact would find it had bitten off more than it could chew.

The professor cleared his throat. "It's time to leave the sled, my dear. We're going to jump and float over there." He pointed at a spot near the apex.

"Float?" Meta asked. "What do you mean *float?* We have thruster packs. We can glide there under controlled flight."

"No packs," Ludendorff said. "We'll jump the remaining distance."

"That's insane, Professor, and there's no reason for it."

"You can stay here if you like. But if you're coming, you'll have to jump. We cannot use thruster packs this close to the nexus."

Meta was silent a moment. "Okay," she finally said. "You have convinced me that you're planning something. What is it this time? You'd better tell me before you get hurt, Professor. Oh," she said in a deeper voice. "You did cause the jamming, didn't you?"

"Nonsense, dear girl," he said. "You've let your husband's prejudices seep into you. It isn't pretty."

Meta brought up the beamer, likely to poke him in the side with it as she'd done earlier.

Ludendorff had been waiting for that and clicked a hidden device.

The hand holding the beamer jerked down hard against the seat.

"What's happening?" Meta said, her voice rising. "I'm magnetized to the sled. So is the gun."

Ludendorff was unaffected by the procedure and climbed up on his seat. He judged the distance and leaped from the sled, sailing through space toward the nexus. As he did, the jack connecting him to Meta snapped so the line dangled behind him. He didn't bother watching Meta. She would free herself soon enough. Of that, he had no doubt. Thus, he needed to use this margin to get inside and lock her out.

You're a clever old boy, Ludendorff told himself.

Then he had no more time to gloat, as the nexus loomed before him. He took out a device, aimed it at a precise spot and manipulated the device, waiting.

Nothing happened.

Wait. What was this? A beam of light flashed past him and—

Ludendorff turned wildly, looking back at the space-sled.

Meta had already freed herself. She aimed the beamer a second time. She must have given him a warning shot. That was her mistake.

Ludendorff pressed an exotic shield-generator button just in time. Her beam struck his personal force field, which reached a little beyond his suit. He lacked a pendant, as Maddox had stolen his only one. This was a temporary shield. It needed to hold just long enough, though.

Her beam kept on target. That was remarkable aiming for the girl. His shield turned red, then brown and went to black. She was going to achieve a burn through too soon.

A *beep* alerted him.

Ludendorff faced forward toward the nexus again, barely doing so in time. A tiny area of the pyramid had dilated open as if it was a miniature mouth. The process must have been delayed. He would have seen it if he'd kept looking at the apex instead of at Meta with her gun.

He had leaped correctly, though, a fine feat for an older fellow like him.

Once more, Meta's beam struck his force field, and the field collapsed. The beam now struck his suit. At that point, he sailed through the opening, and it closed behind him. The beam did not follow him through, blocked by the closed entrance.

He was in total darkness, sailing inside the control area of the nexus. For a moment, giddy laughter bubbled from his throat. He'd done it. He was actually inside. Now—as he clicked on a helmet lamp—he had to see if he still knew what to do in here.

***

Meta cursed furiously as she holstered the beamer. She'd almost cut down the traitor before he'd escaped into the apex. He'd had some kind of force field, but she'd achieved a burn through. Unfortunately, she'd done so several seconds too late.

The good news was that she was no longer magnetized to the sled.

Scooting forward, Meta studied the controls. In less than thirty seconds, she'd figured it out. Slowly, she eased the sled toward the nexus where Ludendorff had gone inside.

She had to figure out how to do the same thing. The professor could do anything in there.

What if I can't get inside?

Within ten minutes, she reached the spot where Ludendorff had entered. She could see where the thing had dilated open. Yet, nothing she had been able to think of had gotten it to open for her.

The jamming was still in place. She hadn't been able to tell Keith or the captain anything.

At fourteen minutes and thirty-two seconds, Meta came to her decision. She had to return to the shuttle and race back to *Victory*. She had to let Maddox know what had happened.

Then… She didn't know about then. She just knew that now she had to warn the others about the professor's black-hearted betrayal.

-65-

Ludendorff sailed through the dark corridors with just his helmet lamp providing a stark beam of light. Primordial hieroglyphs lined the walls together with eons-old Builder controls. Some needed special kinds of light to activate. Others were sound-controlled. The professor thus shut off the lamp at times and made sure to glide soundlessly through other corridors.

It was one of the reasons he hadn't brought a thruster pack. Its hissing would have triggered too many controls that would do who knew what.

After a time, he dropped through what some might have called a hole in the ceiling. He floated "downward" into a vast area. His helmet-lamp beam washed in all directions without striking a wall or bulkhead. A terrible sense of loneliness curdled his stomach. He was like a gnat having dropped through a cavern hole falling toward a subterranean lake deep under the world.

Then, he was moving through a…substance, not just air. The substance was less dense than water but more than mere nothing. It provided enough friction that his momentum slowed until at last he floated in the stuff in the middle of the vast cavern.

The professor shut off the helmet-lamp, making it pitch black. He took several deep breaths while contemplating his next move. There was a feeling of ritual to this. And the sense that he was already connected to the Builder stone became overpowering.

That troubled him…until he recalled that he was Professor Ludendorff, the most cunning human in existence. Would that be enough to outthink or outmaneuver the ancient Builder artifact? He believed so.

In the darkness, he shrugged off and opened his pack as he floated in the strange substance. He suspected that there were many unseen marvels around him. As he touched the stone with his gloves, awareness of the marvels increased. The awareness induced fear to such a degree that his hands began to shake.

"Come now," Ludendorff whispered to himself. "That's no way to challenge the gods."

Despite his trembling hands, Ludendorff grinned tightly within the helmet as he pulled the stone from the pack, holding it aloft like an Earth wizard from prehistoric times.

The white polygonal Builder stone shone eerily. It allowed him to see his spacesuit's gauntlets and the crinkly silver arms. More than that, the eerie shine caused the substance around him to glow with a phosphorescent color that dwindled the farther it was from the stone.

What caused the stone to shine as a thing alive—no, to come on, to turn on like that? It was a machine, nothing more.

He pulled one gloved hand away and then the other, leaving the stone to float weightlessly. With one hand, he reached to the edge of the glove on the other, and halted abruptly.

The professor groaned in dismay. He'd just about removed a glove so he could touch the stone with his skin. But he couldn't remove the gloves or he would suffocate as all his air hissed from his breached spacesuit.

There was no breathable atmosphere in here. He'd come on a fool's errand. How was he supposed to activate the stone to give him the heightened intelligence to use the ancient Builder controls if he couldn't touch it?

The longer Ludendorff pondered the problem, the more he wondered how he'd made such an elementary error.

Did the error indicate that the stone already had a hidden influence on his mind? He would never have forgotten such a thing on his own. He was Ludendorff, not a forgetful old—

A jolt in his mind made him wince. He could feel the alienness of something slithering through his thoughts connecting with his neurons. That wasn't anything like the Builder stone in the past.

The polygonal stone no longer just shone eerily, the light pulsed brighter and weaker in beats like a heart.

Was the connection solely with the Builder stone or did it now link him to something much more bizarre? As he wondered, the professor waited for an entity to contact him mind-to-mind.

That did not happen. Instead, as he waited, he realized his brainpower had expanded exponentially. He knew—

In a flash, he understood what had been happening. This was the great Linkage Chamber. The substance around him had helped a Builder connect to the brain enhancer—the polygonal stone—without having to touch it or insert it into his Builder body.

Did that mean the stone had been connected to his brain all this time? Or did it mean the stone had put a post-hypnotic command into him? The idea of *that* was enraging. He'd used the stone to rid himself of un-professor tinkering in his mind. To now discover—

Wait, wait, this was more interesting than impotent anger.

Ludendorff realized that he controlled the stone. With it, he was able to tap into the greater nexus controls. His brain and the enhancer linked to such a degree that many pseudo-memories flooded into his consciousness.

This wasn't alien control of his mind, but his subconscious having *learned* certain processes and guiding him to do the right thing.

Ludendorff wanted to laugh with delight and relief. Instead, he moaned. The moan escaped him because the expanded power of his mind had engaged the part of the nexus he had come to use.

He'd turned on eons-old computers and engines. They had cycled with growing power until they'd engaged the systems he'd wanted to use, and that hurt his mind.

This was the reason he'd brought the stone with him. It had not been to double-cross the captain and crew. Ludendorff was one of them. But he knew they still didn't really trust him. How could he blame them? He'd practiced deceit throughout the ages, and certainly while with them during many of the voyages.

Without the stone providing the needed knowledge, the professor had known he could not use the nexus in the manner it could perform. That might have been a subconscious understanding, as he'd learned this in hidden ways.

Now, though, Ludendorff engaged the nexus so it reached out with an incredible power, linking with other nearby nexuses—well, near in galactic terms.

The process was mindboggling. Without the brain enhancer, none of this would be possible.

Ludendorff didn't know it, but his heart rate had dramatically increased and he breathed rapidly as if having sprinted for miles. Sweat poured from his body, draining the water in his cells. The suit's air-conditioner was already purring with power, seeking to cool his heated skin.

The polygonal brain enhancer caused the professor's mind to operate at such high levels that it was over-taxing his body. He was an old man, a Methuselah Man. If he kept this up for long, his ancient heart might give out.

Unaware of the personal danger, Ludendorff reached out with his enhanced mind, learning more and more so he could see what had happened here two weeks ago.

-66-

Among their many predilections, the Builders liked to record events. Ludendorff had tripped this function of the nexus.

With unusual clarity of mind, the professor "saw" Strand and several New Men roam inside the nexus, as had occurred two weeks ago. They had not come to this particular location in the pyramid, but to other areas. Ludendorff might have laughed at Strand's stringing together various aspects of the ancient machine. Strand worked so backwardly and in such a convoluted manner when compared to how he should have done it if he'd understood the nexus.

That was the Builder part of Ludendorff's mind "talking." The human half recognized the Methuselah Man's amazing brilliance to cobble together such a plan. It frankly stunned the professor that Strand knew so much without a brain enhancer.

Could he have so profoundly underestimated Strand's brilliance? How had the Methuselah Man come to learn these concepts?

Ludendorff did not sigh. His heart raced far too fast for that. He was not aware that he was close to hyperventilating. A heart attack certainly seemed a likely event in his near future.

Another part of Ludendorff realized he probably did not have much time. He should get on with this instead of absorbing each detail. The over-arching scheme was the priority, not the minutia.

Eleven star cruisers had waited outside the local nexus. Strand had created a hyper-spatial tube. The fantastic FTL object grew into existence, linking the local nexus system to the Deneb System 2,634 light-years away.

The eleven star cruisers entered the swirling hyper-spatial tube and vanished as they sped to the Deneb System.

In the flash of an instant, the eleven star cruisers appeared 2,634 light-years away. Strand's hyper-spatial tube faded away soon thereafter, stranding the eleven New Men crews at a Swarm-territory nexus.

Fortunately, that nexus had recorded some of the events that had occurred over there and let the local nexus here know. Oh, this was intensely interesting.

Deneb was the brightest star in the constellation of Cygnus, the swan. It was a blue-white supergiant belonging in the Orion Spiral Arm. Deneb was also in the fringe area of the Swarm Imperium, the closest Swarm nexus to Human Space.

The supergiant star's luminosity was 200,000 times that of the Sun, and it had a diameter 200 times Earth's star, meaning that if Deneb traded places with the Sun it would reach out to Earth's orbit.

Deneb was nineteen solar masses and had a surface temperature of 8,500 Kelvin. That being the case, the Deneb nexus was much farther away from the star than this nexus. The nexus there was farther than Pluto's farthest distance from the Sun.

The eleven star cruisers appeared twenty million kilometers from the Deneb nexus, making Strand's aim better than perfect, particularly given the distance of the shot.

What was this? Several hundred Swarm science vessels were farther out from the Deneb nexus than the star-cruiser flotilla.

As the recording continued to play, Ludendorff scanned a "memory" of a weeklong running battle that ended in the complete annihilation of the bug science ships, but cost six of the eleven star cruisers, leaving five to complete the daring mission.

New Men had entered the Deneb nexus, as Strand had taught them well. The supermen also learned how to activate the nexus so they could study other nearby Swarm nexuses.

After drawing lots, the New Men created another hyper-spatial tube. This one reached 2,300 light-years to a nexus in the Sagittarius Spiral Arm.

Four of the five star cruisers entered the tube, vanishing to the new nexus.

The remaining star cruiser approached the Deneb nexus. New Men placed many antimatter warheads in the ancient structure. They used other explosives, too. Finally, the commander detonated the many warheads and destroyed the great and primeval structure that had lasted for so many millennia.

That meant the last star cruiser was stranded almost three thousand light-years from home. Instead of despairing, the lone ship had started in the direction of the Throne World. Likely, the ship would never survive long enough to reach home, but they were going to damn well try.

The four other star cruisers reached the next nexus. Ludendorff knew, because this nexus and that one had linked message centers through Ultrix Pulses and Ultrix Receivers. That was an ancient failsafe feature embedded in the nexuses, triggered when aboriginals from one region used a hyper-spatial tube to travel to a nexus far beyond their home territory.

Ludendorff frowned as he tried to absorb all this data. There were some conflicting messages here.

He realized why. That nexus no longer existed. It would seem the four star cruisers had succeeded there as well and at one other nexus, but Ludendorff did not believe that any of those star cruisers had reached yet a fourth nexus, as he did not sense any Ultrix recording of further hyper-spatial tubes.

It had been a fine and daring plan. The New Men had expended eleven badly needed star cruisers for an amazing mission. They had destroyed three primary Swarm-territory nexuses, and had—

At that point, the professor ran a self-diagnostic of himself by wrenching his awareness from the brain enhancer and thus from the Builder machines, and he felt the sweat soaking his clothes, his madly beating heart and that he felt faint and sick.

In a flash, Ludendorff realized the problem, and he weighed his options at lightning speed.

"Data dump," the professor whispered.

He swallowed hard, readying himself. Then, he howled in agony as the Builder machine, aided by the polygonal brain enhancer shoved memories into his mind faster than he could comprehend.

"More," he whispered.

At that point, Ludendorff went rigid as memories flooded him. His body rebelled as his eyes watered and he grunted, farted, vomited—it was a sickening process.

The event lasted mere seconds, but it was inconceivably intense. Then, the professor unfolded and he vomited violently within his suit. A mini-vacuum engaged, scooping up the foulness lest he choke on it.

I'm killing myself. I have to stop the process.

Ludendorff struggled to make the brain enhancer understand. The thing refused to sever the connection, however. In the past, the professor had Maddox with the foam. Here—

I UNDERSTAND.

That was a clear, alien thought in his mind. Ludendorff knew the words hadn't originated in his brain. Did that mean on some fundamental level that the mind enhancer was more than a machine?

The possibility might have frightened Ludendorff before. Now, though, he was on the verge of death.

Before that happened, the linkage severed. The polygonal stone broke contact, and the fantastic memories and connection to the greater nexus ended.

Ludendorff's heart immediately began slowing down. The sweat no longer oozed from his pores so readily. And he finally had the consciousness of mind to suck on the water tube in his helmet. He drank his water supply dry, but he likely saved his life by doing so.

I need to get out of here, Ludendorff realized groggily.

First, though, he had to create a hyper-spatial tube of his own to reach yet a different nexus far away from here.

The professor closed his eyes, thinking, or trying to. He had absorbed so much knowledge. What was the right course of action now? If he—

He reached for the stone. As his gloved hands touched it, the stone stopped shining. The professor put it away and shrugged on the pack. He floated in the substance. How was he going to get out of this vast chamber, as he lacked a thruster pack?

Even though he was exhausted and his head hurt, the professor made swimming motions in the substance, slowly using friction to work his way to a place where he could make a hyper-spatial tube five thousand light-years in length.

That was dangerously long. He really needed the stone's guidance to do this, but at this point, relinking would surely kill him.

What was the right thing to do?

As Ludendorff struggled through the substance, he began a moral and philosophical argument with himself as to his next decision.

-67-

As Ludendorff arrived at his decision in the local nexus, hundreds of light-years away in a different area of the Beyond, the Nerva Hauler *Sulla 7* orbited a Mars-like planet.

The saucer-shaped ships Mako had seen before no longer rested in the cargo bays, but flew around the hauler in a protective screen. At the same time, heavy shuttles continued to move from the hauler as they bore their cargos down to the sandy red surface below.

On the planet, winds howled as super-fine red dust whipped around six gigantic obelisks arrayed in a perfect circle. Each obelisk was shaped exactly like those found in ancient Egypt and later in old-style America in Washington, DC. One of the two key differences was that of scale. Those on Earth would have been puny compared to these giant structures. The alien obelisks with their strange symbols on the sides towered over the red desert and made the shuttles passing them look tiny, like miniature toys.

The second difference was that each obelisk shone as if made of polished steel.

The fine red particles swirling around the six obelisks slid off the smooth metallic surfaces. The dust particles had zero ability to mar the material or the symbols, although the wind and fine dust buffeted each of the heavy shuttles bearing Usan crystals and varth elixir.

Each shuttle landed in the circle created by the gigantic obelisks. Bay doors opened, and heavily clad Spacers staggered through the howling wind. Each bore a box, bringing it to a trapdoor that sprung up as they approached. The bearer immediately climbed down ancient stairs, soon disappearing so the trapdoor snapped shut behind him.

The procession seemed endless. Shuttles lifted off. More shuttles landed. Slowly, by degrees, the Spacers emptied the orbital hauler's cargo bays, bringing down purified crystals and recalibrated varth elixir to the forbidden planet.

Mako 21 and the Visionary landed on the third day of endless hauling. Like everyone else, they bundled up heavily and braved the howling wind and flesh-tearing sand. Each staggered, reaching the trapdoor, hurrying to the stairs and beginning the climb down.

The trapdoor slammed shut above them, causing Mako to look up.

"Keep going," the Visionary said. "More people are on the way. I don't want the sand to get a second chance to ruin my goggles."

The Spacers had rigged interior lighting down here. Ancient alien hieroglyphs on the walls followed the stone steps down. A few of the hieroglyphs could have been representations of humans. Those held swords or glowing spears.

Mako now did as the Visionary asked, climbing down the steps—she shook her head at her stupidity and activated the anti-gravity meshes in her body. Mako floated off the stairs, although she continued to descend at the same rate as the Visionary. This gave Mako a better chance to study the hieroglyphs.

"You do that well," the Visionary said.

For a moment, she feared that the Visionary knew she understood some of the hieroglyphics. Then, she realized that old woman had meant her flight.

As they continued to descend, the Visionary began to breathe hard from her labor.

"Should we pause and rest?" Mako asked.

"No!" the Visionary said, and there was bite in her word.

Mako hid her smile. The Visionary had taught her many hard lessons. It thus did Mako good to see the old woman suffer, if only a bit.

During the voyage here, Mako had learned even more precisely what it meant that she was the Spacer egg of destiny. All her ordeals until now had been in preparation for the coming event. Even waiting in the life-pod had been a lesson. Even now, even with her superior abilities and intellect, she marveled at the subtlety of the Visionary. The woman had prepared the Spacer egg of destiny with ruthless dedication.

She has prepared me, Mako knew. Out of millions of Spacer candidates, she had passed the many secret tests better, proving that she had a greater chance of success later. The Visionaries, old and new, had watched and channeled her for many years already.

Few knew the awful Spacer secret and thus the terrible responsibility that awaited her.

The Visionary had told her a week ago, "This time we're going to succeed. This time we have the means to defeat our enemies and ensure our wonderful progress into something completely new."

As Mako floated down the ancient stairs—those never made for human feet—she recalled the Visionary's revelation.

"Instead of allowing evolution to take its course," the Visionary had said, "we're going to shape ourselves into a higher form. We're going to transcend even the Builders of old. Think about that, Mako. We're going to be greater than our originators. We're going to ascend the mountain and sit in judgment over all other beings. We will not be like the Builders, we will be something unbound by gravity and air. Every creature we have seen or studied has been planet-bound. But what are we, Mako? We are the Spacers. Is it not time to turn us into *real* Spacers?"

Mako pondered that as she heard the workers toiling farther below. This planet, this place, was going to help them achieve the impossible. They were going to evolutionarily leap across millennia to produce the new form of the galaxy, the form to rule them all.

In a sense, the Spacers were going to do it through force of will. Part of that will was learning ancient tech and applying modern technology in novel ways. The other part was in the sheer daring to attempt… maybe not godhood, but something akin to it.

First, though, the workers had to achieve their task, repairing the ancient machines and using the varth elixir to awaken the Old One to perform the technological marvel that would propel her—

Mako frowned. The Usan crystals and varth elixir were of paramount importance. She knew, now, that the antimatter radiation had been critical to transforming the substances to the correct settings. The Visionary had been searching future paths, working diligently to reach this chosen way. The radiation would ensure that the Old One did not survive his awakened use. He would be too dangerous otherwise.

The crystals—

"The time is near," Mako said.

The Visionary was puffing hard as she continued down the steps. She looked up at Mako, but did not have the breath to answer.

They were almost to the bottom. The chamber ahead glowed eerily through the last arch. Many toiled and had toiled for weeks to prepare this dreadful place for her.

Would the Great Machine be ready in time?

"Visionary?" asked Mako.

The old woman looked up again.

"What are our chances of success?"

The Visionary seemed to age before her eyes. It was a sad sight.

"Don't ask that, Mako," the Visionary said. "It is the Path. Success is assured."

Mako nodded absently. It was what she'd expected the old woman to say. With a pang of greater sadness, Mako realized that she had almost outgrown the Visionary. How lonely to become more than your parents, to see farther and know so much more than they could. There were many future paths, but not all would be realized.

Yes. Mako believed she was ready. The Visionary's company would become tedious in several more days. The others…Mako could hardly stand the others now.

Except…she found the clone's company interesting. The Strand clone knew more and understood with keener insights. Maybe she would speak to him again and ask him several questions.

The Visionary kept the Strand clone very busy down here. The clone of the Methuselah Man knew things no one else did. He was the master technician that made all this possible. Wasn't that strange?

Mako shrugged.

The clone would attempt his treachery soon. That was obvious. He was a devious little man. Luckily, she saw so much deeper than he did now that his treachery would be meaningless.

As Mako approached the last arch to the glowing chamber, she anticipated her great elevation and evolution. She wondered if a caterpillar felt anything like this before it began to spin its cocoon to start the metamorphosis into something so much better.

-68-

Far away from the Red Planet of destiny, Captain Maddox had led a second shuttle from *Victory* and toward the nexus. Lieutenant Noonan could watch the three star cruisers for now. The greater danger was Professor Ludendorff.

From the parked shuttle, Maddox maneuvered a space-sled, leading three others behind him. Meta was with him on his sled. Armored marines followed on two others. Doctor Dana Rich rode behind Keith Maker on the last sled. The marines did not wear spacesuits, they wore full battle armor. Everyone else had regular spacesuits.

"How are we going to get inside the apex?" Meta asked via helmet comm.

"We'll blast our way in," Maddox said past clenched teeth.

"Blast in with *what?*" asked Meta. "You still haven't said."

"A disrupter beam," Maddox replied.

"What? Is that…is that prudent?"

"No."

"Oh. Well. At least—you could damage the nexus doing that."

"Yes," Maddox said.

"Husband—"

Maddox cut her off. "Ludendorff has just become the most dangerous man in the galaxy, at least as far as humanity is concerned. We have to reach the other nexuses. What swindle is that devil Ludendorff practicing now? Did the stone hijack his mind? I deem that more than probable. We should have set up more safeguards."

"That's true," Meta said. "Why didn't you?"

Maddox almost told his wife to shut up. If anyone else would have dared question his orders like that—no. That was sheer pride snapping like that. He'd made a mistake with Ludendorff. If he wanted to win, he had to own up to his mistakes. To try to mask them, especially to himself, was suicide on such missions. Cold reality was the key. He had to see events for what they were.

"I really thought he'd fixed his mind," Maddox said. "The professor seemed so...genuine. I'm a good judge of character, but I failed the most critical test."

"You're mad at yourself. That's what this is about."

"Maybe," Maddox said. "No. I am angry. I made a mistake. I should have—"

"No one is perfect," Meta said, interrupting.

"That's a poor excuse for not doing my job. But I'm not using the disrupter cannon because I'm so angry that—"

Maddox cut himself off. He was the captain. He did not need to explain his actions to anyone, not even to his wife.

"Sir," Keith said.

The ace's voice was scratchy in the captain's headphones. Whatever Ludendorff had done earlier was still in effect. They had more powerful transmitters than before, able to pierce the jamming at these short distances.

"What?" Maddox asked.

"Someone is coming out of the nexus," Keith said.

Maddox scanned the apex area that Meta had described earlier.

"Are you sure?" Maddox asked. He didn't see anything.

"You're looking in the wrong spot, sir," Keith said. "It's near the base of the pyramid."

Maddox looked down along the mighty object, using a zoom feature of his visor. He saw it then. A space-suited human had come from a small opening down there.

"What in the—?" Maddox said.

The sled team was near the apex, which meant it was difficult to scan the entire nexus, as the bottom was far away from their present location and they were almost to the pyramid.

"What made you look down there?" Maddox asked, curious.

"I'm a strikefighter pilot first of all, sir," Keith said. "Too many fighter pilots concentrate on one spot. The place you don't look is the most dangerous. Far too many dead pilots never see the enemy fighter that kills them."

"It's Ludendorff," Meta said, sounding surprised.

"Of course it's Ludendorff," Maddox said testily. Then he realized that he *had* lied to himself. He was positively furious at the Methuselah Man. He wanted to throttle the man. It was like the time he'd pummeled Strand. That had felt so good…

"Should I pick him up?" Keith asked.

"Not with Dana on your sled," Maddox said. "No. Return to the shuttle. Get her out of here."

"But—yes, sir," Keith said.

The ace's sled peeled away from the others, making the turning maneuver and picking up velocity.

Maddox twisted the controls of his sled. "Follow me," he told the rest.

"What's the plan?" Meta asked him.

Maddox did not reply. He didn't have one yet, and he was tired of being…off. Ludendorff had done something in the nexus, and now, the Methuselah Man fled the place. What did that indicate?

Maddox couldn't figure it. They needed to capture Ludendorff and interrogate him good and hard. But maybe the Methuselah Man had already played his trick. If the stone guided the Builder-enhanced human…

What would a Builder device want out of Ludendorff?

Maybe the device had warned the Swarm in some way. The Builder in the Dyson Sphere had claimed the bugs were the superior species—that the Imperium deserved to thrive because it's realm had grown fantastically larger than Human Space.

Maddox pondered shooting Ludendorff while he could. He would kill the professor, not because the man had tricked him, but because the alien stone had likely used Ludendorff. The captain remembered their last voyage all too well. If he'd acted sooner then...

"I can't do it," Maddox said.

"Can't do what?" asked Meta.

"Marines," Maddox said, ignoring his wife's question. "Keep your weapons trained on the professor as we approach. If any of us dies from something in the nexus, kill Ludendorff and annihilate the stone."

"I don't see a stone, sir," the marine lieutenant said.

"If you happen to see the stone, destroy it."

"Yes, sir," the marine lieutenant said.

Maddox felt strange sledding down the side of the gigantic pyramid. The silver structure—its ancient cracked side—slid past at an ever-increasing rate. The sled team zoomed after the floating Ludendorff. The professor did not seem to have a source of propulsion. Rather, it seemed he'd shot out of the nexus like a cannonball.

What had happened in there? Had Ludendorff been trying to slip away from them unnoticed?

"Captain," Maddox heard in his headphone. It was a very scratchy noise, worse than ever.

"Professor?" Maddox asked.

"Can you hear me?" That was definitely Ludendorff speaking.

"Barely," Maddox said. "What did you do in there?"

There was no answer.

"Can you hear me?" Ludendorff said, his voice a little more discernible than before.

"I can hear you, you slippery bastard. What treachery did you practice today?"

A hoarse chuckle was the reply.

"Are you sane?" Maddox asked. "Did the stone suborn your will?"

"A reasonable conclusion," Ludendorff said, his voice sounding better than ever. "I had to do it the way I did, as I needed the Builder stone to properly access the nexus. I knew you would never agree to that."

"You're right," Maddox said.

"I see your team. You must hurry. We're running out of time."

"Is the nexus going to explode?" Maddox asked.

"What?" Ludendorff asked. "Why should it explode?"

"What did the stone force you to do?"

"No, no, my boy, you have it all wrong. I used the stone. The stone did not use me."

"You played us false on your own then?" Maddox asked.

"Think, Captain," the professor lectured. "We have a gargantuan task before us. I simply lacked the brainpower to know what to do. I needed the stone to help me, as it's a brain enhancer."

"It must be something more," Maddox said.

"A reasonable conclusion but quite wrong," Ludendorff said, sounding grumpy. "Now quit arguing with me and hurry. Pick me up. An unstable hyper-spatial tube is about to appear. We must enter it. That means we all must be aboard *Victory*. If we don't enter the tube in time, I doubt I'm going to be able to create another that long any time soon. This is a one-shot event."

"Does he think we're going to trust him now?" Meta asked, cutting in.

Maddox almost looked back at his wife. Yes. That was the question, wasn't it? Ludendorff had just made a wild claim. Why would—?

"Why is the tube going to be unstable?" Maddox asked.

"Length, my boy, extreme length," Ludendorff replied. "The nexus is charging up to create it. That will expend—I don't have time and the right language to explain it all to you. Either we get in that tube, or you can forget about stopping the Swarm. We have to act before they do."

"You know what's happening at the other nexus? I assume we're going to another nexus."

"Yes, yes, yes," Ludendorff said. "I know far more than you can understand. Time is running out. Now speed up. For the love of humanity, get a move on or go home."

Maddox blinked inside his helmet.

"Don't trust him," Meta said. "This is a trick. He's been lying all along. His latest actions prove that."

Maddox considered that, and from what they'd seen— "Oh, Hell," he said. "Hang on, Meta. Listen up," he told the others. "Return to the shuttle. I'm getting Ludendorff myself."

"Sir?" the marine lieutenant asked.

"No arguments—from anyone," Maddox said. "Like the man said, let's get a move on."

-69-

As the marine sleds peeled away, their lone space-vehicle sped toward the professor.

"How can you trust him?" Meta asked.

"Who says I do?" Maddox replied.

"But…you sent everyone away. You're picking him up."

"We have Dana as a hostage in the shuttle," Maddox said. "If you and I can't contain the professor by ourselves—"

"But we're doing exactly as he suggested."

"What if he's telling the truth?" Maddox asked.

"You can't believe that, not after what he just did."

"His explanation about why and what he did fits better with what I've seen of him the past week than the reverse."

"You mean it fits your pride better," Meta said.

"No," Maddox said. "It fits what I know better."

"What if the nexus kept the real Ludendorff and sent out a robot replica in his place? That's happened before with the professor, when we were in the Xerxes System."

"It did," Maddox agreed, and it was a reasonable question, as the professor might say.

The answer to Meta's question was his gut. He'd been wondering how he could have been so wrong about the professor. The truth was that he hadn't been wrong—if Ludendorff was telling the truth right now. If the professor was indeed telling the truth, the Methuselah Man was still on their side, and had acted like his old self, doing what he thought was best. "Don't ask for permission; ask for forgiveness." The professor knew that he—Maddox—would never have let him take the stone along. But Maddox could see how having the stone inside the nexus might have been the key to everything.

Strand had always seemed to know more about nexuses and the Builders than Ludendorff had known. The polygonal stone would have been the equalizer between them. It probably gave the professor much more knowledge than Strand had. If Ludendorff had explained the stone correctly—

Maddox felt his old power exuding through him. He'd been feeling off lately. Was that due to his loss of spiritual power against the Ska? Or was it simply that he'd become very tired?

Why would he feel better now all of a sudden?

In an instant Maddox knew. They were finally getting it done. If Ludendorff had accomplished his part, a hyper-spatial tube should appear soon. The professor had said it was five thousand light-years long. They would go deep into bug territory soon.

Maddox grinned tightly. His goal was to save humanity. It had cost him far too much with the Ska. To have seen his sacrifices go down in vain, knowing the Swarm would take out humanity the moment the bugs could get their act together—

That was it. That was what had changed things around for him these past few minutes. The Swarm held all the advantages. They had numbers, nexuses and willpower. Humanity was living on bug sufferance. If they could knock out the local nexuses, though, the bugs wouldn't be able to reach them.

Sure, the Swarm could send a fleet the hard way, but that wouldn't be masses of hundred-thousand-warship fleets one right after another. Maybe it would mean one or two such fleets. *That* humanity *might* be able to defeat if they had enough advance warning. After all, they'd defeated an eighty thousand strong bug fleet invasion. They could possibly take out two more such fleets, yes, with warning, and if the bugs came one fleet at a time.

First, though, they had to destroy the local nexuses. The thought that he was finally on mission invigorated him. He'd bulled through the dross and junk strewn in his path in order to get to the main event. Somehow, that calmed the pent-up energy in him that had been coming out as anger.

It was time to straighten out the professor. If the Methuselah Man was in his sights down the barrel of a gun, he believed he could manage Ludendorff. It was when the professor went off on his own that the old bugger became truly dangerous. That all changed, however, if the nexus—meaning the Builder stone—had given him a robot or a clone instead of the real thing. In that case—

"Let's find out what he is," the captain said.

Once more, Maddox veered off course, zooming away from the ancient pyramid, heading straight for Ludendorff still rocketing off into space. Maddox gunned the vehicle, building up velocity.

"We're going to squeeze him in between us," Maddox told Meta.

"Should I shove the beamer against his back once he's aboard?"

"Good idea," Maddox said. He didn't think it was necessary for the professor, but he knew it would make Meta feel better.

Soon, the space-sled approached Ludendorff. He waved to them and motioned that they hurry.

Ninety-three seconds later, Maddox brought the sled even with Ludendorff.

"Meta is going to drag you down to us," Maddox said.

"Good thinking," Ludendorff said.

Soon, by first grabbing a boot, Meta hauled the Methuselah Man to them, forcing him to squeeze between them. A few seconds later—

"Ow," Ludendorff said. "That hurts."

"Does it?" Meta asked in syrupy voice. "How does *this* feel?"

The professor cried out in pain, twisting away from the beamer shoved even harder against his back.

"I'll force it through you," Meta said, "if you try any more funny stuff."

"Please, dear girl," the professor panted, "ease off, ease off, will you?"

Ludendorff cried out again, no doubt because Meta increased the barrel pressure against him for a third time.

"Captain, I beg you," Ludendorff pleaded.

"Don't maim him, Meta," Maddox said.

"He makes me so angry," she said.

"Meta," Maddox warned.

The professor gasped a fourth time and then his breathing evened out. Maddox supposed Meta had given the beamer a final shove and then eased the pressure.

"I'll have a knot there for weeks," Ludendorff complained.

Maddox had already changed heading, gunning toward the nearest shuttle.

"Faster, my boy, faster," Ludendorff said. "The tube is going to appear in less than ten minutes. We have to be aboard *Victory* by then."

"We're not going to make it then," Meta said.

"We'll see about that," Maddox said, trying to hail the first shuttle. He could barely get through, and it was difficult to understand the other person because of the jamming inference. Talking slowly and deliberately, Maddox gave the comm operator her instructions.

"I understand," the comm operator said at last.

"The shuttle's coming," Maddox said. "That should shave off some time in our favor."

"I hope you're right," Ludendorff said.

Maddox waited three seconds before saying, "You'd better start explaining, Professor. What's going on? Where are we going in the hyper-spatial tube? And what can we expect on the other end? If I don't like your answers, I'm aborting the hyper-spatial jump."

"You can't do that, my boy."

"I can. And I will," Maddox added, "unless you can convince me otherwise."

"Yes, yes, I understand," Ludendorff said. "You're still sore at me for my play."

"Professor, you'd better get to the point while we have options."

"Quite right, quite right," Ludendorff said. "Well, here is the situation…"

-70-

Ludendorff began to explain what had happened to him inside the nexus. Afterward, he told them about the eleven star cruisers that had made the jump to the Deneb System two weeks ago.

"After the Golden Nexus we entered," Ludendorff said, "where the Chitins battled the Swarm, the Deneb nexus is the closest Swarm-territory pyramid to Human Space. We know now that the Golden Nexus exploded after eighty thousand Swarm warships went through its projected hyper-spatial tube. Why that nexus exploded, I don't know. I have several theories—"

"I'm not interested in theories," Maddox said, interrupting. "I want facts. You were giving me those. Stay on track, Professor."

"I am on track," Ludendorff said in a querulous tone. "Ow! What was that for?" he asked Meta. "You know the captain said to stop poking me with that thing."

"Listen to what he says then," Meta told him.

"I can't concentrate if you keep—"

"Professor," Maddox warned.

"Oh, very well, stick to the point—you are two of the most unimaginative people I know."

"An occupational hazard as an Intelligence operative," Maddox said blandly.

Ludendorff grumbled under his breath as the space-sled zoomed toward the nearing shuttle.

"In any case," the professor said, his voice smoothing out, "the eleven star cruisers reached the Deneb System two thousand six hundred light-years away."

He told them about the Swarm science ships at the Deneb System, the weeklong battle and how one star cruiser had remained behind while the remaining four used a hyper-spatial tube to reach two other nexuses in the Sagittarius Spiral Arm.

By the time Ludendorff finished telling them about the nexuses destruction, Maddox had maneuvered onto the shuttle. Once they were secured, the shuttle accelerated toward the approaching starship.

"Now, you must listen carefully," Ludendorff said.

They still wore their spacesuits although minus the helmets. Each of them clutched his or her helmet as they sat on a bench in a cargo hold.

Maddox nodded. He was listening. The New Men had brought one hundred star cruisers to the joint defense against the original Swarm invasion. To lose eleven star cruisers destroying nexuses was a costly price for the New Men.

"I received what you might refer to as a data dump from the nexus computer-core," Ludendorff said. "I did not have time to receive the data the slow way. Thus, the nexus shoved a vast quantity of information into my mind. The stone helped to channel the informational mass. It's an amazing device, by the way, a wonderful tool—"

"I'm *listening*," Maddox said sharply, interrupting once more.

"Er…well, yes, the enhancer helped to channel the data—what I'm trying to tell you is that I learned amazing facts. One of the most critical was advanced knowledge about the Swarm and the Imperium in particular. The nexuses do much more than act like galactic freeways with their hyper-spatial tubes. They gather intelligence on the species in their vicinity. That, in Builder terms, is actually their most useful function."

"I don't understand," Maddox said. "The nexuses are spying on us?"

"You're wrong. You clearly do understand. That's exactly what they do. The computer core in the nexuses is startling, amazing—how could it be anything else, once you think about it? A nexus creates a hyper-spatial tube. That is far beyond our science and understanding. How is such a thing even possible? By our sciences, it is not."

"Does the local nexus know anything about humanity?"

Ludendorff chuckled. "It knows everything about us. Not that I learned what it knows. That would be far too much information for even my advanced brain to contain.

Meta rolled her eyes.

Ludendorff scowled at her, muttering, "Savage."

"What was that?" Meta demanded.

"Forget it," Maddox told her with a wave of a hand. He regarded Ludendorff. "You spoke about the Imperium as if you learned something important about it."

Ludendorff made a scoffing sound. "I learned many important facts. I'm still sorting them out. It might be *years* before I process everything shoved into my brain. Fortunately, the enhancer helped to bring two important points to my immediate attention. These are critical in our dealing with the Imperium, and critical to our present endeavor."

"I'm listening," Maddox said with emphasis.

"First," the professor said in a lecturing voice, "the Imperium is not a monolithic empire. That is hyper-critical to us."

"In what way?" asked Maddox.

"A myriad of ways," Ludendorff said. "Consider. Until Commander Thrax Ti Ix reached the Imperial Queen, the Imperium did not use jump gates or possess a star drive. That meant, naturally, that the great Imperium used Not-As-Fast-As-Light—NAFAL—drives. Do you know what that means in an interstellar empire? It means that most star systems rule themselves. As one heads inward toward the galactic core, star systems are often closer together. That allows NAFAL drive ships to reach neighboring systems in a matter of years instead of decades."

"Right," Maddox said. "I see what you mean. How can the bugs have an Imperium at all?"

"Swarm genetic behavior patterns for one thing," Ludendorff said. "Still, your question has merit. The bugs cannot have a monolithic empire such as we envision they have. Do you realize what has been happening? The Swarm Imperium is under vast turmoil as the Queen and her Hive Masters restructure the essence of the great Imperium. Given the size of the task, because of the size of the empire, that will take years, maybe even centuries."

"Which is why they haven't rushed multiple invasion fleets at us yet," Maddox said.

"Precisely," Ludendorff said. "You're a keen one, Captain, much keener than your—"

Maddox cleared his throat and shook his head.

"Yes…" Ludendorff said. "I take your meaning. In any case, Commander Thrax appeared in the Imperium nearest to Human Space. The Builder's Dyson Sphere was approximately halfway between our two political entities. You left the Dyson Sphere one way, and Thrax went the other. The commander surely had to travel inward to reach the Queen and the Imperial Planet, but he set a precedent. Thrax showed the bugs that our region of space is of deadly importance. It's where they received FTL drives, among other things. I suspect they wonder what other marvels could come from this region if they invaded it in strength."

"That's clear," Meta said, "*not*."

"You didn't let me finish," Ludendorff said. "At the present time, the Imperium is like a kicked over ant colony. In other words, it is in turmoil as I said. But it is a special type of turmoil. They are reordering the Imperium to make it more efficient. Once that process is complete, we can expect a great leap forward in planned Swarm conquests."

"And that reordering will take the Swarm centuries?" Maddox asked.

"At the most it will take that long," Ludendorff said. "I think the more likely probability is a single century should suffice for the reordering. You must keep in mind, though, that even though the Imperium is in turmoil, it will still send out various invasion fleets. It is merely the size and rate of those fleets that will increase once the turmoil ceases."

"So you're saying we're going on a Deep Beyond mission in vain?" Meta asked. "That we don't even need to be doing this because the bugs are already going to keep themselves busy for one hundred years?"

"Didn't you listen to what I said?" Ludendorff asked. "This is not a vain pursuit at all. Consider what's happened. The Imperium has sent an invasion fleet and two science fleets into Human Space and the nearby regions, which includes the Throne World System. That is small potatoes to the Swarm compared to the vast fleets maneuvering in and around the Imperium. Laumer Point tech is new to them. Star-drive ships are even more amazing. But the extent of their empire is immense. They have star systems in three or four different spiral arms. Can you really conceive of what that means?"

Meta glanced at Maddox.

The captain did not appear impressed.

"*That* is another reason why I call you two unimaginative," Ludendorff said. "Human Space is a tiny fraction of territory in the Orion Arm Spur. Ours isn't even a full spiral arm, but a spur. The Imperium has star systems in the Orion Arm Spur, the Perseus Arm outside us, and the Sagittarius and Scutum-Crux Arms inside ours. That is an unbelievable stretch of territory. It's mindboggling in extent. Only a tiny portion of the Imperium is close enough to Human Space that any nexus in or near their territory could reach us."

"Because of the five thousand light-year limit that a nexus can create a hyper-spatial tube?" asked Maddox.

Ludendorff pointed at him, nodding.

"That must still leave us lots of nexuses to destroy," Maddox said.

Ludendorff chuckled, shaking his head. "Not according to what I've learned," the professor said. "For the near future—let us say for the next fifty years—we don't have to worry about any Swarm invasions coming from the Perseus Spiral Arm."

"Why not?" asked Maddox.

"Sheer distance," the professor said. "I'm not talking about the distance from certain areas in the Perseus Arm to Human Space. I'm talking about the extent of bug territory in the Imperium. At present, the Perseus Arm Swarm are the most backward technologically speaking. Nor has the Queen sent any of her reordering fleets in that direction yet. Thus, for now, at least, we don't have to worry about any nexuses in the Perseus Arm. That's good because there are quite a few of them out there."

"Someone will have to go in time," Maddox said.

"Thirty years from now should be soon enough," Ludendorff said. "That means you might be long dead by then, or surely retired from the service."

"Riker will be glad to hear that," Meta said dryly.

"Sir," the shuttle pilot said over a wall-speaker. "We're preparing to land in Hangar Bay "C"."

"Thank you," Maddox said.

Ludendorff stared up at the shuttle ceiling as if he was thinking about something else.

"Keep talking," Maddox said. "I want to hear the rest. Use every second we have."

"Right," Ludendorff said. "You're going to want to hear the next part."

-71-

"I understand the first point," Maddox said while hurrying through a starship corridor. "Now give me the second important point."

Ludendorff jogged to keep up with the captain's long stride. "I can't talk if I have to run like this," the professor said, panting.

The captain slowed his normal stride, pacing himself so Ludendorff did not have to run to keep up.

"Better," the professor said. He dragged a wrist before his mouth. "I need something to drink. I'm thirstier than you can believe."

"Talk," Maddox said, "or I'm sprinting to the bridge, and you can tell me this later."

"No, no, I'd better tell you now. First, the Imperium isn't monolithic. Second—I've already told you the second part. Some parts of the Imperium are quite backward compared to others. The Perseus Arm Imperium lacks Laumer Point technology and star-drive tech. As far as the nexuses have reported, none of the Queen's Imperial warships have crossed over to the Perseus Spiral Arm. There are intricate genetic reasons for what I've been saying. The Perseus Arm Swarm is distinct from the rest. I can't remember this moment why that's so. The reasons go back centuries. The point is that the Perseus Arm Swarm might actually fight the rest of the Imperium."

"The nexuses told you all that?" Maddox asked.

"Not told, but data was given to me from the local nexus. The computer core running our nexus—well, normally it's dormant. The AI is waiting for further instructions from genuine Builders. There was only the one living Builder in the Orion Arm, remember?"

Maddox nodded. He remembered the Dyson Sphere Builder all too well. "So we don't have to worry about Perseus Arm nexuses for a time?" the captain said.

"Precisely," Ludendorff said, who had started puffing despite the slower pace. "Now, there was the Golden Nexus, the Deneb nexus, the Gamma 9-74 nexus and the Alpha Kappa 3 nexus that the last star cruisers reached. The Deneb, Gamma 9-74 and Alpha Kappa 3 nexuses are all gone, by the way. The New Men destroyed them."

"That's just four nexuses. There are two—were two in Human Space before the Xerxes nexus blew up, which clearly has a much smaller area than three spiral arms."

"You're making false assumptions," the professor panted. "First, we're not talking about entire spiral arms. We're talking about nexuses in a five thousand light-year range of Human Space plus the near Beyond. Given that Human Space is tiny compared to the larger Imperium, it means that only a small part of the Imperium is near Human Space."

Maddox frowned at the professor. "That's convoluted."

"That's why you must pay attention, my boy. I'm trying to make this as easy as possible for you to understand. Remember, my brainpower soared less than an hour ago. I have concepts and ideas impossible for you to grasp with your limited intellect."

Maddox turned away as fast as he could lest the professor see him smile. Clearly, the Methuselah Man hadn't liked the reprimand a second ago.

"Sir," Valerie said over a loudspeaker. "A hyper-spatial tube is beginning to appear. The power levels emanating from the nexus are incredible."

Maddox felt his gut clench. "This is it," he said over his shoulder. "Is there any last minute warning you need to give me?"

"We're heading to a key nexus," Ludendorff said in a rush. "Not counting Perseus Arm nexuses, there are or were seven Swarm-territory pyramids in the regions closest to Human Space. Four are gone; three are left. Of those three, this is the most important, as the others are almost out of range for safe travel. There are three more nexuses beyond that that might prove to be a problem, if the Swarm accepts impossible risks—"

"Professor," Maddox said. "Spit it out in three seconds. I'm leaving you behind because it's time to leave this system, and I want to be on the bridge when we do it."

"There are Swarm warships near the Omega Nebula nexus. You must be ready for evasive maneuvers the instant we appear."

"There's always some Jump Lag when we use a hyper-spatial tube," Maddox said.

"Find a way to avoid the lag. It's imperative that you think of something."

Maddox cursed softly. Then, he nodded and broke into a sprint, leaving the professor behind as he raced for the bridge.

-72-

Maddox reached the bridge at a dead run, sprinting through the opening hatch. He barely slowed down in time, passing his command chair, coming to a halt before the main screen.

It showed a giant silvery whirlpool. It was bigger than any hyper-spatial whirlpool he'd seen before.

"I can't believe the power radiating from the nexus," Valerie said as she vacated the captain's chair. "Look, the pyramid is glowing."

Maddox did look, and the silver structure glowed with increasing pulses of power.

"I'm recording the process," Andros Crank, the Kai-Kaus Chief Technician, said from his board. "Maybe we can use the data to help us make our own hyper-spatial tubes someday."

"Good thinking," Maddox said automatically. He backed up until he sat down in the command chair. "Is the whirlpool drawing us toward it?" Maddox asked the pilot.

"Yes, sir," said the pilot, who had grown pale.

"Where's Lieutenant Maker?" Maddox asked.

"He's still in the hangar bay where he landed his shuttle," Valerie said.

"Tell him to get up here on the double," Maddox said.

Lieutenant Noonan nodded as she sat down at her board.

"Golden Ural's star cruisers are heading away from us," Andros said. "They must not like what they're seeing."

"Is the nexus going to explode?" Maddox asked.

"The power pouring from it is…" Andros shook his head. "It's crazy, to use a precise technical term."

"Understood," Maddox said. "But is it going to explode?"

"Your guess is as good as mine."

"That better not be true," Maddox said, "or I'm getting a new chief technician."

"In that case," Andros said, as he studied his board, "I don't see any indications of overload. But the truth is, I don't understand what I'm seeing."

Maddox chewed on his lower lip. "Galyan." He looked around. "Where's Galyan?"

"Here, sir," the holoimage said, popping into view beside him.

"What were you doing?" Maddox asked.

"Speaking with the professor," Galyan said.

"Concerning?" asked Maddox.

"He has a suggestion for you, sir. Would you like to hear it?"

Maddox nodded.

"Use an antimatter missile instead of a thermonuclear explosive," Galyan said.

Maddox stared at the holoimage.

"That's standard operating procedure before going through a hostile Laumer Point," Valerie explained.

"Right," Maddox said, getting it. In the old days when jump gates were the only form of FTL travel, a ship or fleet risked enemy annihilation when using a Laumer Point to enter hostile territory. Jump Lag had been extreme then. A crew exiting a Laumer Point was defenseless against an immediate enemy assault. Thus, a nuclear warhead set with a spring-driven timer went through first, detonating on the other side, hammering any nearby, waiting enemy warships. Shortly thereafter, the ship or fleet came through, using the cleared area to recover from Jump Lag.

"Launch an antimatter missile at the whirlpool," Maddox said.

"In order for the warhead to be effective…" Valerie said.

"Belay that order," Maddox said. "Lieutenant," he told Valerie, "have someone attach an old-style timer to the missile. Tell me when the altered missile is ready to launch."

"Yes, sir," Valerie said, as she manipulated her board.

"I will," Galyan said.

"What's that?" Maddox asked, turning to the holoimage.

"Oh," Galyan said. "I am still in communication with the professor. He told me to tell you that we do not have much time. The hyper-spatial tube is highly unstable. The sooner we enter, the more likely we will exit in one piece. The longer we wait—"

"I understand," Maddox said, cutting Galyan off. The captain bent his head in thought. If Ludendorff said this was an unstable hyper-spatial tube—

"Lieutenant Noonan," Maddox said. "Launch the antimatter missile at once. That means you can forget about the mechanical timer. Set it to detonate the moment it exits the tube."

"The missile and warhead will experience what will seem like Jump Lag," Valerie explained.

"I'm aware of that," Maddox said. "But we don't have the luxury of time. Launch the missile now."

Valerie nodded, turning to her board.

The seconds ticked away as the nexus glowed even more dramatically than before.

"The star cruisers are accelerating," Andros said. "They're really running from this thing."

Maddox checked a chronometer and looked meaningfully at Valerie. It was 74 seconds since he'd given the missile launch order.

"The missile is almost ready," Valerie said.

Maddox refrained from speaking as eleven more seconds passed.

"Ready," Valerie said. "The antimatter missile is launching."

On the main screen, the huge missile left its bay, accelerating toward the swirling whirlpool.

"What if it Jump Lags too much?" Galyan asked. "And detonates just as we arrive on the other end?"

"We have to time this right," Maddox said. "It's as simple as that."

The whirlpool pulled and the missile pushed, and in seconds, it zipped into the hyper-spatial tube, disappearing from view and sensors.

"Sir," Galyan said. "The professor suggests we leave the system now. He says that—"

"Galyan," Maddox said. "Inform the professor that I run my ship my way. He will refrain from giving me further advice on the hyper-spatial tube."

"Yes, sir," the holoimage said.

More seconds passed.

"Sir," Galyan said. "The professor would like me to inform you that—"

"Stow it," Maddox said, interrupting. "I'm not interested. That's an order."

The little Adok holoimage nodded, falling silent.

"The whirlpool is swirling faster," Andros said. "That is increasing the pull on our ship."

Maddox observed the increased speed on the screen as the whirlpool grew larger and larger as they neared it.

"We'll enter the whirlpool in thirty-four seconds," the pilot said in a quavering voice.

Maddox could feel everyone watching him, waiting for his next command. What would the antimatter missile do? It was rigged to resist normal Jump Lag. Was that enough against the incredible leap of five thousand light-years? How much was enough margin for error? The missile would lag a little. If it lagged too much, it could well detonate as they appeared. Wasn't there anything he could do to help increase their odds for survival? Ah.

"Lieutenant Noonan," Maddox said.

"Sir?"

"Start praying."

Valerie didn't answer; she bowed her head and began to audibly ask God for a safe hyper-spatial tube voyage. "Amen," she finished, looking up.

"Ten seconds until we enter the tube," the pilot said.

"Ten seconds," Maddox said. "Let's hope God heard our lieutenant, because here we go."

-73-

Victory entered the hyper-spatial tube. While in the non-Einsteinian tube, the starship flashed from the middle-Beyond near the Throne World System. There was no recognition of the passage of time and space while in the tube. No stars were visible to any person or any sensor. The hyper-spatial tube was its own space with its own bizarre rules that did not align with normal physics.

One thousand light-years, two thousand light-years, three thousand—the starship zoomed across vast distances while in the strange tube realm. Finally, five thousand one hundred and seven light-years from the origin point, Starship *Victory* exited the humming, badly vibrating hyper-spatial tube to vomit out into the Omega M17…region.

The tiny mote of ancient Adok technology had successfully made the fantastic voyage. Now, could they survive this far out in the Deep Beyond to complete their mission?

***

Maddox was the first to raise his head as he shook off the exhaustion or the Jump Lag of an interstellar, hyper-spatial tube voyage. His first attempt to stand failed as he collapsed back into his chair.

The captain panted, collecting himself. He grunted as he stood, staggering toward Valerie.

The lieutenant was slumped against her panel, unmoving at the moment.

Gently, Maddox eased her aside as he began studying the readings on her board.

Victory was in the Omega Nebula. The interstellar matter making up the nebula was approximately 15 light-years in diameter and had a mass of 800 solar masses. Thirty-five hot young stars that formed an open cluster illuminated the gases and debris of the nebula. The captain had no idea how many planets and asteroids were hidden in here. Not that he was interested.

He wanted to know what had happened to the antimatter missile—ah. He found a heavy concentration of radiation. The warhead had detonated. What he couldn't find was any sign of Swarm warships. Ludendorff had told him the system…

Maddox straightened. This wasn't a star system. This was a nebula. There was ambient light from nearby stars, but he couldn't "see" any particular star because thicker than normal gases and debris hid it. Nor could he find any nearby—*any*—Swarm warships.

Maddox closed his eyes in frustration. Had Ludendorff deliberately lied to them? Or did the fool of a Methuselah Man not know what he'd been talking about? Ludendorff could sound so convincing, and Maddox realized he wanted to believe the professor.

Was there even a nexus out here?

With a rapidly beating heart and an inability to breathe right now, Maddox began to scan the nebula. He did not find any nexus. But then, it was difficult to scan very far with all the debris around the ship. The gases and debris, including dust, were worse than the worst parts of the Tau Ceti System.

Calm down, Maddox told himself, finally taking a breath. They'd successfully traveled over five thousand light-years. The unstable hyper-spatial tube had held long enough to allow them to reach out here. That much was right. This was the Omega Nebula—

What was this?

Maddox hunched over the board as Valerie dragged herself upright. The lieutenant blinked at him as he adjusted her panel.

"What are you doing using my board?" Valerie asked sluggishly.

"Scanning," he said.

"I can see that," she said querulously. "Why are you—oh? We're alive. We made it. Did the antimatter—?"

"The warhead detonated and we're alive," Maddox said.

"Did the Swarm warships—?

"There are none out there," he said.

Valerie blinked at him, and a little more liveliness entered her bearing. "Oh no," she said. "Did—?"

"I don't know. That's what I'm checking."

As the captain continued to check, the bridge personnel began to stir around him. More of the ship's functions also began to work.

"Why not let me do that?" Valerie said.

Maddox forced himself away from the panel.

Valerie slid into position. "What are you looking for?" she asked.

"A nexus," Maddox said softly.

Valerie looked up at him sharply. "If there's no nexus out here—"

"Yes," Maddox said. "Now you know why I was using your board."

Valerie nodded as she rubbed her lips with the back of her right hand. Then she hunched over the panel and began searching in earnest.

"Sir," Andros said. "I'm not detecting any Swarm warships or the debris of Swarm warships."

"Keep checking," Maddox said, as he settled into his command chair.

Galyan moved then. The holoimage had been motionless until that point as he'd stood rigidly beside the captain's chair.

"Galyan," Maddox said under his breath.

The Adok holoimage looked at him.

"Find Ludendorff," Maddox whispered. "Tell him we did not reach a star system, but a nebula. There are no Swarm warships here nor is there any nexus. I want an explanation, and I want it now."

"Sir," Galyan said. "I believe that the correct answer is that we are screwed."

"Maybe," Maddox said, not missing a beat, "or maybe the professor has an answer. Tell him to get his sorry butt up here now. I want to know what happened."

"I am on it, sir," Galyan said, disappearing.

Maddox wanted to run a hand over his face, but he didn't. This was one of those moments when the captain had to remain stoic. He had to stay calm so his people stayed calm. They were far, far from home. They might be screwed, as Galyan had suggested. He wondered now…

"No," Maddox whispered to himself. There would be no more negative self-talk. He was the captain of the deepest-voyaging Patrol vessel in human history. It was time to get it done no matter what it took.

Galyan reappeared.

"Speak softly," Maddox said out of the corner of his mouth.

Galyan floated a little closer to the command chair. "I spoke to the professor. He says—are you ready for this, sir?"

"Don't make this worse, Galyan. Just tell me."

"He made a mistake, sir."

Maddox could feel emotions in him trying to break free. Through force of will, he held himself in check. "How big of a mistake?" he whispered.

"Ludendorff is not sure," Galyan said. "The professor seems confused. In fact, after speaking a few words, the professor started uttering gibberish. If I were to render an opinion…"

"By all means," Maddox said.

"I think his great learning has driven him mad, sir. I do not think his mind can contain all the data the Builder nexus shoved into it. He is walking against bulkheads as he talks gibberish to himself. Ludendorff is badly off, sir."

Maddox slid off his chair as he stood. "I'll be right back," he said loudly.

Valerie whirled around in her seat. "Where are you going?"

Maddox refrained from reprimanding her. Instead, he gave her a calm look. "I need to use the head, Lieutenant. I shall be right back."

"Oh," Valerie said.

"You have command until then," Maddox said.

-74-

Maddox didn't feel pity for the Methuselah Man, but he was worried.

Ludendorff was lying in a corridor, facing a bulkhead. He spoke gibberish as Galyan had described. Maddox supposed some might call it speaking in tongues. Yet, according to what he'd read in the Good Book, others had been able to interpret what those speaking in tongues had said.

"Galyan," Maddox said.

The holoimage appeared beside him.

"Scan the passage in Acts in the New Testament where the apostles first spoke in tongues."

Galyan's eyelids fluttered. "What version would you like, sir?"

"A contemporary one," Maddox said.

"I have it."

"In the passage, do others understand those speaking in tongues?"

"Are you referring to the Day of Pentecost, sir?"

"Right," Maddox said. "That's what it's called. Thank you."

"Yes. The apostles spoke in a variety of languages. Some watchers claimed they were drunk, though."

"Drunk and likely speaking gibberish," Maddox said.

"I see your connection, sir. You are referencing this to Professor Ludendorff. But I am not sure I understand. You are not likening his condition to those in Acts?"

"I wouldn't dream of saying Ludendorff is filled with the Holy Spirit," Maddox said. "My point is quite otherwise. Some of the people during Pentecost claimed those speaking in other tongues were drunk. Maybe Ludendorff isn't speaking gibberish but a Builder language he learned while in the nexus."

"An interesting theory, sir," Galyan said.

"Record the professor's words. Maybe later it will help us understand the Builders. Or maybe it will jog something in the professor's memories later hearing what he said now."

"What about this moment, sir? The professor is in a bad way."

"Now—" Maddox said, approaching Ludendorff. He bent down, grabbed the professor and hoisted him up and onto his left shoulder so the old man lay like a sack of wheat.

Maddox headed for the professor's quarters. "Maybe the hyper-spatial journey was too much for Ludendorff's already overtaxed mind," he said. "Maybe this is how a mind bleeds off Builder-induced stress."

"Or the professor has gone insane," Galyan suggested.

Maddox didn't want to believe that. They needed Ludendorff. But if the Methuselah Man had become insane— the captain hurried as Galyan floated beside him.

"I have been wondering, sir," Galyan said. "What happens to us if there is no nearby nexus?"

Maddox shook his head. "There has to be one. Ludendorff couldn't have been that wrong. I want you to begin scanning for a local nexus."

"I have been while we have been speaking, sir. Unfortunately, the nebula's interstellar debris is much too thick to make that an easy task."

Maddox turned a corner and redoubled his speed. Galyan floated faster to keep up.

"Might I make a suggestion, sir?" Galyan asked.

"Please."

"Why not push the Builder stone against the professor? That should reconnect his mind to the enhancer and give him the extra brainpower to…to sort out these language problems."

Maddox halted, turned and peered at the alien holoimage. "That's an excellent idea, and it's fast, too. Good thinking, Galyan."

"Thank you, sir," the holoimage said, standing a little straighter. "I try to help when I can. I hope my suggestion works."

"Agreed," Maddox said. And with that, he broke into a trot. The sooner they found the nexus, if it was out here—he started sprinting, holding onto Ludendorff so the old man didn't slid off his shoulder.

***

Ludendorff was lost inside his brain. He tried to shout for help. He tried to walk. But nothing seemed to work right. The overload had happened when the starship entered the whirlpool. Something about the awful process of ripping through the hyper-spatial tube had mixed his mind so he tasted sounds, heard sights and saw flavors. Everything had become mixed up in his mind.

The professor had not been able to afford that with all the compressed Builder thoughts and data in his mind. The stress had opened channels that should have remained sealed. Now—

Ludendorff bolted upright as he roared at the top of his lungs. It was as if a bright light had struck him as he popped out of a dark cave. To follow the metaphor, the blinding light made his eyes water—in this case, it made his mind throb with pain.

In that moment, Ludendorff realized that he clutched the Builder stone. It was hot and had begun to sear his palms. The addition of the brain enhancer helped him sort the millions and billions pieces of data that had all unloaded at once in his mind. He understood that he was blind and knew nothing.

He roared again, and he tried to shake the stone from his hands. It was like a man blinded by light throwing his arms over his eyes so it wouldn't hurt so much.

Once more, the professor shouted, and this time, he spewed profanities.

"Stop, make it stop!" Ludendorff shouted.

That was what Maddox had been waiting for: to understand the Methuselah Man's words. The captain aimed the nozzle and let the foam gush against the white polygonal stone.

At that point, Ludendorff heaved the thing from him so it smashed against the deck. He was bathed in sweat and he felt horrible, but he blinked several times before opening his eyes.

"Captain," the professor said in a hoarse voice.

"You're back," Maddox said.

Ludendorff frowned.

"Don't worry about it," Maddox said. "You should rest. Yes. Eat and drink something and then get to sleep."

"Is something wrong?" Ludendorff asked.

Maddox shook his head.

Ludendorff yawned, stretched and looked as if he'd fall asleep that moment.

A medical technician handed the professor a protein bar and a large container of water.

Ludendorff ate the bar mechanically, chewing, drinking water and yawning between each bite.

"I'm exhausted," the professor said. Finally, he couldn't stay awake as he turned his head and fell asleep.

"I thought you were going to tell him," Galyan said.

"Not yet," Maddox said. "He looks too horrible."

"You were merciful to him," Galyan said.

Maddox shrugged as he turned to go. "Tell me when he wakes up," he told the medical tech.

"He needs plenty of rest," the woman said. "He's been through too much, and he's old. He's going to need more recuperative time than you or I would need."

Maddox understood. They needed Ludendorff, but they shouldn't overtax him or the fellow might die on the spot.

Maddox and Galyan exited the chamber and headed for the bridge. Before they made it, a comm buzzed in the captain's jacket pocket.

He fished out the comm and clicked it on. Valerie appeared on the tiny screen.

"There's bad trouble, sir," she said.

"You found a destroyed nexus?" Maddox asked.

"What? No. That's not it, but it might be just as bad. We've run into the back of a Swarm fleet." On the tiny screen, Valerie turned to the side before facing Maddox again. "This is an early estimate. There could be more, but so far, we've counted one hundred and ten thousand Swarm motherships."

"Motherships?" asked Maddox, wanting clarification.

"Motherships," Valerie said, "heading deeper into the nebula. Now, I'm not a Methuselah Man, but I'm betting these Swarm are searching for the nexus. Once they find it, it wouldn't surprise me to learn they're on their way to Human Space."

"Is that why Ludendorff said this was the important nexus?" Galyan asked the captain.

Maddox frowned at the holoimage. He almost whirled around to go and shake the professor awake and ask him just that. But that wouldn't change the fact of 110,000 Swarm motherships heading deeper into the nebula, likely searching for the nexus just like they were doing.

"I'm on my way," Maddox said.

"Good," Valerie said. "Because people are starting to freak out up here. What are we going to do?"

Maddox didn't answer. Instead, he clicked off the comm and shoved it in a jacket pocket. Then, without another word, he headed for the bridge.

-75-

Maddox stood dumbfounded on the bridge as he saw the fantastic extent of the Swarm fleet.

Valerie had proven inaccurate—incomplete—as to the count. Andros Crank had already numbered 143,000 Swarm motherships. That was approaching twice as many Swarm warships as had attacked Tau Ceti last time. In fact, it was more than twice the tonnage as had invaded Human Space then.

These were 143,000 motherships. Each mothership dwarfed *Victory*, which was bigger than the largest Star Watch battleship.

Surely, not all the motherships held attack-craft. Many would have heavy hull armor and heavy laser cannons. Swarm ships did not normally have electromagnetic shields. So that was something. The rest of the motherships would spew hundreds of deadly attack-craft each.

The sight caused the captain's gut to clench. If this was an invasion fleet, and if all the warships reached Human Space—then, it was over. Humanity would die. Possibly Spacers might survive, and maybe the New Men as well if they fled elsewhere soon enough. But normal people living normal lives in Human Space would become extinct.

Not that Maddox considered himself normal, but he'd thrown in his lot with the normals and rather liked them as companions.

The amazing thing was that none of the Swarm craft appeared to have spied *Victory* yet. The very gases and debris that had hidden the Swarm fleet from her sensors had also protected the starship from the bugs' eyes.

If the nexus was nearby, and the Swarm surrounded it, Maddox could forget about getting inside until their fleet left. By that time, it might not matter anymore, if the Swarm left by going directly into Human Space from here.

The captain put his hands behind his back. He made sure to stand as tall as he could and to keep his shoulders squared and his head erect. He breathed deeply, practicing calm control.

It almost felt to Maddox that he could *feel* the pressure of the 143,000 Swarm motherships, feel the pressure of the Deep Beyond trying to squeeze his soul into nothingness. Who was he but a mote of existence in a vast, cold and decidedly unfriendly universe? In the end, did it matter what he did? Humanity could not resist such mass. This was too much. How could they defeat the endless Swarm?

Maddox blinked, and he clenched his jaw. This wasn't about defeating the Swarm. This was about survival for another few years. Maybe that wasn't as glorious, but it was a worthy goal.

The captain cleared his throat. Deliberately, he turned around so the main screen was at his back. He scanned his bridge personnel. There was stout Andros Crank with his long white hair. There was Keith Maker sitting at Helm, trying to grin at him and failing. Valerie Noonan was pale-faced and likely trying not to tremble. Galyan waited by the command chair. The holoimage's Adok eyes kept flashing to the Swarm motherships. Doctor Dana Rich had come onto the bridge. She was Indian by heritage, with radiant dark skin and long, jet-black hair. Dana seemed weary with too many lines in her face, but her dark eyes burned with curiosity. She would not quit, especially not as long as Ludendorff lived. Had the professor sent her up here? There were others, a comm operator, two marine security men and a weapons officer.

Riker was staying with Ludendorff, ready to call the captain if anything untoward happened.

"We know one thing," Maddox told the bridge crew. "If a Swarm fleet is here, it must be looking or heading for the nexus."

"Do we really know that?" Dana asked. "Might there be Swarm colonies in the nebula that need a taste of Imperial Swarm discipline?"

"You have a point," Maddox said. "However, I doubt the Imperium would have sent this massive a fleet to do that. Until you can give me concrete evidence otherwise, I'm going to assume this is an invasion fleet."

Maddox faced Keith.

"Figure out the fleet's exact heading," Maddox told the ace. "Then, figure out the fleet's outer limit in that direction. I mean the limit of their scouting ships. We're going to use the star drive to jump ahead of them. Then, we're going to search like crazy for the nexus. If we have to make twenty jumps—"

Galyan's head jerked up.

"What is it?" Maddox asked the holoimage.

"Twenty star-drive jumps should take us out of the Omega Nebula," Galyan said.

"Good point," Maddox said. "The nexus has to be close, very close maybe. We need to find it first, people. And we need a greater margin of time. If we can get there first and soon enough—"

Maddox raised his left hand, indicating the main screen behind him. "If we get there first and in time, that fleet won't matter to us anymore. If we fail to destroy the nexus in time, though, kiss good-bye everyone you know. There is no trying hard and failing and calling it a valiant effort. There is only winning and losing, and on this ship, I only accept winners."

It might have seemed surprising, but the others visibly derived strength from his calmness and hard-nosed attitude. In a situation like this, they wanted a stern taskmaster. They obviously liked the idea of a winning attitude driving them.

"Questions?" asked Maddox.

No one had any, not even Doctor Dana Rich or Galyan.

"Then let's get ready for the first star-drive jump," the captain said. "The Swarm may have more ships, but we're the better vessel, and we're going to prove that today by beating them to the punch."

-76-

More than five thousand light-years away in the Orion Spiral Arm on the alien Red Planet, Mako floated soundlessly through a subterranean corridor of stone.

She no longer noticed the endless *thrum* and *drum* of the Great Machine around her. It almost seemed as if she'd lived here a lifetime. That might have something to do with her last times inside the Educator. Subjectively, she'd been through thousands more hours of special training.

The Visionary had ordered the Educator brought down to the planet. Each time Mako exited the teaching device, the world and especially the people seemed so much duller than before. They thought so slowly. And they thought upon such mundane matters and took eons to arrive at the most obvious conclusions.

In a word, several words, actually, the others here were deathly boring companions.

Mako had come to despise boring. Her mind soared with concepts too grand for ordinary mortals to comprehend. Yes. She understood so much better how the Visionary had attempted to guide her growth for this important moment of time. Without the multi-mind entity, though, the Visionary couldn't have attempted her training, as it would have been impossible. The multi-mind entity had necessitated the Meditation Machines. The genesis for those machines had come from this world called the Forbidden Planet in Spacer lore.

As Mako floated through the subterranean corridor, she wondered yet again why the Visionary wouldn't allow her to speak with the Old One. Surely, that ancient alien could tell her interesting concepts and marvels that might unlock even more jewels of wisdom in her.

Several times now, Mako had almost broken the rule and gone to find the Old One in order to converse with him. A last...*stricture* from her earliest upbringing had held her back. Had the Visionary known that would be the case?

Mako nodded. Obviously, the old woman believed that. How else would the Visionary ever have dared to make her—Mako—so wondrously awesome? And yet, the Visionary, all the Spacers, for that matter, needed her wonderfulness for the next stage in evolution to take place.

That was why Mako floated down the stone corridor. She had become impatient. No. She would not go and visit the Old One. That was against regulations. She could if she really wanted to. But she also knew a theorem from the school of hard-knocks concerning these sorts of things. A small or weak being becoming a bigger or greater being often took unnecessary initial risks because of arrogance and ignorance. Mako called this the Theorem of 'Ances.

She wasn't going to make those terrible and elementary mistakes. She loathed mistakes and missteps, and—

Mako's head jerked up, and a single word flashed in her mind: *Maddox*.

She was going to teach that vainglorious, pompous halfbreed of a human a thing or three. Wasn't he going to be surprised upon meeting her again? He'd had the gall to leave her behind in the Usan System. She still couldn't believe it. She'd had to go through such lengthy training to do it this way, when all of that could have been bypassed if Captain Maddox had just picked her up when he was supposed to.

Why didn't you pick me up, hmm...?

Abruptly, Mako halted her flight and floated down to the stone floor.

She felt the *thrum* and *drum* vibration against her feet. By this point, it was a comforting sensation. Originally, she'd found it suffocating.

A half smile slid onto her face. The Visionary didn't know that she knew about this place. Wouldn't the old woman have a stroke if she could see Mako now?

The petite Spacer shrugged. Then, she raised her right hand and made a gesture.

Bolts moved in a stone door and a mechanism activated. Slowly, with the grinding sound of granite-on-granite, the heavy stone portal opened.

Mako made another gesture. Lights appeared in the cell. She glided through the portal, her shoes less than a centimeter from the floor.

The small, wizened Strand clone blinked and rubbed his eyes as he raised his head. He was prone on a stone shelf and raised himself up on his elbows.

The Visionary had ordered him confined to the cell until further notice.

The clone spied her, blinked again and then struggled to hide a superior smile.

Mako didn't mind. She understood motives so much better these days. She could also see the electronic functions of his body with her transduction. She knew his emotional state to a nicety—anyone's for that matter.

The clone slid off the stone shelf and indicated the chairs. The cell was small, with three rooms, the others likely as stuffy as this one. The Visionary should let the mad scientist have a bath now and again. They owed the clone that much for all the technical work he'd done for them.

"Can I get you anything?" the clone asked her.

"Sit," Mako said.

The clone frowned before hurriedly sitting in the nearest chair. He hunched forward as if to attend to her every utterance. That was false. He was thinking furiously, no doubt how to use her arrival to his advantage.

"Is the Great Machine ready for transference?" Mako asked him.

The question caught the clone by surprise. A second later, he bobbed his head up and down like a nasty little goblin.

Mako almost asked her next question. He beat her to the punch.

"Would you like me to send you through now?" the clone asked.

Mako cocked her head. Was it possible to go now? She hadn't believed that it would be yet.

"It is possible," the clone said, as if he could read her mind.

Lancing suspicion bit Mako. She held herself perfectly still as she scanned his body thoroughly. No. He did not have any modifications. He could not see her electronic patterns like she could see his. Could he read her face?

He was the clone of Methuselah Man Strand. She should remember that he was considered to be the slyest human in existence.

"Why would you send me through now?" Mako said. "You know the Visionary is waiting for the perfect moment."

"There's your answer," the clone said. "I don't like the Visionary. I don't dislike you. What's *your* perfect moment, eh?"

Mako smiled.

He smiled with her, likely hoping for the best.

"What a truly horrid little worm you are, Strand clone."

For a second, his face betrayed his shock. Then, he grinned again like a little monkey, more than willing to laugh at himself if it would get him what he wanted.

"Do you think I'd trust you?" she asked.

"What's to trust?" he countered. "The Great Machine is almost all fully automated. I'd only have to make a few adjustments."

"What?" she said. "Explain that."

He shrugged, flashed the nasty goblin smile again and made an admission of truth. Mako saw that in his body.

"I, ah, have added a few modifications here and there," the clone said. "If you used it as is…" The clone shook his head. "That would be bad for you."

"You've tampered with the Great Machine?"

"Indeed I have. If you want to use it, you need me."

"You're a treacherous scoundrel."

He tried the goblin smile a third time, figuring it was a charm. He must have seen that it wouldn't work, though. That brought a vicious scowl to his features.

"Who do you think I am?" he snarled. "Your clown? No. I am Strand."

"You're a clone."

"Same difference. A Strand is a Strand is a Strand, if you get my meaning."

"You will—"

Mako halted and closed her eyes. She sensed…ah…she sensed a hidden spy device that she hadn't detected earlier. That seemed inconceivable, but there it was. The device indicated a watching Visionary. Was the old woman going to try to teach her a final truth?

Mako opened her eyes. "You are in error, Clone. You will learn what it means to be in error soon enough."

She turned to go.

"Wait," the clone said.

Mako regarded him.

"I have a proposition for you," the clone said. "Help me escape. Give me a weapon, and I'll show you how to fix my few…adjustments to the Great Machine."

"You poor deluded clone," Mako said. "You don't understand the Spacers at all. You think we're crazy mystics, don't you?"

"No," the clone said. "You have advanced tech, alien tech, even. You're more than mystics, although I'll admit you're all as crazy as loons."

"Such words do not endear you to me," Mako said.

The clone cocked his head at her, and there was madness in his eyes. "Maybe you're the craziest of the lot. Well, you know what? Screw all of you."

"No, clone," Mako said, making another gesture. "That will not happen."

He laughed wildly, grabbed a hidden dagger and attempted to turn the knife on himself. His intention was clear. He would kill himself, thus ensuring they could not fix the Great Machine in time. Instead of plunging the dagger into his chest, the clone cried out, dropping the suddenly white-hot metal.

"Did you do that?" he shouted, holding his burned hands gingerly in the air.

"I did."

"Why?" he pleaded.

"Because you must serve the Spacers before you die, worm," Mako said. "You are the clone of a Methuselah Man, and we hate all Methuselah Men."

The clone stared at her with hatred, and she shuddered to see the depth of his passion.

"I won't forget this," he said in a grating voice.

"Good," Mako said. "Neither will I."

At that point, provost marshals entered the room, converging on the clone, picking him up and carrying him away to whatever fate awaited him.

Mako looked around. Then she levitated off the floor, floating away. Soon now, she would be ready to make the transfer.

-77-

Seventy-five hours of grueling and endless searching hadn't produced a nexus in the thickening gases and dust of the Omega Nebula.

They weren't in the Orion Spiral Arm anymore, they had moved into the Sagittarius Arm. That made the distance seem even farther. Home was years away if they failed to find a nexus.

Maddox was stunned at how quickly the Deep Beyond had wilted crew morale. Having a massed alien invasion armada behind them hadn't helped them any. The starship was within the Swarm Imperium. Every hand—every tentacle and clacker, the captain supposed—would be turned against them. No one would aid them. No one would help repair damage no matter how much money they offered.

Where was the nexus? Ludendorff didn't know. Maybe as bad, probes had proven useless in the search, as the little drones had soon lost their laser-link connection with the starship because of the thick gases and clouds of dust. Maddox didn't dare try anything else, as the bug scouts behind them would undoubtedly pick up ordinary comm signals.

There was nothing else for it but dogged searching with *Victory* alone.

"Can't you remember *anything* about the nexus?" Maddox had asked the professor in a padded cell.

The Methuselah Man had looked the worse for wear after seventy-five hours in the Deep Beyond. Galyan seemed to have guessed the right of it earlier. The great learning from the Builder computer-core had turned the normally decisive Ludendorff into the proverbial absentminded professor. It had driven him mad in a sense. Ludendorff was just as apt to give Maddox a bewildered stare as to babble in gibberish. It was daunting.

Maddox stood perplexed on the bridge, staring at the main screen, trying to forget about the professor. They searched and searched for the Builder nexus, finding nothing. Soon, they would have to double back and try a different exploration angle. Unfortunately, heading back toward the mighty Swarm armada, even obliquely, would strain the increasingly fragile crew morale.

Traveling in the Deep Beyond was unlike normal space travel. It was definitely a psychological thing, but true nonetheless. Knowing that one mistake could strand them here forever, turning everyone into bug-food, had a daunting effect.

It was the difference between practicing for a championship football game and actually being out there, on the field under the floodlights as tens of thousands cheered or booed and millions, perhaps billions, more watched on the vid-screen. Running downfield as the football barreled at you became an act of will in the big game. Your palms grew sweaty as the football rocketed at you from above. On the practice field, the pass would have been nothing...but few people could act normally under such tremendous pressure.

But what if that pressure lasted not a few hours, but for days on end? Most people cracked fast then.

Maddox was very aware that they had to succeed soon or crew performance would begin to sink dismally. Against 143,000 Swarm motherships, they couldn't afford *any* mistakes.

The trouble was that he had no idea which direction to search next. Ludendorff was supposed to be their ace in the hole. He was the directional finder, and he was broken. Ludendorff had reached for the Sun, as it were, and it had burned his fingers and maybe blinded him forever.

Maddox chewed at his lower lip as he studied the main screen. *Victory* neared the edge of the Omega Nebula. From her station, Valerie glanced at him sidelong. Galyan fidgeted. Andros rechecked his board, being obvious about it.

All three knew he should order a new heading. Was maintaining their Patrol-like routine, sticking to a pattern chart, the answer? Under normal circumstances that would be true. But what about here and now, in the Omega Nebula with time running out on humanity? Was it time to gamble and choose a random search direction?

The strain had tightened Maddox's stomach for some time now.

The captain almost jumped in alarm as a hand grabbed him from behind, clutching an elbow. He whirled around as his right hand dropped to his holster. He found himself staring down into his wife's green eyes.

"You need a break," Meta whispered.

Maddox licked his lips.

"You should go to the gym and lift," she suggested.

He raised his eyebrows.

"You're like everyone else, wound too tight. You can't do anything well like that."

With a lurch, he strode past his wife as he headed for the exit. "I'll be back in thirty minutes," he said.

"But…" Valerie said.

"Keep searching," Maddox said. "I'll give you a new heading once I'm back."

That seemed to mollify the lieutenant, although it didn't help the holoimage's fidgeting or Andros Crank's panel examination.

After leaving the bridge, Maddox hurried to the closest gym, changing in the locker room into shorts and a T-shirt. Once in the gym itself he did arm and shoulder stretches, several rounds of jumping jacks to get his blood pumping and three sets of deep-knee bends to get his legs and glutes ready.

By that time, Meta had joined him.

The captain racked up several hundred pounds and did some warm-up deadlifts. The warm-up weight felt incredibly heavy to him. He couldn't believe it.

That only forced him to add more weight. He needed to push himself if he was going to relax.

Soon, he had a solid, deadlifting load on the bar. He waited a few minutes to let his muscles revive. Then, he put his feet into position, bent his legs so his shins bumped against the bar and set his grip.

Mentally preparing, Maddox suddenly lunged upward, straining to lift the weight. He strained, and quit, releasing the bar without having lifted it off the floor.

Maddox straightened and flexed his hands. He couldn't believe this. He should have easily hoisted the bar off the floor. What was wrong with him?

"You're tired," Meta said. "I didn't realize just how tired until seeing that. What you need is sleep."

Maddox shook his head. "I can't sleep. I've tried. I just..." He just stared at the ceiling while in bed, but he didn't want to admit it aloud.

Meta stepped near and took his right hand with her left. She tugged him. He didn't have the will this moment to resist. She led him back to the locker area and into the showers. Then she began to take off his clothes until he was naked. At that point, she began to take off her clothes, but did it slowly and seductively.

Maddox watched his wife, absorbed with her beauty. Soon, she too was naked.

Meta came to him, and she began to touch him, stirring the primordial instincts in him.

Finally, Maddox came to life. And there in the showers in the locker area, the captain became reacquainted with his wife.

The release came in time, and it seemed to do more than affirm his love for her. All the anxiety, worries and fears fled him at that moment. With her beauty and love, Meta had helped to ease him and shown him how to enjoy the moment once more.

For the first time in days, Maddox relaxed, holding his wife. This was his mate, his love, his companion. She cared about him. She cherished him, and he cherished her. As he held her, as he kissed her slowly, enjoying the afterglow of love, a fierce resolve began to stir in Maddox.

If he failed out here, he would lose Meta. His beloved wife would die and there would never be another like her, ever. The idea of Meta ceasing to exist because the Swarm devoured all humanity in its ceaseless quest to grow—

"No," Maddox said.

"What's that, love?" Meta asked.

"The Swarm isn't going to win."

"Can't you think about something else at a time like this?"

Maddox looked down into his wife's eyes. "I did," he said. "I had a moment of—" He grinned. "I wouldn't call this rest."

"You'd better not or I'll make you do it again."

He hugged her tightly, and he thrilled that this beauty was his woman. He'd chased and caught her, and the hunt for her love had been worth every effort to achieve it.

He was Captain Maddox, and he had a duty to perform out here in the Deep Beyond. He had accepted the post of captain on Starship *Victory*, and he was here as the champion for humanity. He could wilt under the pressure or he could perform.

In that moment, Maddox determined to go down swinging, if go down they had to. He would not lose by indecisiveness. It was time to reach the nexus—and it was time to figure out why the Swarm fleet hadn't been able to reach it yet, either.

The enemy fleet had changed direction several times. That had thrown him off.

Maddox released his wife, stepping back from her as he snapped his fingers.

"What is it?" she asked.

"This nexus is mobile," he said.

"Meaning what?" Meta asked.

"Meaning..." He stared at her. "I think the nexus is steering away from anyone coming too close to it. That means someone or something is steering it."

"Is that important?" Meta asked.

"It has to be," he said. He almost turned to go. Instead, he reached out, grabbed his wife's hand and pulled her against him one last time. He pressed her naked body against his, kissing her. Then he let go and turned away.

It was time to go to work.

-78-

This was frustrating. In the padded cell, Maddox told Ludendorff his theory. The professor stared at him as if he understood, and then the Methuselah Man began speaking alien gibberish.

Maddox tried another two times. It made no difference. He brought Dana in, but neither her presence nor her ideas helped.

Riker was there because the sergeant had the unenviable task of watching the professor.

Maddox still wasn't completely convinced that Ludendorff wasn't playacting in some manner.

"Why not explain all this to Draegar 2?" Riker asked. "The Bosk overlord is in it with the rest of us. Maybe his supposed genius can see what we're all missing."

"How would he communicate any of his understanding with us?" Maddox asked.

"I've seen him scribble mathematical formulas," the sergeant said. "Maybe that's the only language you and he can both understand."

"I can't believe it," Dana said. "The sergeant has a point."

"I don't see it," Maddox said. "How do you speak to the Draegar through math equations?"

"Is that a serious question?" Dana asked Maddox.

"Yes."

"That's ridiculous," she said. "We should get started on it right away. It might take the Draegar some time to figure it out."

"Figure what out?" Maddox asked.

"Oh, come on," Dana said. "I'll show you."

The doctor proved as good as her word. She wrote out a complex mathematical formula and presented the paper to Draegar 2 in his cell. Then, she showed the Draegar a video as Andros Crank explained the same thing through visual aids.

Maddox stood back and watched. This sounded as nutty as the professor's craziest ideas.

The bronze-skinned Bosk paid careful attention to Dana, and frankly, seemed more interested in her as a woman than in her math paper. The Bosk overlord only paid half attention to the demonstration Andros showed him. Once or twice, though, Draegar 2 looked up sharply and followed the maneuvering of the giant Swarm armada on the video screen.

Maddox glanced at the screen then, wondering what the supposedly genius Bosk saw that he didn't.

Finally, after Dana and Andros completed their briefings, Draegar 2 sat back in his chair. The Bosk didn't acknowledge their presence anymore, except for the few brief times Dana switched her position. The brainy Bosk then paid the closest attention to her breasts, or the fabric covering them, as if he might have X-ray vision. Otherwise, Draegar 2 was motionless. Suddenly, however, he clapped his hands and made writing motions. He did this several times.

"Communication," Dana whispered. "He's never done anything like this before."

Riker got pen and paper, placing them before the Draegar.

The Designer Bosk began to write formulas on the paper. They were tiny numbers and equations. After a time, he stopped, and turned the paper around, looking at the equations at various angles.

How that helped him think, Maddox didn't have the slightest idea.

The Bosk began to write even faster, making scratching sounds as the three of them watched. It was a large cell, and maybe too comfortable in Maddox's opinion. The bronze-colored humanoid scrunched his brow and made faces. Three times, he stuck out his tongue as if he was thinking deeply. Finally, Draegar 2 took his last blank piece of paper. He studied the others careful and wrote slow and much larger equations on the blank paper.

"It's like he thinks we're stupid," Dana whispered to Maddox. "We might miss it if he doesn't write it big enough."

At last, Draegar 2 set down the pen, turned the paper and shoved it in front of Maddox.

The captain peered at it. The paper was filled with numbers and strange squiggles. He reached for it, searching the Draegar as he did so.

The Bosk nodded.

"More direct communication," Dana said. "I'm going to have to reevaluate my thoughts about him."

Maddox didn't know why she said that, but he didn't really care at this point.

"Do you understand his equations?" he asked Dana.

The doctor stood beside the captain as she stared at the equations.

"No," Dana finally said. "I haven't a clue what that all means."

"Chief Technician?" Maddox asked Andros. While the Draegar wrote his equations, the captain had summoned the Kai-Kaus chief to join them.

Stout Andros Crank now looked at the paper. He even took it from Maddox and scanned the equations. Afterward, he gingerly set the paper on the table and turned to Maddox.

"The equations baffle me," Andros admitted.

Maddox's shoulders slumped. He'd thought the Chief Technician was about to solve their problem.

"Let me look," Riker said.

"Be my guest," Maddox said, saying it in such a way that maybe pigs might fly after all.

Riker moved up, standing over the paper, turning it several times and finally beginning to nod.

"You know what that means?" Maddox asked, stunned.

"I do," Riker said. "It means we should give the paper to the professor and hope the Methuselah Man knows what it says."

"Sergeant," Maddox said.

The captain reached out, and it seemed he was going to strike his assistant. At the last moment, Maddox appeared to change his mind as he patted the old Intelligence agent on the left shoulder. "Good idea. Let's give it a try."

-79-

Ludendorff was in a bad way, and the professor almost knew it.

He woke in a dreaming state. No, wait. That wasn't quite right. He dreamed in an awakened province. That seemed better than the original statement, and yet...it was wrong.

Ludendorff bumped against a padded wall as he considered the ramifications of the idea. He staggered backward, hardly aware of what he'd done.

He ached all over, and he wasn't sure why. An outside observer could have told him. He'd been walking into padded walls for over three days. He had bruises all over his body and face. He—

The professor's fingers of his right hand made sharp motions. Maybe he was trying to snap his fingers. It was such a pathetic attempt, however, that it was impossible for others to tell what he attempted to do.

The professor tried it three more times, finally making a clumsy approximation of a finger snap.

"Eureka," he said.

He dreamed in an awakened state. He moved like a sleepwalker here and there, working through strange equations and formulas. He saw past events that had nothing to do with humanity. He floated in ether among hundreds of fellow Builders. They had a Council of Ways and Means, deciding on these puppets called Methuselah Men.

That council meeting had taken place four thousand years ago, but to Ludendorff with the myriad of memories jammed in his skull, it seemed as if it had just taken place. To juggle that memory with the events going on around him now—

Ludendorff staggered backward yet again because he'd crashed against a padded wall…yet again. As he staggered backward, he tripped over his own feet, slamming his back and the back of his head against the padded cell floor.

He lay there for a time, reliving an event that had taken place a mere one thousand, seven hundred and thirty-two years ago.

Sometimes, it felt as if he was going mad. He had such random thoughts and so freaking many of them that he was finding it difficult to sort one from the other. Maybe the worst thing of all was that he was having trouble remembering who he was.

He believed he might be a minor Builder in a Morning Sect of the Afternoon Culture. At other times, he believed he was the Methuselah Man Trainer. The trouble with that thought was having to indulge his time with the apish brutes of the third planet of an insignificant star system—

Ludendorff chuckled to himself as he rolled over onto his belly and slithered across the floor like the deceiving serpent.

Serpent or Sergeant Riker, that was the question. He'd told that oaf a hundred times—

Ludendorff froze as a moment of clarity struck. He was a man, a human, to be precise, the wisest and most profound of the Methuselah Men that had helped dimwitted humanity climb into the Space Age.

"Help," he whispered.

Ludendorff realized that he badly needed help because he had woefully miscalculated not so many days ago. He had shoved—

Ludendorff sat up in a cross-legged yoga pose as he bent his head, clutching it and moaning. He had damned himself by overachieving again. This time, he had gone too far. He could not hold all the Builder memories in his ape head. He had—

The very pads opened before him as several people rushed into the cell. It almost seemed as if they had timed their appearance with one of his brief spells of sanity.

"Darling," the prettiest among them said to him.

Ludendorff mouthed the word, "Dana?" without adding voice to it.

"He's lucid," the pretty thing said.

"Show him," the tallest of the trio said. That one seemed domineering and pushy. Ludendorff supposed he might know that one, and he believed he had reason to dislike him as well.

Ludendorff began to chuckle to himself.

"What's so funny?" the oldest of the three asked.

"Not now, Sergeant. Show him," the tall one told the pretty one.

"Half-breed," Ludendorff said, and he began chuckling once more.

The old one—Sergeant Riker—glanced at the tall one.

"It doesn't matter," Maddox said between clenched teeth. "He doesn't know what he's saying."

"I do," Ludendorff said.

"Darling," the pretty one said. "What does this mean?" And she shoved a sheet of paper at him.

Ludendorff snatched the paper from her, holding it between his hands and scanning fast. He began to rock back and forth as he read and analyzed the formulas and equations.

"Who wrote this?" Ludendorff said.

"Who do you think?" the tall one asked.

Ludendorff peered at… "Maddox," he said. "You're Captain Maddox."

"That's right. Now, who wrote that?"

Ludendorff glanced at the paper in his hands. Suddenly, in a swift fit of rage, the professor tore the paper into pieces and threw the pieces into the air.

"That was just a copy," Maddox said.

"Draegar 2, the Designer, wrote the formulas," Ludendorff said. "A child could see that."

"But you're no child," Maddox said.

Ludendorff almost lost his connection with this waking dream as a dozen new ideas knocked on his consciousness.

"Darling," the pretty one said. "Hang in there. We need you so desperately."

Ludendorff swallowed hard. "Dana," he whispered. "Help me. I need help."

"I'm trying, Professor," she said.

"I helped you come back," Ludendorff said. "You have to help me."

Dana glanced at Maddox.

"Go away," Ludendorff told Maddox. "You're spoiling everything by your presence."

"What did Draegar 2 say in the paper?" Maddox asked. "Once I know that, I'll leave you alone with Dana."

Ludendorff almost lost it there—who did the damn captain think he was?—but he held onto his sanity for a few more moments because Dana had asked him to.

"The nexus is mobile," Ludendorff said. "Draegar 2 figured out its propulsion system and how to track it. It's ingenious, but it has a limited scope."

"Can you show us where the nexus is?" Maddox asked.

"I told you what the paper means," Ludendorff said querulously. "You have to go now, you promised."

"Yes," Maddox said. "I did promise. And I will go. But we need the coordinates. I'm going to have Dana use the Builder stone to fix your mind. That might hurt her—"

"No!" Ludendorff shouted. "Don't do that. I'll kill you if you force her to do that."

"Then, restore your sanity through force of will," Maddox said. "Otherwise, I'm risking Dana to fix you, just like you fixed her."

At that point, Ludendorff turned sullen, putting his head down and concentrating like he'd never concentrated before.

"Stone," the professor whispered. "Give me…the…Builder stone."

-80-

Ludendorff screamed as he clutched onto the white polygonal stone. He stood in a stark room with both hands gripping the slowly heating object.

The connection with the ancient stone expanded his mind, but it still wasn't enough to contain all the compressed Builder data in his gray matter. He raved because the process was daunting and bewildering, and he shouted because he knew what he had to do, but he just couldn't get himself to do it.

He had to erase most of the alien data in his mind or he would never be sane again.

Yet, that was unthinkable. He was Professor Ludendorff, the one who *knew*. All his life, he'd striven to learn more and understand more deeply. Now, he possessed knowledge as he'd never known it. He could solve a thousand mysteries…if he had enough time to sort through all this data.

It was all there in his mind, swirling and bumping up against his previous knowledge.

As he gripped the polygonal stone, using the increased brainpower to think and sort, he realized a proverbial lesson. He was like the storybook man who had found a magic lamp, rubbing it until a genie appeared. "I want a mountain of gold," the man said, using one of his wishes.

The genie waved his blue arms, and a mountain of gold buried the man, killing him.

Ludendorff had his mountain of knowledge, and it was killing him, or incapacitating him. He would never have believed that a man could know too much. His brain was simply too puny to contain such a bewildering mountain of knowledge.

Ludendorff stood in the stark room, weeping. He could fix this if he wanted to, but the idea of it drove him crazy with frustration.

"To delete or not to delete," Ludendorff whispered. "That is the question."

He laughed sadly afterward as the tears continued to stream down his cheeks.

He was like the dwarf-king who had searched for the fabled diamond of his clan, and found it just as the dragon who had stolen it came zooming down from the heavens. The fabled diamond was too heavy to allow him to run away in time. He could have the diamond and lose his life, or he could lose the diamond and save his life.

Ludendorff could almost hear Maddox ask him a question from the Good Book. "What does it profit a man to gain the whole world and lose his soul?"

The obvious answer was that there was no profit in that.

"But I want to keep my knowledge," Ludendorff shouted.

Even though it's driving you mad? a different part of him asked.

"Yes, damnit, yes," the professor wept.

As he struggled with his dilemma, the polygonal stone continued to heat up.

Then, a hatch opened.

Ludendorff expected Maddox to come in and berate him, or Dana to plead with him. He wouldn't listen to Maddox; the captain had ordered him around for too long. And he hoped Dana would not ask him this, for he might come to hate her over time for what he'd lost.

Neither of them showed up, though. Instead, Sergeant Riker waltzed in, nodding slowly as if this was exactly as he'd expected things to be.

"What do you know about this?" Ludendorff snarled.

Riker smiled so his old, seamed face wrinkled up.

"That's not an answer," Ludendorff said.

Riker used a hand and tapped his other arm.

"What's that mean?" Ludendorff asked.

"That arm is bionic," Riker said.

Ludendorff frowned.

"I lost it in a blast," Riker said. "The doc said he had to amputate what was left or I'd die. Do you know what I told him?"

"That you can't live without your real arm?"

Riker chuckled, shaking his head. "I said, 'What are you waiting for, Doc? Cut the damn thing off. Give me one of them fancy bionic arms in its place.'"

"I can't attach a bionic brain to my head, you oaf," Ludendorff said.

Riker shrugged. "So you lose a little knowledge. Big whoop-de-do. You're alive and able to think. What's more important, knowing so much you can't think, or knowing enough and being able to use it cleverly to achieve your ends?"

Ludendorff blinked at the sergeant even as smoke began to smolder from his hands.

"It's up to you," Riker said. "If it were me, I wouldn't hesitate. But just in case you can't let go, good-bye, Professor. It was interesting knowing you."

"You think I'm making a mistake?" Ludendorff asked.

Riker glanced at the smoke curling from underneath the professor's hands. "I think you're running out of time. We all are. Kind of ironic, don't you think?"

"Get out of here," Ludendorff snarled. "I don't need your—"

No, the professor told himself. What did it profit him to have all this knowledge and be unable to use it? The sergeant had a point.

Ludendorff sighed deeply. He knew what he needed to do, and he was going to do it. If he didn't—

The professor shut his eyes. He squeezed his eyelids tightly and began to delete one ancient Builder memory after another. He chose a spot in his mind, and he began shoving knowledge out of his brain from there, erasing, erasing and erasing treasured memories that had never rightfully belonged to man.

Time was running down, so he mass-deleted hordes of compressed memories, losing some of his own in the process.

He kept some of the ancient knowledge, as well, but it was hit and miss because time had run out on him.

Then, Ludendorff truly began howling in agony as the stone cooked his poor hands.

The hatch slid up once more, and Maddox rushed in, spraying foam that hissed and sizzled against the stone. Luckily, Riker tackled the professor then, ripping his melded palms from the polygonal object, swaths of burned flesh going with it. There was blood, far too much blood, but the two Star Watch operatives freed the professor from the killing linkage with the ancient Builder stone.

-81-

Twelve hours and a surgery later for Ludendorff found Captain Maddox on the bridge, directing the starship onto yet another heading.

He had a link with Ludendorff, who was in a medical facility surrounded by med-techs and a fawning Dana.

On a side-screen near Maddox's command chair, Ludendorff sat up in bed. The Methuselah Man was wearing a white gown and had heavy mitts over his healing hands. He looked paler than usual, but there was sanity in his eyes, although he seemed unbelievable sad.

"What a loss," the professor said again. "Gone into the ether—the lost knowledge—a shame, a true and irreparable shame."

Maddox might have told the professor to cheer up, but he'd heard the Methuselah Man's complaints far too often during these past twenty minutes. It was getting tedious beyond endurance.

"Sir," Valerie said from her station on the bridge. "The scouts…"

Maddox looked up at the main screen. Through heavy gases and swirling dust particles, he spied fifty-plus Swarm scout-ships. From what they had been able to observe so far, the Swarm armada had been sending more such scouting teams in all the directions of the Omega Nebula. It would seem the bugs were sick of being lost and had found their own answer to the missing nexus problem.

Maddox turned to the side-screen, "Professor, your new heading will take us toward Swarm scouts."

"I can't help that," Ludendorff said. "According to Draegar 2's analysis, that's what these readings are telling me to do."

Andros and his team had set up a special panel and rigged it beside the professor's bed. As Dana, or other techs, manipulated the board, Ludendorff interpreted the data. He did so, he said, according to Draegar 2's formulas.

"If the Swarm scouts see us..." Maddox said.

"I know very well what you're implying," Ludendorff said in a bad-tempered voice. "But that's not my problem. I'm here telling you how you can find the nexus. It's in the direction I just said."

"But according to our sensors nothing's there," Maddox said.

"I'm telling you, something *is* there; you just can't see it. You have to go closer if you hope to see it."

"But closer will bring us nearer the—"

Ludendorff shouted obscenities as he slapped his mitted hands against his bed-sheeted knees. The hard contact made him stretch his neck and howl with pain.

Dana looked up angrily at the screen. "Can't you listen to him, Captain?" she shouted. "He gave up so much to give us our chance. You mustn't hound him like this."

In a flash, Maddox realized how Ludendorff would play this day for the rest of his long Methuselah Man life. Ludendorff would talk about his great sacrifice to save mankind. He would go on and on about lost knowledge. Well, that didn't matter either way. Let the professor tell his stories. How did that hurt him? Each man had to live with himself. And maybe Ludendorff had made, for him, the ultimate sacrifice.

"Captain," Valerie said from her station.

Maddox tore his gaze from the side-screen and concentrated on the fifty-plus Swarm scouts out there. He had another painful decision to make.

Swarm scouts were small vessels, maybe five times the size of a Star Watch tin can. Fifty of them were a few too many to take out just that like. This group had strayed from the main armada farther than some but not as far as others.

"I don't know," Maddox whispered to himself.

"Captain," Galyan asked, floating nearer the command chair.

Maddox gave the holoimage a suspicious glance. A person that far away shouldn't have heard him mutter. The alien AI seemed to pay far too much attention to his every utterance.

"Maybe I could help, sir," Galyan said. "Before my deification, I was considered a tactical genius. That is how I became the Driving Force for the Adok Home Fleet."

"No doubt," Maddox said absently. He already knew all that.

"Do you suggest I am fabricating, sir?" Galyan asked.

"What?" Maddox asked. "No. Of course not."

The little holoimage glanced at the main screen. He didn't need to do that in order to see the Swarm scouts. Galyan was linked to the starship's sensors and always "saw."

"A direct attack, sir," Galyan suggested. "Ram the starship down their collective, scouting throats and obliterate them."

"That's your tactical-genius advice?" Maddox asked.

"Yes. A direct blow is often the best blow."

"But they'll send a message back to the fleet before I obliterate them," Maddox said. "That will let the main fleet know our exact position."

The captain stared at Galyan with something approaching astonishment. A second later, Maddox slapped his armrest with his left hand. "Thank you, Driving Force. You've given me an idea."

"I did?" Galyan said. "Ah. I did. Shall I order Keith to begin acceleration?"

"No," Maddox said. "Instead, here's what I want you to do."

-82-

At different intervals, four big drones launched from *Victory*. The drones did not accelerate normally, but used stealthy maneuvers, dumping gravity waves to change heading and quietly increase speed.

"Anything?" Maddox asked Valerie.

"Not that I can tell, sir," she said, while studying her board.

Maddox and Valerie referred to the Swarm scouts. None of the enemy vessels seemed to have detected the starship or the four drones yet. The nebula's thick gases and cloud debris still hid them.

"Captain," Ludendorff said from the side-screen. "I suggest you get a move-on. I have come to believe that the nexus is only partly in our universe. That means it will take us longer to reach it."

Maddox frowned at the professor. "No… I don't think so."

"You doubt my analysis?" Ludendorff asked, obviously surprised.

"I know what being partially in the universe is like," the captain said. "That is a tactic of the Nameless Ones. It has never, to my knowledge, been a Builder tactic."

"Are you suggesting your knowledge of the Builders is superior to mine?"

"Not at all, Professor," the captain said smoothly.

"I may have dumped massive amounts of Builder knowledge from my mind…but that doesn't mean I know any less than I did before my encounter with the nexus computer-core."

"I'm sure that's true," Maddox said.

"Don't you dare," Ludendorff said. "I won't accept anyone talking down to me, and certainly not from you, you young pup."

Maddox stared at the Methuselah Man until a slow smile slid onto the captain's face. "Welcome back, Professor. You survived your ordeal with vast extended knowledge driving you insane to return to us as the same pain in the ass you've always been."

Dana's head whipped up. "Captain—"

"No!" Ludendorff said. His frozen features glared at Maddox. "No," he said more softly, as his features lost some their granite quality. "No," he said a third time. "Maybe I deserved that. The great loss of knowledge has been grating on me, Captain."

Maddox nodded.

"You have no idea how I can—"

"I'd like to indulge you," Maddox said, interrupting. "But I have to run a small skirmish. If we can't pull this off, we'll have the entire armada on us too soon."

"Yes, quite right, quite right," Ludendorff said. "Call me when you're ready for further data on the hidden nexus."

With that, the side-screen flickered off.

Galyan gave Maddox a meaningful glance. "I believe the correct phrase is that he is a touchy devil."

"That's it," Maddox said, standing, moving toward the main screen. Galyan floated beside him, also watching the screen.

With his hands behind his back, Maddox observed the enemy scouts as the minutes ticked away. Far too slowly, the drones maneuvered into battle position. They had a ways to go because they needed to come from a direction completely different than *Victory's* location. That was part of the point of the drone attack. He wanted to keep the starship's location hidden from the enemy.

"Oh-oh," Valerie said. "The bugs are detecting that something's out there."

Five of the Swarm scout-vessels detached from the rest, accelerating and turning toward the drones' hidden position.

"This is too soon," Valerie said. "The drones—"

"Turn the drones toward the bugs," Maddox said.

"But—yes, sir," Valerie said. Her fingers flew over her panel. Afterward, she looked up. "We don't have much choice anymore, do we, sir?"

Maddox shook his head.

Valerie studied her panel. "Three different scouts are decelerating. I think those three are going to head back to the fleet and tell them what's happening."

Maddox nodded absently. He'd already divined that.

More time passed. The three decelerating scouts now maneuvered as they began to turn more sharply, heading back toward the main fleet.

"Now," Maddox said. "Have the drones attack now."

The four drones accelerated with a hard burn. Even through the gases and debris clouds, they were now easily visible to the enemy.

"The three messenger ships are accelerating, sir," Valerie said. "One of them has engaged in long-range communication, presumably with the main fleet."

Maddox sighed quietly.

"I understand your choice better now," Galyan said. "Did you assume the scouts would see us too soon for our own good?"

Maddox shrugged.

Galyan became thoughtful. "Are you being modest in order to further highlight the professor's vainglorious—?"

"Galyan," Maddox said, interrupting. "Give it a rest."

"A rest?" the holoimage asked.

"Don't ask so many questions," Maddox said out of the side of his mouth.

"Oh. Yes. I see. I am sorry—"

"Galyan," Maddox said. "Stop talking."

The holoimage blinked as if startled. Then, he fell silent.

Maddox focused on the main screen as the drones roared at the remaining Swarm scouts.

"Their weapon ports are beginning to heat up," Valerie said.

A soft smile twisted Maddox's lips. It wasn't going to be that kind of fight. "Distance?" he asked.

"They are in range of the rods, sir," Valerie said.

"Ignite the drones," Maddox said. "Let's see if this is going to work or not."

Each drone carried a heavy thermonuclear warhead near its cone. The drones were also staggered for just this reason and had begun to spread out. As Valerie's signal reached them, tiny rods sprouted from each cone. A targeting computer aimed each rod. The next instant, the first thermonuclear warhead exploded. It sent gamma and x-ray radiation speeding ahead of the slower EMP and heat. The gamma and x-rays climbed each rod, focusing at a target, and sped at the speed of light at each distant objective just before the nuclear blast destroyed the rods. The nebula's gases and debris made it a less than one hundred percent shot as some of the intervening substances weakened the radiation attacks.

The warhead on the second drone now exploded, sending in advance another arrow mass of directed gamma and x-rays.

The third and fourth warheads performed likewise.

The spears of radiation struck one Swarm scout after another. Many of the small bug vessels crumbled like overtoasted bread in a monkey's hands. Other vessels blew apart as some vital area of the ships' interiors ignited.

Valerie kept a keen watch on her board. "Thirty-three, thirty-four—forty destroyed so far, sir."

Maddox remained motionless, waiting for the end.

The next few seconds saw the annihilation of the Swarm advance threat as forty-five of the enemy scouts died to the exploding drones. Three of the five survivors were already heading back to the main bug fleet.

"What are we going to do about the rest?" Valerie asked.

Maddox appeared not to hear the question.

Galyan made a throat-clearing noise.

Maddox's head turned, and his body followed it, facing the lieutenant. "Leave the last bug scouts," the captain said.

"But—" Valerie said.

"Our drone attack was the best we can do," Maddox explained. "The drone attack came from a different heading. The last two scouts will go to investigate the drone debris. Launch another drone to meet those two, destroying them."

"The Swarm fleet is going to show up soon," Valerie said.

"You're probably right," Maddox said. "But maybe we bought ourselves a small margin as they head in the wrong direction. They'll likely search in the heading from where the drones appeared. If I use *Victory* to try to destroy the three messenger vessels, the odds are the last scouts will be able to tell the main fleet about us. Then, the bugs will head in the right direction instead of veering in the wrong direction."

"I see what you mean," Valerie said. "This was about delaying them, not necessarily stopping them."

Maddox nodded and said, "Bring up the professor again. It's time to see how the nexus has been hiding from us."

-83-

After the skirmish with the scouts, the ancient Adok starship maneuvered according to Ludendorff's specifics. The professor followed Draegar 2's formulas, and the bridge crew found nothing, nothing at all.

Maddox slouched back in his chair, glancing at Valerie. She slowly shook her head.

"The professor is wrong," the lieutenant said. "The nexus isn't there. This was a boondoggle."

"I don't understand this," Ludendorff said in the side-screen. "I followed Draegar 2's instructions. The nexus has to be out there. It's close. It simply must be."

"How could we have missed the nexus if it's there?" Maddox asked.

"Yes," Ludendorff said, as he rubbed his left eye with an edge of a mitt. "If it's there…ah, I think I know. Space is vast. Even here in the nebula, space is incredibly…big. How close did we come to the nexus during our latest search? Possibly as close as several hundred kilometers. In our normal terms, that's right beside a thing. But that's because our sensors can usually easily spot an object one hundred kilometers away. In our terms, we could have moved right past the nexus and not seen or sensed its presence."

"That is illogical," said Andros Crank, who had moved to the command chair.

"That's nonsense," Ludendorff said. "My logic is impeccable, as always."

"You're not listening to me," Andros said patiently. "The Swarm armada is in the nebula. That is a fact. They wouldn't have come to the nebula unless they knew about the nexus. They can't know about the nexus unless a Swarm ship has seen it before."

Through the side-screen, Ludendorff stared at the Kai-Kaus Chief Technician. "By George, you're right. You're absolutely right. The Swarm have been to or sighted the nexus before. Why are they having trouble finding it again then? They must know its general whereabouts…"

The professor stopped talking as he hunched his head, obviously in deep contemplation.

"Yes," the Methuselah Man said shortly. "The nexus must have perfect camouflage—perfect stealth technology, in other words. Even so, we could know it's there if we tried to fire a beam and the beam halted for an inexplicable reason, meaning the nexus blocked the shot."

"Or if we blasted an area with sand," Andros said, "and the sand wall shifted strangely, revealing the hidden nexus."

"In that case, the very gases and dust of the nebula should reveal the nexus," Ludendorff said. "The substances are already a wall of sand, so to speak."

"Perhaps that's part of the stealth technology," Andros said. "The nexus produces extra gases and dust, spewing it away from itself as it…ingests the gases and dust bumping up against it."

"That would be difficult to do perfectly," Ludendorff said, "but it would be workable in theory. We simply lack the time and likely the energy to fire twenty thousand beams in twenty thousand directions during the next few hours."

"It would take damn fine concentrated observation to see the change of gaseous intake and outtake," Andros said.

The little holoimage cleared his throat. "I believe I have the necessary concentration," Galyan said. "I could recalibrate my sensors—"

"Yes!" Maddox said, interrupting. "Get on it, Galyan. How long will it take you to recalibrate?"

The holoimage stood perfectly still as his eyelids fluttered faster than they ever had before. He opened his eyes a moment later.

"The recalibration is done, Captain," Galyan said. "When shall I begin scanning?"

"Now, please," Maddox said dryly.

"Andros's theoretical proposal isn't necessarily how the nexus has remained hidden," Ludendorff said. "It would be a cumbersome process at the best of times."

"Yet it fits all the available data," Andros pointed out. "The bugs found the nexus once. They believe they can find it again and yet haven't found it. There's a reason for that."

"Possibly, possibly," Ludendorff said. "However, I am of the opinion that—"

"I found it," Galyan said. "It is rather easy to spot once you know what to look for. That was well thought out, Chief Technician."

Andros kept his features even, although he stood taller and held his shoulders squarer.

On the side-screen, Ludendorff gingerly crossed his arms and made a grumpy face.

"Where is it?" Maddox said.

"Look on the main screen, Captain," Galyan said. "I have outlined the area in yellow."

Maddox turned to the screen. A yellow triangular outline of gas slowly moved leftward and downward on the main screen. It moved away from the Swarm armada in the distance.

"You're sure that's the nexus?" Maddox asked.

"Oh, yes," Galyan said. "I have found the next Builder pyramid."

"Have you scanned the nexus for life-forms?" Ludendorff asked from the side-screen.

"Yes," Galyan said. "It is empty, likely on automated."

"Yet the nexus is moving," Ludendorff said. "I don't like that."

"Like it or not," Maddox said, "we have to board the nexus and set the next coordinates."

"What coordinates?" Ludendorff asked. "Oh, yes, I understand. You want to get to the next nexus in the near-

Swarm territory. That means another hyper-spatial tube so *Victory* can dash there. But someone will have to stay behind to blow up this nexus."

"Unless we can rig an automated explosive," Maddox said.

"No, Captain," Ludendorff said. "Someone will have to remain behind. We can't leave it to a machine that could break down. We've gone to tremendous effort to get here. We have to be sure we destroy it."

Maddox nodded. It was hard but accurate logic. "First we have to see if we can make a hyper-spatial tube. Are you up to a quick voyage to the nexus, Professor?"

"No!" Dana said from his bedside. "He's injured. He can't go."

"Nonsense, my dear," Ludendorff said from the bed. "Give me a few drugs, and I'll be fit as a fiddle, as they used to say. Oh, and we'd better bring the Builder stone with us just in case."

"He can't go," Dana repeated stubbornly.

"We're all expendable," Maddox told the doctor. "This is a matter of human survival. I'm not going to use second best when the best is available."

Through the side-screen, Dana glared at Maddox. "You're heartless, Captain. You don't care about anyone."

"Yes to the first and no to the second," Maddox said calmly, as he stood.

"Are you also expendable?" Dana asked sharply.

"Of course," Maddox said. Then he pointed at Valerie, telling her that she had the bridge. After that, he hurried for the exit.

-84-

Everyone knew the drill. That didn't make it easy—this was like the pass rocketing downfield as the receiver sprinted toward the end zone during the last minutes of the championship game.

Keith piloted the shuttle as it rose from a hangar-bay deck and headed toward the opening. Within a minute, the Star Watch vehicle left the mighty ship, gliding toward the wall of gases and clouds of debris.

There was no yellow outline in space. There were just endless nebula substances shifting in apparently random patterns.

"This is like flying by radar," Keith said cheerfully. He meant using *Victory's* special sensor data sent to his helm board. "To a great pilot, radar or sight makes no difference."

"Luckily we have you, then," Maddox said from his seat beside the ace.

"True, all too true," Keith said, nodding.

The space-sleds were in the shuttle's cargo bay. Meta was back there, along with Ludendorff and Sergeant Riker, to help the professor when and if the Methuselah Man needed it. A marine and a tech would remain in the shuttle with Keith.

Maddox pressed a switch on his screen for a backward camera glance at *Victory*. Gases and dust were already getting in the way. Maddox inhaled deeply as he realized this would probably be one of the last times he would ever see his starship. He felt a pang of loneliness squeeze his chest. They

446

were in the Sagittarius Spiral Arm, alien space, Swarm territory. After all these years, he'd never found his father. He would have liked to accomplish that, but he'd met his true love and gotten to do many of the things that he'd desperately wanted to do.

Still, life seemed too short all of a sudden. He didn't want to remain behind and detonate the nexus. But he wasn't going to order someone else to do it. He was the captain. He would take the dirty job, the needed job, and make sure it was done right.

The New Men had made the tough choice. They'd understood a soldier's task. Sometimes, one had to guard the bridge alone while the rest of the army fled. That was a glorious honor. It would be his honor to detonate the nexus and make sure this huge bug armada never made it to Human Space.

His mother had died to protect him. He would now willingly lay down his life to protect his mother's people.

"Hey, mate, what has you so gloomy looking?" Keith asked. "Can't you see it? There's the crazy nexus."

Maddox shook off his reveries and looked up. There indeed was the nexus, a silver pyramid like all the others he'd seen. There was a unique addition to this nexus, though. Some kind of pressor field or ray guided incoming gases and debris through three giant sucker discs. The three giant discs were like jet intake props, sucking down gases and dust. How that transferred to three huge ports on the other side of the nexus, Maddox didn't know. More pressor fields or rays smoothed the out-coming gases and debris ejecting from the three back ports.

"That must be how the nexus moves around," Keith said.

"That doesn't make sense," Maddox said. "The law of equilibrium demands greater energy—"

"Of course it makes sense," Keith said, interrupting. "It's like an ancient Bussard ramjet. The nexus scoops up the gases and debris and blows it out as reaction mass. The nexus supplies the additional energy, possibly with antimatter engines or something more elegant. It does it all slowly enough, though, that it remains hidden in the nebula. Now, sense or not, mate—sir—how close do you want me to go to it?"

Maddox eyed the intake discs and blast ports and eyed the swirling gases around the nexus. "Do you think you can bring the shuttle to within fifty meters of it?"

Keith laughed. "Is that a joke?"

"Can or can't you do it?" asked Maddox.

"Consider it done, sir."

Maddox eyed the discs sucking down gases. He didn't trust the three big apparatuses. Could those turn on the space-sleds and suck them down?

"You want me to do it then?" Keith asked.

"Yes, proceed with care," Maddox said.

"Aye, aye, sir," Keith said. "We're going in."

-85-

As he was suiting up in the locker area of the shuttle, Ludendorff knew he should have stayed in bed. He felt lightheaded and nauseous. His hands were useless, and he doubted he could undergo another session in the depth of the apex. But he wasn't going to let the half-breed outman him. This was the moment of decision, of keeping the Swarm from invading Human Space.

Clearly, the vast armada had targeted humanity for extinction. The little he knew about the Swarm led him to that inescapable conclusion. What made it all so galling was that he knew exactly how to shut down the nexus without fanfare. Correction, he *had* known how to do that. But he'd tossed aside the critical knowledge along with other priceless information. All he'd wanted to know about the Builders had been inside his brain.

"I threw it away like trash," he whispered to himself.

The professor shifted his shoulder as Sergeant Riker pulled up the spacesuit. This was ridiculous. He was helpless and couldn't even dress himself.

Ludendorff kept staring at the nexus outside the shuttle. This one was different from all the other nexuses he'd seen. The discs that sucked down debris and the ports on the other side that spewed it out—what a clever system.

"That's it," Ludendorff said. "That's what I do not understand."

"What's that?" Maddox asked. The captain was already wearing his spacesuit. He spoke through the open visor of his helmet.

"That's what I don't understand about this," Ludendorff repeated. "*Why* is this nexus hidden? No other nexus hides like that. What caused the Builders to make those inhalers here and the exhalers on the other side? Why would they go to such effort—?"

"The Swarm," Riker said, as he pulled up the left shoulder of the professor's spacesuit.

"Are you suggesting that the Swarm Imperium sprawled everywhere when the Builders fashioned the ancient nexus?" Ludendorff asked the sergeant.

"Why not?" Riker asked defensively.

The professor rolled his eyes. "I can't believe this. It's obvious why not."

"To you it's obvious," Riker said. "Not to the rest of us."

"The Builders fashioned the nexus before the Swarm Imperium existed," Maddox said.

"Yes, that's what I'm saying," Ludendorff told them. "There wasn't any need then to hide a nexus from the Swarm Imperium, because no imperium existed when the Builders constructed the nexus."

"So they hid the nexus from someone else," Riker said. "Big deal."

"Who else?" asked Ludendorff.

"How should I know?" Riker asked.

"The Nameless Ones?" Maddox guessed.

"No," Ludendorff said. "The Nameless Ones never reached this part of the galaxy."

"A Builder foe we've never heard of then," Maddox said.

"Possibly," Ludendorff said, having grown uneasy.

"Spit it out," Maddox said. "What do you suspect is going on?"

"We shouldn't enter this place," Ludendorff said suddenly. "The Builders…" the professor shook his head. "There's something about this particular nexus the Builders didn't want anyone to learn. That's why they went to such effort to conceal it."

"If it's that dangerous," Riker said, "why construct it in the first place?"

"I don't know," Ludendorff said. "But that's a good question. Captain, I suggest we torpedo the nexus with massed antimatter missiles. Destroy it from the outside."

"That's all well and good," Maddox said. "But first we need a hyper-spatial tube to reach the next nexus. Remember, we have three of these things to destroy. This is just the first one."

"We'll never reach the others if we enter this place," Ludendorff said.

Riker, Meta and Keith glanced at the captain.

"Professor," Maddox said as he eyed the Methuselah Man closely, "you're becoming superstitious. We have no choice about this. Our mission parameters force us to take the risk of entering."

"I have a bad feeling about this," Ludendorff said. "We're…we're possibly treading where humans weren't meant to go."

"This advice is coming from you?" asked Maddox. "You're the one who is always taking insane risks. You must be tired, Professor. I don't blame you. You've been through a lot in a short amount of time. Plus, this is the Sagittarius Arm, not the Orion Spiral Arm."

"What difference could the latter possibly make to me?" Ludendorff asked.

"Pressure," Maddox said. "This is the Deep Beyond. Here, the pressure goes off the charts."

"Bah," Ludendorff said. "If you're not going to listen to reason, then let's get on with this and go to our doom."

"Agreed," said Maddox. "Not the doom part, but let's get started. Sergeant, get a move on if you would."

Riker nodded, pulling up the other shoulder of the professor's spacesuit.

-86-

After a short journey outside the shuttle, Maddox floated several meters from the ancient nexus. Keith had towed him, Meta, Riker and the professor with a space-sled. Each of them wore a spacesuit and carried plenty of extra air-tanks, and supplies on their thruster packs.

The reason for having Keith tow them was simple. He wanted the expert for each part of the mission. No one flew better than Keith Maker. Thus, the ace flew them to the location. If that meant the shuttle lacked a pilot for a little while, so be it.

Riker now guided the handicapped professor before the area the Methuselah Man had indicated. Maddox couldn't see any difference in this part of the nexus, but this wasn't his area of expertise.

Maddox was growing anxious again. The Swarm fleet should be moving up soon and they hadn't even broken into the ancient structure. Why did every stage out here seem to take longer than normal?

"Do you see that point?" Ludendorff asked over his helmet comm as he waved in the desired direction.

Riker grunted an affirmative over his own comm.

"Aim my device at it," Ludendorff said.

The sergeant did as bidden, aiming a clicker at the nexus point. Nothing seemed to happen. Suddenly, however, a small section of the pyramid wall dilated open.

"Now," Ludendorff said, "while it's open, jetpack us inside."

Riker first hooked the professor's suit to his. Then, the sergeant used his thruster pack, squirting white hydrogen particles.

Maddox was more adept at thruster-pack flying than the sergeant. He sailed past the duo, heading for the dark opening. Behind him, Meta surely followed. Maddox clicked on his helmet lamp, washing the area with a beam of light. He sailed through the opening, flying into a large chamber with star fields shining electronically upon the interior bulkheads.

The captain rotated and braked gently until he floated weightlessly in the large chamber—it was half the size of a *Victory* hangar bay.

Meta glided in next and then Riker brought himself and the professor inside.

"Keep going," Ludendorff radioed. "This—" He abruptly stopped talking.

Behind them, the entrance closed, sealing them in the nexus.

"What's wrong?" asked Maddox.

"This place," Ludendorff said in an odd voice.

"What about it?"

"It's...it's different."

"Meaning what?" Maddox asked.

As Riker and he floated weightlessly, the professor twisted toward the captain. "Listen carefully. This is not a normal nexus. We should...we should reopen the entrance and leave while we're able."

"We're staying until we get the job done," Maddox said firmly.

"Do you sense a Ska?" Riker shakily asked the professor.

"What?" Ludendorff asked. "No. I feel something worse than a Ska."

"Worse than a Ska?" Riker whispered. "Worse? You're saying worse? How could it be worse?"

"You need to be precise," Maddox said. "Tell us exactly what you're sensing."

"I-I don't know exactly," Ludendorff said. "It's on the tip of my tongue, but…" He swore afterward. "This is maddening. I'm certain I knew once. But I tossed the knowledge, the precious knowledge. Now, I'm like everyone else, making wild guesses."

"No one is like you, Professor," Maddox said, his voice as calm as he could make it.

The captain looked around, his beam moving as his helmet rotated. The star fields shining on the walls must have been alien constellations—he didn't recognize any—as seen from a planet in the Sagittarius Arm. That vantage-point world could be ten thousand light-years or more away from here.

Yet, there did seem to be something eerie about this nexus. Was that the power of suggestion? Had the professor's words molded his thinking? How could he know? Ah. He had an idea. The power of suggestion could work two ways.

"This nexus is different," Maddox said in an agreeable tone. "It's different because we're in a different spiral arm. Look. We've learned the Swarm Imperium isn't monolithic. Surely, the same holds true for Builders. These are Sagittarius Arm Builders, distinct from the Orion Arm Builders that trained you, Professor."

Ludendorff's silvered visor kept focused on Maddox. Finally, the professor said in a calmer voice than before, "That's an astute observation, Captain. Yes. That makes more sense." Ludendorff chuckled nervously. "I've been making myself and possibly the rest of you nervous for no reason. Five thousand light-years means something after all, doesn't it?"

"I don't like it in here," Riker said over his helmet comm.

"That's because you're a superstitious old coot," Maddox told the sergeant. "Do you still think you know your way around in here?" he asked Ludendorff.

"I believe so," the professor said. "There are a few differences I'm noticing, but the basic pattern still seems to hold. Yes, I recognize the way. Sergeant, if you will rotate us twenty-five degrees, we should enter through the third arch. That should lead us to the Linkage Chamber."

Maddox hoped he was correct about his so-called observation and the professor wrong about his earlier statement. He didn't want to run into a Ska, and he certainly didn't want to run into something worse than a Ska. This was a Sagittarius Arm nexus, and that's all the difference there was to it. Maybe the discs and ports outside helping to hide the nexus were common out here in the Sagittarius Arm.

Maddox squeezed his trigger-throttle and jetted after Riker and Ludendorff. He looked back. Meta was following him.

The four human motes moved through the ancient nexus, with its maze of pitch-black, oversized corridors. With varying degrees of success, the four tried to explore boldly. Yet, despite the captain's words, they each flew warily. According to Galyan's earlier scan, there were no life forms waiting for them in here. Why, then, did Maddox feel so tense? Was it a premonition of a coming disaster? Or was it the fear of having to stay behind soon? He hadn't told anyone about that yet. In a sense, the disaster of his life was fast approaching. He could call holding the way while the others left *glory*, but the closer he came to having to do it, the less glorious it was feeling.

-87-

While the four explored the alien nexus, over five thousand light-years away in the Orion Arm of the galaxy, beneath the surface of the forbidden Red Planet, the Great Machine roared and shook.

The Old One, Nay-Yog-Yezleth—awakened and revived by tainted varth elixir—controlled the Great Machine. The mighty worldwide mechanism did not use thermonuclear or even antimatter energy. Instead, long shafts running through the planetary crust tapped the thermal energy of the red-hot mantle. The mantle had absorbed some of the heat radiating upward from the center of the world—the core that was as hot as some stars.

Mako 21 waited in the transfer chamber inside the heart of the Great Machine. She wore a Spacer suit with oxygen tanks and stood near a large thruster-pack. This pack was different from those Maddox and his people used. The Spacer thruster-pack was bigger, carried more fuel and could act, in some instances, like an independent space vehicle.

The diminutive Spacer had radically changed since her last conversation with the Strand clone some time ago. She was much more capable now than before and had evolutionarily advanced, making her different from the Visionary and other higher-ranked Surveyors First-Class.

Certainly, Mako still looked much as she had when first entering the Meditation Machine that had propelled her on the fateful astral journey when she'd joined the multi-mind entity.

In other words, she still seemed human. But looks could be deceiving. In Mako's estimation and that of the Visionary, she was not *Homo sapiens* any more. Neither was she *Homo superior* as the New Men considered themselves to be. She had become *Homo sapiens enhanced*. She thought differently than Spacer humans did. She possessed extra senses and extra powers provided by her modifications and the extreme training under the Educator.

Mako had also become an artificial being. She could not reproduce herself by mating. If a man lay with her, Mako could conceive, but only an ordinary Spacer-human baby. Yet, even though that was all true, she was the Spacer egg, seeking to mutate into a superior form as conceived by the Visionary's astral voyage dreams and other Visionaries' dreams before her.

The two had spoken about this as the Visionary shared some of the possible paths awaiting Mako. The good ones foretold an amazing transformation, a mutation or, more likely, a metamorphosis from a human into a godling. First, Mako must make the incredible journey to the targeted nexus. She was the pod, the seed of the Spacer future, of a galactic super-being that would transcend even the Builders of old.

Three hours ago, for a reason known only to the Visionary—at least she believed only she knew the reason—the Supreme Spacer had given the word, "It is time to start the Great Machine."

The Strand clone had made his adjustments to the Great Machine some time ago, fixing his alterations. Afterward, provost marshals had returned the clone to his cell where he could contemplate his sins.

With the word given, other Spacers had awakened the hideous Nay-Yog-Yezleth, giving the Old One his final injection of varth elixir. Once the gross being indicated that he was awake, the others had prodded the ancient alien to his great and final task.

Throughout all this, Mako waited in the transfer chamber. Now, she was becoming impatient. She wanted to get on with it, as she was excited and more than a little worried about all the things that could go wrong. As more time passed, the excitement, waiting and worry became too much. Using a combination of transduction and other modifications, the Spacer egg probed outward with her heightened senses. With a radar-like ability, she "saw" and studied the massive activity around her.

Probing farther and farther, Mako "saw" for the first time the mighty alien that had been awakened from his ancient slumber. Nay-Yog-Yezleth was a gross blob-like creature with many tentacles and a ring of hideous eyes. Despite the inhuman appearance, Mako felt his towering intellect.

In turn, Nay-Yog-Yezleth sensed her probing, and he directed a portion of his personality at her.

Mako grew faint as the weight of his presence avalanched upon her. He was old beyond reckoning and callous…not in a reptilian way, but in an alien manner that chilled Mako to the core of her being. Nay-Yog-Yezleth possessed…cosmic awareness, a cold intellect that dwarfed human thought and had soared above the Builders.

Like a sick person flailing against a strong man using a pillow to suffocate her to death, Mako struggled pitifully against the ugly weight of Nay-Yog-Yezleth's searching intellect.

During the overwhelming contact, Mako sensed a malignant will and a demonic hunger to consume. Nay-Yog-Yezleth's mind-power was gigantic compared to hers, and his inhuman vitality had kept him alive in a slimy pit in the hottest abyss of the Forbidden Planet.

A normal Spacer would have wilted under the intense alien onslaught. But Mako was no longer normal, and she had sensed such darkness before. She suffocated under the being's mental weight, but she struggled, and while struggling she sensed more about the Old One. He practiced deep cunning, and in some sly manner, Nay-Yog-Yezleth had helped to *shape* the Spacers.

How did he do this? Mako yearned to know. Her mind was suffocating, but she wriggled a thought here and another there.

Nay-Yog-Yezleth had rejected conscious logic to mold the Spacers. Instead, he'd helped another greater than him who used nightmarish dream-truths that had invaded Meditation Machine-formed multi-mind entities.

Yes! Mako had sensed dark undercurrents flowing through the universe. One piece of that darkness had joined their former multi-mind entity. She realized now that that darkness had come from a greater Old One hidden out there in the Sagittarius Arm.

While her mind gasped under Nay-Yog-Yezleth's mental weight, Mako sought to learn more. Was she a pawn in a Great Game beyond her understanding? Did Nay-Yog-Yezleth use the Spacers instead of the Spacers using the Old One?

In a moment of time, Mako saw Nay-Yog-Yezleth in the control pit, his tentacles whipping about with bewildering speed as he energy-focused the Great Machine.

Mako now received dark secrets of ancient interstellar lore. The Old Ones had installed the Great Machine eons ago during a grim time in galactic history. The subterranean caverns containing the machine snaked throughout much of the continental crust. Heat power from the mantle surged through turbines so giant cogs whirled and spun, and kilometer-long pistons furiously rocketed up and down. Sizzling electronic connections joined with gouts of phantom energy. There were other energies and mechanisms driving the Great Machine that Mako could not conceptualize. The combined forces shook the planetary surface, causing quakes in places.

As Nay-Yog-Yezleth studied her with his immense, cold intellect, Mako received more shocks of knowledge.

The majority of the Great Old Ones had perished in eons past. They had used the Great Machine here in their cosmic conspiracies. A horrible backlash of energies had devoured many of the gross creatures, sending some on long interstellar journeys, while turning most into puddles of slime.

Mako wondered if that was true. Something about the mental images she received now seemed false, off, a distraction. The particular image of the devouring energies showed massive destruction to much of the Great Machine. The idea, then, was that the Spacers had worked for over a hundred years to repair the machine. Mako saw in her mind Spacers toiling like ants, ceaselessly repairing the terrible damage.

"I don't believe that," she managed to gasp. "It isn't logical or true."

The brutal heaviness of the alien's thoughts abruptly pulled back. Just before the retreat, Mako sensed unease, the possibility that he'd made a mistake with her, sensed, if there was a way to repair the mistake? Possibly.

"Mako," a man said.

Mako withdrew her radar-like senses from out there—she could do so now that Nay-Yog-Yezleth had stopped mentally suffocating her—pulling her consciousness back into her mortal body. She was supposed to be alone in the transfer chamber. It was inconceivable, then, that anyone had breached the sealed area to physically join her at this weighty moment of destiny.

As she stood inside the heart of the Great Machine, Mako's blind eyes opened. They used the optic sensors of the goggles, peering through the closed visor of her spacesuit helmet.

To her shock, the Strand clone stood in the chamber with her. He also wore a spacesuit. How he'd achieved this entry and gained a suit, Mako did not know. Could it have anything do to with Nay-Yog-Yezleth's unease with her? That seemed inconceivable. No. That was laughable. This was something else entirely, right?

It didn't matter. She would know soon enough how the Strand clone had snuck in here, and she would teach the clone a bitter lesson about protocol. Only…that lesson might not happen because the clone was aiming a gun at her. That was a joke, of course, because she had her new powers.

Within her helmet, Mako smiled indulgently—the clone was a pathetic, predictable little weasel, thinking he could cow her by waving a weapon. She reached out with her modifications, and recoiled in surprise.

The Strand clone did not hold a beamer, a pistol-weapon she could easily cause to malfunction. Instead, he held an old-fashioned chemical-reaction-driven slugthrower. He had an old .45 pistol of ancient manufacture, an actual 1911 model.

This was highly irregular. Where had the clone found such a thing? Nay-Yog-Yezleth couldn't have produced that. Why would she even think the Old One could?

No. Forget about the Old One. Nay-Yog-Yezleth did his appointed task. He was a cog, a thing the Spacer Nation used in its quest for…for something.

Despite the fear caused by the Colt .45, Mako spoke imperiously through her helmet speaker. "Lower your weapon, Clone."

"I want to know one thing first," Strand said through his helmet speaker.

"What is that?" Mako asked.

"How did I get here and where are we going?"

"That's two questions."

"Where are we going then?"

Ah. Mako realized that the Colt wasn't an insolvable problem. Still, she should humor him a moment or two as she figured out how she would eliminate him.

"I'm going to my destiny in the Sagittarius Arm," Mako said.

"And?" the clone asked.

The question was maddening and insulting. The clone did not deserve to know about her future greatness. Still, if he died soon—as in several seconds from now—what did it matter if she told him?

In a controlled voice, Mako answered, "Once in the Sagittarius Arm, I will transmute into a new being of great power."

In the background, there was a flickering sense of Nay-Yog-Yezleth sighing with relief. What did that mean? The sense of the watching Old One vanished, however.

"I'm speaking to you," the clone said. "I'm not in the habit of repeating myself."

"What did you say?" Mako asked, realizing he'd been talking while she'd sensed Nay-Yog-Yezleth's sigh.

"How will you do this…this *transmuting?*" the clone asked.

That was too much. The clone sought to learn the deep Spacer secrets and asked highly embarrassing questions to boot.

"Why do you care about any of this?" Mako asked haughtily. And then it slipped out. "You're not going to live much longer."

"Oh, but you're wrong," the clone said. "There's no future for me here. That's clear enough. Thus, I'm coming with you. I remember now how I slipped in here. It was quite ingenious and obviously, I must have been planning it for some time. You see, this is an urgent matter for me. The questions are because I want to know what to expect on the other side."

"You're a fool, Clone. The Great Machine cannot propel both of us that incredible distance. There is only power to send one. Thus—" Mako stopped talking because she realized the clone already knew that. He had said all of that to distract her.

Strand pulled the trigger. The Colt boomed as the chemical reaction took place. The explosion hurled a lead slug through the barrel at her.

Mako reacted swiftly and decisively, reaching out with her telekinetic power. She did not stop the bullet cold. It was likely she lacked the power to do such a thing, as the bullet had great force behind it, and this process occurred in a fraction of a second. Instead, Mako deflected the bullet just a trifle.

The bullet still flew at her but missed the spacesuit by a millimeter. The slug crashed against the wall of the transfer chamber, and that was bad. The process needed incredible precision. Another—

Boom!

The clone fired again.

Once again, Mako deflected the bullet.

Now, the Strand clone used two hands to hold the weapon, and he fired one bullet after another. He seemed desperate to kill her, almost maniacal.

She deflected each shot like a gun-fu master from an old vid. She *was* a master at this. Unfortunately, each shot marred the interior of the transfer chamber.

"You fool," Mako said.

Strand snarled and charged her, hurling the Colt .45 at her helmeted head.

Mako used her telekinesis on the metal gun. It lacked the brutal velocity of the bullets, as the clone was weak-armed.

Thus, she deflected the gun's flight, T-lifted the automatic high in the chamber and brought it rushing down against the clone's helmeted head.

The blow disoriented the clone and caused him to stumble. He grunted through his helmet speaker, tangled his feet, tripped and skidded across the floor. He raised his helmeted head.

Mako concentrated, and she used the Colt .45 like a hammer as it rose and fell, repeatedly knocking his helmet. He managed to work up to his feet once and stagger toward her.

She skipped out of his path, but kept her concentration as she continued to hammer his helmet with the T-controlled gun.

"Stop it," the clone said. "Let's make a deal, a pact. We can both live."

That was a lie, and Mako knew that he knew. The process continued, therefore, and finally his helmet cracked.

"No!" he shouted. "Have mercy. I never meant you any harm."

Mako did not laugh. Instead, she continued to use the dented and twisted gun like a hammer. Now, however, she broke open the helmet and dashed the gun against his skull.

The Strand clone fell to the floor and screamed for mercy, begging her.

The gun continued to rise and fall, making grotesque sounds now as it struck his bleeding head. The clone's begging finally ceased and soon so did his groans. At last, the clone's space-suited legs kicked and twitched and then they stilled.

The gun clattered to the floor. According to Mako's quick radar-like scan, his heart had stopped as his brainwaves ceased. The clone was dead. It had taken long enough. The problem was that he'd left a dilemma for her.

The old Mako would have been mentally exhausted by the ordeal. The new mutated Mako had power to spare. Once more, she used her modifications, looking around and knowing that the mission was in serious jeopardy. Because of the bullet marks along the interior walls and the excess mass in here, the Great Machine would transfer her elsewhere than the great goal.

"I cannot allow the project to fail," Mako intoned.

Sitting cross-legged in the center of the chamber, Mako bowed her helmeted head. She gathered her resolve and opened an outer hatch in the transfer chamber.

The hatch had been sealed. Meaning that what she did should have been impossible. She was the Spacer egg, however. She was the proto-god in the making. With her telekinesis, Mako shoved the corpse and the gun and the spent bullets from the chamber. Seconds later, the hatch slammed shut for good.

Then, with great patience and skill, Mako began to repair the bullet damage along the interior walls. It was slow and tedious work. But what else did she have to do?

Once done, Mako exhaled and raised her helmeted head. She had barely completed the repairs in time. For, at that precise moment, the energies of the Great Machine reached its pitch, and the incredible transfer began to take place.

-88-

Vast energies flowed through precisely calibrated Usan crystals. It was a storm of power. This storm wasn't controlled by computers, but by the monstrous entity in the pit of the Great Machine.

Nay-Yog-Yezleth whipped his tentacles with bewildering speed as he sat in the control pit. The mind deep in the blob-like bulk sped through long-string equations as he followed matrix mechanics of eldritch complexity.

The heat power of the Forbidden Planet changed into quantum-5 energy as it passed through one ring of Usan crystals after another. The quantum-5 energy moved great levers and tripped turbines of elder science. That built up the transcendent power source until huge crackling balls of ethereal dynamism merged into one another.

A well opened in a subterranean pit. The massive crackling ethereal dynamism surged down into the last generator. No metal or plastic, nor any material substance of any kind, made up the parts of this machine. Energy walls and phantom circuits flowed with molten power.

On the surface of the Red Planet, the six giant obelisks glowed with power. The symbols along the sides pulsed like a beating heart. The obelisk tips shone sun-like until the luminance became too savage to see.

Now, the elder being in the great control pit—Nay-Yog-Yezleth—swiveled around as panels flipped over to their targeting sides. His slimy tentacles sped through complex sequences. The Visionary had given him the target—so she thought. She'd received the data while using a Meditation Machine as she'd joined another multi-mind entity. The Visionary believed that she had seen the target in her future visions. This target was a great nexus in the Omega Nebula in the Sagittarius Spiral Arm.

Nay-Yog-Yezleth knew the secret truth. Spacers using the Meditation Machines used an astral process that made them susceptible to the cosmic dreams of slumbering Old Ones. Monkey-driven brains floating through the cosmos on astral journeys were easily manipulated. The apish creatures had a high gullibility factor. The Spacers were more prone to this than other humans were because they loved esoteric science and offbeat mysticism.

Thus, Nay-Yog-Yezleth accepted the targeting. He recognized the nexus of their ancient foe, the Builders of hard science insights. The Spacers believed they could soar to evolutionary heights through these forbidden means.

Yes, yes, Nay-Yog-Yezleth told himself. *I shall free you, father. You shall rule again, and the night of the Yog-Soths will descend upon the galaxy once more.*

In the control pit, a myriad of holoimages appeared before Nay-Yog-Yezleth. His hideous ring of eyes observed the many images, and he made squishing sounds and octopus-like croaks as his tentacles whipped faster and faster, the tips touching masses of switches.

The tainted varth elixir gave him the needed energy to perform at this prodigious level. He had not felt like this for ten thousand years. He had been here before the damning era of the Builders. He had hidden during the surge of the Nameless Ones and slumbered as the Builders slowly waned in ability and presence. Now, awakened from his ancient slumber, he knew that he helped in a great process driven by his father's nightmarish dreams.

He silently laughed at the notion that the tainted varth elixir would kill him. That was a Spacer conceit, a last piece of caution against the possibility that they had made a grave mistake in wakening him.

It was no mistake, but it would end miserably for the monkey-beings originating from Earth. It wouldn't be the last time an Old One corrupted a race by promising the power to defeat their foes. Nay-Yog-Yezleth easily recognized his father's dream-manipulations. The Swarm Imperium out there would be the perfect race to serve them as mindless slaves. It was almost as if the bugs were custom-built for the Yog-Soths.

Now, Nay-Yog-Yezleth's contemplations ceased as he began the final process. This would take every erg of his cosmically aware intellect. He had to concentrate, concentrate—

Now, now, now! It was about to happen once again. This was a glorious moment in the greatest saga of the galaxy.

In the transfer chamber where Mako waited, ethereal dynamism boiled in like misty lava. It wasn't hot, no, it was cold—freezing cold—to a woman of flesh and blood. The ethereal dynamism continued to flood the chamber until it compacted. As more churned within, it condensed to an incredible degree. That heated the dynamism and transformed it into metaphysical energy that had no mass. As the transformation occurred, it caused Mako to turn translucent.

An outside observer would say that she was becoming invisible. Yet, that would not be precise. She was losing mass as her mass turned into metaphysical energy. Soon, Mako had disappeared, as had the thruster-pack and all other substances in the strange chamber.

With the faint sound as of a million subdued voices arguing, the metaphysical energy charged up into Quantum-9 Transformers. Seconds passed. Then, the Quantum-9 Transformers beamed the Q9 charged M-energy at the speed of thought toward the six great obelisks on the screaming, stormy surface of the planet.

The six giant obelisks glowed like points on a star. A swirling power appeared between the tips. This was Q9 charged M-energy and it sped faster and faster until it exceeded the speed of thought.

Some might have called this the *scream of ghosts*. It was ethereal, and, arguably supernatural. The science of the Yog-

Soths was unlike any other in the galaxy, except perhaps for the Ska.

In the control pit of the Great Machine, as the vigor of the tainted varth elixir gave him greater concentration, Nay-Yog-Yezleth targeted the Omega Nebula nexus. This was a moment for uncanny precision. He sighted the fantastic distance and tapped a control, releasing the scream of ghosts.

The swirling mass of supernatural energy lofted into the cosmos like a pure beam of light. But it traveled incalculably faster than any light or even thought. It flashed across five thousand, eight hundred and twenty-one light-years. The ghostly scream speared at the nexus. Since the beam had neither mass nor matter, being entirely formed of metaphysical energy, it easily passed through the nexus's walls.

That caused a tripping chain-reaction within the Q9 charged M-energy. As though activated by a sorcerer's spell, the bizarre energy began to coalesce and take shape. That caused ethereal power to shed from it in misty wisps. A strange and inexplicable process—to humans, at least—began. Bit by bit, as if by the hand of God, pieces of matter and mass fit together into a pattern, a three dimensional puzzle. A white cloud enshrouded the process, so no more could be seen—were there an observer.

Seconds passed, and in that time, the white cloud dissipated. A form twitched, and residual ethereal excess faded away as if it had never been.

At that point, Mako 21 and her Spacer thruster-pack appeared, fully formed, in the Calling Chamber inside the Omega Nebula nexus. She stretched, breathed from the suit's tubes, and knew herself to be alive again in the normal, accepted manner.

Mako was aware that she had made an incredible journey. Perhaps equally incredible, she'd been reassembled. She recalled other data. The Strand clone was dead. The Forbidden Planet was over five thousand light-years away. She would likely never see the Visionary again. It was possible she would never see another Spacer. At least not in the next thousand years.

As Mako inhaled her tank's air, she realized that the final step still lay before her. At this point, strangely, she seemed to have forgotten about Nay-Yog-Yezleth. But no matter, Maddox was here, or so she deemed likely.

Mako moved in a slow circle, examining the chamber. The idea of crossing from one spiral arm to another might have wilted the old Mako. This Mako, the Spacer egg Mako, accepted the journey as part of the process.

She'd faced Maddox on Usan III and then again in the Usan System. He would believe her long dead, if he thought about her at all. Instead, he was about to face his doom at the hands of the Spacer he'd refused to rescue.

"I am here, *di-far*," Mako said aloud.

Then she stopped talking as she climbed into the thruster-pack. Once she wore it, she activated the controls, lifted off the floor and thrust toward the exit in the ceiling.

This would be the day of her great metamorphosis. She would finally transmute into the being she was destined to become.

-89-

As Maddox followed the professor's instructions, he squirted a bit more thrust, turning "down" at a helmet-lamp-lit intersection.

Like all nexuses, this one was huge, with a feeling of great antiquity. The sensation was different from a Nameless-One-created Destroyer. There wasn't that pervading sense of death and evil that the giant craft of the Nameless Ones had emanated. Yet, there was a sense of inhumanity to this place, an alien-ness beyond anything of Earth.

Maddox had expected that much. What he hadn't expected was a continuing premonition of otherworldly danger. It reminded him of meeting the Ska in the Alpha Centauri System. That had been an awful confrontation. The fight had cost him in ways he didn't yet understand. It wasn't like facing overwhelming odds where you knew your enemies could maim and possibly kill you. No. That had been more insidious, a demonic sensation, he supposed.

Within his helmet, Maddox's face twisted wryly. Was he becoming superstitious like the others? He told himself that it was just that he was far from home. That was all. Who knew what strange forms life took in the Sagittarius Arm? The Swarm thrived here, but he'd faced the Swarm before and defeated them. So the bugs didn't really count as something unwholesomely different. He'd met a Builder in the ancient Dyson Sphere and had survived to tell about it. So the feeling couldn't come from a Builder. Just how different would a Sagittarius Arm Builder be from an Orion Arm one anyway?

Hmm... The more he tried to analyze the feel of the emanations, the more it reminded him of the Destroyers and the Ska. It did not have the same sensation as that, though, not even close, really. It was simply foreign in a fundamental way that...made his skin crawl and his heart pound unnaturally fast.

Why would the Omega Nebula nexus be causing him to feel this way?

Maddox hesitated to ask the others if they felt likewise. This was different than the first fears that both Riker and Ludendorff had articulated.

Maddox thought about that, about his hesitation to ask the others about their sensations. Did he care what they thought about him? Was that what was stopping him? Yes. He supposed he did care, and that was odd. He'd been an island for so long that he never thought he'd ever really be used to being part of a team and caring what others thought about him.

Still, worrying unduly about his image was weakness. Weakness led to defeat. Above everything else, he needed to win today. The necessity of victory meant he should gather information. One man could easily feel something strange because he was off. That meant—

Maddox cleared his throat.

"Something wrong, my boy?" the professor asked via helmet comm.

"Maybe," Maddox said. "I'm...I'm beginning to feel that you had the right of it earlier. I mean the odd sensations from our surroundings." And he went on to describe the Destroyer-like similarity to this place.

"I know you poo-pooed that before," Riker said in a shaky voice. "But I'm feeling the same in spades. Something evil lives here. It reminds me of Kauai."

"What?" Ludendorff asked. "That makes no sense. Kauai is an island on Earth. It's part of the Hawaiian Chain."

"I know where Kauai is, Professor," Riker said. "And what I feel makes total sense. Kauai was where the Ska-infected person tried to infect me. I'll never forget that night. I'd love to forget it, believe you me. My nightmares..."

"And you feel the same thing here?" Maddox asked into the ensuing silence.

"I do," Riker said. "It's giving me the willies. I can't stop shaking."

"Bah," Ludendorff said. "I'm actually ashamed about what I said earlier. I can hardly believe I uttered those words. This place has a tranquilizing effect on me. It's uncanny, really. The more I travel around in here, the better I feel."

"That's weird," Maddox said.

"Nonsense," Ludendorff said. "The truth is that your minds, all three of you, are too malleable, too susceptible to impressions. A disciplined mind like mine rejects the impressions and logically deduces that it is nothing more than overwrought emotions. That is the trouble with most people—"

"You no longer feel anything untoward?" Maddox asked, interrupting the lecture.

"Surely you just heard what I said. I had similar sensations before. Don't you remember your argument then?"

"I remember," Maddox said.

"Exactly," Ludendorff said. "*You* had the right of it, my boy. I believe the calming effect on me has been the hidden process of my rejecting any unease as I focus my logical mind on reality. Mystical pulsations such as you're implying—"

"Excuse me," Maddox said, interrupting again. "Mystical pulsations? Is that what you just said?"

"Do I stutter?" asked Ludendorff.

Maddox said nothing.

"Logic," Ludendorff said. "Stick to logic. It will bring you greater calm every time."

Maddox wondered if he detected an odd inflection in the professor's voice that had never been there before. It was hard to tell.

"Logic is good," Maddox said. "But I also have an intuitive side that often works from my subconscious. To ignore intuition is folly because sometimes our body or even our hindbrain recognizes something that our logical half is too dense to see."

"Bah, you're spouting pure emotionalism," the professor said. "I wouldn't have expected that from you, Captain."

"You must be joking," Maddox said. Then, he fell silent. What was wrong with him? Why would he argue like this with the professor during the most important part of the mission? Was there something in here influencing his mind, influencing *all* their minds?

The captain looked around into the darkness. They floated slowly through yet another large corridor. The four of them had on their helmet lamps—their only illumination in this place. Otherwise, the giant nexus was as dark as a tomb.

At that moment, Maddox's lamplight struck a weird glyph on the nearest wall. He had no idea what the symbol meant, but he'd seen it before. Perhaps he should be concentrating on those. He'd seen many glyphs during their journey throughout the corridors. It reminded him of the symbols on the Fisher world.

Maddox frowned. Glyphs? What did he care about glyphs? They needed to reach their destination as fast as possible and make a hyper-spatial tube.

"Professor?" asked Maddox. "Are we still headed in the right direction?"

"Of course," Ludendorff said. "Why would you think otherwise…?" The professor trailed off as his helmet swiveled back and forth, causing his beam to move like a searchlight through the darkness.

"That's most odd," Ludendorff said. "We've taken a wrong turn. Yet, I've followed the same path as before, as I know the route by heart. But I've…I've forgotten to tell you to swing left at the last junction."

"Uh-huh," Maddox said, his suspicions fully aroused. He'd talked a big game about following his intuitions. If ever there was a time to listen to his gut, this was it. He concentrated. It felt as if something…studied him.

Maddox looked around wildly, causing his beam to flash here and there.

"What's wrong?" Meta asked over the helmet comm.

"I-I don't know," Maddox said, the feeling of a sniper-scope trained on him fading away. What had he been thinking before he looked around? Why couldn't he remember? He concentrated—oh, right, the glyphs.

"Professor," Maddox asked, "do you understand the meaning of any of the glyphs along the walls?"

Once more, the professor's helmet swiveled as his beam played upon various hieroglyphics.

"Most are a mystery to me," Ludendorff said a few seconds later. "A few I know precisely. Those—" The professor's voice began taking on a shaky quality before he quit talking.

"Are you experiencing emotionalism like the rest of us?" Riker asked.

"This is an ill time to throw anything back into my teeth," Ludendorff said. "Why, I have a mind to—"

"Professor," Maddox said, interrupting. "Something is trying to confuse us."

"Eh?" Ludendorff asked.

"We're not going to argue about it," Maddox said. "You recognized two glyphs. What do they mean?"

"Oh, yes, the hieroglyphs," Ludendorff said. "I almost forgot about them. That's odd, because the two I recognize are terrifying. One is an emblem for an ancient entity frozen in embryo. The Builders knew them as the Old Ones."

"That's not an original name," Riker said.

"But it is apt," Ludendorff replied. "The Old Ones were also called the Yog-Soths…" His voice cracked as it trailed off.

"Are the Yog-Soths like the Ska?" asked Maddox.

"The Ska are nonphysical entities," Ludendorff said. "The Yog-Soths were as physical as you or I. They had terrifying powers of mind, however."

"Like telepathy?" Meta asked.

"Not psionic as we think of it," Ludendorff said. "They had great intellectual prowess and something more, something primordial. They could conceive of things that baffled the Builders. I do not know this except as an ancient memory. I must have kept this tidbit of knowledge from the nexus computer-core, the downloaded information."

"You said the glyph tells of a Yog-Soth embryo?" Maddox asked.

"Precisely," Ludendorff said. "The being is in stasis, in storage, likely has been in such storage for thousands upon thousands of years."

"Could the Yog-Soth be influencing our thoughts or our emotions?" Maddox asked.

"It's in storage," Ludendorff said. "That would necessitate it being asleep. I don't see how it could—"

"Is the Yog-Soth alive?" Meta asked.

"The hieroglyphic indicates that it is quite alive, if frozen in time."

"Is there a machine here that can thaw it out?" Maddox asked.

"I would think so," the professor said, "but I am not certain."

"What does the second hieroglyphic mean?" Riker asked. "You said you recognized two of them."

"That is correct," Ludendorff said. "The second one means melding, a combination of different things that makes one."

"Uh...*what?*" Riker asked.

"I do not understand completely," Ludendorff said. "Part of the meaning is lost to me. A machine could cause the melding, though. Think of a teleportation device that breaks down atoms and recombines them at a different point in space. The idea here is a machine that breaks down atoms of various things and melds them into something new as it recombines all the atoms."

"Why would the Builders have something like that?" Maddox asked.

"I have no idea," Ludendorff said.

"Husband," Meta said. "Why are we talking about all this instead of backtracking and getting to where the professor needs to be?"

Maddox looked back at Meta in her thruster-pack harness. She cradled a heavy rifle that launched small rocket shells.

Maddox frowned. He was off, not himself. He'd already reached the reason why. "Something is diverting our thoughts," he said.

"What something?" Ludendorff asked. "Galyan did not detect any life-forms, remember?"

"The AI has been wrong before."

"An AI malfunction?" asked Ludendorff.

"Or something deliberately shielding itself from Galyan's sensors," Maddox said. "You've read the glyph warning us about a Yog-Soth entity. We're all feeling something unhealthy. We're not just imagining it, and it's not emotionalism as you suggested before. Perhaps the Yog-Soth is the reason the Builders hid this nexus. Maybe the Builders wanted to hold the last of the Old Ones for reasons we don't yet know."

"Perhaps," the professor admitted. "But I don't recall saying it was the last."

"You did," Riker said.

"No," Ludendorff said. "I definitely did not."

"I feel that, too," Meta said.

"Feel?" asked Ludendorff.

"That this is the last of the Old Ones," Meta said.

"That's confirmation the Yog-Soth can influence our minds," Maddox said. "Maybe it can do these things in its sleep."

"How?" asked Ludendorff.

"I don't care how," Maddox said sharply. "None of that matters now. We'll avoid the Yog-Soth or kill it if we run across it."

"Destroy the Yog-Soth together with the nexus?" asked Ludendorff.

"Now that I know something is attempting to sidetrack us," Maddox said, "I'm no longer going to allow it. We have one mission. We make a hyper-spatial tube before the Swarm fleet closes in on *Victory*. It's time to backtrack so you can reach the Linkage Chamber, Professor. Once we've made the tube, *Victory* can be on its way to the next Swarm-territory nexus."

"It strikes me as a terrible shame to destroy such an ancient entity as the Yog-Soth," Ludendorff said.

"No more arguments," Maddox said, realizing two things: First, he felt likewise. That meant the alien was still trying to sway him. The second truth was that he could no longer fully trust the professor.

"We stick to the script," Maddox said, "so we can buy humanity an extra century or two from the Swarm."

-90-

Mako 21 cruised through the depths of the nexus as she piloted her thruster-pack. The size of the Builder pyramid overwhelmed her. That she had crossed more than five thousand light-years in a bound struck her as technologically spectacular. The planetary machine that had propelled her to this exact spot in the Sagittarius Arm—

Mako frowned inside her helmet. She cruised through the nexus's corridors, knowing that she should immediately seek her destiny as the Spacer egg. She knew how to go about that, too. But a spark of…she would call it *concern*. Fear or worry was too strong for the tiny speck of—yes, she would call it concern. That was her decision and she was going to stick to it.

In any case, the idea of Nay-Yog-Yezleth using the Great Machine on the Forbidden Planet to launch her to this location—something about the process troubled her, and she hadn't been able to pinpoint why.

Why had the Old One chosen this nexus in particular? Yes, this nexus held her destiny, but why did it do so? How could Spacer visions accurately foretell the future? What did Spacers possess that other humans did not that gave them this future-telling ability?

Mako had her concern about this place and her part in it, and because of the concern, she wandered around the nexus, letting it awe her as she avoided her final critical decision. She didn't want to go just yet to the place of transmutation.

Besides, how many Spacers had traveled five thousand-plus light-years in a second of time?

But I'm not a Spacer anymore. I'm the Spacer egg. I am Homo sapiens enhanced.

That was an intriguing idea, and so was another.

How did the Visionary learn or know how to modify me correctly?

As Mako cruised from one huge corridor to the next, she pondered about the ability of visions to foretell the future. She wrestled with the concept and realized that such visions would need a source.

Was there a being supplying the supernatural *power*, for want of a better term? Did that imply God? Not necessarily, she supposed. It could be any being with enough power.

The more Mako pondered the ability of a Spacer multi-mind entity reading the future that she could then chart, the more that seemed like a supernatural thing. Surely, she didn't believe that the multi-mind entity itself did the future reading. That implied far too much ability or power within the multi-mind entity.

Mako decided that she must be having these thoughts because she was much more intelligent now than she used to be. At the same time, some innate caution kept her from using her Spacer modifications to search the nexus with her radar-like sight.

She did not realize, and possibly never would, that the genesis for the accurate future visions came from this place. How had the Spacers stumbled onto the Forbidden Planet and uncovered the carefully hidden and slumbering Nay-Yog-Yezleth? How had the Spacers learned about the Great Machine when even the Builders had never suspected what lay inside the planet?

The Old Ones—the Yog-Soths—had tremendous power of mind. That power meant an uncanny ability to think ahead, to play out millions upon millions of possibilities.

The Yog-Soth "embryo" in the nexus was the result of an incredibly long chain of moves, countermoves and plans made thousands upon thousands of years ago. Instead of the Visionary pulling accurate future visions from the ether, she and other Spacers had tapped into the various Yog-Soths' mental plans and mind-generated dreams—nightmares—that rebounded throughout the galaxy like ancient radio transmissions. The embryo in the nexus had added certain moves of his own into the grand scheme of the Yog-Soths and thus now into the Visionary-led Spacers.

Most of the ancient Yog-Soths plans had failed eons ago. But this one yet remained. The stasis-frozen creature in the nexus—Ghar-Yog-Tog—had powers of mind unsuspected by even the Builders. His dreams had shaped and subtly altered Swarm Imperium plans, human plans, Spacer plans and lost Builder plans into a moment of awakened rebirth.

Ghar-Yog-Tog needed to bend the little Spacer's will another few degrees. She had become the egg indeed, the one who could give him the kiss of life anew, who had the modifications to run the eons-old technology hidden on this unique nexus.

However, Mako 21 still possessed a sense of self-preservation. It was time to tickle her vanity with the greatest conceit for any thinking creature—to become a god.

Mako flew through yet another corridor…and she grunted, as something oily seemed to reach out for her. Within her spacesuit, she grunted again and shook her body like a cat shaking off water, but the feeling remained.

It dawned on her that she was wasting time flying around like this. Captain Maddox was near. She could feel him, and knew he'd often thwarted Spacer plans. And he'd left her behind in the life-pod, in the Usan System, uncaring whether she lived or died.

"I'm here," Mako told herself, smiling at the obviousness of the statement. She *was* here as the Spacer egg of possibility, and here she was, cruising around like a fool who might let the greatest possibility of the universe pass her by.

She could become the new thing and skip thousands of years of evolution to turn into the most powerful being in the galaxy. All she had to do was find the machine, wake the embryo and steal the white polygonal Builder stone. Then, she could combine it all and create a being so powerful that she would jump into godhood, the ultimate human yearning.

Mako wondered for a moment if that was true. Hadn't many people fallen horribly because they'd reached for godhood, been wildly puffed up by pride and hubris and then taken a horrible fall into certain destruction?

But I am the Spacer egg. I'm doing this as my destiny. This is the reason for the Spacers. I'm the chosen one. I cannot wilt when no one but me can take the next step in gigantic evolution.

Mako rotated her thruster-pack and pressed a throttle-trigger, spraying white hydrogen mist. That slowed her velocity until she came to a stop in the middle of a huge, dark corridor.

Her helmet scanned first one way and then a different way. She sensed the correct direction, and yet, she hesitated. Why should she hesitate? It made no sense. She had suffered so much for this opportunity. She'd even killed the meddlesome clone that had tried to take her place.

"I won this right by killing the clone," Mako told herself. "I need merely take the next-to-last step."

If she became this new thing, could she go back to Human Space and let others see what she had become?

Why not? a voice asked in her mind.

Mako's smile grew. Why not indeed? She would go back to Human Space, and she might do more than just show herself. Perhaps she would rule the humans and guide them in superior ways. They would come to worship her, and she would make them into a powerful race, supreme in the galaxy.

"Yes," Mako said. "I accept."

At that instant, the oily sensation vanished, and Mako felt better than she'd ever felt in her life. She'd made the right decision and soon, everyone would know it.

With a greater sense of purpose than ever, Mako reactivated the controls, accelerated and headed for a dangerous area of the nexus. No. That wasn't right. She was heading for the most glorious part of the nexus there was. The ancient Builders had made it a fortress because it held the great—

I am the egg, Mako thought to herself.

The sperm, something said in her mind. *I am the great sperm of possibility that will propel you into godhood.*

As Mako realized this, the excitement in her grew. She added more thrust and began zooming through the corridors. She made the turns with supreme confidence as the excitement grew unbearably. Why had she dallied so long wandering the corridors? It made no sense to her now.

Finally, Mako slowed down until she reached huge sealed doors blocking the path. Through them awaited her apotheosis into a greater being of great power. Her helmet lamplight washed over bizarre symbols on the hatch. One of the symbols looked like a monster with tentacles. Other symbols radiated danger.

Mako pondered that until an inner thought assured her of the silliness of fear at a time like this. She'd just journeyed over five thousand light-years. What could possibly be behind the sealed doors that could hurt her?

Mako inhaled deeply through her nostrils and began to concentrate. A thought of warning kept her from searching past the sealed doors. She must save all her power to open the trick locks. Yes. Using her modified powers to look ahead was a waste of talent.

A small part of her asked why it would hurt to look ahead. Surely, looking ahead was wise.

A sneering laugh at such stupidity stilled the cautious feeling. She'd come across the gulfs of space to do mighty deeds and to show that cock's crow Maddox a thing or three.

"That's right," Mako said.

She closed her eyes and concentrated her modified Spacer abilities. Then, working one interior lock at a time, she began to undo what a Builder had put in place two thousand, four hundred and ninety-one years ago. She had to do this exactly right or a process would start that would murder the sperm of possibilities inside the armored area.

Finally, with a shove of technologically powered telekinesis, Mako caused the mighty doors to open. It was dark in there. For a moment, it seemed like stygian darkness, too much for Mako's helmet-lamp to penetrate.

Why do I need light anyway? I can see perfectly in the dark with my transduction.

With a squeeze of the trigger-throttle, Mako released hydrogen spray, propelling herself deeper into the nexus.

-91-

Professor Ludendorff, along with the others, had reached the great cavern called the Linkage Chamber. Ludendorff admitted to himself that he was feeling trepidation about this, and he wasn't completely sure why.

"What is that cloud?" Maddox radioed.

"The cloud, as you call it, is the substance that will allow me to link with the Builder stone without my having to touch it," the professor said. "It will also allow me to disengage from the stone through an act of will."

"So, we've been using the object wrong all this time?" asked Maddox.

"In a manner of speaking," Ludendorff said.

"Should we fly into the substance?" Maddox asked.

"On no account should you do so. I will go in alone. Oh, and I'll need the stone now."

"Sergeant," Maddox radioed.

"Are you sure about this, sir?" Riker asked.

"Not completely," Maddox admitted. "But my sense of urgency has grown because something is tugging at me to slow down and take it easy."

"I feel the urgency in the pit of my stomach," Meta said.

"Agreed," Riker said, sounding surprised. "I almost feel sick."

"This is curious," Ludendorff said. "I have no physical symptoms, but I do feel…concern is probably the correct word."

"Wait a minute," Maddox said. "Do you realize that we're delaying by discussing this? Sergeant, give him the stone at once. Professor, are you ready?"

Ludendorff didn't answer, but watched as Riker shrugged off the pack that held the Builder stone. Riker gave the pack to Maddox and the captain held it out for the professor to take.

But Ludendorff hesitated. Why was he delaying? He had no logical reason to hold back. It almost felt as if an outside source fed him growing concern so he—

"That's it," Maddox said. "I'm going into the cloud with you, Professor. Otherwise, we'll be here until Doomsday."

"I've already said I must go alone," Ludendorff replied.

"Yeah," Maddox said. "You've told us a lot of things. I'm going with you. That's final."

"And if that causes the linkage to fail?" asked Ludendorff.

"Then, at least I'll know that you tried."

Ludendorff stared at Maddox in his spacesuit. The captain could be far too stubborn at times. He knew the half-breed considered it as one of his strengths, but it simply wasn't so. Well, there was no working around this.

"Very well," Ludendorff said. "But I will not be held responsible for the failure."

"Good luck, sir," Riker said.

Maddox nodded his helmet.

"Be careful, husband," Meta told him.

"I will," the captain said.

"What about me?" Ludendorff complained. "Will no one wish me luck?"

"Isn't that emotionalism?" Riker asked.

"Confound you, you oaf," the professor said.

"Good luck," Meta told Ludendorff.

"Thank you," the Methuselah Man said stiffly.

"Fine," Riker said. "Luck to you, Professor."

"I don't need luck," Ludendorff said petulantly. "But I accept your sentiment."

"Enough," Maddox said, as he piloted the two of them into the misty substance.

***

Later, the captain unhooked the professor, gave him the Builder-stone pack and shoved him away. Maddox and the thruster pack moved back minimally while Ludendorff sailed off much faster.

Ludendorff did not look back. The captain could take care of himself. The feeling of trepidation had grown, but he still did not exhibit any of the physical symptoms that the others had spoken about.

Logically, what did that mean? Ludendorff refused to accept any intuitive sensations to guide him. He didn't know what the growing fear meant. It was no longer a matter of mere concern. He was beginning to feel true fear. It was like the time Governor G.A. Stannous of Cygnet Carious IV had entombed him in a underground chamber for two and half years. The dread of the closing door had almost induced panic.

It was a wonder he had remained sane. Two and a half years alone in the chamber had nearly driven him over the edge. Strand had saved him. Strand had slain the governor and the man's extended family on both sides. His fellow Methuselah Man could be unbelievably brutal at times.

"Don't give them a chance to come back," Strand had told him back then. "It's always a mistake to trap someone and throw away the key. When I have the upper hand, I kill all of them, even the seed corn."

By seed corn, Strand had meant the children. Children grew up in time and often sought revenge. Strand wouldn't give them the opportunity.

As Ludendorff "swam" in the mist to slow himself, he wondered why he would think such a thing now. Did it *mean* anything?

Ludendorff breathed deeply, holding it, wondering what was going on. There was a primordial sense to all this. He exhaled. Yes. Primordial fears, superstitions, atavistic sensations… The dark urges of man had crept to the forefront in this nexus.

The professor shrugged off the tote bag and removed the white polygonal stone. With his mitted gloves, he gingerly set the ball in the substance so it floated before him as though weightless.

Using his burned hands caused them to ache and throb, and it almost made him shy from mental contact with the stone.

Ludendorff shook his head. He was not going to put it off any longer. Maddox was right. It had begun to feel as if the Old One worked against him. But he was the professor, driven by logical ideals more than primitive emotionalism.

Calming himself, Ludendorff reached out with his thoughts and attempted to link with the stone.

That was odd. Something blocked the connection with the stone. *Maddox*, the professor thought.

Only...it didn't feel like that. This felt dark and sinister, felt like a giant octopus swimming toward him in the depths of a murky sea.

Ludendorff recalled the octopoid hieroglyphic of the Yon-Soths, the Old Ones out of time. This was something one of those would do, could do.

Ludendorff focused his considerable intellect on the white polygonal stone. He thought of nothing else and refused to relent. When other thoughts popped up, he ignored them.

A glimmer of connection radiated to him. That increased the professor's ability to concentrate, and in seconds, he linked with the ancient Builder object as he had before. The process quickened further as Ludendorff's mind opened up like a flower taken from deep shade and set in hot and glorious sunlight.

Ah. That was much better. As the linkage opened the professor's mind, he accessed the hieroglyphics about the Yon-Soths. He used the Builder stone to tap into the Omega Nebula nexus's computer core.

He found an ancient file, a corrupted file, no less.

Ludendorff began searching for backup files on the Yon-Soths. Every one of them had been corrupted. That wasn't mere coincidence. That was deliberate sabotage.

There had to be— *Ah. Yes. Here we go.* Ludendorff's expanded mind linked to an old and hidden file deep in the Omega Nebula nexus's computer core.

In those precious seconds, Ludendorff grunted as his mind absorbed the known story of the Yon-Soths. This was awful beyond belief. Why, Maddox had had more of the right of it than he'd had.

The grunts became groans and Ludendorff began to perceive what was at stake here in the Omega Nebula nexus.

With undue haste, Ludendorff linked to the nexus recording systems. He—

The professor began to curse profoundly as he saw the beam of M-energy and watched it turning into a—

"Spacer?" Ludendorff asked aloud. "A Spacer is in the nexus?"

Blinking, realizing there was far too much he didn't know, Ludendorff almost made the same error he had in the last nexus. He almost crammed his mind with zipped files of Builder data. Instead of doing that, he concentrated again, trying to decide what he needed to know to combat this terrible descent into one of the most hideous horrors of the Milky Way Galaxy.

-92-

Maddox had moved outside the radius of the misty cloud in the center of the giant Linkage Chamber. For a while, the cloud radiated with intense brightness and then became dark again. Then, regions of the cloud brightened like distant lightning. It was sudden, and there was no telling which area would light up next.

The cloud and the lightning flashes in it vaguely reminded Maddox of something. He tried to place it, and with a start, he realized the cloud was like a giant brain. The sudden light in areas was like neurons firing up, causing thought.

Could the misty cloud be a disembodied Builder brain? No. That was preposterous. Maybe it acted *like* a brain, but it couldn't be anything more than that. And yet, the more Maddox observed the brightening areas of the cloud, the more it struck the captain as firing neurons.

Then, Ludendorff swam clumsily out of the cloud. "Maddox," the professor said urgently over the helmet comm. "Maddox, can you hear me?"

"I can now," the captain replied.

"This is a trap," Ludendorff said. "No, no, that's not right. We must hurry. A Spacer is wandering through the nexus. She's no doubt planning to set Ghar-Yon-Tog the Great free."

"That's the name of the Yon-Soth embryo?" Maddox asked.

"Yes!" Ludendorff said. "And Ghar-Yon-Tog the Great is no embryo. That's a, a, joke. It's like calling a huge man Tiny.

The Old One is massive and ancient, possibly the progenitor. I don't understand half of this. I don't understand why the Builders kept the most dangerous Yon-Soth in the galaxy on ice. But the Spacer plans to use the transfer portal."

"The what?" asked Maddox.

"Hurry," Ludendorff said. "Hook me to your suit and fire up your thruster pack. We have to stop the Spacer. We have to kill Ghar-Yon-Tog."

"No," Maddox said. "We have to make a hyper-spatial tube and leave this star system while we can, making sure the nexus blows up behind us."

"There's no time for that now."

"Wrong," Maddox said. "Humanity comes first."

"Don't you understand?" Ludendorff shouted.

"No."

"I don't have time to explain."

Maddox calmly drew a blaster, aiming it at the approaching professor. "Give me the Builder stone. I'm going into the cloud. I'm going to talk to the computer core and find out what's going on for myself."

"We've run out of time," Ludendorff said in a highly agitated state. "The Old Ones are making their last play. I don't know how many of them are left—no!" Ludendorff said in horror as he clutched his helmet. "I'm finally beginning to understand. Yes! The Builder memories are becoming clearer in my mind. Oh, this is monstrous, monstrous. The Builders defeated the Old Ones, or they mopped up the last Yon-Soth strongholds eons ago. They must have captured Ghar-Yon-Tog, imprisoning him."

"If he's so dangerous, why didn't the Builders kill him back then?" Maddox asked.

"Why are you aiming a blaster at me?" Ludendorff demanded. "You already know that an alien mind is influencing yours. I know how to defeat Ghar-Yon-Tog. He knows that and wants to kill me to buy himself time."

Inside his helmet, Maddox licked his lips. He did feel a growing desire to burn down the meddlesome professor. Ludendorff had played one trick too many on the most illustrious Intelligence agent in Star Watch history. He was the best, the greatest of the undercover operatives—

"No," Maddox whispered to himself. "There's your mistake, Ghar-Yon-Tog. I'm not a braggart. You just revealed your thoughts in my mind."

Pain struck Maddox's head as an oily sensation hit and threatened more agony if he didn't obey orders.

Maddox laughed harshly at the threat.

"What's wrong with you?" Ludendorff shouted.

"Ghar-Yon-Tog is making an open play for my thoughts," Maddox said through gritted teeth. "But he's using the wrong levers, trying to force the wrong man. Yes, I'm coming nearer, Professor. It's time to hook up and travel. Tell me more about the Old Ones while we go—where are we going, by the way?"

"To the transfer portal or, as it's more properly called, the star gate," Ludendorff said. "We have to reach the nexus where Ghar-Yon-Tog is imprisoned.

"What?"

"We have to use the star gate linking our two nexuses. It's the only way we can reach the Old One in time to kill him before the Spacer awakens him."

"Let's go," Maddox said.

***

A few minutes later, Maddox led the way, with the professor hooked to his spacesuit. Riker was in the middle of the thruster-pack caravan, while Meta brought up the rear.

The oily sensation no longer plagued Maddox. Riker and Meta had both admitted to similar impressions. But with the captain explaining how to defeat the Old One's insinuation attacks, the other two resisted, and finally the mental influences stopped.

The professor had told them such influences would become irresistible once Ghar-Yon-Tog woke up, as these were just dream-induced stimuli.

As Maddox took another turn at speed, piloting almost recklessly, his focus sharpened yet again. He was going to kill this thing. It reminded him of the Ska, and he had come to hate these monstrous aliens, whether from other dimensions or the primeval times of the universe.

"There is one problem I haven't broached," Ludendorff radioed abruptly. "Partly it's a lack of coherent memories. I might have taken on a few too many Builder recollections too quickly. They aren't zipped remembrances, but they are cumbersome nonetheless."

"Spit it out," Maddox said. "What's the problem?"

"The Old Ones—the Yon-Soths—have or had a unique function in our galaxy," Ludendorff said. "I don't quite understand that function. No. Here at the possible end I'm not going to lie. I have *no* idea what that special function might be. It has to do with…aliens, possible machines or quantum matrix technologies either in the galactic core or on the edge of the core."

"Meaning what?" Maddox asked.

"The Yon-Soths are…advanced techs, I suppose you could say."

"They're like Kai-Kaus technicians?"

"That's likely a poor analogy," the professor said, "but it's the best I can do under the circumstances. I have the feeling it's not an immediate problem. But the Builders wanted to keep one galactic tech around in case the problem ever cropped up again."

"Okay…" Maddox said.

"If we kill Ghar-Yon-Tog and Nay-Yog-Yezleth on the Forbidden Planet—"

"Where?" asked Maddox, interrupting. "Who is Nay-Yon-Yezleth and where's the Forbidden Planet?"

"There's a second if considerably weaker Old One in the Beyond," Ludendorff said. "It's where the Spacers went when they fled Human Space, or where some of them went, anyway. They've been working on a special project inside the Forbidden Planet."

"This world in the Beyond is near Human Space?" Maddox asked.

"I believe so," Ludendorff said, groaning afterward. "Oh, my head hurts. I'm sick of shoving Builder data into my mind. I want this to end."

"No doubt," Maddox said. "Well, I'm not going to worry about alien super-science techs having work to do in the galactic core. Likely, in time references, this is meaningless to humanity. Likely, whatever trouble these Old Ones were or are supposed to fix won't take place for thirty thousand years or more. So, who cares about it now?"

"That's a cavalier attitude," the professor said.

"As a Star Watch officer, I worry about the Commonwealth first and foremost," Maddox said. "We kill Ghar-Yon-Tog, make the hyper-spatial tube, leave and make sure to blow the nexus after us. That's the plan. That's it. We don't worry about anything else."

"I cannot be party to that," Ludendorff said.

Maddox scoffed. "Then you'd better damn well change your mind quickly, Professor. You're on my team, which means you're going to obey orders for once. Do I make myself clear?"

Ludendorff did not respond.

"Dana dies if we do this differently," Maddox said.

Ludendorff mumbled.

"I can't hear you, Professor."

"Fine," Ludendorff said sullenly. "Let's murder the future so we can save ourselves—"

"Right," Maddox said, interrupting as the professor tried to say more. "Now, we're finally on the same page. How much farther to the star gate?"

Ludendorff did not answer.

"Professor?" Maddox warned.

"Take a right at the next intersection," Ludendorff said, "and go down at the second intersection. After a few more turns, you can't miss the gate after that."

Maddox gripped the trigger-throttle of his thruster pack. It was too bad he hadn't brought Keith along. Then, an idea struck. "Can anyone get a comm signal through to *Victory*?"

After a few moments, each of them gave him a negative reply.

"Keep trying," Maddox said. "If you do get through, tell them to ready a heavy salvo of antimatter missiles. If we can't win here, we can't allow the nexus to survive us. That way, this

Swarm invasion fleet can't hit Earth. Maybe other Swarm fleets will attack later, but not this one. We'll buy our side a few more years at the worst."

With that, the team fell silent as they zoomed through the ancient nexus.

-93-

Outside the Omega Nebula nexus aboard Starship *Victory*, Lieutenant Valerie Noonan was becoming increasingly anxious on the bridge.

No one aboard the ancient Adok vessel had seen the beam sent from the Great Machine on the Forbidden Planet. So that wasn't what worried Valerie. Instead, it was Galyan's steady reports of the approaching Swarm fleet moving en masse in their direction.

"Okay," Valerie said, as she sat in the captain's chair. "Now, I want to see them. Show me."

Galyan made an internal adjustment, and the scene on the main screen changed as the nexus vanished. In its place was a gaseous, dirt-debris cloud nebula with patches of open space. By degrees, motion occurred behind all that gas and dirt.

"Do you see, Valerie?" Galyan asked.

"I see movement but can't see exactly what's causing the motion."

"Those are approaching Swarm motherships."

"Where are the advance scouts?"

"The Swarm appear to have forgone sending out more scouts," Galyan said. "Perhaps the Hive Masters running the fleet have decided they know our location."

"Are you getting sensor pings?" Valerie asked.

"A few," Galyan admitted.

"When were you going to tell me about them?"

"I am telling you, Valerie. That is partly why I have been pestering you—using your own term for my repeated warnings."

"You've made your point," Valerie said. "The Swarm is coming for us. Why aren't they going the wrong way? The captain used the drones to trick them as to our true location."

"I will give you a simple reason," Galyan said. "The Swarm sensors likely see just enough to know our position. Perhaps our presence has given away the nexus's position as well, making us doubly visible."

"Perhaps," Valerie said gloomily. She drummed the fingers of her left hand on the left-hand armrest of the command chair.

"We must do something, Valerie," Galyan said.

"I know that. But I don't know what to do. I'm open to suggestions."

"On Earth, certain parent birds will squawk and carry on," Galyan said. "They will flop on the ground to draw a predator away from their vulnerable young. We can draw the fleet from the nexus and use the star drive later to jump near the nexus."

"I understand the procedure," Valerie said. "The hyperspatial tube should appear any second, though. We have to wait for it or we'll be stranded out here in the Sagittarius Arm for the rest of our short lives."

"Lieutenant," Andros said, looking up from his board. "I'm receiving a strange signal from the nexus. It's weak—"

"From whom?" Valerie asked, cutting off the Chief Technician.

"It's…Sergeant Riker," Andros said. "Lieutenant, this is incredible. Riker is instructing me to tell you to mass antimatter missiles outside the ship."

"How will a few antimatter missiles help us against 143,000 Swarm motherships?" Valerie asked.

"The missiles aren't for the Swarm," Andros said. "You're supposed to get ready to destroy the nexus. Riker says under no circumstances are you supposed to let the Swarm board it."

Valerie stared at Andros Crank, and a moment later, she nodded sharply. "Tell Riker I understand, and I'll comply."

"Valerie," Galyan said. "You can't destroy the nexus."

"Why not?" she asked.

"That will kill the captain," Galyan said. "We must save him."

"Orders are orders," Valerie said grimly. "These also happen to make perfect sense."

"No," Galyan said. "You must gain communication with the captain."

Valerie and Galyan looked at Andros. The Chief Technician shook his head. "I've lost the connection," he said. "I'm not sure I can get it back anytime soon."

"Valerie, please," Galyan said. "You are the acting captain of the ship. You have to do something smarter than just blowing everything up."

"Why?" she asked. "It's what you Adoks did against the Swarm when you faced them six thousand years ago."

The little holoimage looked crestfallen as his ropy shoulders slumped.

"I'm sorry, Galyan," Valerie said. "I shouldn't have said it like that."

"It does not matter," Galyan said sadly. "My friends want to destroy themselves. Everything I touch dies. It is my curse."

Valerie stared at the holoimage. "Are you trying to use psychology on me so I'll change my mind?"

Galyan would not look up.

"When did you become so devious?" Valerie asked.

The holoimage shrugged listlessly.

Valerie drummed her fingers more relentlessly on the armrest. "Andros, can you pinpoint the team's location inside the nexus?"

"I can tell you where they were—or Riker was—when he sent the message."

"Put in on the main screen," Valerie said.

"What is your plan, Valerie?" Galyan asked.

"I don't have one yet. I'm thinking."

Lieutenant Noonan studied the graphic Andros Crank superimposed upon the nexus.

The lieutenant slapped the armrest the way she'd seen Maddox do on occasion. And just like the captain, Valerie stood up and put her hands behind her back as she approached the main screen.

"Mr. Crank," Valerie said, mimicking the captain once more. "We're here to destroy the nexus no matter what else happens. Therefore, we're going to burn down some of that structure beforehand."

"Why would you do that, Valerie?" Galyan asked. "You risk destroying the nexus before it creates a hyper-spatial tube."

"I want a direct link with the captain, and that's the best way I can think of to get one," Valerie said. She looked around, walked back to the command chair and sat down, instructing the weapons officer to begin heating up the disrupter cannon.

-94-

With her large Spacer thruster-pack, Mako 21 dragged a huge weightless cylindrical container through a dark corridor on the Omega Nebula nexus. The container was ancient beyond reckoning and had a unique engine within to power a portal—a star gate—between nexuses.

Not that Mako gave undue conscious consideration to what she did. She had found an attachment in the darkness some time ago. A tug in her mind had bidden her to plug the attachment to her suit. She had turned the attachment over and over with her gloved hands. The debate had proven tedious, but in the end, the thought of becoming a godling had beaten down her innate caution.

Mako had plugged the attachment to her suit, and she had not remembered anything since then. Instead, a new will several thousand light-years away guided her body.

Mako's blind eyes used her goggles to peer through the visor of her spacesuit helmet as she dragged the last piece of the star gate to its rightful location. This piece was massive, making her thruster pack look like a harbor tug dragging a great ocean liner.

The Old One—Ghar-Yon-Tog—resided in a different nexus and was in deep stasis sleep. But he was nothing like a hominid or an insect-like Swarm creature or even like a Builder of old. The Yon-Soth was from the dawn time of the universe, a monster many would say, with primordial powers and energies that dwarfed those of puny humanity. His intellect was cold, possibly evil as seen from a human perspective, and immense. Yes, he slept in a real sense. Yes, his city-block long tentacles did not move but for the odd twitch of the very tip. And like a human, Ghar-Yon-Tog dreamed constantly while asleep. But his dreams were not like a man's dreams.

The Old One's dreams could slither along the undercurrents of the universe, traveling in an astral sense throughout far regions of the galaxy. At times, given the right conditions, Ghar-Yon-Tog could tug a mind or insert a thought. If one journeyed near enough to his prison nexus, he could drive thinking beings mad, causing them to commit insane acts. Such had happened to a Swarm Hive Master and his science fleet.

By adding the ancient attachment to her suit, Mako had committed a fatal blunder. The appeal of godhood had been too powerful to resist. The attachment had been her apple, but instead of knowing good and evil, she fell under the dominating power of the Old One's dreaming intellect.

After eons in the Builder trap, Ghar-Yon-Tog would be free again to practice his deceptions on the universe. He would go to the galactic core, to the ancient machines, and there rob the god-tombs for the weapons to make a galaxy burn in unholy horror to pay for his unjust imprisonment.

The only glitch to this perfect plan was that the little Spacer piloting the thruster pack was proving a more difficult pawn than he'd anticipated. It had caused more of Ghar-Yon-Tog's dream concentration to turn on her.

He remembered her, and her former resistance, when she had unplugged from the Meditation Machine multi-mind entity with the Visionary and other properly duped Spacers. No matter, Mako 21 was still here to do what needed doing.

Inside her spacesuit and behind her goggles, Mako had a fixed stare. She had entered the dark chamber behind the locked hatches, moving through wondrous equipment, found the attachment, plugged it in—and she'd remembered nothing since then. However, a tiny spark of her ego-id had darted into the deepest recesses of her modified brain. There, Mako yet lived. There, she realized with sick understanding that all of this had been a dreadful trick and a trap. Ghar-Yon-Tog and later, Nay-Yon-Yezleth, had guided the gullible Spacers into one folly after another.

She was the key that was going to unlock a monstrosity. She knew deep in the recess of her ego-id fortress that Ghar-Yon-Tog had plans for the Swarm Imperium. As the Ska guided the Nameless Ones, Ghar-Yon-Tog was going to mold the bug Imperium, turning them into an even greater all-conquering nightmare that would consume the galaxy in a growing tide of Yon-Soth revenge.

There were thoughts about galactic-core machines that she did not understand. There were histories and knowledge of such primeval vastness and age that she could not grasp their meaning.

Ghar-Yon-Tog would awaken and enact a reign of horror as he revived the Old Ones out of time. She would use the star gate to travel to the other nexus and start the machine that would loosen the shackles chaining the ancient master in stasis sleep.

Mako cringed as she considered this. She was going to unleash a demonic reign onto the galaxy. The Visionary had much to answer for—the long line of Visionaries were like foolish and lonely girls listening to a pimp's promises and envisioning a life of love and pleasure. Instead, this was the reward: enslavement of the worst kind.

Mako wanted to weep. The old Mako likely would have wept, if the old Mako would've had the power to resist Ghar-Yon-Tog even to this little degree. But she was the new Mako, a hardened individual with great innate and modification powers. She would bide her time and take her opportunity—if it ever arrived. Then, she would strike for her mind's freedom.

That vainglorious thought brought a wave of horrors knocking on the last citadel of her personality. Through the attachment, Ghar-Yon-Tog was knocking, demanding utter servitude from her.

In that last recess of thought, Mako fought to hang on. Just a little longer, she told herself, a few more seconds of mental liberty, that was all she wanted.

Thus, as her Spacer body, the transduction and other powers did the sleeping Old One's bidding, a final spark of self watched as the cylindrical container neared the star gate.

-95-

"Now please, if you would, Galyan," Valerie said from the command chair. "Begin firing the disrupter cannon."

The Adok holoimage hovered beside the captain's chair. He stared at the Omega Nebula nexus with its discs and ports.

The starship was close to the silver pyramid. At Valerie's orders, Keith had returned to a hangar bay with his shuttle. Behind *Victory*, the advance guard of the Swarm horde was minutes away from their long-range firing distance. The crew of *Victory* had just about run out of time.

The great antimatter engines in the starship built up power. The disrupter cannon was primed and ready to fire.

Galyan aimed. The destructive yellow beam burst from the cannon, striking the nearest hull of the ancient nexus. The Builder-made hull resisted for a moment, and then it began to crumble under the annihilating power of the disruptor ray.

That tripped several processes.

In the advance ships of the Swarm fleet, messages began to fly back to the Hive Masters. Quick orders raced ahead to the lead vessels.

Almost immediately, the advance motherships accelerated faster toward the alien starship. Their actions told one thing. They wanted to destroy the vessel that was attempting to annihilate the great machine that forged hyper-spatial tubes.

The second action was inside the nexus. Despite his dreaming state and actual distance from the battle, Ghar-Yon-Tog was aware of the assault primarily due to Mako and her attachment. The Old One thrashed in his dream for an answer, and he found it almost immediately.

His dream reality turned on the little Spacer. She used her modified powers amplified by the Old One's mind.

Inside *Victory*, Galyan turned to the lieutenant. "Valerie, there is an outside source battling me. It is shutting down the disrupter cannon."

The lieutenant had leaped up as the disrupter beam stopped striking the nexus. She turned to Galyan. "What did you say?"

"The electronic interference is coming from the nexus, Valerie. I am powerless to countermand the cease firing order."

"Fix it!" Valerie shouted.

"I do not know how," Galyan said.

Valerie stared at the holoimage. As she did, her mouth opened. Slowly, the lieutenant closed her mouth. She whirled around.

"Weapons officer," Valerie said, "activate the antimatter missiles. Send them at the nexus. We're going to destroy it while we can."

"No," Galyan said. "Do not do it. The captain is still in the nexus."

"Do it, Weapons Officer," Valerie said sternly.

The weapons officer hesitated a moment longer. Then, his fingers blurred over his board.

***

Mako still towed the giant cylindrical container toward the star gate. She felt exhausted, was exhausted by what she had done to Starship *Victory*.

Now, fear bolted through her. Antimatter missiles accelerated for the nexus. She would die soon under their annihilating blasts.

Ghar-Yon-Tog also realized—in his dream state—that he was about to lose the key that would allow him to awaken after many millennia. The knowledge of that loss had weakened his power over the key.

Mako wondered what she should do. She wanted freedom, but she did not want to die. The question did not last long, nor her ability to choose.

Ghar-Yon-Tog resumed control of her body, although he did not reach the small spark of self in her mind citadel.

The Spacer bent her head, and she used more Old One-amplified modification power against the enemy. She adjusted the antimatter missiles' targeting computers. It took several seconds of concentration—then the body of Mako 21 gasped and slumped unconscious from serious over-straining of her abilities.

***

Aboard *Victory*, Lieutenant Noonan watched in dismay as the huge antimatter missiles began sharp turning maneuvers. They no longer sped at the nearby nexus, but swerved aside and continued turning.

"Are they targeting us?" Valerie asked.

"No, Valerie," Galyan said. "They are going to speed past us. I suspect they are heading for the Swarm advance guard. But there are too few missiles to make any difference against them."

"Use the neutron cannon on the nexus," Valerie said.

"The neutron cannon does not respond," Galyan said. "The thing in the nexus has shorted it for the time being."

"Launch more antimatter missiles."

"The launch tubes are now locked," Galyan said.

"Isn't there anything we can do?" Valerie shouted. "I know, launch the strikefighters. Launch the tin cans."

"I have a different idea," Galyan said.

"Spit it out, Galyan. We're running out of time."

"I can attempt a computer virus attack against the nexus."

"That can work?" Valerie asked.

"It is doubtful, but at least I can attempt it."

"Then do it, Galyan."

"It will take a few minutes to ready the needed boosters."

"Do it. Do it."

The holoimage disappeared from the bridge.

"What about us?" Andros asked. "We have to help."

Valerie pressed a comm button on her command chair. She ordered the strikefighter pilots to launch as soon as demolition teams blasted open the frozen hangar-bay doors. *Victory* might be crippled with the disrupter and neutron cannons out, and the missile launch tubes frozen, but the starship still had some fight left with strikefighters and fold-fighters.

And if that didn't work…?

Valerie sat in the captain's chair, deciding that if that didn't work, she would use the star-drive jump and appear inside the nexus, destroying it from within, so to speak. It would be a kamikaze strike, but, whatever it took, she wasn't going to let the bugs use this nexus.

-96-

Three Star Watch thruster-packs spewed hydrogen spray as the four humans inside the nexus sped with velocity down the dark corridors.

"How much farther is the star gate?" Maddox radioed.

"What?" Ludendorff asked.

"The star gate?" asked Maddox. "How far away is it from here?"

"I-I appear to have made a mistake," Ludendorff said.

Maddox groaned. "You gave us the wrong directions?"

"No, no," Ludendorff said. "Nothing so easily fixed. Some of the memories I took have been corrupted."

"How in the world can you tell something like that?" Meta asked.

"It is a tedious process," Ludendorff admitted. "I have been correlating various theories—"

"Never mind how you do it," Maddox snarled. "What's false? What did you tell us that isn't true?"

"It concerns the star gate," Ludendorff said. "Not its position in the nexus, but its existence in reality."

"Say that again," Riker growled.

"There is no star gate," Ludendorff said. "It is a myth, a falsehood. I believe Ghar-Yon-Tog has infected the nexus computer-core here."

"How can he do that when he's in stasis and in another nexus?" Maddox asked.

"I'm sketchy on that," Ludendorff said. "His dream state is not like our dream state. It can warp reality...sometimes directly and sometimes—"

"You're making him sound like some kind of cosmic devil-monster," Maddox said.

"Yes," Ludendorff said. "He is, he most certainly is. But the star gate is a falsehood. I don't know why he would put such a mistruth in the computer-core..."

"What? What?" Maddox demanded.

"It must be part of a larger or bigger gambit," Ludendorff said. "I doubt the falsehood was meant for our consumption, but for others. Yes, of course, for the Spacer here."

"Explain that," Maddox said.

"I don't have enough data to make a coherent theory," Ludendorff said.

"We're missing something," Riker said. "If it isn't a star gate, what is it?"

"It's some kind of transforming chamber," Ludendorff said. "The Spacer—oh, now I'm beginning to comprehend. I think Ghar-Yon-Tog goaded the Spacers by promising to turn them into something greater."

"So...what's the point?" Maddox said. "The Spacer is working for a reward?"

"That is my new theory," Ludendorff said. "It fits with the diabolical nature of the Yon-Soths, the Old Ones."

"A cosmic devil-monster," Maddox said. "So, Ghar-Yon-Tog has manipulated events while asleep in stasis. I'm thinking awake he's going to be a hundred times worse."

"A million or a billion times worse," Ludendorff said.

"Right," Maddox said. "But...but what you're saying can't be right. Is Ghar-Yon-Tog really going to turn the Spacers into something better?"

"I find that doubtful," Ludendorff admitted.

"Then...wait," Maddox said, his head hurting. Was Ghar-Yon-Tog still trying to confuse them but doing it in a more subtle manner than before? "The Old One corrupted the computer-core so the Spacers would believe they could turn into something better through a transforming machine. Is that correct?"

"I don't know anymore," Ludendorff said miserably.

"But that was the trick, right?" Maddox asked.

"Trick?" asked Ludendorff. "Oh. Yes. I suppose so. The Old One is tricking the Spacers."

"Then, the machine we're heading toward probably isn't a transforming machine, but is actually a star gate as you originally guessed."

"I'm tired," Ludendorff said. "It's becoming increasingly difficult to think."

Inside his helmet, Maddox's eyes narrowed. Maybe the closer they came to the star gate, the more powerful Ghar-Yon-Tog's dream powers became. The Old One was trying to confuse them so they didn't try as hard or maybe didn't try at all.

"How far away is the chamber, whatever it really is?" Maddox asked.

"I think it is close now," Ludendorff said.

"Good," Maddox said, with bitter determination in his voice.

-97-

The body of Mako 21 stirred once more. Unconscious in the thruster pack, it had arrived at the star gate, a huge perfect rectangle of ancient black stone.

Blinking behind her goggles, the body of Mako unlatched itself from the thruster pack. The huge cylinder she'd dragged here was in place, even though she didn't recall using the thruster pack to brake the massive thing's slow velocity. It was here, stopped, in place, ready for her to attach the power lines.

She pushed off the floor, sailing toward the engine she had brought from a locked area of the nexus. As events unfolded around her, the body of Mako 21 worked furiously. All the while, the last spark of identity hidden in her mind watched helplessly. She'd actually had a chance to do something a little while ago but had flubbed it. With growing bitterness, the last spark of ego-id of Mako 21 vowed to do it right if she ever got a second chance.

***

As Mako's body followed the directions of Ghar-Yon-Tog's dreaming will, Galyan, aboard Starship *Victory*, began his virus attack into the Builder nexus computer-core.

He was a mere Adok AI, however, an electronic, deified personality driven by half-Builder technology. That meant he was weaker technologically speaking than the master computer-core that ran the Omega Nebula nexus. While it was true that Ghar-Yon-Tog had weakened the great core through various corruptions, it was still more than a match for an Adok/human hybrid computer attack.

The process was computer fast and unseen by human eyes. The dreaming Ghar-Yon-Tog was vaguely aware of the virus assault, and that caused him unease. There was a possibility this Galyan could jeopardize his plan.

Thus, the dreaming Old One halted Mako 21. Once more, Ghar-Yon-Tog used her like a weapon, utilizing the wonderful modifications in her Spacer mind and body.

The nexus computer now reacted faster and smoother than before, and in seconds, it ejected the AI personality of Driving Force Galyan, sealing the great computer-core against further virus attacks of this nature.

Immediately, the body of Mako 21 went back to work on repowering the ancient star gate.

***

Outside the nexus, clouds of Star Watch strikefighters began zooming at the Builder structure and unleashing their ordnance. Small missiles and shells hammered the silver surface, barely denting armor that had withstood centuries of space debris.

Starship *Victory* had maneuvered closer to the nexus. From blasted-open bay doors, hangar tugs towed big antimatter missiles, rushing them into space as fast as they could.

Lastly, two fold-fighters hovered nearby. Keith Maker piloted one of them. He argued via comm with Valerie, demanding permission to fold into the nexus and attempt to rescue the captain's party.

"We need a signal from them first," Valerie said.

"Screw that," Keith said. "Let's just get it done."

"No," Valerie said. "I'm not sending you to certain death where you fold into an interior structure."

"It will be a calculated rescue," Keith countered.

"Galyan failed. Now, the nexus knows we're here. This has just become more dangerous for all of us."

"I don't see how," Keith said. "The nexus hasn't done anything against the strikefighters. What do you mean it knows we're here?"

"The strikefighters haven't done anything to truly damage the nexus. That's why it hasn't hit back at us yet."

Keith didn't respond to that, although he did say a moment later, "The Swarm motherships are going to be in firing range—theirs—in another two minutes at most."

"I know," Valerie said.

"That means we're out of time," Keith said. "Let me fold into the nexus. At this point, what do we have to lose?"

This time, Valerie didn't answer right away.

"You know I should do it," Keith said.

"Not yet," Valerie said. "We'll wait a few more minutes."

"Why? That doesn't make sense."

"Because I want you to take two antimatter missiles with you," Valerie said quietly.

"Oh," Keith said, getting it. "We're out of options, aren't we? This is Suicide King time, huh?"

"Something like that," Valerie said. "Get the antimatter missiles attached to your fighter. Tell me when you're ready."

"Roger that, love," Keith said, trying to sound as cheerful as ever.

-98-

Mako 21, under the Old One's influence, used her Spacer modifications, turning on the great star gate in a process no human could have done otherwise.

The huge cylinder engine hummed with power and the big rectangular block of black stone shimmered in an eerie manner. Seconds passed, and then, several thousand light-years away, an exact replica of the towering block of black stone activated in a haunted nexus.

Mako shivered in her spacesuit, and she noticed a tug of gravity at her feet. It wasn't a powerful source of gravity, but it was there nonetheless.

The real Mako hidden in a recess in her mind, attempted to move an arm, but she failed.

There was a heavy, evil chuckle in her mind. Ghar-Yon-Tog toyed with her in delight because the time of his awakening was at hand.

Mako tried to resist him, but it was fruitless. Her spacesuited body began to walk toward the towering edifice of black stone. She made croaking noises, all her body could do as she tried to scream in horror.

The inhuman chuckling grew into evil mirth echoing in her thoughts. This was a delight to Ghar-Yon-Tog.

Mako's arms lifted as she reached out to touch the surface of the towering black stone. Then, she did touch it, with her spacesuit gloves pressing against the alien stone. A horrible shock went through her.

Her croaking renewed while the surface of the black stone swirled before her. Mako 21's hands sank into the awful stone. It felt as if some space goblin grabbed her wrists and yanked hard, pulling her entirely within.

Mako stumbled into the towering dark portal, and she vanished from the Omega Nebula nexus. She tumbled end over end as lights flashed around her. There were roaring comets and slithering things of darkness with yawning mouths. The teeth snapped. Mako screamed, but they swallowed her with ghostly mouths that made her shiver and moan.

Then, Mako popped out from another towering black stone and she slid along a slick floor. When she finally stopped, she lay on the floor gasping within her suit. She felt exhausted and her mind throbbed with pain. But she dragged herself upright and turned in amazement.

She was in a vast chamber with great towering statues of alien things in various poses. There were mighty arches around her, leading to different corridors and chambers. One of the huge arches glowed with an evil light. Mako found herself walking robotically toward that arch. She wanted to whimper and hide, but she could not. It was time to unleash the Great One.

Mako entered an even larger chamber with hundreds of gigantic shadowy machines around her. They towered often two hundred meters or more. This was the revival chamber, and it had been the stasis chamber eons ago.

Like a timid mouse, Mako's space-suited body crept toward the master controls. She did not fear the controls, and the pulsating evil of the dreaming master actually weakened Ghar-Yon-Tog's hold on her mind. It should have been the reverse, but the reaction of her body was elemental and uncontrollable.

The dreaming Old One struggled to master her, and Mako almost had her second chance. Then the progenitor of the Yon-Soths found the needed control of her flea-bitten mind.

Ghar-Yon-Tog asserted himself in her.

Mako froze rigidly as her skin crawled in revulsion. This was horror beyond understanding. She was far, far from any help. She was deep in the Sagittarius Spiral Arm, more than twice the distance she had previously been from the Forbidden Planet.

Ghar-Yon-Tog used her Spacer modifications, and lights began to snap on in the great chamber, revealing the enormous machines and various pieces of Builder medical-equipment in stark detail. The machines had odd shapes and unknown functions. Some moved slowly and some reacted instantly as power surged through them for the first time in eons.

Using the anti-gravity meshes in her body, Mako drifted up to a vast machine with a small hatch. The hatch opened and Mako entered the control chamber.

Like a sleepwalker, she began to press switches, using her modifications to help speed the process. She had waited so, so long for this day to arrive. Once more, the universe would know—

Inside her helmet and beneath her goggles, Mako blinked wildly. She wasn't Mako anymore. She was Ghar-Yon-Tog. She was the master tech of the galaxy. The Builders had tricked her—him—so long ago. Those bastard aliens had thought to gain his great and galactic core knowledge. He hadn't given it to them. He had made them pay in a thousand ways for their treachery.

Now—

Through Mako 21, Ghar-Yon-Tog manipulated the mighty machine. An entire section of wall drew back, revealing a monstrous creature three times the greatest Earth whale that had ever swum the prehistoric seas. Behind a second wall, this one of glass, the slimy thing had great if lifeless-looking tentacles and a ring of monstrous closed eyes.

As the glass parted and slid away into hidden recesses, a colossal robot moved from an even bigger alcove across the room. An intense buzzing sounded as it floated on anti-gravity processors while extending unbelievably huge robotic arms. Soon, it reached the cryo-sleeping monster, and with care, the robot arms encircled the vast Yon-Soth. Gently, as the buzzing noises increased, the robot withdrew the colossal thing. Frozen tentacles dragged on the floor even as the ring of eyes remained closed and the Old One continued in stasis sleep.

Once more, the buzzing intensified, this time to an intolerable level. Within the control room, Mako winced painfully. The robot raised Ghar-Yon-Tog higher and slowly swiveled around. At the same time, an impossibly vast glass cylinder rose up from the opening floor. Once the cylinder reached its full height and halted, three great tubes lowered from the high ceiling and began pouring a yellow solution into the gigantic container.

The process took time, Mako realized, but not too much. Finally, the robot arms moved the frozen bulk once more, gently sliding the interstellar monster so Ghar-Yon-Tog splashed into the solution. The great creature floated downward, his tentacles slowly following him.

With its job complete, and the buzzing noises back to tolerable levels, the robot used its anti-gravity processors to put itself back into the gigantic alcove.

Now, all through the enormous chamber, power surged through the revival machine as the time of awakening neared. After eons of sleep, after endless millennia of dreaming that had attempted to alter the living aliens of the fringe galaxy, Ghar-Yon-Tog was going to emerge whole again. The Spacer Nation had been an incredible find. Ghar-Yon-Tog doubted there was a more gullible assembly of fools than the mystic Spacers. Imagine the Visionaries believing they could leap millions of years ahead in evolutionary progress. That was unbounded folly, but useful folly nonetheless.

"What was that?" Mako asked, as she sat in the revival control chamber.

Ghar-Yon-Tog ignored her question. She had served her purpose. There might be another use for her—

"What did you say?" Mako asked, newfound rage giving her greater ability to resist the alien invasion in her mind. "There never was a Transformer Chamber? That was a lie? We couldn't become gods through fast evolutionary means? How dare you lie to us?"

You are a gnat, the still dreaming Ghar-Yon-Tog told her.

"I'll show you want a gnat can do," Mako said, collecting her transduction powers.

515

You will do nothing of the kind. Sleep, little Spacer, until I need you again.

As Mako attempted to rebel, using spurned rage, an overpowering sleepiness caused her eyelids to flicker with heaviness. She wanted to resist. She wanted the monstrous alien to pay for all his lies and deceits against the Spacer Nation. Most of all, she wanted to kill him because he had used and deceived her so badly. But instead of any of those things, Mako 21 fell forward in the control chamber, fast asleep.

-99-

In the Omega Nebula nexus several thousand light-years away, Captain Maddox felt the tug of gravity first as Ludendorff and he began to sink toward the corridor floor. They flew with the thruster pack toward a shimmering, towering black stone rectangle in what had been a non-gravity corridor.

"What is that?" Maddox shouted.

"That must be the star gate," Ludendorff said. "And it appears we've entered a gravitational area of the nexus."

"Quick," Maddox radioed the others. "Land, land. We have to land before the gravity increases and we crash against the floor."

The captain had guessed right. As the thruster-pack-propelled group zoomed closer to the star gate, the gravity increased dramatically. Maddox with his quicker reactions had already taken Ludendorff and himself lower than the others were.

"Hurry," Maddox radioed the others. "Hang on," he told the professor. "This could get rough."

The two of them wobbled as they zoomed lower. With amazing dexterity and despite Ludendorff's dead weight, the captain rotated them around and used all the thrust he could to slow their velocity.

As it was, the two of them struck the floor hard, tumbling end over end, taking a fierce beating. At last, they came to a tangled halt.

Maddox stirred slowly. He hurt all over. "Professor?" he said.

There was no answer from the unmoving Ludendorff.

Maddox carefully untangled and unhooked the professor from him. Afterward, he took off the shattered thruster pack. He hadn't broken any bones, although his joints were stiff and some of his muscles throbbed painfully.

He had no time to check on Ludendorff. They might have all already run out of time.

Farther ahead in the corridor, Sergeant Riker crashed against the floor. Part of his thruster pack exploded off him, the rest remained as he tumbled endlessly, finally coming to a dead stop. The sergeant did not groan or twist. He, like Ludendorff, was either unconscious or dead.

Meta crashed last, although she unhooked from her thruster pack while airborne. The heavy pack sailed ahead of her, hitting, bouncing, tumbling and sparking, going for quite a ways across the floor. Luckily, it missed the huge rectangular stone that seemed to be the star gate and it missed the humming power source as well. Even though Meta was wearing a spacesuit and its weighty helmet, she tucked and rolled, taking minimal damage from the crash landing.

Maddox had already begun limp sprinting for the star gate. His left calf muscle hurt every time he set down that boot, but he could manage. The captain reached Meta as she climbed to her feet.

"Impressive," Maddox told her. "Are you ready?"

She picked up her rocket-firing rifle. Maddox had his slung across his left space-suited shoulder.

"Let's do this," Meta said.

"Let's do this," Maddox agreed.

Husband and wife—both of them stronger than normal humans, with spacesuits and rocket-propelled rifles—raced clumsily for the pulsating black stone star gate.

"Is that the portal?" Meta asked.

"We're going to find out," Maddox said. For once, he didn't sprint ahead of her, as he babied his left calf muscle.

The two ran for the star gate. A second later, something invisible struck, making both of them stagger.

For Maddox, it challenged his will to keep himself running. Could this be Ghar-Yon-Tog's dream will battling his?

Meta had already begun to gasp. "I can't keep going," she whispered.

Maddox grabbed one of her gloved hands. "Yes, you can. Come on."

"My head throbs. No…" Meta moaned. "He sees me. This is awful. I feel his eyes."

"Fight him."

"How?" Meta whimpered. "I want it to stop."

"Think of past injuries, how others hurt you, how you always wanted to get back at them."

"It's not helping."

"Get mad, Meta. Get pissed, really pissed."

"Oh, Maddox, I want him to stop seeing me."

Maddox could feel his wife digging in, resisting the run. "Meta," he said, yanking her, forcing her to keep up with him.

"No," she said, in a deeper voice, a dreadful voice. "No. This will not happen."

Maddox tried to yank his hand free, but Meta gripped fiercely, using her considerable strength, holding him, and holding him back.

"Fight him, Meta. Everyone dies if we fail."

Meta tried. How did Maddox resist the awful Old One? The grim stare—

Meta, she heard as from far away. The voice told her to shoot Maddox. The captain was evil.

With tears in her eyes, using her love for Maddox to resist the inhuman monster, Meta lessened her handgrip.

No! something said in her mind, and it hurt so much that she screamed.

At the same time, Maddox pulled his hand free. His heard his wife's scream over the comm link in his helmet, and it almost broke through his resolve. He could feel Ghar-Yon-Tog whispering in his mind, promising and threatening. Maddox's neck shivered, and he wanted to listen to the promises and avoid the threats.

But Maddox drummed up the prejudices of his youth, how he'd always had to stand alone. The others would try to force him to do what they wanted. But he said no and endured the insults and the fistfights with the bigger boys. He had endured and had bottled everything up in his heart.

Now, Maddox poured out the scorn and hatred that had robbed him of a normal youth. He'd stood alone. He'd been an island, a rock that had resisted the waves of united peer pressure trying to make him submit. But he hadn't submitted. He had fought back. He'd always fought back. So, although his mind throbbed with the intensity of Ghar-Yon-Tog's demonic will and the terror behind it, Maddox limp-sprinted for the towering black stone. Sweat oozed from the strain and his gut tightened as if a bigger boy was going to kick him the stomach over and over again. Maddox clenched his jaw. He was almost to the towering flat stone.

With a snarl, Maddox dove headfirst, lifting off his feet, aiming at the flat surface. His better sense told him he'd dash himself senseless doing that. Then he reached the stone—the star gate—and vanished from the Omega Nebula nexus.

He was…somewhere else, a place without gravity. He tumbled end over end through a bizarre realm of…what the heck? He saw comets and strange sights that did not fully imprint upon his mind. The insidious whispering was gone. That must mean Ghar-Yon-Tog couldn't touch his mind here.

That was interesting. What was this place? How did a star gate operate?

Maddox snarled again. The physics didn't matter. *Get ready*, he told himself. *The biggest fight is about to start.* He drummed up rage. *Show the alien monster he shouldn't have screwed with the human race. Make him suffer.*

As the captain tumbled through the between realm, he saw a huge opening ahead. Through the opening and a farther arch—a vast entrance—he sighted exotic and impossibly gigantic machinery. He fell toward the opening and it seemed as if he fell through molasses or maybe it was a time warp. He didn't know how to make sense of it. Maybe it was a last way for the dreaming, sleeping Ghar-Yon-Tog to influence reality. Was this another trick of the mind or was it really happening like this?

Then, Maddox saw the vast tentacled monster in a yellow solution. It—

Maddox remembered seeing a speeded film once, a nature show. In the film were bare winter trees with snow on the ground. The snow melted at a phenomenal rate, and grass sprouted. Then, buds appeared, leaves, and in no time, fruit that ripened and fell onto the ground. By that time, the leaves changed color and one by one dropped to the forest floor.

That's what it was like through the opening and the farther arch as the frozen space monster in the yellow solution became supple again and began twitching ugly tentacles.

Abruptly, Maddox fell through the opening, and reality twisted around him. He staggered on his feet, stumbling toward an unbelievably huge archway.

He looked back and saw a pulsating, towering black stone, the other end of the star gate. He was here, wherever here was, and it looked as if the Yon-Soth creature was beginning to wake up after eons of sleep in the Builder nexus.

This was it. This was the final showdown.

-100-

Maddox felt insignificant and puny in this gargantuan place. He was like a mouse in a museum, a mouse scurrying past vast alien statues that represented who the heck knew what.

But a mouse had teeth. It could bite. Maybe it wouldn't be much of a bite, but Maddox would try to make his a rabid one.

Sliding the rocket-rifle strap from his space-suited shoulder, gripping the weapon in both gloved hands, Maddox advanced toward the great arch that led to the gargantuan revival chamber.

The ugly monster in the yellow solution stirred. Maddox did not think the thing was asleep anymore. Ghar-Yon-Tog had almost completed his awakening.

Maddox had a glimmering then of what Ghar-Yon-Tog awake meant. While asleep, the creature had exhibited fantastic powers, however he generated such powers. Clearly, the Old One wasn't mortal in the accepted sense of the word. The monster was from the primeval era of the universe. Had the laws of physics been different then?

Maddox had studied a little ancient Greek history. In the beginning of Time, according to the Greeks, had been Father Sky and Mother Earth. Their brood had been giants, monsters of all kinds. They had been the firstborn. Was that super-sized creature stirring in the yellow solution like that? Was it a firstborn, with primal abilities that made a mockery of intelligent beings in this era?

The Builders had kept it alive, Ludendorff said because it was an original tech to work galactic core machinery of some importance. Might that be true?

Maddox shrugged. He didn't care. This thing would destroy humanity. Maybe it would first usher in a nightmare world for the human race. With the powers that it had possessed while asleep and dreaming, there was no telling what Ghar-Yon-Tog the Great, the progenitor of a foul race of monsters, could do awake. Thus, the wisest course was to kill him before he could fully awaken. Maybe the Yon-Soth was groggy from his long slumber. Maybe this was the critical moment that gave Maddox the only opportunity to save humanity from Hell on Earth.

With his heart resolved, Maddox limped through the great opening. A glance around failed to show him the Spacer anywhere. For all he knew, the Spacer was dead.

Maddox's heart was beating hard as he skidded to a halt. He was only partway to the glass container. That container was far larger than any football stadium.

Maddox raised the heavy rifle and sighted down the scope—and he saw the most horrible thing possible. Ghar-Yon-Tog was far larger than any blue whale, Maddox estimated, three or four times larger. Whales had tiny eyes compared to their bulk. The same was true for Ghar-Yon-Tog.

As Maddox sighted down the scope, the first of the Old One's ring of eyes opened. Then more opened. They were red with yellow irises, and they radiated hellish intelligence. Worse, a thousand maybe even a million times worse, the first, and then the second and third, fourth and fifth eyes all fixed on him.

As a sense of sick fear washed over the captain, he steeled himself and pulled the trigger. The first rocket shell popped out of the opening. The rear of the shell ignited and roared as the rocket sped the HEAT warhead at the great glass container holding the Old One.

Maddox grinned tightly even as his heart raced, and he fired again and again. It felt awesome to shoot at the monster that had caused him so much grief and frankly, terror.

Then, Maddox watched something horrible. The first rocket shell abruptly halted in midflight. The second and third shells also stopped. Each warhead blew up in turn, the shrapnel flying through the gargantuan chamber and doing absolutely no harm as some of the metal pieces tinkled against the gigantic glass container.

The mighty and demonic will of Ghar-Yon-Tog, a groggy will from eons of stasis sleep, fixed on Maddox.

Maddox might have wilted and given up, but that wasn't in his nature. He had come this far, and yes, maybe compared to Ghar-Yon-Tog he was at most a mouse. But couldn't a mouse rush forward, get itself gulped and gnaw the monster's innards while the mouse still had life?

Maybe there was a touch of madness about Maddox here deep in the Sagittarius Spiral Arm. Maybe the haunted nexus tore away the calm, rational aspect of the Star Watch Intelligence operative. This was the elemental Maddox that he usually kept buried deep in his heart. He was going to die, but he was going to die with rage glinting in his eyes while charging the enemy.

Maddox shook the heavy rifle at the monster. The action said, "I'm not done with you yet, Beast." The captain tore out the empty magazine and inserted a fresh one. Then, as David had done against Goliath, Captain Maddox ran at the Old One. Maddox chambered the next rocket shell as he limp-sprinted closer. Could Ghar-Yon-Tog stop the rocket shells from close range? Maddox aimed to find out.

The captain did something, then, all out of proportion to his power to hurt the awakening Great One. What could he truly hope to achieve? Maybe a glorious way to die—if battling insane odds really was glorious instead of just plain futile.

What Maddox did was cause the Old One to concentrate *all* his awakened will on him. The very courage of the act might have worried Ghar-Yon-Tog. Or maybe it wasn't that, but instead that the Old One had been asleep for eons. He was groggy now, prone to make an error he otherwise would never have made. For Ghar-Yon-Tog most certainly made an error in this moment.

As the Old One fixed the entirety of his awakening will on puny Maddox racing at the glass container, Ghar-Yon-Tog inadvertently withdrew his former dreaming will that had tentacles of thought throughout various part of the Sagittarius and Orion Spiral Arms. That daunting will had included the Omega Nebula nexus several thousand light-years away.

With the lifting or disappearing of the Old One's will from the Omega Nebula nexus, others who could never have acted were now starting to think bravely about how they could save the day for humanity.

-101-

On the bridge of *Victory*, Valerie ordered the helmsman to take the starship behind the nexus in relation to the advancing Swarm super-fleet.

The first long-range, heavy-laser beams of the motherships had already turned the starship's shield a red-tinged color. That was only going to get worse with each passing second.

Victory maneuvered toward the nexus and already began turning around it. The effect on the Swarm ships was practically instantaneous. The barrage of enemy heavy lasers quit. Clearly, the Hive Masters controlling the fleet did not want to damage the nexus in any way.

"That gives us a tiny tactical advantage," Lieutenant Noonan said.

"Valerie," Galyan informed her. "It does more than that. The electronic blockage to the disrupter and neutron cannons is gone. I have begun warming up each. You should be able to fire in several minutes."

"What difference does that make for us now?" Valerie asked. "We can possibly destroy a handful of enemy ships—"

"Or break through the nexus hull," Galyan said, interrupting.

"Right," Valerie said, as she slapped an armrest. She turned to communications. "Recall the strikefighters. They're not doing any good now."

"Yes, Lieutenant," the comm officer said. "By the way, sir, Lieutenant Maker is asking permission to fold into the nexus."

Valerie stared at the main screen, obviously thinking about the request.

"Lieutenant," Andros said from his station. "I have Meta on the line."

"Put her on the speaker," Valerie said.

Andros tapped his panel.

"Meta," Valerie said.

"Maddox went into the star gate," Meta said in a rush. "I wanted to join him, but Ghar-Yon-Tog wouldn't let me."

"What?" Valerie asked. "What star gate? What are you talking about?"

"The Old One is on a different nexus," Meta said. "Maddox went through a star gate linking the two nexuses. He went to try to kill the thing. I don't think he succeeded, but I'm not feeling Ghar-Yon-Tog's will stopping me from acting anymore. That's got to mean something good."

"I heard that," Keith said from a different comm link. "This is it, Valerie," he said. "We have the away team's location. Meta," Keith said, "is there room for me to fold the tin can to your position?"

"Barely," Meta said, sounding doubtful.

Valerie was shaking her head at Keith's insistence on going in there.

"I have to go get them," Keith said over the comm. "If nothing else, I can be there when the captain returns, and pull him out."

"He's not returning," Meta said. "Didn't you hear me? He went after Ghar-Yon-Tog, and he has a peashooter to kill an elephant."

"What does that mean?" Valerie asked.

"What kind of weapon did the captain take with him?" Keith asked from the fold-fighter.

"A rocket-firing rifle," Meta said. "But he can't kill an evil monster with that."

"I have just the thing to help the captain," Keith said. "Lieutenant Noonan, I'm asking permission to fold into the nexus."

Valerie heard the conviction in the ace's voice. "Will you go in if I don't give you permission?" she asked.

"I'm asking first," Keith said. "I know how to kill the Old One. I have just the weapon to do it."

Valerie swallowed hard, because she thought she understood what the hotheaded fighter jock planned to do. He had two antimatter missiles attached to the fold-fighter. If a mere rifle was a peashooter…

"Permission granted," Valerie said in a whisper.

"I heard that," Keith said. "And thanks, love. You won't regret it."

"If you don't come back, I'll regret it for the rest of my life," Valerie told him.

"Roger that," Keith said. "Meta, are you ready?"

"I don't know about this," Meta said.

"I do," Keith said. "This time, I'm going to be the hero."

-102-

Maddox had charged the glass container with a fresh magazine of rocket shells. He hadn't gotten a chance to test his theory, though.

Ghar-Yon-Tog had fixed the entirety of his will on the puny human, with predictable results.

Without any visible means for doing so, the space-suited Maddox presently dangled in midair before the Old One. The rocket rifle had smashed itself against the floor just before an irresistible and invisible force had grasped the captain and raised him into the air.

Maddox twisted in the grip of the invisible force, but he wasn't having any luck. He did have a horrible bird's eye view of the proceedings. He was like a kid shoved up against a glass window, looking down at the quadruple-whale-sized monster watching him.

It was either scream in terror or roar in rage. Maddox wasn't shouting, but froth bubbled at his lips and his throat was sore from previous shouting. There was still some of the detached Maddox left—the anger had burned away, leaving the molten core of the captain's personality. As a highly trained Intelligence operative, he observed for future references—not that he had a future, but old habits died hard.

With his tentacles—abnormally long and strong looking—Ghar-Yon-Tog pushed against the bottom of the colossal glass container, propelling his gross bulk toward the surface of the yellow solution. In moments, he breached it and eyed the captain from closer range.

You have committed blasphemy against the new order, Ghar-Yon-Tog mentally told Maddox. *You tried to slay a god.*

Hearing the Old One's awakened thoughts directly in his brain was an agonizing experience. Maddox's face scrunched up as the thoughts boomed with throbbing intensity, making the veins on the side of his temples swell with blood.

It took longer for the captain to understand the words' meaning. Finally, he did. Inside his helmet, Maddox's lips twisted as he tried to reply. His voice came out harsh and gasping.

"You're no god."

Ghar-Yon-Tog appeared to enjoy the talk. *Will you spout yet more blasphemy, gnat? Compared to you, I am the master of the universe.*

Maddox groaned as the words boomed in his brain. He could not take much more of this. Soon, he would develop an aneurism and it would surely blow.

With his huge tentacles, Ghar-Yon-Tog grasped the edge of the glass container and pulled himself higher yet. He revealed a gaping maw of a mouth and slowly lowered Maddox toward it.

You shall be my victory snack, gnat. Think upon that in your last seconds of life. You went against the greatest and now shall join me as sustenance and then as a smear of excrement as I shit you out. You are nothing, Captain Maddox. You are a worm—

Ghar-Yon-Tog the Great—the progenitor of the Yon-Soths—abruptly stopped forcing his thoughts into Maddox's tiny brain, for at that moment, a terrible calamity impinged upon the Great One's mind. He realized his earlier error of withdrawing his dream-state will from the vast reaches of space. It was a simple and understandable error, as he had been groggy from eons of sleep.

Lieutenant Keith Maker's daring now showed itself. An antimatter missile zoomed out of the towering black stone star gate. The missile's sides barely made it through the star-gate monolith, but make it through it did. The exhaust from the missile propelled it at great velocity toward the great arch that led to the revival chamber.

At the last moment, Ghar-Yon-Tog had sensed the incoming missile through the star gate. He'd made an error, but he also had masterful powers that these frail creatures likely did not even imagine he could possess.

With a thought, the Great One froze the missile's exhaust and energy supply and forward momentum. Just like the rocket shells earlier, he halted the missile's advance. There was a critical difference, however. This act took more power. But wasn't he Ghar-Yon-Tog the Great? He had power to spare.

Do you see, gnat, Ghar-Yon-Tog thought at Maddox.

I see, a new thought mind-spoke. *Do you see this?*

Maddox was vaguely aware of a new entity, one with soft mind-thoughts.

Oh. With his peripheral vision and through the visor, Maddox saw a tiny Spacer in a spacesuit walk boldly across the floor toward the gargantuan glass container. He silently applauded the daring—wait. He recognized the thought as coming from Mako 21. That was inconceivable. He'd left her behind in a life-pod in the Usan System.

I haven't forgotten that, Maddox heard softly in his mind.

The captain might have given that more consideration, but the force keeping him up there abruptly quit. With a sick lurch in his gut, Maddox began falling from twenty-two meters up. He flailed for a second, surprised.

Instead of feeling elation that Ghar-Yon-Tog had cut the invisible moorings, Maddox looked down. He wasn't headed for the gaping maw or the liquid of the yellow solution. He was headed straight for the floor. He stopped flailing and braced for impact, keeping his knees bent. This was going to hurt. It might cripple him.

The floor rushed up with startling speed. Then, Maddox was there. He hit the hard floor and managed to land like a cat—on his feet. His ankles did not twist. He had bracing space boots and they were on tight. His knees buckled even as he attempted to use parachute-landing technique. The bruised left calf exploded with agony and the rest of his body thumped down so hard he bounced.

Maddox clenched his jaws in order to keep from screaming at the pain jolting through him. Despite his best efforts, he was sure he'd broken bones and torn muscles. Maddox groaned then because the pain was too much.

Through tear-filmed eyes, Maddox saw the Spacer halt beside him, looking down at him.

Maddox made a feeble gesture with one of his gloved hands.

The Spacer—Mako 21—ignored him as she resumed her approach to the towering glass container. Maddox couldn't understand how she resisted Ghar-Yon-Tog's power to raise her airborne as he'd been airborne. Maybe the Old One had pegged him up there, but now that Ghar-Yon-Tog held the antimatter missile in place, he could not easily grasp someone with his powers.

With a soft groan, Maddox twisted his prone position on the floor. Some of the pain was fading. He could think a little more, even as he was aware of sweat drenching him. Had the spacesuit's conditioner unit broken?

Mako aimed her visor up at Ghar-Yon-Tog. Maddox looked up too. All of the Old One's eyes peered down at Mako from the top of the gargantuan glass container.

Maddox was no longer privy to the thoughts flashing back and forth between the two. He heard a buzz in his mind, so he figured they were speaking at each other. A glance to the left showed him the motionless, midair antimatter missile. Wait. The missile was not utterly motionless. It shifted minutely as if shivering, and that told something of the powers at play.

That bothered Maddox so his forehead furrowed. Mako had her modifications. That was nothing compared to the awakened Ghar-Yon-Tog, though. How could she stand free before the monster?

Then it dawned on Maddox what must be happening. It was the best answer as it fit the facts. The Spacer must have triggered the antimatter warhead. She must have caused it to explode. Ghar-Yon-Tog had then used his considerable powers to dampen the explosion—at least for the moment. The fantastic strain against the Yon-Soth allowed Mako's slight power to come into play.

Correct, Maddox heard in his mind.

The captain frowned. Ghar-Yon-Tog kept the missile from flying at himself and kept its fuel from igniting. The frozen moment could not last long. Mako used the fantastic strain against the Old One and attempted to do something with her modifications. Soon, the monster or the Spacer would win.

Maddox looked around. He had to help Mako against Ghar-Yon-Tog. Ah. He spied his broken rocket rifle on the floor. Maybe he could salvage something there.

Maddox began dragging himself across the floor. His right knee had ballooned up, and his left leg wasn't responding to his will. It hurt to pull himself like this, but—

Maddox chuckled throatily instead of groaning. It felt as if ants crawled across his body, biting him. Was that how he sensed the unleashed forces around him?

He eyed the broken rifle and felt sweat pouring off him, stinging his eyes. He panted, and he dragged himself faster.

Mako faced a monster from the deep time. Maybe he could figure out a way to launch the rocket shells at the thing. He had to tip the scales toward the Spacer. So what if it meant he blew up in an antimatter blast? This would be his final act. He would save his crew, the best crew any captain had ever had. He would save Meta, his love, save Brigadier O'Hara who had been like a mother to him. He'd save old Sergeant Riker, the best Intelligence operative high command could ever have given him.

Maddox no longer chuckled and no longer groaned. He'd fixated his sights upon the heap of a rocket rifle and was almost there. He could see the magazine, a dented thing, but full of rocket shells.

"Yes," Maddox said through gritted teeth.

He saw something else in the background. It looked an awful lot like Meta in her spacesuit coming out of the star gate. He must be hallucinating. He would have liked to say goodbye to her.

Meta veered toward him, and she slammed her helmet with a gloved hand. Was she talking to him through the helmet comm? Was his broken?

"Meta is not there," Maddox whispered to himself with a head-shake. The broken rocket rifle was there, though. Meta couldn't be there, not after they'd launched an antimatter missile into this place. That would mean Meta had entered the star gate after they had launched the missile. She would have known that she would be coming here to almost certain doom.

Would Meta do that for him?

That was when Maddox realized he really saw his wife. She was no longer looking at him, but at the vast monster in the equally huge glass container.

***

Meta raced into a bizarre chamber and could hardly credit her eyes. She saw her poor husband dragging himself across the floor in a battered spacesuit. She saw the antimatter missile hanging in the air, making slight side-movements as if struggling to continue its flight at the, at the—

What was that ugly, tentacled monster in the glass container? Was that Ghar-Yon-Tog? He had warty skin and horrible eyes and locked his gaze on—

That was a Spacer spacesuit and therefore had to be a Spacer, a human, standing up to the grim monster from the early times of the universe. Meta gulped noisily and shivered in her spacesuit. She moaned in dread—

Then Meta tore her gaze from the awful monster. If she looked at Ghar-Yon-Tog, she would fall under his spell. Instead, she focused on Maddox. What had happened to him? Why didn't he stand up?

Meta swerved aside and ran to him. She hit her helmet again with a gloved palm and told him to hurry up. He wasn't listening or his helmet comm didn't work. He dragged himself toward a useless rocket rifle on the floor. Maybe her husband's fabled poise had broken under the strain. No. She didn't believe that. He wanted to keep fighting and went to the only weapon he could see.

The fight was over in here. Now, it was time to go home.

Meta reached him. Maddox did not acknowledge her, but kept dragging his space-suited body to the heap on the floor.

She grabbed him. Maddox tried to fight free of her grasp, and he was weak. That told her the extent of his injuries. Maddox normally had iron strength. Given his lack of power, he must be critically injured.

"Stop it," she cried. "Don't make your injuries worse."

Maddox didn't listen.

Meta hunched her shoulders, all the acknowledgement she was willing to give the nearby monster. Then, using her 2G strength, knowing this was it, she turned Maddox onto his back. She grabbed his arms and hoisted him onto her back in a fireman's carry. He was heavy, and she staggered under the load.

Meta turned away from the monster, and she was only vaguely aware that Maddox had torn her sidearm blaster from its outer holster. How had he managed the tricky maneuver? He had to be in great pain.

Carrying Maddox on her shoulders, staggering for the star gate in the other chamber, Meta headed there one lurching step after another. Through her helmet, she heard the power whine of her blaster firing. She twisted to look.

Maddox aimed the blaster and fired at the monster. The beams struck Ghar-Yon-Tog's warty hide, the area that was higher than the edge of the glass container. Black spots appeared at the location of each beam strike. Smoke roiled up, and the warty skin flinched like a cat's furry hide shaking off water.

There was something much more ominous. Each blaster shot against Ghar-Yon-Tog caused the giant antimatter missile to belch a wisp of smoke from the rear port as it inched closer, in midair, toward the glass container.

Each blaster shot broke a little of Ghar-Yon-Tog's concentration.

Meta heard a crackle of comm noise over her helmet comm.

"Die, Beast," Maddox snarled in a tinny voice. A harsh laugh sounded next, a second harsh laugh that might have carried a tinge of madness in it. "Hit him harder, Mako. I'll keep firing."

Another blaster shot singed the great monster.

With a sob of effort, realizing Maddox wanted to kill Ghar-Yon-Tog more than survive, Meta began screaming. She moved faster than a lurch at a time now, and began trying to run in a staggering fashion.

Meta hated this place. And she knew they were out of time. If she didn't reach the star gate soon, they would fail to make it onto the last fold-fighter out of the Omega Nebula nexus.

Meta's space-suited boots rang against the floor of the statue chamber. She looked back as Maddox hurled the empty blaster at the monster. Then, through her helmet, Meta heard an octopus-like squeal that would haunt her for the rest of her life. That couldn't have come from a blaster shot. Did Ghar-Yon-Tog expend his last strength holding back the missile?

The hideous squeal gave Meta a final burst of energy. Then, the wretched squeal happened a second time. With a grunt, Meta dove through the star gate with her husband, leaving the haunted nexus of the Sagittarius Arm.

-103-

The two Star Watch officers disappeared through the star gate, leaving the frozen moment behind them.

A blaster-pimpled Ghar-Yon-Tog strove to smother the antimatter explosion even as he kept the missile from speeding forward. He hated Maddox. The wretched human had used him for target practice, striking his flesh again and again. Each blast-hit had upset his concentration and caused the antimatter explosion to slip one notch nearer to happening.

Now, Ghar-Yon-Tog struggled to reassert his former control over the warhead. A growing rage against Maddox kept him from doing it as fast as he otherwise might have. How dare the puny human do that to him? Maddox should be mashed protein in his stomach and headed for his sphincter. Instead, the arrogant human who had used him for target practice was safely back on a distant nexus.

That was too much, too galling—

Ghar-Yon-Tog struggled to release his anger against the starship captain. He could feel the Spacer's miniscule transduction power lever the antimatter explosion one particle closer to completion. He needed to put an end to this now.

Ghar-Yon-Tog was stunned to find that the explosion was a hair's breath away from happening in real time. How had it gotten this close?

The Old One knew the answer. Those last blaster shots had brought catastrophe to the brink. The last shots had multiplied

Mako's modification strength, allowing her to wedge destruction to the very tipping point.

Ghar-Yon-Tog concentrated all his might, but now it was like stopping an avalanche in progress instead of seconds before it started. Incredibly, Mako was still making incremental headway.

As the black spots on his skin finally stopped smoking with raw hurt, Ghar-Yon-Tog began to furiously reason with himself. The moment was on a knife's edge. If he made one false move, it would all end in disaster. He had the power to do this, but it would be so much easier if the stubborn little Spacer would quit. Maybe it was time to negotiate his way out of trouble.

While dampening the antimatter blast and keeping the missile relatively motionless, the Old One opened mind-channels between them. It was delicate work, and no doubt, the Spacer could recognize that. Still, it was time to bargain. He could—no, Ghar-Yon-Tog would be sweet reasonableness and think of nothing else.

Dear little Mako 21, Ghar-Yon-Tog mentally said. *I'm sorry for what I did to you earlier. It was wrong of me. You have greatly aided me in my quest. That deserves a reward, one so huge that the universe will see that I recompense justly those who help me.*

There. That sounded good. The little minx should fall for that.

Are you truly sorry? Mako mentally asked.

Good, good, he'd started her talking. The rest would be easy. He still needed to frame this correctly, even if hers was a prideful rejoinder.

I have said I am sorry. I am more than big enough to admit my errors. I realize others will serve me willingly if they see how generous I am. I yearn to show you vast generosity as a showcase to the rest of the universe. That is how you can know I mean what I say.

Ghar-Yon-Tog waited, but she did not reply. Maybe she was thinking this through. No doubt, she feared for her safety, as well she should.

Come, Mako, why continue with this foolishness? You and I will both die. You do not want to die, do you?

No.

Good, good. That is a reasonable attitude. Now, tell me what you want, little Mako, and I will grant it in such stunning abundance that you will marvel we ever had this incident with each other.

Do you know what I want?

Ghar-Yon-Tog checked his anger at her snotty little question. How dare she talk to him like this?

He glanced at the missile and the terrible warhead. Already the delay was helping him. The blaster shots no longer stung so much. Damn Maddox with his blaster fire. The little minx with her transduction had been losing to him before that. If Maddox hadn't fired…

Well, no matter, no matter. With Mako's help, they could take care of this deadly problem.

Tell me what you want, little Mako, Ghar-Yon-Tog told her.

Her thoughts boiled at him with furious rage. *I want you to burn in Hell, fiend, and remember that I, Mako 21, did this to you!*

What? he asked.

She threw her final dregs of power into the fray. That caused the blaster burns on his skin to itch horribly. The itching made it that much more difficult to concentrate.

Once more, the missile slipped a little closer.

Now, Ghar-Yon-Tog knew Mako meant to kill him if she could, even at the cost of her death. If only those burn marks didn't inflame his tender skin—

Ghar-Yon-Tog thrust the thought aside. It was time to do this the hard way. Then, he would seek out Maddox and exact a fearsome retribution for all this bother. He would show Maddox the real fury of a Yon-Soth.

For the next thirteen and half minutes, Ghar-Yon-Tog struggled against Mako 21 and the avalanche-levered antimatter missile.

At the end of the time, Ghar-Yon-Tog's incredible but still-groggy power had wilted just enough under the terrible forces unleashed against him. The antimatter explosion finally shoved forward to completion. The eruption roared through the chamber with annihilating, star-bright force. The missile would have resumed its flight, but the detonating warhead obliterated it and Mako 21. The blast also eliminated one of the oldest creatures in the Milky Way Galaxy, burning him out of existence in a flash of time. The explosion began a chain reaction that blew up the ancient but haunted nexus deep in the Sagittarius Spiral Arm.

Ghar-Yon-Tog the Great, the progenitor of the Yon-Soths, had woken up, and through the efforts of Keith Maker, Mako 21 and Captain Maddox, the Old One had died.

-104-

Meta and Maddox tumbled through the between realm linking the two star gates. Maddox fought for consciousness as his injuries threatened to overwhelm him. Grabbing and firing the blaster had taken his last reserves of strength and will. Meta, on the other hand, prayed they had escaped in time.

Finally, Meta, with Maddox over her shoulders, staggered into the Omega Nebula nexus. She stumbled toward the grounded fold-fighter, grinning at the sight of the open hatch. The hatch moved then, shutting decisively. Meta's grin threatened to dissolve into tears of frustration.

After all this effort, to be so close and yet so far—it just wasn't fair!

Meta had seen the fold-fighter land earlier, detaching two antimatter missiles. Keith had guided the one through the star gate. The other waited peacefully on the floor, its warhead near the towering rectangle of black stone.

Through the vibration of the floor and through her space boots, Meta could feel the fold-fighter powering up. It was going to fold back to *Victory* soon. She staggered toward the tin can, wanting to wave her arms but unable to unless she dumped her husband. This, she refused to do.

It was too much. Tears leaked from Meta's eyes and her face screwed up inside her helmet. At that moment, the fighter's outer hatch reopened. A Star Watch marine in a spacesuit stepped forward and beckoned her with an arm wave.

Hiccupping as she cried and laughed all at once, Meta lowered her helmet and charged toward the tin can.

The marine moved out of the way. Meta gathered herself and leaped the distance between floor and hatch, hurtling within as she clutched her husband against her.

Maddox slid with her across the interior deck of the fold fighter. The marine jumped above them as they slid underneath. The marine landed, reached toward the hatch and slapped a button. The hatch slammed shut, locking into place.

The marine must have communicated through a helmet comm and on a different channel. The marine crouched low to the deck, bracing himself for liftoff.

"We're folding," Meta radioed Maddox.

The captain grunted, likely all he could say.

Then Meta waited, wondering if they could escape from the Omega Nebula in time.

***

That was exactly what Lieutenant Noonan was wondering as the massed Swarm fleet accelerated for the nexus, with Starship *Victory* hiding behind the ancient Builder structure.

The insect fleet had become much more visible now, seen through probes. The starship had launched several rather than expose itself to direct sight and thus direct enemy fire. Flotilla after flotilla, more and even more motherships zoomed out of the concealing gases and debris clouds. There were literally thousands upon thousands of the Imperial Swarm vessels approaching.

As Valerie sat on the command chair, the number of visible enemy warships awed her. To see such massed might on the main screen heading toward the starship to kill her and the crew, and then everyone in Human Space after the bugs took over the nexus—it was one thing to say that 143,000 huge space-capable warships were in a single enemy fleet. It was quite another thing to actually see the vessels filling up space before you. Valerie had fought in her share of space battles. She had fought small actions and huge fleet actions. But she had never even once seen anything remotely like this.

The lieutenant felt small and insignificant, and she realized that humanity could not cope with such an enemy. If the bugs could reach Human Space, the bugs could wipe out the human race. It wouldn't be a matter of probabilities, but of cold hard facts.

The strategy of destroying nexuses made utter sense now. Humanity needed time, decades, centuries, maybe even a millennia or two to get ready to face the Swarm Imperium.

Yet, as Valerie studied the continuously growing and advancing invasion fleet, she wondered if even several millennia would be enough time for mankind to prepare for the Swarm. Well, she would be long dead by then. Her job was to save humanity today. That meant blowing up this damn nexus before the invasion fleet reached them and made that impossible.

The grim thought of using the star drive to jump into the nexus—"I'll do it if I have to," she said quietly.

"What was that, Valerie?" Galyan asked, as he hovered nearby.

Valerie swiveled the chair to face the holoimage. "Where's Ludendorff?"

"In the fold-fighter," Galyan said.

"Is he awake yet?"

Galyan's eyelids fluttered. "Ludendorff is still wearing his spacesuit and helmet, and has not yet responded to queries."

Valerie cursed softly. They needed Ludendorff to make a hyper-spatial tube for them.

"However," Galyan said, "you may be interested to know that I have communicated directly with the nexus computer-core."

"You did what?"

"I am unable to hack its software," Galyan said. "But I have convinced the core to make a hyper-spatial tube for us."

"What did you say?"

"I requested permission to flee the advancing Swarm."

"What did the computer core say to you?"

"That it would be better for us to leave so it could greet the new owners peacefully."

"The nexus computer core really said that?"

"It appears to be confused, Valerie. I must assume that is due to the corrupting nature of Ghar-Yon-Tog's interference with its software."

"Why would a Builder computer core side with the bugs?" Valerie asked.

"We already know the answer. The Builder that Captain Maddox spoke to several years ago assured us that the Swarm are the superior life-forms because they had created the largest political organization in the galaxy. The Swarm also have vastly superior numbers to humanity. Thus, in Builder thinking, they are the superior race."

"That's a poor way to decide it."

"What metric would you use, Valerie?"

"I don't care about metrics," the lieutenant said. "Is the fold-fighter back in the barn yet?"

"If you mean back aboard the starship, yes, Valerie."

"Are the antimatter warheads primed and ready?"

"Yes, Valerie."

At that moment, on the main screen, a growing swirling silvery mass appeared on the other side of the nexus.

"That's just great," Valerie said. "The hyper-spatial tube entrance is on the wrong side of the nexus. Now what do we do?"

"I would suggest that we fly, as fast as we can go, directly to it," Galyan said.

Valerie's nostrils flared. She swiveled the command chair toward the helm. "You heard the Driving Force," she told the watching pilot. "Take us around the nexus and head for the tube entrance."

The helmsman stared at her in shock.

Valerie shrugged. "Either we survive a massed laser barrage or we don't. Let's not fret about it, though."

"Roger, Lieutenant," the helmsman said. With shaking fingers, he began to set the coordinates.

"Valerie," Galyan said. "I have an important question for you."

"What's that?"

"Who is going to stay behind to make sure the antimatter warheads detonate?"

"No one is staying."

"Captain Maddox planned to stay," Galyan told her.

"Bully for him," Valerie said.

"Are you not the acting captain now, Valerie?"

She stared at the little holoimage. "Are you suggesting that it's *my* task to stay behind?"

"I do not *want* you to stay behind. But I know what Captain Maddox wants."

Valerie frowned as she stared at Galyan. Her eyes narrowed and she finally shook her head. "I'm the acting captain. You agree with that, right?"

"I have said so, Valerie."

"Right," she said, just as Maddox might have done. "If I'm the acting captain, I'm making the decisions around here. No one is staying behind, as we're going to trust our Star Watch-made equipment. That's how we're going to beat the bugs in the end, by having superior weapons. Because I'll tell you one thing, we ain't ever going to do it through a war of attrition."

"That strikes me as self-evident," Galyan said.

"We're moving around the nexus, Lieutenant," the helmsmen shouted.

Valerie looked up at the main screen, waiting for a glimpse of the massed Swarm vessels out there.

"I have another point to make," Galyan said.

"Stow it," Valerie said. "I'm busy."

"Ah," Galyan said. "Stow it. Yes, I understand. The captain taught me the meaning of the phrase."

The lieutenant glared at the holoimage.

"I am shutting up—now," Galyan said.

Valerie gave the holoimage a second look. Then, she concentrated as the starship made its dash for the swirling mass out there.

-105-

The ancient Adok starship accelerated from behind the nexus as nine decoy buoys did exactly the same thing.

Those nine decoys emitted ghost signals and projected pseudo-*Victory* holoimages that confused the Swarm commanders. How could ten alien starships now be where only one had been originally sighted?

Orders came down swiftly from the Hive Masters: "Fire, fire on the starships."

Fully one thousand eight hundred and sixty-three motherships were in the fleet's vanguard, but only one thousand six hundred and nineteen targeting computers locked onto their objectives. Seconds later, one thousand five hundred and eighty-nine laser cannons emitted heavy beams of harsh light. The rest malfunctioned in some manner.

The lasers flashed at the speed of light. Most hit, and nine decoy emitters winked out of existence. That just left Starship *Victory*.

One hundred and thirty-seven heavy lasers from a little more than outer medium range struck *Victory's* reinforced shield. The results were predictable. The shield did not change through the usual color progression, but went black and blacker still. The saturation laser assault was too much, too fast, and the shield collapsed.

Thus, one hundred and thirty-seven heavy lasers struck the armored hull of the starship. The armor was some of the very best of Star Watch. But it was no match for such a massed onslaught. The armor wasn't like the shield, however. With the shield, the combined energy quickly overwhelmed the electromagnetic defense. The armor heated up in one hundred and thirty-seven separate locations on the hull. Soon, extremely soon under these conditions, the combined wattage would cause the entire armored hull to heat up and glow red-hot.

The key today was that the motherships did not have the time to lazily hammer the enemy vessel. Here, seconds counted. The short but appreciable delay in firing because of the shock of seeing ten starships likely helped *Victory* more than any other factor, compounded by the fact that there had been ten separate targets to begin with, thus ensuring far fewer hits on target for the first few seconds.

During that short spell, the starship had raced at super-acceleration for the nearby swirling entrance to the hyper-spatial tube.

The second that the shield had lasted also gave the starship a tiny edge.

Those edges combined allowed an intact starship, albeit with a quickly heating hull, to dive into the swirling mass. Then, *Victory* disappeared from the Omega Nebula nexus region. As importantly, none of the Swarm laser beams was able to follow it into the hyper-spatial tube—they all fizzled at the edge of the silvery swirling mass instead.

***

The starship hurtled through the hyper-spatial tube toward the destination that Galyan had cajoled the Omega Nebula nexus's computer-core to program.

***

Meanwhile, inside the Omega Nebula nexus, a brace of antimatter warheads waited as an old-fashioned timer ticked down toward zero. The timer moved second by second and then there was a *click*. The click caused a detonation device to activate, which sent an electrical pulse to the waiting warheads.

At that instant, the warheads detonated simultaneously.

A gigantic antimatter fireball ballooned into existence, obliterating all matter in its path. In this instance, that meant the nexus's computer core, the star gate with all of its varied components and then one Builder system after another. The final combustible was the nexus's outer hull, which burned and disintegrated as the antimatter blast devoured that as well.

The gigantic blast sent waves of gamma and x-rays, heat and EMP, but those didn't matter in the greater scheme of things. The front motherships took damage. But, given the massive number of ships present, that mattered very little.

What did matter was the destruction of the nexus. It was gone. Thus, there would be no more hyper-spatial tubes from the Omega Nebula to anywhere else in the Sagittarius or Orion Spiral Arms.

-106-

The severely battered starship sped through the hyper-spatial tube, journeying one thousand, eight hundred and sixty-eight and a quarter light-years before *Victory* exited the tube.

Seven minutes and thirteen seconds later, the tube faded away, leaving *Victory* alone in a distant star system in the Sagittarius Spiral Arm.

At that point, people began to stir on the starship. Maddox wasn't one of them. He'd barely made it to medical before the ship raced for the tube entrance in the Omega Nebula. In medical, a doctor had given Maddox a shot, inducing sleep so his body and mind could start healing.

Ludendorff was worse off, with broken bones, torn ligaments and a severe concussion, although the professor would live. Sergeant Riker had been rendered unconscious earlier, but had sustained relatively minor injuries compared to the professor.

All three of them were under sedation.

From the bridge, Lieutenant Noonan initiated an investigation of the new star system. Data quickly flowed in. The system had a giant red star, one terrestrial planet—the star had probably devoured any other inner terrestrial planets when it had originally expanded. There were three outer gas giants with two asteroid belts mixed in and a thick Kuiper Belt beyond the last ice giant.

"I'm not finding any indication of Swarm ships or colonies," Andros Crank reported from his station.

"That's a relief," Valerie said from the command chair. "I want you to analyze our hull next. I have to know if we have a ship or not."

"Clearly, we have a ship, as we're intact," Andros said. "While we've taken heavy damage, we have hull integrity."

"I need to know more," Valerie said. "Lots more. We're far from home, and I don't see any nexus—"

"Found it," Andros said. "This nexus is just beyond the terrestrial planet's orbital path. Makes you wonder if the nexus used to be closer to the star, when the star was younger, I mean."

Before Valerie could comment or ask why Andros was checking for nexuses when she'd just given him an order concerning the hull, the hatch to the bridge opened.

Lieutenant Keith Maker waltzed onto the bridge. He had a huge smile, and his uniform jacket was open all the way. With his right-hand thumb, he loudly popped off a champagne cork from a glistening bottle in his right hand. He gripped the bottle by its neck.

"Congratulations, mates!" Keith roared. He watched the cork sail against a station, laughed, and raised the gushing geyser of a champagne bottle. He must have shaken it pretty hard on the way up.

With another laugh, Keith moved the bottle to his lips as he slurped bubbling champagne.

"Just what do you think you're doing?" Valerie demanded, with her arms crossed.

"Cheers!" Keith roared, raising the bottle high, marching toward the lieutenant.

"Mr. Maker!" Valerie shouted. "This is the bridge."

"Right you are," Keith laughed, guzzling more champagne. "This is the bridge and you're the finest acting ship's captain any vessel in Star Watch ever had." Keith looked startled, blinked with theatrical showmanship and nodded. "Yes, yes," he said in a different voice. "She is a fine one, lads, and with an ass that never quits."

"Keith!" Valerie shouted. "Behave yourself."

The ace hunched his shoulders and wagged a forefinger at her.

550

"I am *not* going to behave myself, sir," Keith said. "Not after I singlehandedly destroyed the great and terrible menace in the other nexus. You know the one I mean. The one Meta and Maddox had to use a star gate to reach."

"You're *drunk*," Valerie declared.

"Drunk on victory, lass," Keith said, grinning wide, taking another healthy swallow of champagne. "We did it," he said, marching up to her and throwing his arms wide—all while keeping hold of the champagne bottle.

"Keith, stop," Valerie said. "We have work to do."

"I sure do," Keith said. He engulfed her in a bear hug and kissed her smack on the lips, and his breath tasted like champagne, all right.

"Keith," she said, after fighting free of the embrace.

The ace grabbed her more forcefully, but he didn't kiss her again. Instead, face to face, he said, "You have to bend once in a while, love. When you win the super victory that just saved everything in Human Space, you're allowed to cheer, kiss the girls—well, I'll do that part—and have a party. Let's party, love."

"Keith," Valerie said, and there was pleading in her tone.

Maybe for the first time, the ace looked around the bridge and at everyone staring at him. He released Valerie afterward. "Where are we in terms of our galactic position?" the ace asked.

"That's what I'm trying to determine," Valerie said.

Keith swigged more champagne. "You gotta admit that we beat the odds."

Valerie nodded, and she wondered if the ace didn't have a point about celebrating their fantastic victory.

"We won!" Keith roared, raising the bottle high and guzzling like a maniac afterward. "You want to know the best part?" he asked.

Valerie shook her head.

"It was my idea to fire the antimatter missile through the star gate. I lined it up and I launched it from the floor. That was slick, don't you agree?"

"I do agree," Valerie said.

"Right," Keith said. "This time—" he looked around the bridge. "This time, I saved the day."

Valerie couldn't help herself. She smiled and said, "You're the hero, Mr. Maker."

"Ah-ha!" he cried. "I hereby request you to join me in my quarters to have a party and celebrate."

Valerie nodded. "I will. Later. You go drink. You deserve it. Sleep it off and later, you and I will—"

"Make out!" he shouted.

Valerie blushed.

Keith blew her a kiss, turned to Andros and aimed the top of the champagne bottle at him. "Figure out where we are, mate," the Scotsman slurred. "I want to get home and tell everyone what I did. This is the best mission ever."

"The ship is seriously damaged," Andros said.

"I figure that's so," Keith said. "Well, don't fret. I'll think of something. First, though, first I'm going to celebrate our victory against this Ghar-Yon-Tog. Who would have thought it would be my missile that finished off the monster?"

"You go and have your celebration," Valerie said. Keith deserved a party, but she didn't like seeing him drink so openly. That wasn't good for him. She'd have to talk to the captain about this. Speaking of—

"How's Maddox?" Valerie asked as Keith left the bridge. "Does anyone know?"

Galyan appeared, and the holoimage gave her a rundown on Maddox, Riker and Ludendorff.

"I have a question, Valerie," Galyan said.

"What is it?" the lieutenant asked the holoimage.

"If Professor Ludendorff is out of commission for a time," Galyan said, "who is going to go and talk to this nexus? How do we make a hyper-spatial tube from this far out that can get us home? Yes, I talked the last nexus computer-core into helping us, but Ghar-Yon-Tog had corrupted it. I do not believe the Old One will have corrupted this computer-core."

Valerie didn't have a ready answer. And she knew Galyan was right about distance.

Andros had already calculated their distance from Human Space. It was outside the safe hyper-spatial tube-traveling limit.

They had beaten Ghar-Yon-Tog and escaped the massive Swarm invasion fleet, but they might never be able to reach anyone in Star Watch to tell them.

-107-

Maddox stirred and realized he felt too groggy. He must be under some kind of sedation. A glance around showed the captain that he was in a medical facility aboard *Victory*.

He scowled. Why did he feel so…so *weird?* Yes. It felt as if his thoughts traveled through molasses.

A jolt of pain in his head—his brain, his frontal lobe—welled up then. The jolt made him wince and rub a spot on his forehead.

"I would leave your head alone if I were you, sir," a nurse told him.

She was a pretty young thing, an ensign. This might be her first voyage out.

"Is something wrong with…?" Maddox stopped talking. His tongue felt as if it was twice normal size, as if he was slurring his words.

"You're highly sedated, sir," the blonde-haired nurse said. "I'm surprised you're talking at all. That has to take great effort. The doctor is hoping you sleep."

"What's wrong with me?" Maddox asked slowly.

"I'm not supposed to say, sir."

"Tell me," he said.

She peered at him, looking frightened, but shook her head just the same.

The questioning exhausted Maddox. He closed his eyes and lay back. His frontal lobe throbbed several times, and it struck him that his mind *ached*. He had a strange memory of screaming—but that couldn't have been him.

He wasn't able to finish the thought as he fell into troubled slumber.

***

Maddox stirred later, and a vision swam before his numbed eyes. He saw a nurse as through a water glass, as if he was a kid leaning his chin on the table and staring through his glass of water at his grandma.

Maddox could barely tell it was a nurse. Maybe she was the same nurse that had refused a direct order.

His head throbbed. He tried to reach up to rub his forehead, but something held his hand down.

It took him a good long while to focus his eyes on his right hand. Was that a strap holding down his wrist? By damn, it really was a strap.

It took far longer for his head to make the journey to stare at the other half of his body, the left half. After a time, he looked down at his left wrist. A strap held it down, too.

"Nurse," Maddox said, although it came out jumbled, as if he'd crammed a ton of marbles into his mouth.

The indistinct nurse hovered over him. Maddox could no longer tell if she was pretty or not, or if she was the one who had disobeyed his direct order.

"What's wrong with me?" Maddox slurred.

"You're under heavy sedation, sir," the nurse said.

"Why?"

"The doctor will tell you later."

"Tell me now."

"I can't."

She didn't seem bothered by refusing him this time. Before he could figure out if it actually was the same nurse, his eyes closed and his world became blank.

***

The days passed like that for Maddox. No one visited him that he could tell. His head throbbed most of the time, but the sedation robbed it of its full power. That was the captain's verdict anyway.

Then, he woke up one day with a startling conclusion. Ghar-Yon-Tog must still be alive. The Old One still screwed with his mind. This was his punishment for what he'd done on the haunted nexus.

After that, Maddox became cunning. He feigned sleep and watched with hooded eyes.

Yes, a nurse, a big beefy fellow, this time, gave him an injection. After that, everything became blurry and indistinct.

When the captain woke up again, he feigned sleep once more, and when no one was around, he worked on loosening his binding straps.

He was a prisoner. *That* wasn't going to last.

Maddox had a secret with one of his fingernails. Some time ago, he'd had it lacquered and then sharpened. Not even Meta knew about it. With the lacquered fingernail, he carefully sawed off one strap.

Later, when it was dark, he worked furiously on the other straps. His head pounded as he toiled, and his mouth became bone dry. He felt nauseous, but he wasn't going to let that stop him.

Finally, with everything sawn through, he was ready, and he feigned sleep yet again.

A beefy nurse came later—Maddox couldn't tell the time. The man approached the bed, and Maddox sat up, whipping the covers over the man's head.

Swiftly, Maddox surged to his feet, and his eyesight swam as he tried to maintain his balance. He had to clutch the side of the bed one-handed, and by that time, the nurse had freed himself from the sheet.

"I have to give you an injection, sir," the nurse said, holding onto a hypo. "It's for your own good."

"Yes, my mistake," Maddox said, feigning total exhaustion. It wasn't that hard to do.

The captain waited as the nurse stepped nearer. Then Maddox sucker-punched the man in the gut and kneed him in the balls, making the poor fellow double over in pain. A last kick and the nurse went down hard.

Maddox bolted from the chamber, walking swiftly through medical. He only spied two others on duty, working elsewhere.

He actually made it to a corridor, hurrying down it as his eyesight swam and as he dragged his left hand along the wall for balance.

A holoimage appeared before him.

Maddox staggered back in surprise, and his head truly started throbbing.

"Captain," Galyan said. "You have to go back to bed. You have received possible brain damage. The medics are trying to cure you."

Maddox decided this had to be a trick, and he charged through the holoimage, hurrying for his quarters.

Meta, in the company of several medics, met him three corridor-turns later.

"Dear," Meta said, with worry etched across her face. "You're still under treatment. You've been getting fractionally better—"

"No more sedation," Maddox snapped.

Meta looked at Dana Rich in her white lab coat.

"Fine," Dana said. "No more drugs."

Maddox would have nodded, but that would have hurt his head too much.

"You don't look well," Dana said.

Maddox did not address that.

"Is your head hurting?" Dana asked.

"Ghar-Yon-Tog did it?" asked Maddox.

"That is the prognosis," Dana said. "You mumbled most of the story in your sleep. You also roared with pain before we figured out why you have these headaches. You've taken some brain damage, sir."

"Where is the ship?" Maddox asked.

"Galyan and I have almost reached the answer," Dana said. "We're far out in the Sagittarius Arm. The real question is, 'Can we go home again?'"

Maddox stared at Dana. The world was starting to grow dim around the edges.

"It's happening again," Meta said.

Dana nodded, but did not comment.

"Sigma Draconis," Maddox whispered. "Take us there."

"To the ship yard at Sigma Draconis?" asked Dana.

Maddox nodded, and that was the last thing he remembered this time around.

-108-

As Maddox endured the sedation—at lower doses now—and his throbbing headaches, the rest of the crew worked on getting home again. The Sagittarius star system was over one thousand light-years beyond the safe traveling distance through a hyper-spatial tube. Five thousand light-years was the limit.

Still, a hyper-spatial tube was the only way *Victory* could hope to reach Earth again. Traveling through the Swarm Imperium with the star drive and with Laumer Points did not appeal to anyone.

At Valerie's orders, the starship maneuvered to the nexus. She held a staff meeting, and agreed with Dana that they might as well try the direct approach. The longer they stayed out here, the less chance they had of surviving. The hull was intact, but that was just barely true. Far too many ship's systems had broken down and every day new ones broke down.

Dana led the expedition to the nexus—this was her show in more than one way. Without the professor's help, Dana figured out how to break inside the silver pyramid. The place seemed dead inside, but that was normal. After several hours of interior exploration, Dana and her team came upon the old Builder computer core.

It turned out that this nexus—or the computer core, at least—did not have any hostility against *Victory* or humans in general, nor did it have any wish for the Swarm Imperium to expand. This nexus's computer core had gone haywire—to use

Dana's precise technical term—approximately three hundred and twenty-one and a half years ago.

Fortunately, Dana and Galyan were able to figure out how to jumpstart the hyper-spatial tube machine inside the nexus. That machine took an entire day to find. Using the starship's computers and working for twenty-nine straight hours, they calculated distance, power and other specifics.

At Dana's request, Valerie held another staff meeting. The doctor went over their chances. This could go wrong in any number of ways. She looked at Valerie.

"Let's vote," Valerie suggested.

Dana nodded.

Everyone voted for trying the hyper-spatial jump. Morale, which had soared after their victory over Ghar-Yon-Tog, had begun to plummet again.

"You all know the odds, right?" Dana asked.

"We voted," Valerie said. "Now, let's do it."

Preparations took fifty-three hours of intense work.

"This is Joe Magee work," Dana said at one point.

"What is that?" Galyan asked.

"The professor uses the term sometimes," Dana explained. "It means this is a makeshift, jury-rig operation."

Galyan's eyelids fluttered. "Yes. I understand," he said.

Finally, the moment came as the starship waited ten and a quarter kilometers from the nexus. Soon, a silvery swirling mass appeared. It didn't quite have the same shiny-silvery sheen the others had shown.

Valerie gulped before giving the order. Keith piloted them. The starship entered the hyper-spatial tube twelve minutes later, leaving the Sagittarius Arm, hopefully for good.

The starship flashed down the tube, and a maelstrom of power emissions crackled against her feeble hull. Sections of battered hull-plating peeled away, but no one knew it yet. They were in the grip of Hyper-spatial Tube Lag.

Victory kept tunneling down the strange conduit, while the sides of the tube shook and shimmered, and things seemed in doubt. But not for long, as *Victory* ejected from the hyper-spatial tube, successfully making an incredibly long journey, arriving at the Sigma Draconis System in one, if severely battered, piece.

**

The star of Sigma Draconis was a main sequence dwarf with a 4.7 magnitude. The star system was 18.8 light-years from Earth and had one of the main warship building and repair yards of Star Watch.

The starship's sudden appearance caused a stir in the Sigma Draconis high command. Three interceptor cruisers rushed out to confront *Victory,* while the main fleet recalled all its personnel on the main planet and the various shore-leave satellites.

Lieutenant Noonan was still the acting captain, and she conferred with Captain Shaw of the *Bremen*. He was the leader of the Sigma Draconis cruiser squadron.

Captain Shaw sent a long-range message to Admiral Hawes, the commanding officer of the Sigma Draconis repair yard. Soon, Shaw received the admiral's reply, and he passed it on to Valerie.

Several hours later, the Sigma Draconis fleet went into a surprise war-game drill. It was a deception plan, with several of the fleet's battleships soon reaching and guarding *Victory*.

Two days later, the ancient Adok starship entered a space dock. There, Star Watch workers began emergency repairs to the hull and the many barely-functioning ship's systems.

A badly hurt Ludendorff continued to receive medical care, while Captain Maddox endured enforced rest and relaxation as his outer injuries healed.

Despite being in dock, and due to tight security, few knew about *Victory's* presence in the Sigma Draconis System.

**

Twenty-seven minutes, on the dot, after *Victory's* departure from the Sagittarius star system, the last nexus had detonated in yet another antimatter holocaust.

**

The reason Dana and Galyan had done the work with the nexus computer-core was that the professor had been under intensive care. Perhaps that was for the best for everyone. Later in the Sigma Draconis System, when Ludendorff heard what Dana and Galyan had done and after the professor went over their figures and calculations, he said they should have succeeded only twenty-three percent of the time. That meant, of course, that *Victory* had had a little better than a one in five chance of successfully completing the long-long-distance hyper-spatial tube journey.

In the end, the only utility to Ludendorff's calculations was to assuage his bruised ego. When Dana attempted to point out they might not have tried to leave the nexus system if they had followed his advice, the professor waved that aside as not germane to the terrible chance she and the Adok AI had taken upon their ill-considered calculations.

"Next time," Ludendorff said in his med-chamber, "leave such matters to the expert, me."

Dana stared at him, finally shaking her head and walking out on Ludendorff. If she hadn't done so, she knew she might have ended up saying something that she would have regretted later.

Dana knew that Ludendorff loved her after his own fashion, and she loved him. But he'd also taken her to that horrible Bosk homeworld and gotten her enslaved. Yes, the professor had gotten himself mentally enslaved, as well, and once he'd gained his freedom, he had done everything he could to rescue her. But still… she was beginning to wonder about their relationship. Yes, the sex was fantastic—but the professor's ego was finally beginning to grate on her.

Maybe she needed a break from him in order to sort out her true feelings.

As the days passed in the repair yard in the Sigma Draconis System, Dana's resolve to leave Ludendorff, for a time anyway, turned into a fixed purpose.

-109-

Maddox left the starship's medical facility on the sixth day after *Victory's* arrival in the Sigma Draconis System.

Gingerly, the captain began exercising the best he was able. His brain still hurt, but not like before.

On the eighth day after their arrival, a security team of space marines surprised Maddox in a *Victory* gym. He was hitting a heavy bag and had actually worked up a sweat.

Maddox lowered his wrapped hands, eyeing the five marines as they approached him. The marines were big boys with thick necks and scarred knuckles. These five would be excellent fighters, and they did not belong to *Victory*.

"You're to come with us, sir," said the oldest marine, maybe in his earliest thirties.

By this time, Maddox had recovered from the physical injuries incurred during the mission, the worst injury from the twenty-two meter fall inside the haunted nexus deep in the Sagittarius Arm. His excruciatingly painful headaches weren't as frequent, but they often came at the worst times. If only Ghar-Yon-Tog hadn't spoken directly into his mind after the monster's awakening.

The truth was that a human brain wasn't meant to endure that kind of trauma. He wondered if he would have headaches like this for the rest of his life. If so…he doubted that he would be much good as an Intelligence field agent or a starship captain.

"Are you from Earth?" Maddox asked the marines. They looked like they were from Earth.

"You're to come with us, sir," the same marine as before said in his same clipped way.

"How about answering my question first," Maddox said.

The marine eyed his men and then looked at Maddox. "We can make this easy or we can make this hard, sir. Frankly, it makes no difference to me which way you want it."

Maddox eyed the tough guy before saying, "Galyan."

The holoimage did not appear.

"Galyan," Maddox said again, looking around.

Once more, nothing happened.

That told Maddox what he needed to know. Still, it surprised him the Iron Lady's protection detail would talk to him like this. Maybe this had something to do with him drawing his gun on O'Hara aboard the *Moltke*.

"Fine," Maddox said. "Show me the way."

The five marines surrounded him as they left the gym. They did not meet anyone in the corridors. That struck Maddox as odd. The starship should still be crowded.

As they marched through the empty corridors, Maddox's head began to pound. It was sudden and it hurt like blazes, and it didn't matter that he'd taken pills to dull the pain. His visual field narrowed and a touch of nausea made him wonder if he was going to throw up. He needed to rest after hitting the heavy bag. Maybe the stress of these marines added to his weakness.

Maddox had really begun to resent the headache and he despised the weakness in himself. He'd always been strong, ready for anything. To be crippled by headaches—

"Is something wrong with you?" the head marine asked him.

"No," Maddox said.

"You look pale," the marine said.

"Don't worry about it."

"You a tough guy, Maddox?" the head marine asked.

"Tougher than you, at least," the captain said.

The marine grinned at his men before saying to Maddox. "Let's keep marching then."

They marched the captain for another five minutes. Maddox began to wonder if that was to test him in some way. Finally, the five marines escorted him to the same gym where he'd been practicing with the heavy bag.

"Surprised?" the head marine asked him.

Maddox said nothing. The pulsating headache seemed to be debating whether it should give him a blackout or not. He'd been trying his damnest to ignore the pounding in his skull. His mouth tasted like bile.

One of the marines pressed a switch so the hatch opened. The head marine indicated that Maddox should go in first.

The captain drew a short breath through his nostrils. A long one would have made the headache worse. Then he strode past the marines and through the hatch. It didn't surprise him that the marines did not follow him in or that the hatch closed behind him.

What did surprise Maddox was seeing the Lord High Admiral sitting behind a table someone must have set up while he'd been marching through the corridors. Maddox had expected Brigadier O'Hara to be waiting for him. Upon arriving in the Sigma Draconis System, Maddox had sent word to Earth for O'Hara to come immediately.

"Did O'Hara make it back to Earth?" Maddox asked worriedly.

From behind the table, the big, white-haired admiral in his white service uniform nodded solemnly. Cook then indicated with one of his huge hands that Maddox should sit on the chair before the table.

Maddox did so, soon asking. "Is Brigadier O'Hara well?"

"The brigadier has taken a leave of absence," Cook said in his deep voice.

Maddox waited, still trying to ignore the pounding headache.

"What's wrong with you?" Cook asked. "You looked…exhausted."

"Nothing is wrong, sir."

"Don't lie to me, son. I detest that above everything."

Maddox nodded slightly. "Yes, sir. My head hurts."

"Has it been doing that much lately?"

"I think you already know it has been, sir."

"That's no answer."

"My head has been hurting ever since I faced Ghar-Yon-Tog on the haunted nexus in the Sagittarius Arm."

"Tell me about the incident."

Maddox started the story.

Lord High Admiral Cook, the leader of Star Watch, listened attentively. Finally, after Maddox stopped talking, the big man made several notations in a small folder.

"Can you function with those headaches?" Cook asked.

"Yes," Maddox said, maybe a little too quickly.

"You mean maybe," Cook said.

"Yes," Maddox said again.

The big old admiral with his mass of white hair leaned back in his chair as he fingered his leathery chin. "You could use an extended leave of absence yourself," Cook said. "Do you want that?"

"No, sir."

"You have some scores to settle, do you?"

"I'm thinking I do, sir."

Cook studied him. "What makes you think that?"

"You're here instead of Brigadier O'Hara," Maddox said. "The Bosks used her, deceived her and took over her mind. I have Draegar 2."

"You *had* the Bosk overlord. I have him now, son."

Maddox said nothing.

Cook tapped his chin before saying, "Brigadier O'Hara might or might not have her normal mind back now. The Bosks tampered with her brain on the direct orders from a faction of New Men. According to the briefing I received, Lord Drakos runs that faction."

"I assume you know Methuselah Man Strand created or modified the Bosk society for his purposes."

"I do indeed," Cook said. "My experts have been interrogating your people for some time now. I had them leave the starship without your knowledge. Under my orders, none of your people were to inform you what was happening."

Maddox said nothing.

"By the way, Captain, you did an excellent job with the nexuses and against Ghar-Yon-Tog. Thank you for your exemplary service."

Maddox dipped his head. "If you interrogated my people, you should already know about Nay-Yon-Yezleth and the Forbidden Planet."

Cook gave him a mirthless smile.

"So you know?" Maddox asked.

"It is being taken care of, Captain. More, at this time, you do not need to know."

"Yes, sir," Maddox said in a clipped voice.

"Instead, if you can really handle those headaches, I want you to take care of the Bosks and catch Lord Drakos for me."

"Take care of the Bosks, sir?" asked Maddox.

Cook eyed him for several seconds. "You're right," the Lord High Admiral finally said. "I want to nail more than a few New Men. Through the Bosks, they tricked O'Hara and took over her mind. I need to know how much they learned about Star Watch. I have a bad feeling that much of Star Watch Intelligence has been compromised. We went through terrible times in the past against the New Men Secret Service. I don't want to go through that with them again."

"Do you feel you can trust me, sir?" Maddox asked.

The big old admiral gave him a wintery grin. "I don't have many choices, now do I, Captain? I'm willing to try you. If you succeed, I'll know I can still trust you. If not…maybe it will be time for you to take a long rest."

Maddox nodded flatly instead of showing any bitterness. O'Hara had always backed him and Cook had humored her. If the brigadier had left Star Watch Intelligence for good…

Bitterness tried to surface to the forefront of Maddox's thoughts. That only made the headache worse.

"You're not going to faint on me, are you?" Cook asked.

Maddox felt like it, but he didn't. Instead—he wasn't sure how—he stood up and tottered out of the chamber—the hatch opened for him.

He had to come up with a plan for catching Lord Drakos, and he'd better do it fast before his brain quit working for good.

-110-

Before Maddox could do anything of the kind, however, he staggered through the corridors, clenching his jaws so he didn't scream at the agony of his excruciating headache. Somehow, he made it to his quarters, gingerly easing himself onto his bed, curling up and enduring.

He woke up later as Meta rubbed his forehead. He was on his back, and his head was in her lap as she sat cross-legged on the bed. He kept his eyes shut, as the light would hurt too much.

"You have to rest," Meta said softly.

He knew she meant more than a few hours, more like weeks or months. "I can't do that," he said.

"Why can't you? What did the Lord High Admiral say to you?"

"Brigadier O'Hara," he said.

"Oh," Meta said. "Did something bad happen to her?"

Maddox did not reply. He just lay there as Meta stroked his forehead, and he fell into a more restful slumber.

When he woke up, several hours had passed.

Meta rolled over to greet him. She must have heard a change in his breathing as she lay with him. "Are you feeling better?" she asked.

Maddox grunted. He felt minimally better, but that wasn't saying much.

Meta waited.

Finally, as Maddox lay there, he said, "Brigadier O'Hara has taken a leave of absence from Intelligence. The Bosks, well, Lord Drakos's brand of New Men, tapped her brain, so to speak. I guess the combined Draegar did it for Drakos."

Maddox fell silent as he brooded.

"And...?" Meta finally asked.

The captain sat up in the dim lighting of their quarters. "I have an idea," he said, with some of the old force returning to his voice.

"Is it a good idea?"

Maddox turned toward his wife. He could sense more than see the worry in her. He reached across the bed and took hold of a shoulder. "Thanks," he said.

"For the forehead rub?" she asked.

"No, for what you did in the nexus. I was out of it, Meta. Ghar-Yon-Tog had won. I'd failed to stop him."

"Failed?" Meta asked. "I don't think you failed. You kept firing at him, and that damn missile kept inching closer. I...I talked to Galyan about it. I hope you don't mind."

"No."

"Good. Galyan spoke to Dana about it. According to them, your initial action must have surprised the Old One. I no longer felt him in my mind as I waited for you to return out of the star gate. No one else felt Ghar Yon Tog's mind anymore either. He...I don't know, drew his mental focus back to the nexus that you and the Spacer were in. You told me you fired rocket shells at him, right?"

"Right..." Maddox said slowly. "With his mind, or however he used his powers, Ghar-Yon-Tog stopped the rocket shells and he stopped the missile, and stopped the antimatter warhead from detonating. Mako 21 started resisting him around then."

"That's what I'm saying," Meta told him. "The point is that you attacked him at likely his most vulnerable moment. Later, you shot him with my beamer, burning his warty skin. You didn't fail, love. You made possible everything else that happened afterward. None of us feels the Old One anymore. That has to mean he's dead, kaput, finished."

Maddox smiled faintly before he let go of Meta's shoulder and turned away. Feeling better, a whole lot better, he climbed out of bed.

"What's your plan, darling?"

"It may be nothing," Maddox said. "First, I have to talk to the professor."

"Ah..." Meta said.

"What's that mean?" Maddox asked.

"Ludendorff is in a foul mood these days. Dana and he are taking a break from each other. He doesn't want a trial separation—"

"I have to go," Maddox said, interrupting. "If Ludendorff can't do what I want..." With that, the captain grabbed his clothes, put them on and rushed out of their quarters.

***

"No!" Ludendorff said while shaking his head. "That's out of the question."

Maddox spoke to the professor in a reading room. Ludendorff lounged on a recliner, wearing a bathrobe and little else.

The professor had several casts—two of them on his legs—had gained some weight and sipped a yellow-colored drink through a short red straw. His face was puffier than usual and his mood was indeed foul, as Meta had suggested.

"You're the only one practiced enough to succeed in doing it," Maddox said.

"I'm never using the Builder stone again," Ludendorff said. "You can take that to the bank."

Maddox frowned, having never heard that expression before. "We need to know more about the Bosk operation and how Drakos's New Men control it," Maddox said.

"Then go about learning it the old-fashioned spy way," Ludendorff told him.

"The old way often takes a long time. We have Draegar 2, or the Lord High Admiral has him. The Bosk overlord is the key to—"

"You're not thinking about trying to trap Lord Drakos are you?" Ludendorff asked, interrupting.

"That's the ideal outcome…" Maddox said, trailing off.

"What's next after that?" Ludendorff asked. "You're dying to tell me something."

"Wouldn't destroying Lord Drakos's Bosk connection make you feel better?" Maddox asked. "Through the Bosks, Drakos took much from you."

Ludendorff squinted at Maddox. "Are you referring to Dana?"

"Among other things."

"Bah!" Ludendorff said. "Do you suppose a knightly retribution would suddenly cause Dana to fall into my arms again?"

Maddox nodded.

"What?" Ludendorff said in a scoffing way. "You think that will work with Dana?"

"I make no guarantees," Maddox said. "But I know one thing. If Drakos and the Bosks had hurt Meta the way they hurt Dana, I would do everything in my power to take the Bosks and Drakos apart until they were all dead."

"That's the old way of doing things, Captain."

"Yes," Maddox said. "And in this instance, the old ways are the best ways."

"Haven't you ever heard that he who lives by the sword dies by the sword?"

"I have, and I accept that. Frankly, I can think of no better way to die than while I'm fighting as hard as I can for what I believe in."

Ludendorff regarded the captain. "No," the professor said after a time. "I'm too tired to do all that. Besides, the Builder stone is too risky, and frankly, Draegar 2 might be too difficult to tackle in the manner you suggest. After I'm fully rested I might consider it."

"Time is critical, Professor."

"I'm sorry," Ludendorff said. "The answer is still no."

Maddox stared at the professor. Finally, the captain stood, turned and headed for the hatch.

"I don't care if my answer upsets you," Ludendorff shouted.

Maddox did not respond. Instead, he left the reading room and headed down the corridor. Ludendorff wouldn't help. That meant he'd have to do this himself.

-111-

No one supported Maddox in his idea. Meta pleaded with him not to do this. She even cried, clinging to him.

"Don't you love me?" Meta wept in their quarters.

"Of course I love you," Maddox said.

"You're going to kill yourself for O'Hara. You love her more than you love me."

Maddox took Meta in his arms, stroking her head. "Brigadier O'Hara…helped me when I needed it most. I can't abandon her when she needs help the most."

"Oh, you stupid man," Meta said. "Don't you even know why you're doing this?"

Maddox frowned down at his angry wife.

"Don't you know why you always do *whatever* O'Hara asks you?"

"She's my patron in Star Watch," Maddox said.

Meta laughed but without any humor. Finally, she turned away. "Fine," she said. "If you want to throw your life away on a stupid gesture, be my guest."

Maddox turned Meta toward him, reached down and took her chin in one of his hands. Gently, he raised her tear-streaked face to his.

"I love you, darling," he said softly. "But I'm an Intelligence agent of Star Watch. I have a duty to perform."

Meta smiled sadly and sniffled, reaching up and wiping tears from her face. "Oh, Maddox," she said, and she clung to him. "You're the tarnished knight."

"Have you been talking to Ludendorff?"

She clung to him even harder. "You're a warrior. I understand that. But I wish...I wish..."

"I can do this," Maddox said. "I know I can."

Meta gripped him with strength so fierce it was a challenge to breathe. "If he hurts you in any way, I'll kill him."

"I accept that." Maddox didn't tell her, but he was counting on it as his final backup.

"Why does it always have to be you who does the dangerous task?" she whispered.

"Meta," he said, and he stroked her hair as her grip loosened just a little, letting him breathe more easily.

"All right," she whispered. "But I'm going to be there."

"Good," Maddox said. "I can think of no one better to be my anchor." *And to kill the bastard if he needs it*, he thought to himself.

***

It had taken the captain a few *mistruths* to convince the Lord High Admiral to let him attempt this. Maybe the old man knew they were lies. Maybe Cook wanted O'Hara back on his staff more than he was letting on.

The point was that Draegar 2 returned to *Victory*.

In a sealed chamber, with Sergeant Riker outside watching through a two-way mirror—Riker had sustained a few injuries in his thruster-pack tumble, but they had been relatively minor and had healed by now—Maddox stood with the Builder stone on a stand. Dana Rich was in here with him. Meta stood on the other side of the cell, with an extinguisher in her hands.

Across from Maddox sat Draegar 2. The bronze-colored Bosk was strapped to a chair. He appeared uncomfortable but kept a dark-eyed gaze latched onto the captain.

In Maddox's estimation, the Bosk knew what was going to happen.

"He looks eager," Dana said.

Maddox wasn't listening. He focused on the Builder stone, felt the stirring of a headache and stepped up to the white polygonal object, grasping the ancient thing with both hands. At first, nothing happened. Then, the captain felt the Wi-Fi-like connection with the object. It was a frightening experience. Ancient tendrils of Builder technology reached inside his mind. It connected with him, and Maddox felt a sudden growing of intelligence and possibilities.

He saw, in that moment, why he had the headaches. Could he fix those with the Builder stone? Before he could contemplate that, another mind struck his.

Maddox wanted to look up, but he was physically frozen. He felt the Bosk, Draegar 2, chuckling in his mind. It was an awful feeling.

You are too bold for your own good, Captain, Draegar 2 said to him mind-to-mind, using the Builder stone as the connection between them. *You are a superb Intelligence agent and even a gifted starship captain. But you are no match for me in a mind-to-mind contest. I am so much your mental superior that this is a joke. I knew right away what you were going to do. This "stone" is amazing. It is just the tool I need to expand my reach. I cannot believe you were that stupid to challenge me in an arena where I hold all the cards.*

"Lord Drakos," Maddox managed to croak.

Ah, yes, the New Man thinks he controls us Bosks, Draegar 2 said through the mind-link. *Is that not a fantastic joke?*

"Drakos does control the Bosks."

Only in a few minor ways, Draegar 2 said mind to mind. *When Drakos took over from the Master, Strand—* The Bosk mind-chuckled. *Let us say that we have a little surprise for Lord Drakos.*

From the Bosk's mind, Maddox caught a glimpse of that surprise.

Oh no, Captain, the Draegar said. *You weren't supposed to see that. I will have to modify you now. Let's see, how shall I begin to do this? Oh, I love this stone. It is simply marvelous.*

Maddox fought back with his mind as best as he was able.

The Draegar parried the mental attempt with startling ease. *Oh, no, no, no, Captain. That's not going to work with me. Let me now demonstrate how to do such a—*

Maddox waited, but nothing bad happened to him. Instead, the Bosk's presence vanished from his mind. Then an icy sensation broke his mind's Wi-Fi like connection with the Builder stone.

It took Maddox several seconds—or so he thought. The captain opened his eyes as his too-hot hands throbbed painfully. He was lying on the floor, and his head…throbbed some, but it wasn't anything like in the recent past.

He tried to concentrate, and he saw Draegar 2 lying on the floor across from him. The man's tongue was sticking out of his mouth and his head was at the oddest angle.

Meta stood over the Bosk, opening and closing her hands as she breathed hard.

Maddox looked around. Dana stood openmouthed and shocked, and she held the extinguisher, with a bit of foam dripping from the nozzle.

"What happened?" the captain whispered.

It took Dana a second to look at him and another to engage her mind. "You groaned pitifully," the doctor said slowly. "The Bosk was smiling too arrogantly. Then, Meta went wild. She rushed the bound man and tore him free of his straps as she twisted and finally broke his neck, killing him."

Maddox looked at Meta. She must have throttled Draegar 2. Then, Dana must have grabbed the extinguisher and hosed the Builder stone. That had allowed Maddox to break free of its mental hold. If he'd been linked to the Bosk through the stone when the man had died, that would have killed him, too. A choking death for Draegar 2 had been perfect for Maddox, giving him time to break the connection before it was too late.

Meta gave him a pleading look. "I couldn't help myself," she said. "The thought of him killing you…"

Maddox climbed to his feet, testing his limbs. His head felt better than it had for a long time. Had the Bosk done something to help it?

"I spoiled everything," Meta said.

"You're wrong," Maddox said. "I was counting on you reacting as you did—if it became necessary. Clearly, it was necessary. The key is that I have a thread of data."

"What?"

"I gained it from his mind. The thread may be enough for what we want." The captain stepped up to his wife and hugged her. Meta was the greatest. Perhaps as importantly, Maddox now had an idea of how to trap Lord Drakos.

-112-

Captain Maddox made his plans. The Lord High Admiral made his.

Cook spent two restless days and nights agonizing over his decisions. He paced. He ate too much and after the decisions were made, he drank far too much whiskey.

Responsibility for Star Watch and thus the Commonwealth of Planets weighed heavily on him. Sometimes, he thought about setting down the burden so someone better suited to the task could take it up. He seriously thought about it, and decided he would wait on the outcome of his latest decisions. If either of his choices failed to bring the needed results, Star Watch was going to have its hands full. He couldn't very well step down then, could he?

Cook's plans entailed two different battle fleets of vastly different sizes going in opposite directions. Both fleets received their orders due to the information that the Lord High Admiral had received from Maddox. In fact, without Maddox's costly won information, neither fleet would have moved.

One set of orders went out via a Builder communication device Cook kept on his flagship. The other set of orders raced away on a fast courier ship that would use a combination of star drive and Laumer Point jumps.

After he sobered up from the hard drinking, Cook wondered why it had been so hard to make the decisions. He mentally offered himself this and that reason. In the end, he realized that he sorely missed the brigadier's common sense wisdom. If Maddox failed to capture Lord Drakos, could he—Cook—ever allow the brigadier to come back to her old job?

It seemed doubtful. As the Lord High Admiral headed back to Earth, he silently wished the captain Godspeed. If anyone could do it, Maddox was the man.

"Use a thief to catch a thief," Cook mumbled to himself as he sat in his study. Or in this instance, use a New Man to catch a New Man.

Cook shook his head, wondering why Strand and Ludendorff had ever thought it would be a good idea to develop so-called superior men to help protect the rest of the human race. Talk about the hubris of geniuses—those two Methuselah Men had caused more heartache through their meddling than anyone else the admiral knew. *A curse on the two of them.*

***

Starship *Victory* left the Sigma Draconis System and headed for the Beyond in the general direction of the Bosk System.

Four days out from Sigma Draconis, Maddox received a message via his Builder communication device. He was in the special quarters for the device, having been summoned by Galyan.

"Maddox speaking," the captain said into the ancient machine.

"This is the Lord High Admiral speaking," said a tinny voice. "I thought I should tell you. I've sent a battle fleet at the Bosk homeworld."

"Sir?" Maddox asked.

"I have an inkling of your plan," Cook said. "So I thought you should know about the invasion fleet."

"The fleet might ruin everything, sir," Maddox said.

"It might," Cook agreed. "But I'm not letting that hotbed planet of super-spies have any more freedom of action. If you can pull off your caper, that's fine and dandy. If not—well, I'll have put a stop to Bosk meddling once and for all."

"The real culprits will go free then, sir."

"I know you mean the New Men. In twelve days, the Bosk homeworld is going to face an invasion by Star Watch. If the defenders make it too difficult, Admiral Piedmont will burn the planet to the bedrock. If the Bosks are sensible and surrender, the Intelligence teams can begin work on the interrogations."

"I doubt those teams will find what you want."

"Don't you think I know that?" Cook asked. "That's why you're receiving this call. Do what you can, Captain. I want to tell you—well, do what you can."

"Yes, sir," Maddox said. "Anything else?"

"Bow your head, son."

Maddox did just that.

"I beseech thee, Lord God," Cook said over the Builder comm device, "grant Captain Maddox success against Lord Drakos and the Strand operatives. Amen."

"Thank you, sir," Maddox said.

"You'll show me your thanks by succeeding. Cook out."

Once the call ended, Maddox stared at the bulky device. This was cutting it too fine. He needed more time to lure Drakos into a trap.

Okay… He would have to send the message sooner, and hope that Drakos raced to his doom. Likely, the message would alert the New Man that something was wrong. But Cook had his reasons for sending the fleet.

"I'm doing what I can, ma'am," Maddox said quietly. "But this time, I don't know if it's going to be enough."

-113-

Maddox and the crew of *Victory* made their plans, using the captain's glimpse into Draegar 2's mind.

The starship did not go the Bosk homeworld, it went to a heavy moon orbiting a gas giant at the same relative distance as the Asteroid Belt orbits the Sun.

The Balak System was 9.4 light-years from the Bosk homeworld and at the edge of the Beyond. The heavy moon, a water moon, held a small colony of Middle-Eastern settlers. The moon was a bleak place with constant sandstorms, but it had rich veins of heavy metals.

The gas giant caused the small bodies of water on the moon to have fantastically high and low tides. Storms swirled most artistically across the gas giant's face as seen from the moon's surface.

Maddox, Riker, Meta and several space marines used a shuttle to land on the moon. *Victory* remained in orbit around the gas giant, staying hidden on the other side.

The team went to the city of Aleppo, a mining community with the busiest spaceport on the moon. It was a rough and ready place where everyone went armed, all with knives, some with guns. Part of Aleppo had an area called Bosk Town as some places on Earth used to have a China Town.

The natives of Aleppo wouldn't allow Bosks to live anywhere else on the moon. The Bosks looked down at what they considered weakling Balaks, while the moon natives thought of the Bosks as lunatic ruffians.

The mining corporations hired Bosks to work the deepest and most dangerous mines, and they paid incredibly low wages to boot. Fortunately, for the corporation stockholders, any Bosk having made it to Balak considered himself a lucky man, and the money he earned deep mining was an unbelievable boon to him. For the Bosk workers, the mining town was paradise compared to the Bosk homeworld.

Having little practice having personal money, the Bosk miners proved easy marks for casino and cathouse owners. The few poker and slot machine winners among the Bosks made the rest crazy to emulate the lucky ones. And the idea of paying a woman for sex—this was the most wonderful world in the galaxy according to the Bosk miners.

Maddox, Riker, Meta and the handful of marines waited near the spaceport. Word had gone out from a noted casino owned by a Bosk crime lord. That man was the front for the New Men. That crime lord no longer lived, however, but was buried six feet under the desert sands.

Maddox had convinced the Bosk crime lord to make the call. Afterward, the crime lord died because he'd made a break for it.

The captain could not allow that. Unfortunately, two of the crime lord's crew had seen the act. Maddox, Riker and Meta and the marines had shot their way out of a vicious casino ambush. One of the marines had died. Worse, there was an uproar at the casino. Fortunately, the Aleppo police had gone in with riot gear, closing the place down and putting the town under interdict. That meant no calls went out of the city.

Maddox had implemented all the moves he'd seen in Draegar 2's mind. The Bosk casino-owner had been the capping touch. It had all turned sour because of two hidden men, however.

"Sir," a marine said, the one sitting at the comm in their rented room.

Maddox had been lying on a bed. He jumped up, nodding.

"Galyan spotted a decelerating star cruiser as it's approaching the gas giant," the marine said.

"Why did it take the holoimage so long to see the star cruiser?" Maddox asked.

"I asked that, too, sir," the marine said. "Galyan suggested the star cruiser was traveling cloaked before he spotted it."

"It could be one of Strand's old star cruisers," Maddox said.

"Yes, sir," the marine said. "That's also what Galyan said."

Maddox looked at the others as he rubbed his hands in anticipation. "The plan is working," he said.

"Maybe," Meta said.

An hour went by. Two hours clicked away. At three hours, fourteen minutes and thirty seconds, the comm marine looked up again from his device.

"A shuttle has left the orbital-parked star cruiser, sir. Someone is coming down."

"Is the shuttle headed for Aleppo?" Maddox asked.

The marine asked a question, listened for a long moment and finally asked, "Are you sure?" The marine waited for an answer and then cut the connection.

"Well?" asked Maddox.

The marine turned glumly to the captain. "The shuttle has reversed course, sir. It's heading back upstairs to the waiting star cruiser. According to Galyan, the star cruiser has activated its weapons."

Maddox cursed as he struck a thigh, and he waited. Two minutes later, he asked, "Is there any change to the shuttle?"

The marine relayed the question. Instead of an answer, Galyan appeared in the rented room.

"Sir," the holoimage said. "We've scanned the star cruiser. It's the *Grazing Lion*. According to my analysis, the name indicates Lord Drakos, with seventy-three percent accuracy."

Maddox didn't bother asking how Galyan had come to that conclusion. Instead, he said, "You're sure about that?"

"I am, sir," Galyan said.

"Right," Maddox said. "We're going to do this the hard way. Tell Valerie to get ready. We're coming up."

"I must point out, sir—"

"Don't bother," Maddox said. "There's an armed and primed star cruiser up there. We're going around the planet—the moon. Pick us up on the other side. One way or another, I'm capturing Lord Drakos."

"*If* he is aboard the star cruiser, sir," Galyan said.

"Why are you still here?" Maddox asked. "I gave you orders."

Without another word, Galyan disappeared.

-114-

The Star Watch shuttle roared from the spaceport with Maddox at the controls. Everyone was strapped in tight. The captain raced across desert sands, trying to circle the moon as fast as he could. He also waited for word from Valerie or Galyan that the star cruiser had spotted them.

No such message came down. Instead, twenty-seven minutes later, Maddox headed up for orbital space.

In relative time, they made it up into a hangar bay at record speed. In subjective time, the rocket ride up had taken far too long. The star cruiser was already moving away from Balak at full acceleration.

Maddox sprinted at top speed for the bridge. He arrived breathlessly as Valerie jumped out of the captain's chair.

"We're following them," she said.

"Get ready to use the star drive, Mr. Maker," Maddox said, as if he hadn't heard a word the lieutenant said.

"Sir?" Keith asked.

"Now," Maddox said. "No discussions," he told Valerie. "Galyan, stow it."

The bridge fell silent as Maddox marched to the main screen. His eyes flashed, and there was an intensity to him that he normally cloaked. Not today—today, he wanted Lord Drakos, and he wanted the New Man badly.

The star cruiser continued its acceleration. *Victory* charged after it.

"We're ready to jump," Keith said from the Helm. "Do you have a location, sir?"

Maddox gave it.

"That will put us ahead of the star cruiser," Keith said.

"Yes," Maddox said, as he stared at the main screen.

"The New Men might attack us during a brief moment of lag, sir."

"Good," Maddox said. "That will give us the excuse we need for fighting back."

"Is this an instance of covering one's ass, sir?" Galyan asked.

If it was possible, the bridge fell even more deadly silent than before.

"What did you say?" Maddox asked the holoimage.

"It is an expression, sir," Galyan said. "Should I not have said it?"

"Who told you this expression?" Maddox asked.

"The professor," Galyan said.

"Ah," Maddox said. He faced the ace. "You will proceed, Mr. Maker. Make the jump."

Seconds later, *Victory* used the star drive, leaving the gas giant and its heavy water moon behind. They appeared suddenly in space.

Maddox was the first to revive. He noted that nothing bad had happened to the starship. That likely meant the star cruiser hadn't fired on them. The captain waited, therefore, until everyone else was functional again.

"Rotate the ship, Helmsman," the captain said. "Let's face the enemy."

"Sir," Valerie said. "The captain of the *Grazing Lion* is hailing us."

"Put him on the main screen," Maddox said.

A second later, Lord Drakos appeared. Maddox had never been happier to see the bastard. Drakos was just as golden-skinned as ever, if not as much as other New Men, and he still had broader than average shoulders.

"Captain Maddox," Drakos said smoothly. "This is a surprise."

Maddox stared at the man, saying nothing.

"I am advising you to move aside, Captain," Drakos said.

Maddox stirred, and there was hatred in his eyes. "Surrender or die," he said in a slow voice.

Drakos eyed him, and he allowed himself an indulgent smile.

"Galyan," Maddox said, as he stared into Drakos's eyes. "Warm up the disrupter and neutron cannons."

"Aren't you going to warn me against stubbornness?" Drakos asked.

Maddox said nothing, although he matched the New Man stare for stare.

"You cannot simply *fire* on my ship," Drakos said.

Maddox said nothing.

"If you do this," Drakos said, "you will have broken the concord between the Throne World and Star Watch."

Maddox did not reply.

For the first time, Drakos appeared uneasy. "You're bluffing," he said.

"The disrupter cannon is ready, sir," Galyan said. "The neutron cannon will take a little longer."

"Fire," Maddox said.

"Wait," Drakos said.

"Are you surrendering?" Maddox asked coldly.

"Sir," Valerie said. "I'm receiving a new hailing signal. This one is coming from three star cruisers that have just appeared from around the second planet of the system."

"They can't save you," Maddox told Drakos. "The three are too far away. If you're not surrendering, prepare to die."

"Sir," Valerie said. "I think you should listen to the incoming message."

Maddox fought with himself. He wanted to capture or kill Drakos. Capturing him was better, as that could help restore the brigadier to her position in Star Watch Intelligence. Killing would do, though. He couldn't let the cunning bastard get away to do more harm.

"Sir," Valerie said. "I urge you to listen to the new message."

It felt as if Maddox's neck moved on rusted hinges. He regarded the lieutenant. She was pale and even trembling.

"Go ahead," Maddox said.

Lord Drakos disappeared from the main screen. In his place appeared Golden Ural.

Maddox blinked in surprise.

"I see you survived your trip into the Deep Beyond," Golden Ural said smoothly. "Were you successful, Captain?"

"Yes," Maddox said.

"Excellent," Ural said. "You have no idea how glad that makes me. Now, unfortunately, we have other business at hand. I, ah, intercepted your message to Lord Drakos. I'm afraid I will have to interrupt your standoff. As a representative of the Emperor, I cannot stand idly by while a Star Watch ship attacks a Throne World vessel."

"Drakos is your enemy just as much as he is mine," Maddox said.

"Events have moved forward since we last talked, Captain. I'm afraid your assessment is no longer true."

"You're siding with Drakos?" Maddox asked, astonished.

"I am following orders, Captain. Lord Drakos now recognizes the treaty between us and your Commonwealth."

"Since when?" demanded Maddox.

Golden Ural frowned. "I cannot allow you to speak to me in such a tone, sir. It doesn't matter when. It is an accomplished fact. Will you recognize your obligation to Star Watch or must we fight a battle and start an incident between our peoples?"

"Drakos has information I—" Maddox almost said information he *needed*. But he did not want to appear weak before any New Man, not even Golden Ural. "Lord Drakos has information I desire," the captain said.

"We all have unsatisfied wants, Captain," Ural said.

Maddox blinked several times. This was outrageous. He had Drakos under his guns. He'd almost snared the New Man on Balak. To fail after coming this close to succeeding—it stung horribly.

Finally, Maddox exhaled. "Good day to you, Golden Ural."

"I have had star drives installed in my vessels," Ural said. "Must I use them to engage your ship in battle? I do not desire a fight with you, but if I must do so to uphold the Throne World's honor…"

The next three seconds were subjectively the longest in Captain Maddox's life. He wrestled with the decision, and it did not come easily.

Finally, Maddox said softly, "No. You do not need to engage your star drives. I will abide by the treaty."

Golden Ural did not smile, but he bowed his head as a gesture. "Until next time, Captain," the New Man said.

Maddox nodded, no longer able to speak.

After Ural disappeared from the screen, the captain moved to his chair and sat down.

"Lord Drakos is hailing us, sir," Valerie said.

Maddox said nothing.

"What do you want me to do, sir?" Valerie asked.

"With Drakos, nothing," Maddox said. "Mr. Maker, set a course for Earth. I'd better tell the Lord High Admiral that I failed."

"Sir," Valerie said softly, "Lord Drakos sends you a message."

Maddox looked at Valerie.

The lieutenant grew red-faced. "But I don't think I'll repeat it. I'll log it, sir. If you wish to hear it, you can do so later at your leisure."

Maddox wanted to threaten Lord Drakos. He wanted to assure the bastard that he would kill him soon enough. But Maddox hated to threaten anyone, and he dearly didn't want to do it when an enemy had just gotten the better of him.

He half suspected that Drakos had agreed to the accord several minutes ago. There was a power struggle going on among the New Men, and maybe this political maneuver had something to do with it.

Maddox sighed. Star Watch was about to invade the Bosk homeworld. That would cut off that avenue for infiltrating enemy agents into the Commonwealth.

But what was he going to do to restore the brigadier to her post? At the moment, Maddox didn't know. But he silently vowed that he would find a way to help his—his former superior in Star Watch Intelligence.

"I'm ready to jump again, sir," Keith said.

Maddox nodded. "Get us out of here, Helm. I'm sick of the Throne World company we've been keeping."

-115-

Several weeks later, across the entire length of Human Space and then deeper into the Beyond, Admiral Fletcher led the bulk of the Grand Fleet. He had been using Laumer Point jumps for some time now.

Ever since Fletcher had received his orders via the Builder communication device on the bridge, the Grand Fleet had raced with grim purpose.

It was difficult for Fletcher to credit what the Lord High Admiral had told him. On two separate occasions, Fletcher had used the Builder comm device to call Cook. Each time, Fletcher had asked for conformation of the kill order.

If anything, Cook had become even more adamant than the first time.

Now, the van of the Grand Fleet intercepted Spacer vessels in the oddly named Terser System. The Spacer commander warned Fletcher to leave this section of the Beyond. According to the enemy commander, this was Spacer territory. If the Star Watch fleet did not leave within seven hours, there would be war.

For the third time since he'd received the kill order, Fletcher used the Builder comm device.

"Yes?" Cook said shortly across hundreds of light-years.

Fletcher told the Lord High Admiral about the Spacer ultimatum.

"Admiral," Cook said, "I want you to listen to me closely. Are you listening?"

"I am, Admiral," Fletcher said, with many of his staff officers around him waiting with bated breath.

"The world the Grand Fleet is seeking is called the Forbidden Planet. The place holds an Old One."

"A what, sir?" asked Fletcher as he glanced at his chief staff officer.

"An Old One—an alien of terrible evil and even worse power," Cook said. "You must not waver in this. Destroy any Spacer vessels that threaten you. If they want war with us, we will give them war. Tell them that. Tell them I said that."

"Sir?" Fletcher asked.

"If you question me one more time, Admiral," Cook said. "I will relieve you of duty. You used to be my *fighting* admiral. Well, I need that Fletcher more than ever. Humanity needs that Fletcher. Is he still there?"

Fletcher gulped. In truth, he wasn't as bloodthirsty as he used to be. But he knew how to follow orders.

"If this alien is as bad as you say…"

"Captain Maddox says he's that bad," Cook said.

"Maddox?" asked Fletcher. "What does Maddox have to do with this?"

"Everything," Cook said with emotion. "The captain has performed wonderfully. He saved the human race several weeks ago. It cost him hard, too. But you have to finish this, Fletch. This planet, it's housing a devil's brood. Burn it down, and then blow it over again with hell-burners. This planet must be dead once you leave. Is that clear?"

"Yes, Admiral," Fletcher said.

"Good. Then do it."

***

The Spacers warned again. Fletcher told his lead squadrons to warn the Spacers once. After that, they were to open fire and destroy every Spacer vessel that came within range.

The squadron commanders did as ordered. Afterward, eleven saucer-shaped vessels were destroyed before the Spacers quit warning the Grand Fleet and fled for their lives.

Six days later, the fleet reached the system of the Forbidden Planet. That was when the Spacers attacked like kamikazes with half the number of warships as in the Grand Fleet. Those saucer-shaped ships were no match for the newer battleships. But then, awful beams rose up from the Forbidden Planet, and they were ship-killing beams of tremendous power.

Incredibly, to Fletcher and his staff, the battle began to turn against Star Watch. When three of his newest battleships blew up like firecrackers to the planetary beams, some of the old fighting fire returned to the admiral.

Fletcher asked for volunteers, and he got them. Thirteen crews of star-drive jump-capable cruisers agreed to the plan.

As even more planetary beams reached up from the surface of this Forbidden Planet, the cruisers used their star drives, appeared behind the awful world and came low into orbital space, curving around to do battle. From low orbit, the cruisers launched antimatter missiles at the sandy surface. Only one in ten of those reached their targets, but those detonated and took out enemy primary beam batteries.

That meant the surface batteries turned on the cruisers. Only three of the thirteen survived the planetary run.

After that, Fletcher sent another wave, and they took out more of the deadly primary beams.

The battle shifted decisively in Star Watch's favor after that.

The surviving half of the Grand Fleet annihilated the remaining Spacers. The last few surviving Spacer ships forgot their valor and fled.

Fletcher ordered his battleships to continue firing at the enemy. Only a handful of the original Spacer ships escaped intact.

Later, the approach to the planet went like clockwork. Enemy, heavy primary beams killed another five battleships. Then, the hell-burners and thermonuclear bombs rained on the Forbidden Planet.

After two hours of saturation bombing, no more enemy beams struck the battered Grand Fleet.

Now, strikefighters flew low, pinpointing targets. For the next three days, heavy orbital beams lanced the surface.

Then, more hell-burners exploded on the Forbidden Planet.

Yes, the rumors were true; Fletcher wept over his losses, but he also got innovative. His battleships went out and began towing small asteroids. For three weeks, they brought all kinds of asteroids near the hated planet. Then, the asteroids and meteors rained down on the doomed world, creating tectonic havoc.

The Grand Fleet did not leave the Forbidden Planet until massive earthquakes had caused huge cracks to appear across the continents. Seas of lava flowed where the heaviest asteroids had broken the continental crust.

Admiral Fletcher wasn't sure how anything could have survived down there. The Forbidden Planet had become the Molten Planet. Was the Old One dead?

There was no way for Fletcher to check. This much had cost Star Watch dearly, with half the Grand Fleet destroyed or too heavily damaged to leave for the trip back to the Commonwealth.

Thus, the crowning signature of the terrible contest was Fletcher sending his worst ships screaming down to the seas of lava to die—after the crews had transported to other ships.

He had done his damnedest against the alien Old One. Now, he would go home and retire from the service. This last fight had taken all the fire he had left. Now, he just wanted to live in peace for the rest of his life.

-116-

In the course of time, Starship *Victory* returned to Earth. There in Geneva at Star Watch Headquarters, Maddox gave his report to the Lord High Admiral.

"I'd rather you'd captured Lord Drakos," Cook told Maddox after the briefing.

They met in the Lord High Admiral's office. It was much starker than Brigadier O'Hara's office had been.

"I know, sir," Maddox said.

Cook studied the captain while drumming his fingers on the large desk.

Maddox kept quiet, waiting.

"Impressive," Cook said at last. "Most men squirm under my stare. They make excuses. Don't you have any excuses to give me?"

"No, sir," Maddox said. "I failed. That says it all."

"Lord Drakos outmaneuvered you, which is different than failure."

Maddox felt heat on his features as he said, "I don't see how, sir."

Cook grunted. "Well, it's a small matter in the scheme of things. I know, I know. We both want Brigadier O'Hara back in her office. She has been badly compromised, however. It was one of the risks she took going out to find Ludendorff. She found the Methuselah Man, and he proved instrumental in Star Watch knocking out the needed enemy nexuses."

Maddox cleared his throat.

From underneath his bushy white eyebrows, Cook studied him anew. "Are you going to tell me the New Men knocked out the other half of the enemy nexuses?"

"It crossed my mind, sir," Maddox said.

"Humph," Cook said. "You're right, of course. In this, we worked together. It would seem that for the moment, anyway, Star Watch doesn't have to worry about the awful Swarm Imperium invading us."

Maddox nodded.

"That's huge, Captain, huge. Humanity could never hope to survive massed Swarm invasions. Now, our species has more time. You performed splendidly out there. I am more than impressed, Captain. I am awed at what you've managed to achieve. Think about it. For years, the Swarm Imperium has been our nightmare. No more, thanks to you and a band of brave New Men. Oh, yes, the Swarm could send an invasion fleet the long way using Laumer Points. But I doubt they'll do that. From the little we know about Swarm thinking, they're rational after a fashion. Besides, the Chitin Empire stands between the Swarm and us."

Maddox nodded.

"We can breathe again, Captain. We can think about expanding, and we've learned to work with the New Men."

"Have we, sir?" asked Maddox.

"Explain that."

"The New Men and Star Watch stood back to back, sir, against a larger threat. If we'd failed to work together, we would have both perished. Now, the New Men have stolen a march on us."

"You're referring to the brigadier, I suppose."

"Golden Ural and the Emperor must have Lord Drakos in custody."

"We don't know that," Cook said.

"There's a lot we don't know about the New Men. We've also never recovered the kidnapped women they took with them after their invasion of "C" Quadrant."

"Are you suggesting we fight a war with the Throne World?"

"No, sir," Maddox said. "I think we should watch them closely, though. They have Methuselah Man Strand. He clearly helped them against the Swarm."

"Hmm…" Cook said.

"We also know the Beyond is filled with aliens," Maddox added. "There are still plenty of threats out there, maybe even more Old Ones. But…"

"The brigadier," Cook finished.

Maddox nodded sharply.

"It's time for some deep thinking, Captain. We no longer have to worry about the Swarm, but it's Star Watch's job to see that nothing else takes the Swarm's place. I suggest you take a few weeks off, young man. By then, I'm sure I'll have something else for you."

Maddox realized the admiral was dismissing him. He stood, saluted and paused.

Cook had unlocked a drawer, pulled out a folder, set it on his desk and opened it. He looked up at Maddox. "Is something wrong?"

"I'd like your permission to visit the brigadier."

The Lord High Admiral's eyes narrowed. "I see you've already been snooping around. You've found out that we're keeping her hidden."

Maddox said nothing.

Cook gave him a mirthless smile. "Very well, Captain, permission granted. You'll find her on the island of Patmos."

"Thank you, sir."

Cook had already started reading the contents of the folder and waved the captain on.

Maddox quietly took his leave, looking forward to telling his…his former superior about the success of his greater mission. When he saw the brigadier again, Maddox was also going to assure her that he would catch Lord Drakos. In fact, he would do everything in his power to help reinstall her in her rightful position.

With his face set, Maddox marched down the corridors. Humanity was going to survive the Swarm Imperium, for another fifty years at least. Now, Star Watch had time to make sure it was regular humanity that came out on top, not the arrogant supermen who kidnapped women to serve their lecherous needs.

Maddox's stride lengthened until he stopped abruptly in the general HQ waiting room. Meta, Valerie and Keith rose from the chairs where they'd been waiting. Galyan floated closer toward him.

"What's the meaning of this?" Maddox asked.

"A night on the town," Meta said. "It's been too long since you and I have gone on a date, and we're always going on our dates alone. This time, let's go out as couples."

"What about Galyan?" Maddox asked.

"Oh," the holoimage said. "I am not joining you on the date, sir. I just wanted to see that the four of you had a good time, and to tell you that I would watch the ship in case you desired to get drunk."

"Drunk?" asked Maddox.

"As a victory symbol," Galyan said. "Tie one on, sir, if you know what I mean."

"I do indeed," Maddox said, as he eyed his wife. "Yes, let's celebrate." He could talk to the brigadier afterward. First, he needed to make sure his friends knew how much he appreciated them. Without his teammates, he never would have defeated Ghar-Yon-Tog and stopped the Swarm Imperium from invading Human Space.

"Come on," Meta said, grabbing one of his arms. "I haven't danced in a long time, and I plan to make you dance until you drop."

"This I have to see," Keith said.

Maddox frowned at the ace until he thought better of it and chuckled appreciatively.

Then, as Galyan went back upstairs to keep watch, the four of them headed for the HQ exit so they could properly celebrate their greatest victory to date.

For a little longer anyway, the human race was safe from the predatory aliens prowling the Great Beyond.

THE END

SF Books by Vaughn Heppner

LOST STARSHIP SERIES:
The Lost Starship
The Lost Command
The Lost Destroyer
The Lost Colony
The Lost Patrol
The Lost Planet
The Lost Earth
The Lost Artifact
The Lost Star Gate

THE A.I. SERIES:
A.I. Destroyer
The A.I. Gene
A.I. Assault
A.I. Battle Station
A.I. Battle Fleet

Visit VaughnHeppner.com for more information

Printed in Great Britain
by Amazon